THE HERBWITCH'S APPRENTICE

THE HERBWITCH'S APPRENTICE

IREEN CHAU

ILLUSTRATED EDITION

THE HERBWITCH'S APPRENTICE

Cover design and Illustrations: Ireen Chau
Formatting: Enchanted Ink Publishing

Hardcover ISBN: 979-8-8028728-4-0
Paperback ISBN: 979-8-8040841-3-5

Thank you for your support of the author's rights.

Illustrated edition June 2022

Printed in the United States of America

FOR ESME

Manbane—Made of the foulest ingredients known to witchkind, this insidious poison sucks years of life from the unlucky human who consumes it–knowingly or not.

1

THE
GENTLEMAN'S
DAUGHTER

1

I was almost certain our neighbor was a witch.

Witches, they say, must be avoided at all costs. Some can turn you to stone with a glance. Some can conjure lightning and fry you on the spot. Some brew foul poisons day and night, hoping to slip them into your supper. When you're dead, they'll chop you up and use your flesh in their wicked alchemy.

They didn't roam the kingdom anymore, of course, and I had never seen Julianna Alderidge brew poisons or turn people into stone. But there was no doubt she was a wicked creature I avoided at all costs.

I just wished my stepmother would stop inviting her to tea parties.

Julianna's laugh rung across the lawn. "Mr. Sternfeld, you are a riot!"

Cedric Sternfeld said something inaudible, his pearly smile a stark contrast to his dark skin. Julianna dissolved into an explosion of giggles.

He was a rather handsome young man, but compared to his wealth, his face was inconsequential. The neighborhood girls stuck to him like caramel on a toddler's tooth the second he moved in across the street.

None more so than Julianna. No doubt she would have hosted a welcome event in her backyard if my stepmother hadn't done it first.

"Does she think he'll marry the girl who laughs at everything he says?" I grumbled to Genevieve as Julianna giggled for the thousandth time. I didn't need to turn to know my stepsister was smiling.

"He just moved in, Amarante," Genevieve said, setting her sketchbook and charcoal onto the grass. The dappled light beneath the apple tree made her blond hair glow. "She's only being friendly."

I didn't think it took more than a pretty face to impress a lord's son, but I hoped for his own sake that Mr. Sternfeld wouldn't fall for Julianna's perfect curls and milky complexion.

"Or she's waiting to pounce once his grandfather passes," I said.

Genevieve coughed. "Amarante!"

"Rumors have it he'll inherit a good mass of land from Lord Gideon Sternfeld."

Genevieve gave me a reproachful look, but her lips were twitching. "Since when do you listen to rumors?"

I rolled my eyes. "Oh, Gen. Stepmother is the biggest gossip in the neighborhood."

My stepmother, Lydia, was too busy playing hostess to notice we were huddled beneath our apple tree, away from the guests. Most of the neighborhood families had shown up this morning with their daughters in tow. Several of them swarmed Lydia now. Only the top of her impeccable

updo was visible behind the heads of our neighbors, who were no doubt complimenting her for organizing such a lovely reception.

Genevieve started sketching again.

I sighed. "Do you *ever* stop drawing?"

"We're in hiding, remember?" Genevieve said. The arched windows of our house took form on the page. "There's nothing else to do."

"Didn't stepmother tell you to pick gowns for the Season?"

"I'll do that later," she said. "I have a month before it starts."

"And you're sure you want to go this year?" I asked, picking at the embroidery on my skirt.

"Yes, Amarante, for the fifth time. I'm already eighteen. The youngest girls attending are your age."

I blew a strand of brown hair out of my face. "Ridiculous. I cannot believe they're asking for marriage at sixteen."

"They are not! The Season is a coming-of-age celebration," Genevieve said. "That is all."

"It's frivolous and overrated."

The scratching of charcoal stopped. "Really? Then how come I remember you dancing in the parlor with a bed sheet around your waist, pretending you were at the Debutante Ball?"

My cheeks burned. "Keep drawing, why don't you?"

"Admit it. You can't wait to attend next year."

I stomped the grass beneath me. "I'd rather kiss a toad!"

"Perhaps it'll turn into Prince Charming," Genevieve said in a singsong voice.

"Gen!"

Before Genevieve could tease me further, Julianna approached with Cedric Sternfeld at her arm. I prayed she hadn't overheard our conversation. The last thing I needed was another rumor about me, this time kissing toads.

I savagely took a bite of my raspberry tart. Our cook, Theodora, always baked the most heavenly pastries, but Julianna's presence soured the taste. She looked infuriatingly pretty in a lilac sundress and her chestnut hair twisted back.

"If it isn't Amarante and Genevieve," Julianna said in a faux-cheery voice. "Why haven't you joined the rest of us in welcoming our new neighbor?"

I tried not to scowl as Genevieve and I stood and curtsied to Mr. Sternfeld.

"Apologies, Mr. Sternfeld. Amarante and I merely wandered off," my stepsister said. "I hope you won't take offense."

Mr. Sternfeld bowed. "Not at all. You're Madam Lydia's daughters?"

He had a friendly baritone voice and a kind gaze which lingered on Genevieve a beat longer than customary. So he *was* impressed by pretty faces. Hopefully he had enough sense to choose the right one.

"Indeed. A pleasure to make your acquaintance, Mr. Sternfeld," Genevieve said.

"The pleasure is all mine, Miss Genevieve," he said with an easy laugh. "I cannot thank your mother enough for such a warm reception upon moving in. Your backyard is lovely."

"Our gardener does a fantastic job with the roses," Genevieve said with a demure smile. A hint of pink stained her cheeks.

Julianna's grip on Mr. Sternfeld's arm tightened. "Didn't you fall into the rose bushes one year, Amarante?" she said. "Madam Lydia almost had that gardener Rhonda fired."

"Her name is Rowena," I said stiffly. "And it wasn't her fault I fell."

"The thorns scratched your face horribly." Julianna

looked up at Mr. Sternfeld with a pout. "Scratches are awfully unattractive on a woman's face, aren't they, Mr. Sternfeld?"

He had the decency to look uncomfortable. "Not at all, Miss Julianna. I find them to be great conversation starters."

I fought the urge to laugh at Julianna's reddening face.

Mr. Sternfeld flicked his gaze about, as if searching for another topic. Genevieve's sketchbook caught his attention.

"You draw, Miss Genevieve?" he said brightly, picking it up from the grass. She had nearly finished the sketch. It depicted the lawn and several figures, one of them Mr. Sternfeld himself.

"A little," my stepsister said.

"A lot," I corrected. "She's been drawing for ages."

Genevieve kicked my ankle.

"Masterful!" Mr. Sternfeld exclaimed. "Tell me, how did you render these forms with so few strokes?"

"Well, I used the broad side of the charcoal to block out the shadows—"

"I doubt Mr. Sternfeld wants to hear about your amateur techniques, Genevieve," Julianna said. She snatched the sketchbook and tossed it over her shoulder. "My mother hired a famous Aquatian artist to paint my portrait. Now *his* work is truly masterful. I would love to show you, Mr. Sternfeld."

Mr. Sternfeld cleared his throat. "Thank you, Miss Julianna, but I'm afraid I'll be busy."

"Why is that? Will you be attending the Season?" Julianna said eagerly.

"I won't. But my sister Olivia will," he said. "I'm chaperoning her."

I hadn't heard about Mr. Sternfeld having a sister. Probably because she wasn't the one with the inheritance.

"Is your sister here too?" Genevieve inquired.

"Ah, yes. She arrived last night, but Olivia is deathly timid," Mr. Sternfeld said, easing his arm out of Julianna's claws. "New places scare her."

"Poor dear," Julianna crooned. She inched closer to him. "It must be so difficult for her."

I rolled my eyes at her poor attempt at compassion.

"That's unfortunate," Genevieve said. "I always find strange places more bearable when I have a friend. Perhaps Amarante and I can meet her sometime."

Mr. Sternfeld beamed. "Now there's an idea! How would you like to join us and Grandfather for dinner next week, Miss Genevieve? You too, Miss Amarante. And your mother, if she deigns to join us."

"That would be wonderful," Genevieve said.

I nodded, knowing that Lydia would force us to go whether I liked it or not.

"I'd love to meet your sister as well, Mr. Sternfeld," Julianna said, batting her eyes.

"Apologies, Miss Julianna. Our dining table is rather small," he said. "Perhaps another time?"

Julianna was fuming when Mr. Sternfeld went off to tell Lydia about the dinner plans. My stepmother would be elated. After all, this was an auction and Mr. Sternfeld, the poor man, was the prize cow we had just won.

"Well, Genevieve, I reckon you're proud of yourself?" our witch of a neighbor said.

"Pardon?" My stepsister looked taken aback.

Julianna's heeled shoe smashed into Genevieve's sketchbook. "Don't act innocent. Mr. Sternfeld is soon to become a lord. You ought to give up. He will never marry a commoner's daughter."

I clenched my fists. "Take that back, Julianna."

7

She merely huffed. "That is a horrid gown you have on, Amarante. Did you raid your mother's closet? Oh, I forget. You don't have one."

Before I could spit out an equally venomous remark, she sneered and stalked away.

"Oh, Amarante! How could she?" Genevieve exclaimed.

"Insulting us in our own home! She gets nastier by the day," I said. "And look what she did to your drawing!"

The sketch was now crinkled and stained with Julianna's filthy footprint. Genevieve frowned and brushed it off with her sleeve. "I wonder why she's like this. Hardships of her own, perhaps?"

I scoffed. Only Genevieve would be concerned about Julianna, who basked in her own sense of superiority because her mother was a dame and her father was a wealthy courtier.

I was more concerned with how to punish her.

A shriek of laughter came from the children playing a few feet away. A boy was chasing his friend with a handful of dirt from the rose bushes, which Rowena had recently fertilized. I grinned.

At the front of the garden, Lydia tapped her glass with a fork, beaming from ear to ear. No doubt Mr. Sternfeld had just invited her to dinner. I took the opportunity to slip off.

"It is an honor...no—a *privilege*, to welcome a new member to our neighborhood, Mr. Cedric Sternfeld!" my stepmother announced.

The guests gave a polite applause as Mr. Sternfeld stepped up. I ducked behind a dense rosebush with pale yellow blooms. The boy chasing his friend now sat on the grass, kneading the dirt in his hands. I tapped him on the shoulder.

"Mind if I take some of that?" I asked.

He shrugged.

"Much obliged." I pinched the dirt between my fingers and emerged from the bushes.

My stepmother was still speaking, praising Mr. Sternfeld's charm and good manners and how he would do wonders to liven up the neighborhood. Julianna sat a few feet away, her fingers inches away from her tea. It was strongly brewed, perfect to conceal something of similar color.

I sprinkled the dirt into my palm and began picking out the roots and gravel.

"Psst! What are you doing?"

I looked down. A couple of ginger-haired boys stared at me from the bushes, their cheeks flushed apple red. They were Tessa Donahue's brothers, Frederick and Teddy.

Tessa, a dear friend of Julianna's, lived a block away. She was in charge of her brothers today since their parents were absent. Unfortunately for her, the boys were the most rambunctious scamps on the block.

"There's a witch in our midst," I said to them, flicking away the last piece of root. "And I'm taking her down."

The two exchanged a glance. Fred gave me a gap-toothed grin and thumped his chest. "We can help."

I raised an eyebrow. "Are you up for the task?"

They nodded.

Lydia concluded her speech and the guests applauded. Julianna began chatting with Tessa, who incidentally was sitting beside her. Neither of them noticed me huddling with the Donahue brothers, or giving dirt to Ted.

"Got it?" I whispered.

"Got it," they chorused.

And then chaos ensued.

Fred darted out and snatched Julianna's straw hat, tearing at the ribbons and crepe flowers with his grubby hands. Julianna shrieked. Tessa's face grew as red as her hair.

"Fred! Stop that at once!" Tessa bellowed.

"Catch me if you can!" Fred sang.

They ran after him. The guests gaped as Fred fled, leaving a trail of shredded ribbons behind him. Julianna's scream was now shrill enough to shatter glass. Ted burst from the bushes and sprinkled the dirt into Julianna's tea, stirring it in with a grimy finger.

Seeing the mission complete, Fred abandoned the ruined hat and dove into the marigolds along the fence.

"You wretched little—ack!" Julianna stumbled over her hat and crashed into the lawn, bringing Tessa down with her.

Tessa squealed as her hands skidded across the grass. "My gloves!"

"Your gloves?" Julianna screeched. "My hat!"

Lydia rushed over. She looked horrified, her impeccable updo now in disarray. "Good heavens! Girls, are you alright?"

"I am not!" Julianna pounded the grass with her fist. "That *horrid* boy tore up my hat! The duchess gifted it to me on my sixteenth birthday!"

"T-the duchess?" Lydia stuttered. "Duchess Wilhelmina? The hostess of this year's Season?" She paled when Julianna nodded.

Tessa whimpered. "How much was it, exactly?"

Julianna shot her a glare. "It was *priceless*. You ought to keep your brothers on leashes, Tessa."

Mr. Sternfeld, who had been watching with an unreadable expression, finally walked over to help Julianna to her seat. She began sobbing unabashedly onto his shoulder and raving about how awful small boys were. Tessa trailed meekly behind them.

"Do calm yourself, Miss. Julianna," Mr. Sternfeld said.

She dabbed her eyes with her handkerchief. "Oh, Mr. Sternfeld. I am so distressed!"

The gentleman chuckled. It sounded forced. "Why not have some tea to settle your nerves?"

I smiled.

Julianna took a sip of tea.

And spat into her handkerchief with an ear-splitting scream. Specks of dirt marked her teeth.

"Tessa! Your brothers will *pay* for this!"

Lydia came over with Fred in tow. He was covered in marigold petals and dirt but looked immensely pleased with himself. I gave him a wink.

"Mr. Donahue, apologize to Miss Julianna at once," my stepmother said.

Fred merely smiled.

"You destroyed my hat and put dirt in my tea, you awful boy!" Julianna said, sobbing hysterically. "You will pay for this!"

Lydia's frown deepened as she looked at Fred. "You put *dirt* in her tea?"

"I didn't. Ted did." The boy jutted his chin to his brother.

"Your parents will be hearing about this," Lydia said, glowering at each boy. "Both of you will be punished severely."

I almost felt bad for the brothers, but only for a second.

Ted pointed at me. "She told us to do it."

2

You have ruined this family, Amarante!" Lydia said for the third time that evening. She blew her nose into her handkerchief as Genevieve gently patted her back. I continued working on my embroidery. It had been two days since the Great Tea Scandal. My stepmother was still livid though I had personally apologized to the Donahues and Alderidges per her orders.

Fred and Ted were punished to spend twice as much time on their studies, but I still wanted to give the little scoundrels a good shake for exposing me. Tessa merely stuck her nose in the air and harrumphed, as if she had been the one to drink fertilized dirt.

Julianna and Dame Patricia Alderidge, of course, were both furious. That was no loss to me. I was never on good terms with either of them. But Lydia fell into hysterics when Dame Alderidge declared the end of their friendship.

"Mama, please," Genevieve said. "It was those boys who stirred up all this trouble."

My stepmother shot me a glare. "I raised you for the better half of your life and this is how you repay me," she said, sniveling. "Patricia won't acknowledge me. She'll tell everyone at court what a horrid stepdaughter I have. And Genevieve! Oh, my poor, dear, beautiful Genevieve! Your name will be dragged down with this scandal!"

Genevieve and I exchanged a look. She was trying not to smile. "This hardly counts as a scandal, Mama, and I am sure Dame Alderidge has other people to gossip about."

"She gossips about everyone. Everyone!" Lydia wailed.

I wanted to remark that Dame Alderidge wasn't a very good friend, but held my tongue.

"And Mr. Sternfeld. Oh, Mr. Sternfeld is sure to take back his dinner invitation." Her words were muffled as she buried her face into her handkerchief again. "The tea party was supposed to be in his honor. And you *ruined* it!"

This time, I couldn't help but speak. "I'm sure I did him a favor. Julianna was clinging to him like a leech."

Lydia glared at me again. It would've been intimidating if her nose were not so red. "I'm sure he prefers Julianna now! I can't blame the man. *She* won't put dirt in his tea!"

Genevieve cleared her throat. "Actually, Mama, Mr. Sternfeld sent us a note today. He wanted to know if we were still available for dinner tomorrow."

"A letter? Helene, have we received a letter from Mr. Sternfeld?"

Lydia's personal maid, who was standing behind the couch, nodded. "It was addressed to Miss Genevieve, Madam."

My stepmother's lips trembled. "A note personally written by Mr. Sternfeld addressed to Genevieve?"

Genevieve colored. "It's nothing, Mama."

Lydia made a high-pitched noise at the back of her

throat. "Nothing, dear? It is everything!" She shot up from the couch, nearly tumbling over the coffee table. "There is no doubt about it! The gentleman fancies you, Genevieve. I knew you weren't so beautiful for nothing!"

Lydia whooped and laughed. Her handkerchief lay abandoned on the armrest, already dry.

Genevieve was now very red in the face.

"That rotten Patricia will have nothing to say if Mr. Sternfeld chooses Genevieve. Her daughter never stood a chance!"

I sputtered. "But I thought—"

"Hush!" Lydia said, pacing before the fireplace. "We must present ourselves properly tomorrow. Especially you, Genevieve! Hurry! Go upstairs and find something flattering to wear."

My stepsister blinked. "Now?"

"Yes now!"

Genevieve shot me an astonished look as she left the parlor. Even she wasn't used to her mother's odd moods.

I tucked the needle in my embroidery, ready to slip off, but Lydia stopped me with a frown.

"Yes, stepmother?" I said nonchalantly.

She put her hands on her hips. "I'm not done with you. Your conduct has been atrocious, Amarante."

"I already apologized to everyone!"

"I am not speaking of this incident alone. For the past four years, you have wreaked havoc for no apparent reason other than to make my life difficult."

"For the last time, stepmother, Julianna—"

"I will hear none of it! Playing pranks as a young lady is most unbecoming. You are almost seventeen, Amarante. It is time to grow up and act like a gentleman's daughter."

I crossed my arms. "Papa is a merchant, not a gentleman."

"He is as good as a gentleman with the wealth he has provided us. Must you be so contrary?" Lydia rubbed her temples. "You and Genevieve are of marriageable age. I will see both of you settled. Genevieve will be no problem, of course. Whether she marries or not, she still has the makings of a great artist. But *you*. What am I to do with you?"

I poked my embroidery with the needle. My flowers looked like shrimp on green sticks.

I had never been good at embroidery. I had never been good at anything except causing trouble, as my stepmother told me countless times. A part of me knew it was true and was ashamed of it.

Dread churned in my gut at the thought of Genevieve married or painting landscapes for wealthy ladies in a foreign country. I would be all alone, left for Lydia to throw at every possible suitor. Papa was rarely home. He would not be there to stop it.

Lydia finally stopped pacing. "I know. You will attend the Season."

I pricked myself with the needle. "What?"

"Yes. You will attend with Genevieve," Lydia said, punctuating her sentence with a nod. "Duchess Wilhelmina is hosting the Season this year. I don't expect you to be her favorite, not after you destroyed her gift to Julianna. But it will do you good to have a strict mentor and well-mannered peers. All the better if you find a young man willing to marry you."

I sputtered at the prospect. "But stepmother, I'm much too young to attend—"

"Nonsense! You will be seventeen in three months. What better age to come out?" she said. "The welcome banquet for debutantes is in a week. That is plenty of time to send your name to the palace."

There was a spring in her step as she headed out the parlor, humming to herself.

A drop of blood soaked my embroidery, but I could only stare at Lydia's retreating figure.

Me? A debutante?

"It's all Julianna's fault!" I said, fuming as Theodora helped me into my nightgown.

Despite being a house away, Julianna's operatic singing reverberated through my walls. I had learned to tolerate her singing lessons for the past twelve years, but tonight I found her voice especially irritating as she went up and down the scale.

Rowena fluffed my pillow. "It's partly your fault too," she said, tucking a stray curl into her bonnet. "Freshly fertilized dirt in tea? Honestly, Amarante. You're depriving my rose bushes."

Theodora began combing my hair. The scent of this morning's raspberry tarts lingered on her apron. Both of them had shirked their duties in the kitchen and garden to see me to bed for the past two days. They usually did when I was upset or in trouble, or both. I was immensely grateful. There was comfort in Theodora's steady hands and Rowena's jokes. It reminded me of my childhood, when the two had been my nannies.

"Your stepmother never goes through with her punishments," Theodora said, meeting my eye in the mirror.

"She seems serious this time." I slumped my shoulders, brushing a speck of dust off my vanity.

"Don't fret, dear," she said. "You're too young to attend."

I shook my head. "I'm turning seventeen in three months."

Theodora dropped the comb with a clack. "What?"

I repeated myself.

Rowena sucked in a breath. "Seventeen? Already?"

The two of them exchanged a glance. Julianna hit the highest note of the scale and held it with a strong vibrato.

"Exactly. I *am* old enough to attend." I hopped onto my bed and sunk into the freshly fluffed pillows with a sigh. "If only Papa were here."

Papa always prevented my punishments, like the time he stopped Lydia from shipping me off to a boarding school for troubled young ladies. But even boarding school seemed tame compared to the Season. Attending would mean passing the threshold from girlhood to womanhood. And there was no going back after that.

"Yes, of course!" Theodora exclaimed, pacing the room with sudden energy. "We will write to him immediately."

Rowena nodded. "Not a moment to lose." She gave the bedsheets one final tug and kissed the top of my head. "Sleep tight, dear."

With that, she exited my room just as Julianna began practicing her trills.

I gave Theodora a questioning look. She, however, was too busy pacing to respond.

"Theodora, you really don't have to worry at my expense," I said at last. "I'm sure Papa will change Lydia's mind."

She patted my cheek. "Of course, dear," she said, sounding distracted. "Rowena and I will write to him immediately."

I was about to tell her that I could write to Papa myself, but the words died in my throat when the door clicked shut.

The next day, Lydia ordered me to help Rowena with the marigold bushes along the fence, which were ruffled after Fred's hasty escape. I knew my stepmother would assign me a more unpleasant task if she knew I actually enjoyed gardening.

Still, last night's conversation with Lydia weighed heavily upon my shoulders, making it difficult to enjoy anything at all. Even Theodora's raspberry tarts tasted bland that morning.

I heaved a sigh as I packed in the loose dirt with a shovel.

"Theodora sent the letter this morning. I'm sure your Papa will get it soon," Rowena said, sweeping away the fallen marigold petals. They burned fiery yellow against the brown and green debris.

"How can you be sure?" I squatted and picked at the weeds around the bushes. Papa had yet to reply to the letters I sent him three months ago. The postman told me they must've been lost at sea. I wondered how many I had to write before one made it to him.

"Those aren't weeds," Rowena said without looking down.

I had unconsciously ripped out a fistful of grass.

"Sorry." I patted the uprooted grass back into the dirt. "I'm just nervous."

"Don't worry about things out of your control," Rowena said, rolling up her sleeves. Her brown skin had tanned even more in the past month. "You'll get a headache."

As I was about to reply, a smudge of color bloomed at the corner of my vision. It drifted beneath a rose bush

18

several paces away, a deep violet vibrating at the edges. It didn't look solid, but neither was it transparent.

I straightened. "What's that?"

Rowena turned, squinting to where I was pointing. "What's what?"

"You mean you can't—?"

The smudge vanished, but Rowena approached the spot.

"Crabgrass," she said when I walked over. A round patch of green was hidden under the foliage. There was a peculiar look on her face as she regarded the weed. "How did you spot this all the way over there?"

"I don't know. I thought I saw a violet…" I trailed off. The base of my head ached as I shook my head. "Never mind. Maybe I have been worrying too much."

Rowena shrugged. "What did I tell you? Go rest. I'll finish up here."

"Are you sure?"

"I'll manage. Besides, you have dinner with the Sternfelds tonight." Rowena gave me a knowing look. "You've forgotten, haven't you?"

I had. With a groan, I trailed back to the house. My stepmother was scribbling a letter in the dining room when I entered.

"Helene, take this to the post," Lydia said, giving the envelope to the maid. Helene curtsied and swept out the door.

"Who was that for?" I asked.

Lydia looked up. "That was—heavens! What are you wearing?"

I lifted my dirt-streaked skirts. "A dress, stepmother."

She gave me a look I was all too familiar with—disappointment mixed with disgust. "Honestly, Amarante. Next time, enter through the back door. I do not want the Sternfelds thinking you're a scullery maid."

As I climbed the stairs to my room, she spoke again.

"That was your application for the Season," Lydia called out. "You'll receive your invitation soon."

I froze. "What?"

"Just think. You'll attend the welcome banquet with Genevieve in a week," Lydia said. "The sooner you surround yourself with proper society the better."

"But Papa hasn't approved yet!"

"Oh, pooh. Julien will approve. You know, he has been saying he wants you to—"

The rest of my stepmother's words cut off as I flew down the steps.

I had to get that letter back.

3

In a flash, I was out the door. There was no trace of Helene's stout figure in the shaded streets of our neighborhood. She must've taken a horse chaise to the city post office, a place I was luckily very familiar with.

I hiked up my skirts as much as propriety allowed and ran, arms full of fabric and heart full of trepidation. Years of fleeing from Lydia's etiquette lessons should have prepared me for the half-mile sprint, but I was still wheezing for air when the outskirts of town came into view. The wooden sign of the post poked out from the tiled rooftops, a welcome sight as I trotted my usual route past several small shops.

I only had one thing in mind as I burst through the door.

"Those letters can't go!"

The dim room with poufs dotting the floor was most definitely not the post office. I blinked, realizing where I was—the boutique called Miriam's Terrariums.

It had been next to the post office for as long as I remembered, though I never knew why such a run-down shop was next to the city post. My stepmother had warned me about such places, where the decaying signs creaked with neglect and rounded architecture recalled times long passed.

"Letters?" A woman with a wrinkled brown face sat behind a low table, wrapped in chiffon shawls that drowned her hunched figure. She gave me a watery smile.

"I-I'm sorry," I said. The scent of ripe fruit and incense overwhelmed my nostrils. "I thought this was the post office."

"That's next door, dearie," she said with a cackle. "My little companions would make terrible postboys."

It was then I realized the shop was full of snails—large, slimy snails with colorful shells too bright to be natural. They lined the shelves in glass terrariums and crowded the corners behind gauzy draperies. There was even a handful of them roaming freely on the woman's table.

I shuddered, recalling my old governess's history lesson of the witches that once roamed the streets of Olderea. Our previous king, King Humphrey, had banned magic and witches from the kingdom two generations ago. But there were whispered rumors of a Witch Market where one could buy cursed items and gruesome poisons. Could this be it?

"Come sit, my dear. Meet some of my friends," the woman said, gesturing to a velvet pouf. A leafy branch lay along her table, the brown bark speckled with several snails.

I sat despite how desperately I wanted to leave. If she were indeed a witch, I could not afford to anger her.

"May I interest you in a pet snail?" the woman asked.

"No th—"

"Well then! Perhaps I can change your mind."

She plucked one off the branch. It was large and shiny with an orange and teal shell. She set it a few inches away from the leaves. The creature wriggled its antennae and crawled away, leaving a trail of mucus in its wake. Seconds dragged on as it inched around.

"See there. Snails are often knocked into unsure paths," the woman whispered. She had lowered herself so her eyes were level to the table. "Nevertheless, they continue on with patience and composure. Plus, they're good for gardens. Clean up dead debris and such."

"Fascinating," I lied.

"So. Would you like to purchase one?" the woman said, popping up. "Each snail comes with a free terrarium. Buy two and get another one free."

"No, thanks."

"Are you sure? I'll offer a fifty percent discount for a bag of specially curated snail food."

I shook my head and stood. "Thank you, madam, but I really must go. I have, er, a rendezvous with someone."

The woman harrumphed. "Very well, dear," she said. "At least tell your swain about my shop. Business has been slow lately."

My skin was still crawling when I entered the post office. Of all the things I expected the strange boutique to be, it was a snail shop!

When I inquired after Helene, Vincent, the mustachioed postman, informed me that I arrived a minute too late. The letters had already dispatched and were unlikely to be called back.

"Then are there any letters from my father?" I asked hopefully.

"Unfortunately not, Miss Amarante," Vincent said. He looked apologetic. I left before he could express his sympathy.

The trip home was slow and cumbersome. I was in no rush to see my stepmother again, as I expected yet another lecture about my brashness and unladylike behavior. However, no one had the breath to scold me when I arrived.

"Hurry and get dressed, Amarante!" my stepmother said when I entered. She was in a flurry of spirits, running to and fro with curl papers in her hair. "Dinner with the Sternfelds starts in an hour!"

I barely had time to breathe before Theodora ushered me upstairs to lace me into a presentable dress, her apron still dusted with flour from the rolls she had abandoned in the kitchen. Rowena fussed over Genevieve's shawl. By the time everyone was properly attired, we set out across the street.

The Sternfelds' dining room was large and cavernous, but sparsely furnished. A short dining table sat underneath a massive, glittering chandelier. There were no servants waiting along the walls. The house seemed to have a sort of stillness to it which the clinking of silverware did little to fill.

I had heard whispers around the neighborhood that Lord Gideon Sternfeld was immensely rich, having acquired his wealth in the bookbinding business. No one said he had a bad case of gout and was perpetually grouchy because of it. I found it immensely hard to enjoy dinner when I knew His Lordship's gouty foot was underneath the food.

I stole another glance at Lord Gideon at the head of the table, trying to find Mr. Sternfeld's open friendliness on his face. If anything, Lord Gideon's face was closed. His many wrinkles seemed to shrivel into a mighty frown, hard and unmoving.

Miss Olivia Sternfeld sat next to her brother across the table. She was a petite girl with large brown eyes and as pretty as Mr. Sternfeld was handsome. There was a timidity to her manner and after our polite introduction, she didn't peep another word. Neither did I, after realizing that eating was the much better alternative.

"You don't seem to keep much staff here, Mr. Sternfeld." Lydia's voice sounded eerily loud in the large room.

"Please, call me Cedric. And Joe here takes care of most things. He's been fantastic serving grandfather all these years," Cedric said, gesturing to the black-haired man standing behind him. He looked about forty, with skin almost as dark as his tightly curled locks. He gave a curt bow and resumed his silent post.

"Will he not join us?" Genevieve asked.

"Absolutely not, miss," Lord Gideon boomed. "Servants at the dining table? How preposterous."

Genevieve looked taken aback. My stepmother flushed. I suspected that once we went home, Theodora and Rowena and our other staff would no longer be allowed to dine at our table.

Cedric coughed and stirred his soup. "What my grandfather means is that it's not customary."

He gave his grandfather a look I could only describe as a blend of pity and frustration. His Lordship was chewing on a mussel, seemingly unbothered by the tension.

"So, Cedric, your sister is attending the Season?" Lydia asked. She had learned ten minutes ago that it was futile to speak to Olivia directly. "Will you not attend?"

"Unfortunately, no. I am looking through some encyclopedias I found during my travels," he said. He chatted animatedly about a book of various herbs and their medicinal properties. I hardly understood half of what he was describing, but I was glad someone was talking at all.

Lord Gideon harrumphed. "You embarrass yourself, boy. You're supposed to bind books, not read them. Especially not ones about plants. Botany is not a real man's hobby."

"Botany is an admirable science," Genevieve interceded. "I'm quite fond of plants myself."

"Really?" Cedric said, leaning forward. "Do you have a favorite?"

My stepsister smiled. "Roses."

"Ah, you did have some lovely ones in your garden."

A loud rustling sounded as Lord Gideon pulled a newspaper from underneath the table and flicked it open. A corner of it soaked into his gravy boat. Lydia stared.

"Anything interesting in the news, grandfather?" Cedric said after a beat.

He grunted. "Some fellow got arrested for buying from the Witch Market."

"Horrid place, that is," Lydia said.

Lord Gideon looked at her with steely eyes. "How would you know? Have you been there?"

"N-no, Your Lordship. I only hear things, that's all."

"I'm sure you do." He disappeared behind his newspaper again.

The clinking of spoons filled the air for a few moments. "So, the welcome banquet for debutantes is in a week," Cedric said. I was impressed by how cheery he still sounded.

"It is," Genevieve said, seemingly eager to converse again. "Olivia could take a carriage with me and Amarante to the palace if she wishes."

Olivia bent lower over her soup. Cedric smiled at her.

"That's kind of you to offer, Miss Genevieve, but my sister and I are moving into the palace tomorrow. I thought it'd be a good opportunity to see the royal grounds while I'm in Delibera."

My stepmother's eyes widened. The palace offered room and board for debutantes who wished to stay close for events, but the cost of living with royalty was a high one indeed. The fact that both Cedric and Olivia could afford to live there spoke volumes about their wealth.

"Well! That is quite exciting," Lydia said. "Maybe you'll catch a glimpse of Queen Cordelia, or the princes."

"Heard that Prince Ash is illegitimate," Lord Gideon said from behind his newspaper.

"How would you know, Grandfather? Were you present at his birth?" Cedric said with utmost politeness.

His Lordship snorted. "Touché, boy."

Dinner went on in this way, Lydia asking questions, Cedric answering, and Lord Gideon throwing in rude comments. I was beyond relieved when dessert was cleared from the table.

Cedric escorted us back home and apologized profusely for his grandfather, but Lydia still muttered about Lord Gideon's ill manners when the doors closed behind us. Genevieve lingered at the threshold, claiming she needed air.

I would've teased her, but the earlier talk of the Season unsettled me. In a few days, I would have to attend the dreaded welcome banquet.

The thought of meeting the Season mentors, especially Duchess Wilhelmina, struck a chord of panic in me. Genevieve and I grew up reading about her. Endless magazines and newspaper articles lauded the duchess as a pioneer of both fashion and politics. Julianna had often told stories of Her Grace as if she were a hero of mankind instead of a duchess. How I would act in the scrutiny of such a woman, I did not know.

My invitation came three days later.

"You will cherish this forever, Amarante," my stepmother said, handing me the crisp white envelope and gold embossed box. Nestled within was a bracelet of silver bells. It chimed when I took it out.

It was an old Olderean custom. Debutantes wore silver bells to mark the beginning of possible courtship. Young men tied gold ribbons around their wrists so the ladies knew they were interested suitors. By the end of the Season, if a couple decided to pair up, the two ornaments would be woven together as a pretty—but useless— symbol of courtship.

As I fastened the bracelet around my wrist, I vowed that a ribbon would not be looped through the chain under any circumstances. I was not attending for courtship, and even if I was, there was little sense in keeping such an ornament.

Lydia had kept hers all these years, locked away in her jewelry box. The ribbon intertwined in her chains, now faded of its luster, was not Papa's.

4

The west wing of the palace was a sprawling mass of marble arches and sky-high windows that extended beyond my vision. It was the only part of the palace open to the public, or the part of the public that could afford to rent the place.

I had only been there once for a soirée hosted by a particularly illustrious personage, but it had been ages since I'd stepped foot inside the banquet hall. A grand crystal chandelier that rivaled the Sternfelds' hung above a long dining table set with twenty-five places of glittering dishes and silverware.

A handful of girls were already seated. I felt smaller and smaller as Genevieve and I approached.

"Relax, Amarante," Genevieve said.

I loosened my grip on her hand, my palms clammy. "I'm sorry. I'm sweating all over you."

"Don't worry. This isn't officially the start of the Season.

Stepfather will let you withdraw before the Debutante Ball, I'm sure of it."

I was glad for Genevieve's assurance, but doubt still gnawed at my mind. Everything *looked* official enough.

A gasp sounded from behind me.

"Amarante? Who let *you* in the palace?" Julianna demanded. She marched toward me in a gown of tangerine orange, a lace fan clenched in her hands.

This was icing on the cake.

"You did," I retorted. "I have to spend two entire months attending these dull events because *you* threw a tantrum in my backyard."

Julianna glared. "I wouldn't have if you didn't ruin my hat and make me drink dirt! And you!" she said, turning to Genevieve. "You seduced Mr. Sternfeld!"

Genevieve was at a loss for words. I scowled. *Seduce* Mr. Sternfeld? Charm, delight, and captivate, perhaps, but not seduce.

"Don't you dare talk to my sister like that."

"Oh?" Julianna said, waving her fan in front of her nose. "You aren't going to start a brawl at the palace, are you?"

I gritted my teeth, tempted to rip the ribbons off her hair and see what she had to say to that, but Genevieve touched my arm in warning.

"Just leave us alone," I said, turning on my heel. But my march away was cut short when I stumbled over something black and furry. A yowl echoed through the banquet hall.

"Misty!" An auburn-haired girl in a scarlet dress rushed over to the black cat I had unceremoniously tripped over. She shot me a venomous glare.

"I-I didn't mean to," I stuttered. The girl's beauty

would've been entrancing if she weren't scowling at me like I was something stuck to her shoe.

Julianna pushed me aside. "Don't mind her, Narcissa," she said to the girl. "That's Amarante. The one I told you about."

Whatever Julianna had told her, it brought a sneer to Narcissa's face. "Oh. Her," was all she said.

Without another word, the two of them glided off to the table.

I was ready to pounce on all three of them, the cat included, before Narcissa settled herself next to the head of the table.

"What is *she* doing so high up?" I asked, aghast, as Genevieve and I took our seats. At the entrance, Cedric Sternfeld came in with Olivia trailing several feet behind, as if this were the last place she wanted to be. I couldn't relate more.

"It appears she's a high-ranking lady," Genevieve whispered.

"More like a high-ranking b—"

Genevieve shot me a look.

"…brat," I finished.

"Some guts you have insulting the duchess's daughter," came a cheery voice.

A girl with mousy-brown hair grinned at us from across the table. She wore a frilly peach dress that looked rather out of place against her plain features and thin arms.

"The duchess's daughter?" I said.

"Lady Narcissa Whittington," the girl said, enunciating each syllable as if savoring it. "Heard she's spoiled rotten. Rumors have it she and the crown prince are engaged."

Genevieve and I stared.

31

"Apologies, let me introduce myself. I'm Victoria Strongfoot, but you two can call me Tori." She stuck hands over the table, one at me and one at Genevieve. Before we could shake them, Tori struck her forehead. "Horse feathers. I've done it wrong."

"Done what wrong?" I asked.

She cleared her throat. "Good evening, I am Lady Victoria Strongfoot. Enchanted to meet you." She punctuated this sentence with a graceful bow of her head and a demure smile. After a beat, she broke the facade. "I'm not quite used to this, if you can't tell."

"Why aren't you?" Genevieve asked politely.

At this, Tori snorted. "Well, long story short, my Pa was a blacksmith who made weapons and armor for the Royal Guard. A couple of months ago, he crafted a magnificent sword for Captain Greenwood."

"The captain of the Royal Guard?" I said. My knowledge of palace personages came primarily from Lydia's gossip. My stepmother said Captain Greenwood once was a desirable bachelor, partly because he was close friends with the king, queen, and Duchess Wilhelmina. She also said he had an affair with Queen Cordelia. I hardly knew what to believe.

"That's the one. Old Greenwood liked the sword so much he asked the king to grant my father the title of 'Lord'. Lord of nothing, I tell you, but Pa was ecstatic. Became a gentleman of leisure right then and there and vowed to never step foot in his workshop again! He told me, 'Victoria, now that your old Pa is a lord, you ought to learn to be a proper lady. Marry proper. Find a nice, wealthy gentleman and start a new generation of Strongfoots who'll never have to work a day in their lives'," Tori looked mistily into the distance. I found myself squinting in an attempt to see what she was seeing. "I'm not too keen on finding a fellow to marry, but I'll do anything for my Pa. So here I am, talking to you two."

"Oh. I'm Amarante, by the way."

"And I'm Genevieve."

"I figured," Tori said with a nod to our place cards.

"Say, since you're technically a lady, shouldn't you be sitting somewhere up there?" I asked, gesturing toward the head of the table.

Tori guffawed, drawing a few disgusted looks from passersby. "Sure, when witches are allowed back in Olderea. The duchess wouldn't want me with my lord of nothing father up there. She's very particular about preserving the distinction of class, ironically."

"Ironically?"

"Haven't you heard? Her Grace came to the palace as a mere scullery maid, befriended the queen, married a duke on his deathbed and became one of the most powerful and well-respected women in court. She's in charge of the Season this year instead of the queen. Said Her Majesty wanted her to do it for some reason." She wrinkled her nose. "I don't expect to like Her Grace very much. My Pa says she's a sharp sort of woman who knows too much for her own good."

"Seems like you know a lot about the duchess," I said, quite drawn in to our new friend's stories. She spoke as if she were a palace insider and not a blacksmith's daughter thrown into prosperity.

Tori's cheeky grin reappeared. "I know about as much as everyone else."

"Not us. We're new to all this," Genevieve said.

"Is that so? I couldn't tell," Tori said. "You two look as proper as anyone else in the room."

"Propriety can be learned," I said with a smile. "Our father is a bit like yours, though he doesn't have a fancy title. He's a merchant."

Tori nodded. "Heard there's been a boom in trade ever since Olderea opened its ports to Aquatia. Who would've thought? That kingdom is full of magic."

"They've arrested someone for going to the Witch Market this week," I said in a lower voice. "Why would we accept goods from Aquatia if magic is illegal here?"

She shrugged. "To keep good relations, I suppose. It's because Queen Cordelia is Aquatian. Olderean merchants are only accepting non-magical items, I heard. But who knows? That may change."

Before I could say more, a dignified woman dressed in a brilliant red gown emerged from the hall. The chatter quieted. She had a thin nose, thick auburn hair, and rosebud lips that curved into a smile when she approached.

Her teeth gleamed like the large gold locket around her neck, stamped with an emblem of a snake twisted amongst thorny roses.

"The Whittington insignia," Tori murmured from the corner of her mouth when she saw my interest in the piece.

When Duchess Wilhelmina reached the table, we all stood. I thought I saw a girl swoon.

"Good evening, ladies." The duchess's voice was deeper than I anticipated.

"Good evening, Your Grace," we collectively murmured.

She inclined her head, her diamond earrings glittering. "Welcome to this year's Season. As you know, it is tradition for all young ladies who have come of age to participate in this two-month event to celebrate their journey to womanhood. This year, Queen Cordelia has allowed me to be your hostess. I have chosen two ladies to help me mentor you during this year's events."

At her word, two women entered, one thin and one plump. They were introduced respectively as Madam Lucille, the music mistress and Lady Hortensia, a courtier. Madam Lucille looked more like a nun in her somber high-necked frock, but Lady Hortensia looked her part, adorned with layers of beaded jewelry and lacy hems.

The two chattered some nonsense about how they looked forward to mentoring us and how they had never seen a prettier batch of debutantes. After Madam Lucille and Lady Hortensia seated themselves with us, Duchess Wilhelmina once again took the stage.

"A catalog of events will be sent out soon. But for now," the duchess said, clapping her hands, "let the banquet begin!"

A row of smartly-dressed waiters filed into the hall, carrying silver platters with shallow plates of leafy green salads.

For the next thirty minutes, Duchess Wilhelmina instructed us on the proper way to sit and the correct utensils to use for each dish. It was all immensely dull and confusing, and time seemed to muddle itself in my brain. In the midst of it, Olivia Sternfeld left the room after whispering to a maid. She never returned. Whether it was the dullness of the event or her crippling shyness, I did not know, but I certainly envied the girl.

At the start of the last course, a few waiters came to replenish our beverages. I watched absentmindedly as one of them refilled a girl's glass, the water rising up and up and…

The girl shrieked when her glass overflowed, water pooling onto the tablecloth and dribbling down onto her violet skirts. "What have you done?" she demanded, frantically wiping her dress. "This gown is worth more than your yearly wages you clumsy cow!"

"Apologies, Miss Samantha." The waiter who spoke couldn't have been older than me. He bowed his head of lustrous black hair and offered Samantha a napkin. She snatched it, dabbed her skirts, and flung it back at him. He caught it with ease and proceeded down the table.

The duchess, oddly enough, did not seem to notice this encounter. Even Madam Lucille and Lady Hortensia were preoccupied chatting amongst themselves.

An arm reached past my shoulder with a water pitcher. I glanced up, recognizing the waiter's black hair. He didn't seem too bothered by Samantha's rebuke. I supposed he had to be thick-skinned to be a waiter.

But apparently not well-coordinated.

A shock of icy water cascaded into my lap. I gasped and jerked up. My chair crashed behind me.

"Apologies!"

Half-melted cubes of ice clattered to the floor as water rained down my skirt. Genevieve and Tori looked at me in horror.

"Good heavens, what is going on?" The duchess's voice cut off the gasps and exclamations. I hardly expected her to speak after her silence during Samantha's episode.

"It was my fault, Your Grace," the waiter said, bowing at the waist. "An accidental slip of the hand."

Two spots of color appeared on Duchess Wilhelmina's face when he straightened. She took a shuddering breath before speaking in an even voice. "Show the young lady to a place she can clean up," she said. "Then leave at once."

He bowed again. Beckoning to me, he walked with decided steps through the arch from which the duchess had entered. I had to trot to catch up, my steps echoing loudly in the dead silence. When we had both safely exited, I finally found my voice.

"Er…Are you sure waiting on the upper class was the right career choice?"

He didn't turn around fully, but a dimple appeared on his left cheek. "You're not angry with me?" he said. Nothing about his manner betrayed any reaction to being scolded. His back was straight. There was even a bounce in his steps.

"Not particularly," I said. Truth be told, I was a little annoyed. Wet skirts didn't put me in the best of moods, but I wasn't going to lash out at someone I barely knew. The waiter kept walking as I held the drenched fabric away from me, leaving a trail of water droplets in my wake. "I would appreciate a napkin, though."

"Here. Take this." Before I could react, the waiter stripped off his jacket and handed it to me, one hand still holding the water pitcher. It was then I noticed he was a rather handsome fellow with almond eyes, sculpted features, and an easy smile.

I blushed, taking his jacket. "Thank you."

The waiter stood by as I attempted to blot my dress. The material of his jacket proved to be less than absorbent. Still, I managed to wring my skirts dry until it resembled a mangled bed sheet.

There was an audible silence when the two of us reentered the banquet hall. Time passed agonizingly slowly as the waiter lifted my chair right side up and gestured for me to sit. I shoved his jacket into his hands. He leaned over to set the water pitcher before me.

"Enjoy the banquet, Miss Amarante."

He winked and departed. I sat for a second to compose myself before looking up. I hoped the exchange went unnoticed, but the curious face of Genevieve, the suggestive one of Tori, and the disapproving look on Samantha's were clear signs that it hadn't.

"Heavens. You were flirting with him," Samantha accused.

"I was not," I said, affronted.

"Looked like he was flirting with you," Tori said.

I flushed. "No, he was not."

"Looked a bit like he was," Genevieve admitted.

"Nobody was flirting!"

I didn't realize how loudly I spoke until the words were out of my mouth. A few debutantes looked my way and I ducked my head, praying that the clinking of silverware was enough to cover my voice further along the table. Heavens forbid the duchess heard! Genevieve stifled a laugh.

Samantha looked at me haughtily, her expression not unlike Narcissa's. "Don't you know better than to tangle yourself with the likes of him? The whole point of the Season is to find an *eligible* match," she said.

Tori turned to her with a sharp look. "What are you trying to say? Working class is dirt to you?" she said. Samantha huffed and turned away.

Tori shot her one last glare before addressing me. "It's a shame nobody here appreciates a working man. If you want to flirt with that waiter, flirt all you want," Tori said generously.

"Thanks, I suppose," I said in a strangled voice.

"There will be no flirting in my presence, ladies," a commanding voice said. I jumped.

The duchess was standing behind me, frowning. Her lips were pressed into a thin line. I craned my neck to look at her.

"I-I'm sorry, Your Grace," I stuttered, startled at being addressed by the duchess herself.

"I expect you all to behave like proper young women tonight." She did not sound pleased. Her eyes flicked to my place card. "Especially you, Miss Amarante Flora."

I bowed my head. "Yes, Your Grace."

"I've heard about you," the duchess said, looking at me through her lashes. "You caused quite a scene in your own backyard, yes?"

My face burned. I could already see Julianna's smug face.

Duchess Wilhelmina took my silence as confirmation. She shook her head. "I cannot blame you for being uneducated, coming from such a family. It is unseemly to isolate yourself with such lowly personage, Miss Flora. Do you understand?"

"Y-yes, but Your Grace, you told me to go with him."

Not even a clink of silverware interrupted the silence that ensued. I wished I hadn't said anything. Arguing with the duchess? I must have gone mad.

"Stand up," the duchess said softly.

My legs stood on their own accord, barely able to support my weight.

"Look at me when I address you, Miss Flora."

I lifted my chin. The duchess's gaze was steely, intensified by her slate-colored irises. I made out the harsh creases between her brows. Hers was not a face that had seen much joy.

"Repeat after me," she said crisply. Her voice rung out in the banquet hall. "I will not flirt with inconsequential men."

My breath caught at my throat. "B-But, Your Grace—"

"I said, Miss Flora, repeat after me."

I clasped my hands behind me, wishing that the silence were not so deafening. "I…I will not flirt with inconsequential men," I said.

"Louder, Miss Flora, for the young ladies in the back."

"I will not flirt with inconsequential men."

Snickers sounded from the head of the table. Julianna's was the loudest. I hated how my eyes prickled.

"Very good. Do well to remember that." The duchess swept away, heels clicking against the marble. She clapped her hands. "Now, let us start dessert."

Throughout dessert, Genevieve threw me concerned looks I pretended not to notice. Tori opened and closed her mouth, as if wanting to speak but thinking better of it. It was a good thing she did because I was too mortified to do anything but eat my slice of cake, hoping that each swallow would push down the tears that threatened to spill onto my plate.

Why should I cry? It wasn't as if I wanted to impress the duchess in the first place.

When the banquet ended, we all were escorted outside to wait for our carriages. The night air and hazy lights eased the tension in my throat and I managed to join Genevieve and Tori's lighthearted debate on whether Lady Hortensia's gown was lime green or chartreuse. My comfort, however, was short lived.

"What a humiliating scene!" Julianna's voice pierced through the murmur of conversation as she sauntered toward me. A few debutantes stopped and stared.

"Julianna," Genevieve said, crossing her arms. "We were talking." My stepsister looked almost hostile, which I would have marveled at if I weren't dizzy with indignation.

"I cannot imagine what Madam Lydia was thinking, letting you attend the Season," Julianna said, tossing a curl behind her shoulder. She sneered at me, her eyes lingering on the wrinkled, wet stain at the front of my dress. "Flirting with the staff. Really, Amarante, have you no shame?"

Tori stepped forward. "Have you no shame bullying people when you know perfectly well they did nothing wrong?" she said.

Julianna scoffed. "And who might you be?"

"*Lady* Victoria Strongfoot, daughter of *Lord* Strongfoot," Tori said.

"Oh. The blacksmith's daughter. You say those titles as if they mean something, peasant girl," Julianna said.

"Repeat that and I'll—"

I pulled Tori back before she did any damage. "What do you want, Julianna?" I said, glaring. Hadn't she humiliated me enough?

"I wonder what the Sternfelds would think if they hear about this," Julianna said with a sly smirk. "How improper for a soon-to-be lord to be associating with such…promiscuous young ladies." Her eyes slid from me to my stepsister. It didn't take long for me to get her meaning.

She was jealous of Cedric's interest in Genevieve. What would happen once news of my blunder spread to the neighborhood? Genevieve and I would be labeled as shameless flirts. Lord Gideon made it evident last week that he disapproved of us. The gossip would no doubt push him over the edge and Cedric would no longer be able to look at Genevieve without judgment.

And Lydia. What would Lydia do once she discovers that my mistakes cost Genevieve her reputation and the affection of a rich suitor?

Julianna grew even more smug at my reaction. I had never wanted to box her face so badly. Even so, I controlled myself. Starting a brawl at the palace wouldn't improve my situation.

"So? You'll gossip whether I want you to or not," I said steadily, though I was anything but.

Genevieve took my hand. "The Sternfelds have better judgment than you think, Julianna," she said coolly. "It's your word against ours."

I squeezed my stepsister's fingers, relieved to have her support. My only hope was Julianna would buy our bluff.

Julianna's face grew tomato red. "Forget the Sternfelds! They clearly have no taste in good society," she said, narrowing her eyes at me. "Just you wait, Amarante. Everyone who is anyone will hear about your behavior tonight." With that, she harrumphed and stomped away.

I let go of a breath. It was just me she wanted to humiliate now, but whether she meant to or not, Julianna would ruin Genevieve's coming out if she ruined mine.

"Nicely handled," Tori said as she watched my neighbor's retreating figure.

Genevieve touched my arm. "Don't worry, Amarante. She probably doesn't mean it."

How I hoped that were true.

5

The cold mornings grew shorter and the sun began to cast its sweltering rays on the earth below. June was fast approaching and with that the Debutante Ball, marking the commencement of the dreaded Season.

A week had passed since the Welcome Banquet Disaster with Duchess Wilhelmina. Lydia had no clue of my blunder as Genevieve left it out when recounting our time at the palace. I spent days brewing over Julianna's threat. I almost expected to wake up to taunts and rotten eggs thrown at our windows, but I was only met with silence. It was the silence that worried me.

It could only mean Julianna was waiting for a bigger, wealthier audience. An audience like the guests of the Debutante Ball. No doubt she decided that exposing me in high society was the more satisfying option.

My mind swam with thoughts of water spills, Duchess Wilhelmina's disapproving face, and the ball of humiliation that loomed over me. I prayed that Papa would write back and tell Lydia I cannot go, that I was too young or he was too poor. But fate disregarded my hopes.

The day before the Debutante Ball, Rowena handed me a letter from Papa.

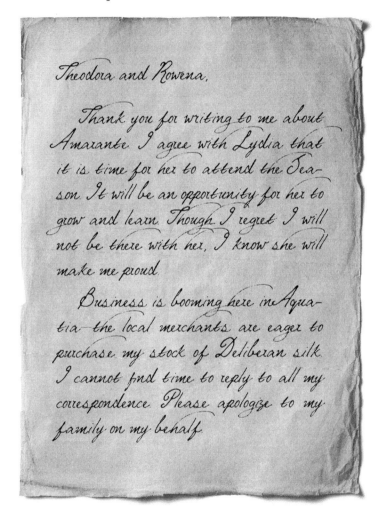

Theodora and Rowena,

Thank you for writing to me about Amarante. I agree with Lydia that it is time for her to attend the Season. It will be an opportunity for her to grow and learn. Though I regret I will not be there with her, I know she will make me proud.

Business is booming here in Aquatia—the local merchants are eager to purchase my stock of Deliberan silk. I cannot find time to reply to all my correspondence. Please apologize to my family on my behalf.

The letter cut off. I flipped the paper over. "Where's the rest?" I asked.

Rowena scuffed her feet. "He was rambling about business matters. I didn't think you'd care for it."

I set the paper on my nightstand, sick to my stomach. Papa wanted me to attend the Season. He believed I would make him proud.

If only he knew the mess I had gotten myself into already.

"What's wrong, dear?" Rowena asked.

"What if Papa doesn't care about me anymore?" I said. It sounded harsher out loud, but it was a reasonable conclusion. He had always been there to stop my punishments. Just a few years back, he refused to have Lydia ship me off to a boarding school for troubled young ladies. Why would the Season be any different?

Rowena tutted. "Don't say that. He's just busy, that's all. Look how hard he works to support us."

"I suppose so," I muttered.

I didn't want to overwhelm her with my real thoughts. Perhaps it was ungrateful of me, but I was more aware of Papa's absence than the wealth that crept into our home in the form of new furniture and ornate rugs.

"Here. Your father sent this too," Rowena said brightly. She set a large box with a satin bow onto my bed.

Inside was a magnificent ball gown of marigold yellow with intricate beading and gauzy fabric. Though beautiful, it solidified my doom, just like the bracelet of silver bells.

As I ran my fingers over the embroidery on the bodice, I recalled the last conversation I had with him.

———•———

"Ah, my flower," Papa said, smiling as I brought in his nightly tea. His desk was in disarray, his fingers stained with ink. "You look like quite the young lady."

The porcelain clinked when I set it down. I made a face. "Really?"

"Why, you act like it's a bad thing," he said.

"My old governess used to call me that." I recalled Mrs. Handel's voice. She reminded me of Julianna, haughty, condescending, and shrill.

Papa took his tea and inhaled its earthy fragrance. "You know," he said thoughtfully, "ever since Mrs. Handel left you've been quite idle."

I sunk into a leather armchair and slumped over the side. "She was a terror. Besides, Genevieve doesn't have a governess. She's doing just fine."

Papa chuckled. "That's because Lydia is tutoring her. And since you refuse to be taught by your stepmother, Mrs. Handel was the only solution. Though I wouldn't have chosen her as your governess if I'd known she would swipe the antiques."

I grinned, recalling the look on my governess's face when Lydia's bronze cat figurines fell out of her purse. I had flirted with the idea of getting rid of her in some way or other, but I didn't expect the old hag to do it herself. It had been four months since I'd received any sort of schooling at all, since Papa was too busy to find a replacement.

In the absence of having to recite historical events or embroider a fish, I spent my time helping Rowena in the garden, lounging outside with Genevieve, and sitting with Papa whenever he was home. The break was a blessing.

Papa took a sip of his tea. "What do you think about attending the Season this year?"

I jerked up. "Papa!"

"Genevieve is going. You won't be alone," he said, adjusting his spectacles. He usually did that when he fancied his own idea.

"I don't want to go," I said. A whine escaped into my voice—hardly becoming for someone my age—but I didn't care. I was not going to the Season, with its socials and dancing and courtship.

"Why not?" Papa said. "It's something a young lady of your status would have to attend sooner or later."

I crossed my arms and scowled. "I choose later." How I wished Papa hadn't gotten so rich, so I wouldn't have to attend at all!

He sighed and gave me a look I couldn't quite read. "I suppose you can wait another year. But promise me you'll spend your time more wisely, my flower. Nothing rots the mind like idleness."

I relaxed into the armchair. "Very well, Papa. I promise."

———•———

I never kept my promise after he left for Aquatia, so perhaps I deserved the punishment.

Lydia's thrill over Papa's approval was nothing when she saw Genevieve in her ball gown. My stepsister looked like a princess in her gown of pale rose dotted with seed pearls. Lydia cried for a whole evening after the fitting.

I was happy for Genevieve. She was clearly excited for her coming out, but I knew she was suppressing her emotions for my sake. Still, as much as I tried, I couldn't keep my sour mood from showing during the long carriage ride to the palace. My ill-fitting corset dug into my ribs and the embroidery on my dress itched. I hated that something so beautiful could be so painful.

When we arrived, Lady Hortensia met us debutantes in the courtyard and told us we had to rehearse our entrance before the ball. The year before, a debutante tumbled down the stairs as she did not know the proper way to descend a royal staircase. I doubted there was a difference between descending a regular staircase versus a royal one, but I followed Lady Hortensia into the ballroom nonetheless.

All twenty-five of us gathered behind the grand steps, each moving forward as the herald called our names. He was a short man with a monocled eye, a bald head, and the most piercing voice I ever heard, second only to Julianna's.

"Miss Amara...Amaran...tee—"

"The 'e' is silent, sir," I said, already halfway down.

The herald sniffed. "Very well. Er...Miss Rachel Estelle!"

A tall girl in a blue dress descended after me at his squeaky call. Her hands were shaking, though the ballroom below was empty aside from the servants setting the refreshments table.

"Posture, dear!" Lady Hortensia trilled from the bottom of the steps. "Remember Rachel, you are a swan gliding along a lake, not a pigeon pecking crumbs on the road. And speaking of pigeons, Mr. Packington," she said, turning to the herald, "are you sure you cannot do anything about those awful birds? They're nesting in the chandeliers."

The herald peered up. A band of gray-blue pigeons was perched on the golden arms of the chandelier above him. They stared back with round, unblinking eyes. Mr. Packington shuddered. "Like I told you milady, the servants have tried everything. They simply wouldn't leave."

"I don't like it. It seems like some sort of...witchery." Lady Hortensia shuddered, wiggling her plump, bejeweled fingers.

"Nonsense!" Mr. Packington puffed up his scrawny chest. "We do not speak of such things here, milady. I'm sure that much you know."

The lady frowned a frown that rivaled Lord Gideon's.

By the end of it, we were led into a sitting room to wait for the start of the ball. Many debutantes spent the time chattering. Genevieve, Tori, and I sat in our own corner. We asked Olivia to join us, but the girl shied away from any interaction and buried her nose in a book.

Perhaps she would disappear again, like she had at the welcome banquet. We decided to leave her be.

As dull minute after dull minute dragged on, Tori excused herself to the lavatory, Genevieve sketched aimlessly on a napkin, and I settled on eavesdropping.

"How do you think pigeons got into the ballroom?" Samantha asked from the other side of the room.

"I heard from one of the servers they entered through the kitchens," Tessa Donahue said, patting her coppery curls. "Someone must've left a window open."

"How irresponsible." Julianna scoffed. "Narcissa, why don't you have your cat take them down?"

The duchess's daughter was perched on an armchair. She narrowed her eyes. "It's the servants' job to take care of such things."

Julianna looked cowed, but she masked it with a laugh. "You're right. Work like that is reserved for clumsy waiters and girls who flirt with them." She threw a glance at me. A few debutantes giggled.

"Ignore them," Genevieve whispered, smoothing her napkin. Julianna's laughter was still ringing in my ear.

"I can't believe her," I muttered, blood rushing to my face. It was true that I had grown used to Julianna's antics. She spread all sorts of rumors about me as a child—that I had a beard I shaved off every morning, that I ate bird droppings, that I had freckles because I was cursed by a witch. At some point I learned to tolerate it by playing pranks and giving empty threats, but this was different.

How would Lydia react knowing my reputation had ruined Genevieve's? What would Papa say if my first day at the Season was a disaster? How could I make him proud then?

"Amarante, whoever she gossips to is going to think worse of her than of you. No respectable lady would say such things about others," Genevieve said, tucking her napkin away. She squeezed my shoulders. "It will be fine. I promise."

I marveled at her calm, especially when her reputation was on the line too. A part of me wished I could be like Genevieve, but the sensible part knew that wasn't possible.

I gave my stepsister a strained smile and stood from my seat. "You're right," I said. "I'm going to the lavatory."

I was in more danger of pummeling Julianna with my bare fists than ever before, but I had since learned to curb my juvenile tantrums. I satisfied myself by marching up and down the hall instead, imagining I was digging my heel into Julianna's face with each step. I passed Tori my fifth time down the hall.

"Where you off to?" Tori said, nibbling on a pastry.

"The lavatory," I said.

"It's over there," she said, pointing to the left. "The kitchen is to the right. They'll let you sneak a little snack before the ball if you ask."

"Great. Thanks."

She went back into the sitting room and I made my way to the right. If there was anything I needed, it was Theodora's signature raspberry tarts, but I would have to settle for the next best thing. The more I walked the angrier I got. What right did Julianna have to hold my reputation against me? That was crossing the line, even for her.

Servants bustled past with arms laden with baked goods. A maid beat at a stray pigeon with a feather duster. A young man strolled by, polishing a green apple with his shirt.

I stopped in my tracks. It was *him*.

"You!" I whirled around, pointing a trembling finger at the waiter who had spilled water on me. This time, he was dressed in a plain shirt and breeches. Those in the hall stopped and stared, but I paid them no mind. My blood was boiling.

"Oh. You," the waiter said. He raised his eyebrows, looking infuriatingly relaxed. "Hello."

"Hello? *Hello?*" My voice raised an octave higher as I stomped up to him. "Do you have any idea what you caused?"

"Woah, easy there." He stepped back, holding his apple away.

"Of all things you *had* to give me your jacket! And you...you *winked* at me!" I sputtered.

I wanted to say a million more things, but surely shouting at a palace employee wouldn't help my situation.

Yet my anger had to go somewhere. I snatched the apple from his hand. Curse him for holding it away from me, like he was afraid I was going to spit on it. I shoved the fruit between my teeth and crunched down.

The servants behind me gasped. The waiter merely stared.

My eyes watered from the acidity of the fruit as I thrust it back into his hands.

"Enjoy that," I said, mouth full of apple, and marched off.

It wasn't long before Lady Hortensia ushered us out of the sitting room to the top of the stairs again. The ballroom was now alive with chattering guests. Somehow, the servants had shooed the pigeons away. The only sign of their presence was a dollop of droppings on an unlit candle.

"Miss Samantha Faas!" Mr. Packington announced.

Samantha descended the marble staircase as several other debutantes had before her. The ballroom burst into a smattering of applause. The waiter's apple soured my stomach, a reminder of yet another humiliating decision I had made in the past few weeks.

The queue shuffled forward. A thousand faces turned toward us.

"Miss Genevieve Bonavich Flora!"

My stepsister descended, the voluminous skirts of her ball gown flaring around her like petals on a rose. She was a tiny figure when she reached the bottom. She curtsied low before the dais and joined the cluster of debutantes on the side of the ballroom.

IREEN CHAU

"Miss Amarante Flora!"

My feet brought me forward at their own accord, seemingly more prepared than I was. The descent was longer than I anticipated. Queasy as I felt, I managed to reach the foot of the stairs and curtsy before the king and queen.

The fact that the rulers of Olderea were merely a few feet before me did not help my nerves. I stole a glance at them as I rose. King Maximus was swathed in golden finery. His bleary gaze and stony expression told me he was already bored with the festivities. In contrast, Queen Cordelia gave me the smallest of smiles. It made her eyes glimmer. I let go of a breath, returned her smile, and joined Genevieve on the side of the ballroom.

It felt like ages when they finished announcing everyone, including the illustrious courtiers and gold-ribboned young men. Silver bells jingled as the debutantes shifted about, restless from standing. When I thought they would finally let us go, a fanfare sounded from the top of the stairs.

"Announcing His Highness Crown Prince Bennett Median of Olderea!"

Squeals and whispers erupted from around me. I peeked over the shoulders of my fellow debutantes to catch a glimpse of the crown prince. He was tall and stately in a deep maroon coat, his crown gleaming from atop his chestnut hair. He looked very much like the king, if the king weren't paunchy and balding. With a curt bow before his parents, the crown prince mounted the dais and took his seat beside his father. His face was stoic as he stared ahead.

"Who put dirt in his tea?" I muttered to Genevieve. She giggled.

53

Another fanfare sounded. "His Highness Prince Ash Median of Olderea!"

A familiar figure came down the steps.

Except this time, there was a crown nestled in his dark hair.

6

As the ballroom erupted into applause, someone grabbed my wrist.

"Is that who I think it is?" Samantha whispered. She smelled like she took a bath in her grandmother's perfume. I tugged my arm out of her clammy fingers.

The other debutantes seemed to have similar reactions. Genevieve looked perplexed. I could only feel horror and embarrassment as I recalled what I had done mere minutes ago.

"Why in the blazing fires was the second prince of the kingdom disguised as a waiter?" Tori emerged from behind us in her magnificent sapphire blue gown. "Do you think he might be a pervert?"

Samantha shot her a glare. "His Highness is entitled to do whatever he wishes."

"Really? I wonder why you had such a fit when His

Highness spilled water on your gown, then," Tori said, tilting her head.

Samantha bristled and glared but said no more.

When the cheers died down and Prince Ash took his seat next to the queen, the orchestra at the balcony began playing a light air. The guests gravitated toward the dance floor, and several debutantes were whisked away by the boldest of the gold-ribboned young men.

A hook-nosed matron I recognized as Lady Thornbush, one of Lydia's friends, approached Genevieve.

"Enchanted to see you, my dear girl! You look as lovely as ever. Have I introduced you to my son, Edward?" Lady Thornbrush said, fluttering a feathered fan beneath her nose. I wondered how she didn't sneeze.

Beside her, a scrawny youth no more than sixteen executed an awkward bow. Genevieve curtsied. "Lovely to meet you," she murmured.

At this, Edward blushed a deep red and stuttered a request for a dance. My stepsister threw me an apologetic look. I motioned for her to go.

Lady Thornbush gave a contented sigh as Genevieve and her son made for the dance floor. After a moment of staring, her ladyship walked off, completely ignoring my presence.

Tori gave a low whistle. "Well then. Off to the refreshments table, Amarante?"

"Gladly."

The other side of the ballroom was filled with platters of sandwiches and cakes, far away from the dais and the dance floor. I was beyond relieved. The last thing I needed was attention on me. Tori grabbed a few cucumber sandwiches and I helped myself to berries and a puff pastry. We devoured our snacks against the wall, observing the chattering groups around us.

My eyes darted around the ballroom for Julianna, but she was nowhere to be found in the midst of opulent gowns and swirling couples. The undercover prince showed no signs of leaving his dais either, his head bowed in conversation with Queen Cordelia.

"How long do you suppose we could go without dance partners?" I said, popping a raspberry into my mouth. I forced my voice to be light, hoping it didn't betray the churning anxiety in my gut.

"However long it takes us to eat this entire table," was Tori's reply. She swallowed her bite of sandwich. "Actually, I ought to find my Pa. He said he would be arriving late."

"Ah. The roads are crowded with carriages," I said.

"Oh, no. He's walking here."

I raised my brows. "All the way to the palace?"

Tori took another bite of her sandwich. "Our place is a quarter mile from the west wing," she said. "I would've walked here if I didn't like these shoes so much." She poked her foot out from her skirts, revealing a dainty high-heeled slipper encrusted with sapphires.

As she bent over, a gold coin tumbled out from her bodice, dangling from a chain around her neck. It bore a stamp of a lion and crossed swords, different from the standard coins of the kingdom.

"This is Captain Greenwood's insignia," Tori explained after noticing my interest. "Illustrious families usually have their own coins to reward to people of their choice. To us Strongfoots, it's a symbol of merit."

"You must really revere the captain," I said.

Tori shrugged. "My Pa certainly does, but I haven't

met him." She straightened. "And speaking of Pa, I think I see him."

I sagged against the wall, picking at my berries. Was I doomed to spend the rest of the night alone?

Tori looped her arm around mine. "Don't think I'm leaving you," she said with a lopsided grin. There was a bit of bread stuck to her teeth, but it didn't make her smile any less bright. "Pa's been nagging me to find some proper lady friends. He'll be over the moon to meet you. That is, unless you want to stay here."

I spotted Lydia's head amongst the crowd. She was probably looking for Genevieve, or worse, me. I had no desire to be forced into a dance with one of her friends' sons.

"Not at all," I told Tori, abandoning my plate.

Tori led me through the crowd to an open space near the exit. A large man with muscled arms and a protruding gut stood aimlessly about, looking extremely out of place with his grizzly black beard. His gray eyes lit up when we approached.

"There's my girl!" he bellowed. "What did I miss? Wait, never mind that. How's the food? Have they got any turkey legs?"

Tori grinned. "No, Pa. But they've got a load of candied pineapples."

"Ah! My favorite. The best thing I ever tasted as a boy," Lord Strongfoot said wistfully. He noticed me standing to the side. "And who is your pretty friend?"

"This is Amarante. Amarante Flora," Tori said.

I dipped a curtsy. "Good to meet you, Lord Strongfoot."

"Now, none of that," he said with a jolly laugh, grabbing my hand and shaking it profusely. My shoulder was nearly shaken out of my socket. "Any friend of Tori's I welcome with open arms and no formalities. Though I do get a kick out of being called 'lord'."

"Don't scare her away, now, Pa," Tori said, giving my throbbing shoulder a pat.

"Impossible. I know you don't make friends who scare easy," Lord Strongfoot said, flashing me a toothy smile. "But what are you girls standing around for? This is a ball!"

Tori and I exchanged looks.

"Ah. Suddenly shy, my girl?"

"I am nothing of the sort!" Tori said, affronted.

Lord Strongfoot tutted. "Now, now, there's no shame in that. Back when I was courting your mother, I was as nervous as any lad, but I got over it. Everything turned out fine." He thumped Tori on the shoulder. She bore it surprisingly well. "Look! Here comes a young man now."

I turned around and found myself face to face with the waiter—no—Prince Ash. He was dressed in a crisp aquamarine waistcoat, his dark hair combed to the side. He had taken his crown off but it certainly didn't diminish his princely appearance.

"Hello," he said, grinning. "Miss Amarante Flora, if I remember correctly?"

I nodded, realizing that I should have curtsied.

"Will you spare me the next dance?"

I nodded again.

"Splendid! I'll see you then." With a smart bow and a polite smile at the Strongfoots, the prince was gone.

Lord Strongfoot grunted. "He looks like a nice chap. See, Tori? It can't be that hard to find a partner. Amarante didn't have to say a word."

The first dance ended quicker than I could've imagined. When a five-minute intermission was announced after one of the violins went horribly out of tune, I excused myself from the Strongfoots and fished out Genevieve from the crowd.

"Amarante? What's the matter?" Genevieve asked as I steered us away from the dance floor to the short hallway outside.

"Prince Ash asked me to dance," I said. Of all the things I imagined would happen tonight, dancing with a prince was not one of them.

"That's wonderful! Where are we going?"

"The powder room."

"You look fine."

"I'm going to hide."

"Amarante!"

I pulled Genevieve inside the powder room. Debutantes and their mothers were crowded in front of a mirror that stretched across the wall, chattering and refreshing their rouge.

"It cannot be wise to shirk a dance with a prince," Genevieve said. We squeezed ourselves through the trailing skirts and perfumed wigs to the last few inches of the mirror.

"You don't understand! I did something incredibly stupid," I said. I told her about my blunder with the apple. Genevieve hid her laugh with a cough. "So you see, I'm doomed!"

"On the contrary," my stepsister said. "Everyone knows the waiter is Prince Ash, so Julianna can't say anything. Now it just seems like the prince favors you."

Her comment seemed to garner some attention. I pretended to adjust my hair, ignoring the familiar faces of those who had attended the dinner. Most of them had snickered when Julianna and Narcissa mocked me. I did not want to know what they thought of me now.

"Is it true?" a girl said. "Did Prince Ash really ask you to dance?"

Several other faces looked at me eagerly and a few matrons whispered. My embarrassment mounted.

"Amarante is too delirious with happiness to answer."

The group parted, revealing Lady Narcissa in all her glory. Tonight, she was wearing a gown of ruby silk and a swath of diamond necklaces at her throat.

Genevieve and I curtsied, though I wanted to slap the sneer off her face more than anything else.

"Lady Narcissa," I said curtly.

"I suppose city girls who cannot recognize a royal when they see one would be similarly elated," she said, rearranging her curls. "But don't forget the advice my mother so kindly bestowed upon you. Do not flirt with inconsequential men." She laughed. A few others joined in, but some looked doubtful.

"But it is His Highness Prince Ash," the girl who had addressed me piped up.

"Inconsequential," Narcissa said, narrowing her eyes. The girl shrank back. "Really, Amarante. If you're going to pursue a prince at least pick the legitimate one. Or not. Bennett is far above your station."

A few gasps sounded at the familiar way she spoke of the crown prince. I merely pressed my lips together and looked ahead.

Narcissa scowled at my silence, perhaps disappointed that I hadn't lashed out and said something foolish. She snapped open her fan, blowing the hair from my face. "Now get out of my way, I have a dance with the crown prince."

I stepped aside to let her pass. When the door swung shut behind her ruby skirts, everyone began chattering about Narcissa and Crown Prince Bennett.

"They knew," I said, scowling. "Narcissa and the duchess knew the waiter was Prince Ash all along."

"How odd," Genevieve said. "I wonder why Her Grace lost her temper with you at the banquet."

I wondered too. Was their distaste for me caused by Julianna?

Staying in the powder room proved to be impossible. All the occupants surged out at once at the commencement of the second dance. I tried to make myself inconspicuous, but a few debutantes pulled on my arms and urged me to go.

Genevieve, after accompanying me back to the ball-room, was bombarded by another one of Lydia's friends and taken away by a lanky youth with a freckled face. I spotted Cedric next to Olivia, following my stepsister with his gaze. Tori, to my surprise, was twirling on the dance floor in the arms of a rather buggy-eyed young guard. From the look of it, she wasn't too happy with the arrangement.

I wandered yet again to the wall behind the refreshments table, this time alone, sipping punch in an attempt to look occupied. I hoped that the whirling couples would obstruct me from the view of Lydia, or better yet, Prince Ash. I was sorely mistaken.

"Ever so eager for our dance, I see," a voice came from behind me.

My heart nearly leapt out my throat. I whirled around and scrambled into a curtsy. "Your Highness."

"You're late," he said, smiling. His teeth were very straight and very white.

"I...got lost."

"Indeed? From one side of the ballroom to the other?"

My face felt like it was on fire. "Yes. Indeed."

"I see." The prince leaned against the wall next to me. He smelled like evergreen trees and peppermint candy. "That's a shame. I suppose we must wait for the next dance."

I glanced at him from the corner of my eye, wondering if he was displeased. He looked cheery enough, just like he had after the duchess scolded him. I was burning to ask what he was doing that day, but found that my voice wouldn't work and I couldn't tear my eyes from his profile. He looked so regal. Too regal to pass for a waiter.

His dark brown eyes met mine. "Well, ask away. We can't very well spend the next four minutes in silence."

I was planning on doing just that, but curiosity—and his permission—got the best of me. "What were you doing dressed as a waiter at the welcome banquet?" I said, and then realizing who I was talking to, added, "Your Highness."

His smile widened as if he had been waiting for someone to ask all day. But instead of answering, he grabbed a puff pastry and ate it slowly. I figured he was teasing me by keeping me in suspense.

"If you must know," he finally said, brushing off the crumbs on his pants, "I was there for research."

I certainly didn't expect that. "Research?"

"For choosing the next crown princess consort."

I furrowed my brow. Was he the royal matchmaker as well as a prince? What business did he have choosing a crown princess?

"It is no easy task. She must possess honorable rank, distinguished manners, virtue, cleverness, and level-headedness to be a good queen," he said.

"You can determine all that by spilling ice water on people's laps?"

"Not all, but some."

I took it that Samantha hadn't passed the test. Emboldened, I asked, "And Queen Cordelia allowed you to carry out such schemes?"

Prince Ash shrugged. "She ordered it."

My eyebrows shot to my hairline. "Whatever do you mean?"

"Tomorrow, Bennett and my father will leave for royal business. I'm attending the Season on his behalf," he said, holding up his arm. A golden ribbon was tied around his wrist with a neat bow.

"I didn't know that," I said.

He smiled. "No one does. But I reckon my mother will make it known soon," he said, tucking his hands behind his back. "Besides, I must past my time with *something*. Father doesn't trust me with royal affairs. I hardly know why."

He was teasing again, but there was gravity to his light tone.

"Now I would like to ask my own question," he said, before I could read more into it. "What was that earlier? With the apple?"

"I'm sorry," I said. The embarrassment of the encounter rushed back over me. "I was…not myself." I explained how our interaction at the banquet was misunderstood and how Julianna threatened me with spreading the rumors. "I suppose it doesn't really matter now."

Prince Ash raised his eyebrows. "Her name is Julianna Alderidge, you say?"

I nodded.

"I'll cross her off the list, then. Gossip and threats are not fitting for a queen," he said.

"If you're looking for a bride for the crown prince," I said slowly, "then the rumors that he's betrothed to the duchess's daughter are false."

"Indeed. But I'm not surprised," the prince said with a shrug. "Narcissa is the obvious choice, solely because of wealth and position. Father certainly approves of the match."

I bit my lip before I could tell him what I thought about Narcissa. I didn't want to contradict the king, after all. "So, there's no point in your list?" I asked, amused.

"Of course there is," he said, grinning. "It gives me something to do."

At that moment, the second dance concluded. Couples bowed and curtsied to each other and split off, some moving toward the refreshments and others elsewhere. Lydia emerged from the crowd.

"Amarante! Have you been here all this time? This is your first royal ball and you spend a quarter of it snacking like a gluttonous social pariah! Come here at once before you—" Lydia stopped abruptly when she saw Prince Ash. She trilled a nervous giggle and curtsied. "Oh. Good evening, Your Highness."

I was too mortified to look at anything but the floor.

"This is…?" the prince asked.

"My stepmother. Madam Lydia Bonavich Flora," I managed to say.

He dipped his head graciously. "Madam."

Lydia giggled again and sidled up to me, wrapping an arm around my shoulders. "I was giving dear Amarante a little motherly advice, Your Highness. She's quite shy, really. Never too good at balls."

"Perhaps a dance will remedy that." He offered me his hand just as the orchestra began playing a waltz. I took it. Lydia looked as if she had seen the gates of heaven.

Prince Ash led me to the center of the ballroom where other couples had positioned themselves for the dance.

"I apologize for my stepmother," I said as he led me through the steps of the waltz.

"I reckon you're not usually 'dear Amarante'?"

I shook my head. "She gets overexcited when I'm not disappointing her."

"Are you in the habit of disappointing her?" the prince said.

I thought back to the Great Tea Scandal. "Absolutely," I said. "In fact, this is my punishment for doing so."

He gave me a wounded look. "You injure me, Miss Amarante! I must say your chances of becoming crown princess are not very high."

"No, I didn't mean—I mean—" I sputtered and stopped, realizing that he was teasing. My cheeks colored. "What I mean is," I said, choosing my words carefully, "attending the Season is my punishment. I really have no desire to be crown princess, or marry anyone."

"Let me guess. Your stepmother thinks surrounding yourself with well-mannered peers will improve you? Even better if a nice young chap decides to ask for your hand in marriage?"

"How did you know?" I said, surprised. He had stolen the words right out of Lydia's mouth.

"Your stepmother and my father are quite similar," Prince Ash said, chuckling. "But I'm afraid he has given up by now."

I couldn't help but smile. "What kind of havoc did you wreak?"

"Most recently? I accidentally set a hedge on fire. The head gardener was furious. But don't tell anyone," he said. "What about you?"

"I put dirt in Julianna's tea," I said. I looked over the prince's shoulder and spotted Julianna's bright magenta dress. Incidentally, she was glaring at me. I ducked back down and pointed her out to him.

"I'm sure she deserved it," he said, letting me go for a spin. "I once put dirt in the Aquatian ambassador's tea, but I mixed it in so well he didn't notice. Afterward, he said he liked the earthy flavor."

The orchestra ended their song. Prince Ash and I stepped back. I gave the customary curtsy and he a bow. He was smiling when he straightened. He smiled a lot.

"Thank you for the dance, Miss Amarante. I hope we will see more of each other."

"I reckon we will."

"I'm crossing you off the list as well," Prince Ash said. "My brother has the sense of humor of a dead fish. You're far too fun for him."

With another bow, he was off, no doubt to find another debutante to cross off.

I was back at the refreshments table when the next song began. My mouth was dry from talking and Lydia seemed pleased enough to leave me alone for a few minutes, so I took some punch and sat on a bench along the wall where other guests were resting their feet. Relishing the respite, I leaned back and watched the ballroom.

My peace was disrupted at the appearance of Julianna. I raised an eyebrow.

"Well?" I said.

Julianna scowled heavily. "Don't think you're safe because you danced with a prince. If I can't punish you, Narcissa will," she said. "She hasn't forgotten that you tripped over her cat."

With that, she went off. I sat back with a grin. To think I spent so many sleepless nights dreading this ball.

Narcissa's ruby gown swirled past. She was dancing with

Crown Prince Bennett, though to my amusement, he didn't seem to be enjoying himself. Behind them, Duchess Wilhelmina was chatting with the queen. I took a sip of punch. Someone approached them with two jewel-encrusted goblets on a silver platter. The duchess offered one to the queen and took the other. Her Majesty smiled and brought the goblet to her lips. Scarlet red smoke billowed out from the rim.

I started, nearly spilling my punch.

But the smoke had disappeared. The queen was still smiling. Had I hallucinated?

Eventually, Lydia found me squinting at the dais and scolded me for gaping like an ape. The ball went on with no more visions of red smoke. Cedric managed to ask Genevieve for a waltz after escaping Julianna's claws for the third time that night. I danced with some of Lydia's friends' sons, who danced more awkwardly than they looked.

By the end of the night, all thoughts of the queen's goblet were gone. My feet were sore and I wanted nothing more than to go home and sleep.

The carriage ride back was blissful for my aching limbs, but not quite so for my ears. My stepmother prattled on about young men and feathered fans and Lady Hortensia's horrid gown. I was so exhausted that I only grunted when she asked me about my dance with Prince Ash. Seeing that she might as well interrogate a dead turtle, Lydia allowed me and Genevieve to stumble to our rooms without another comment.

7

The next morning, Lydia was in very high spirits. "Ah, my girls! Last night was a raving success, if I say so myself," my stepmother said as Genevieve and I took our seats at the dining table.

"It was a lovely ball," Genevieve said, stifling a yawn.

I grabbed a roll and began to eat.

"I'll never forget my Season. King Maximus was quite the catch back then," Lydia said, sighing.

Genevieve and I exchanged faces.

"All the girls vied for his attention, but sadly he was engaged to Queen Cordelia," Lydia said. "It was rumored that she and her sister, Nerissa, were great beauties in their kingdom. Strange place, Aquatia."

"Have you ever been there, Mama?" my stepsister asked.

Lydia shuddered. "Never. I heard it's full of magic and odd creatures. If they're anything like witches, I'll never set foot there. Thank goodness the queen was one of the normal ones. But never mind that. I've received wonderful news today!" My stepmother shuffled through the pile of letters next to her and pulled out a creamy envelope.

"Who is that from?" I said, setting down my roll.

"A Lord Strongfoot," Lydia said. "His daughter is a friend of yours. Why haven't you girls told me you're acquainted with a lord's daughter?"

"Oh, Tori!" Genevieve said. "She's a lovely girl."

"Well, her father has extended an invitation to the two of you to stay with them during the extent of the Season. They say their manor is only minutes away from the palace. Can you believe it? Minutes!"

Lydia's eyes gleamed as she looked at us. The woman was clearly having the best month of her life. Cedric favored Genevieve and I danced with a prince. And now, a lord was offering us free food and lodging at his manor minutes away from the palace. I wondered what my stepmother would say if I told her the duchess hated me, the prince spilled ice water over my dress on purpose, and Lord Strongfoot was actually a blacksmith with a great deal of money.

"Are we going to accept the invitation?" I said.

"Is there any question?" Lydia said, waving the letter in the air. She looked ready to fly off her seat. "Helene! Start packing the girls' things. They're going to a lord's manor!"

The prospect of a change of scenery and an escape from Lydia's delirium were extremely appealing. I was eager to meet Tori again and curious to see the Strongfoot manor, and how generous Captain Greenwood's reward had been.

The news lightened my spirits and I bore the rest of the day relatively well, despite my frustrations at Helene crowding my room with suitcases and folding my gowns wrong.

After hearing the news, Theodora and Rowena insisted on coming with me, but Lydia told them that a lord would have enough handmaids to serve a dozen young ladies.

"Plus," my stepmother said begrudgingly to Theodora, "your baked goods are unmatched. I couldn't possibly find a replacement."

That night, Genevieve and I sat cross-legged on the floor in her room, repacking our suitcases. It seemed that Helene, after nearly a decade of working for us, still did not know how to fold silk gowns correctly.

Genevieve shook out the skirts of her rose-colored riding gown. The split skirt was slightly creased from Helene's folding. Her stomach let out a loud growl.

"Oh my. I feel like I could eat a horse," Genevieve said, rubbing her stomach.

I stood and stretched. "I'll go down and see if Theodora can spare us something to eat."

"Maybe a few of her raspberry tarts?"

"Perfect."

I descended the stairs and traversed the hall to the kitchen. It was almost an hour past ten, so Theodora would still be preparing tomorrow's breakfast. But when I entered, there wasn't a soul in sight. The oven was lit and the smell of baking bread permeated the air, but the counter was empty. I turned on my heel, ready to tell Genevieve the bad news, until I heard voices from the servants' break room. It was usually deserted this late at night, yet a light shone beneath the door.

"…poor girl. She wouldn't have to do this alone if her mother were still alive."

"Hush. We promised not to bring that up as long as we're here."

"I know. But now that her magic is emerging, we'll have to break that promise. You say it happened in the gardens?"

I stilled, recognizing Theodora and Rowena's voices. They were speaking of magic! I tiptoed past the counter and flattened myself against the wall.

"Yes. I'm sure it's her Emergence. She said she saw something purple. Lo and behold it was a patch of weeds too far away for anyone to see, much less identify."

Someone's shoes scuffed along the floorboards. Theodora was pacing. "Is there any other explanation?" She sounded desperate. "Has our spell really worn off after a mere sixteen years?"

"It was bound to. Magic cannot be suppressed for long."

My breathing became uneven. Was Rowena talking about the purple smudge I had seen in the garden? It had been a mere hallucination—a result of poor sleep. What were they going on about with spells and magic?

"What do we do, Rowena, if we can't come with her? What did Master Flora say?"

Paper crinkled. "He told us to suppress it again by any means possible. He wants us to remove her magic for good." Rowena's voice shook. "How could we do that to her? Without her knowing consent?"

"She won't know what she has lost. It'll be painless for her."

"Seraphina would never allow it."

"Seraphina is dead."

Rowena sobbed.

"Now, now, Rowena. It will all be over soon," Theodora said, her own voice shaking. "Amarante will never know she has magic. To her, it'll be like nothing has happened."

I couldn't stay quiet when Theodora finally said my name. I wrenched open the door.

"What are you two talking about?"

Rowena spun around, a crinkled letter in her hand. She tucked it behind her.

"Amarante, let us explain—"

"There's nothing to explain," Theodora interrupted. Her lined face was emotionless, but the crease between her brows told a different story. "You must be tired. Go to bed, dear. It's nearly midnight."

I stepped further into the room, shaking my head. "No. I-I heard everything," I said. "You can't tell me to go to bed when I heard everything. The magic. The spell. Tell me what it means." My voice went an octave higher. I was sure I sounded raving mad.

Rowena wiped her tear-streaked cheeks. "She's right, Theodora. We have to tell her."

Theodora's stoic facade crumbled. "Amarante," she said, taking a breath, "Rowena and I are witches. And so was your mother."

I fell back into a chair. It sounded even more absurd out loud than in my head. Witches were wicked creatures. Everyone knew that. I stared at Theodora's warm, wrinkled hands. But my nannies weren't wicked. I wasn't wicked. And I was sure, with my whole heart, that Papa could never love someone who was.

My vision spun. "Prove it, then," I said, raising my chin. "If you're witches, then why are you in Olderea? Everyone knows they were banned two generations ago at the inception of the Non-Magic Age." History never was my forte, but King Humphrey's witch ban was a piece of Olderean history everybody knew.

"Much of the history involving witches are skewed beyond recognition, Amarante," Rowena said.

"Prove it," I repeated.

Theodora sighed, exchanging a look with Rowena. Then, before my eyes, the air around them shimmered and shifted. Theodora's brown eyes became golden and strands of Rowena's wild curls gleamed metallic champagne.

I tightened my jaw. I didn't know if I was on the verge of screaming or laughing. "This is a joke, isn't it?" I said. A giggle burst out in spite of myself.

"That was an enchantment," Theodora said, pulling up her sleeve. Her mosaic of sun spots shimmered like gold leaf. "We were hiding our witch traits—all witches have to if they dare stay here. The enchantment dissolves when we willingly reveal ourselves to others."

"Ha! Witch traits? Enchantment?" I said, my cheeks aching from laughter. "This is a joke!"

"Amarante…" Theodora's voice died off. I kept laughing.

Rowena slammed her hand on the table, rattling the silverware. I stopped at the sight of her flashing eyes.

"Is this proof enough?" She jutted her finger out at a vase across the room. It levitated and fell back down with a heavy clink. "Or this?" She waved her arm toward the curtains. They swung shut on their own accord. "And this?" My chair began spinning, blurring the room before me. I clutched the armrests as it went faster and faster and faster and—

"Rowena, enough!" Theodora's angry voice halted the spinning. I lurched to the floor on my hands and knees, limbs trembling. A choked sound erupted from my throat and wouldn't stop.

"Oh, Amarante! I'm so sorry." Rowena knelt next to me. Her hands were shaking too. "I didn't mean to lose my temper."

"W-well I believe you now," I sobbed. My tears dripped onto the carpet and I hastily wiped them away. I was bound to believe them. A part of me believed them the moment I walked into the room. But I simply couldn't bring myself to accept it.

Theodora offered me her handkerchief and sighed. "There, now. This is going all wrong isn't it?"

"It's my fault," Rowena muttered. "You're half witch, Amarante. Magic is a part of you and the fact that you had to grow up without it…" She shook her head and withdrew the crinkled letter from her pocket. It was the other half of Papa's letter.

"But I thought…"

"Read it, dear," Theodora said.

> I must thank you for alerting me to the other situation. I don't know how long I can conceal the circumstances of her own birth from her. Sometimes I forget she is like her Mama. Each year I convince myself that deception is the right thing to do and each year I succeed. Have I become too comfortable being a liar, knowing that cheating my daughter is for her own protection?
>
> Forgive me, I am rambling
>
> If there is anything you can do to suppress her powers a little longer, or for good, please do so.
>
> All the best,
> Julien

"Papa always told me Mama was a nobleman's daughter who left us," I said. My mind flashed back to the first time I had asked him about my mother. I wasn't too introspective at eight years old and his spectacles obstructed my view of his eyes. Now, I fancied that there was a glimmer of tears behind the frames.

I knew enough then not to pry. Over the years I assumed that she had broken off the marriage and went off without caring a wit for me or Papa. To think she was a witch!

"Ridiculous thing to say to a child," Theodora said.

I gave the letter back to Rowena. "So," I said shakily. "Are you going to get rid of my magic?"

"We cannot get rid of it for good," Rowena said, helping me back into the armchair. "But we know someone who can."

I tried to calm myself. "Who?"

Theodora fiddled with her apron. "We'll have to find her first, of course." She shook her head at my panicked look and said, "There is no reason she wouldn't do it."

"Will everything go back to normal after that?"

"It will, dear," Rowena said. "As long as you never tell anyone about this."

I nodded. I didn't ask for this secret, but there was no doubt I had to keep it. To think I came here for raspberry tarts and got all this instead.

That reminded me. Genevieve!

Wiping my eyes, I said, "Do you have any raspberry tarts, Theodora?"

After thrusting a generous amount of pastries in my hands, Theodora and Rowena ushered me upstairs with gentle smiles. I excused myself to bed after dropping a few tarts off to Genevieve, leaving my portion untouched.

I rearranged my blanket, staring out the spot between

my curtains. The chirping of crickets was the only sound that filled the silence. At the gap under my door, Genevieve's light doused. I wondered what she would think of the whole affair. That I was half witch. That I possessed magic—actual, dangerous magic.

But the purple smudge at the garden didn't seem dangerous. Was my magic merely seeing strange colors?

Rowena had made things move on their own accord. I squinted hard at the ottoman a few feet away from my bed, willing it to spin as she had done to my armchair.

Nothing happened.

I was too exhausted to know whether I was relieved or disappointed.

8

When the sun rose, we set off to the Strongfoots. I had almost forgotten last night's ordeal until Theodora and Rowena met me outside.

"Are you sure you don't want us to come with you?" Theodora said, gripping my hands.

I looked earnestly at my nannies. I was half-tempted to take them with me but I knew Lydia wouldn't be pleased. "I'll be fine," I said.

They looked doubtful, like how I felt.

Rowena pulled me into a hug and pinched my cheek—something she hadn't stopped doing even after my face lost the chubbiness of girlhood. "We won't be far. Write us if anything disastrous happens, alright?"

I pulled back. "Will anything disastrous happen?"

"Now look! You've gone and scared her again," Theodora scolded.

Rowena put her hands on her hips. "Well, better expect

the unexpected. During my Emergence I set a house on fire."

"You what?"

"It was harmless fire. It was quite pretty, actually, from what I remember."

"What Rowena means to say is that some things will take you by surprise," Theodora said, nudging her out of the way. "But I doubt your magic will misbehave at this stage. Remember to stay calm."

"I will." I took a deep breath and gave each of them a tight smile. "I'll miss you two."

"As will we."

Before I knew it, Genevieve and I were rattling down the road, waving goodbye to a tearful yet ecstatic Lydia. My stepsister gazed out the window, eyes shining.

"Well, Amarante. Are you ready?"

Her question, though I knew only applied to the Season, resonated on many levels for me. "Ready as I'll ever be," I said. I hoped very much that I wouldn't set the Strongfoot's house on fire.

When we arrived, I realized their residence could hardly be called a house—it was a mansion. Our footman drove us through ornate iron gates into a well-paved courtyard. We stopped in front of a short flight of steps that led to a massive structure of arched windows and creamy pillars where Tori and Lord Strongfoot stood waiting for us.

"Took you long enough," Tori said as a greeting when Genevieve and I exited the carriage. She grabbed one of our suitcases from our footman and lugged it inside.

"Ah, welcome Amarante! And this must be your sister Genevieve!" Lord Strongfoot came forward. His beard looked even bushier and more impressive in broad daylight.

"I regret Lady Strongfoot isn't here to greet you two. She's in the country tending to her old mother."

After brief introductions and inquiries about the health of our respective families, Lord Strongfoot guided us inside.

Tori came down a spiral staircase. "Come on. I'll show you where you're staying."

The guest room was enormous, big enough to fit two comfortably sized beds with quite a bit of room to spare. Along the far side was a lovely arched window that overlooked the front yard and a bit of the busy streets below. Potted plants lined the windowsill and two dressing tables, complete with a mirror and stool, were set across the foot of the beds. Beside the door were two armoires, in which we hastily shoved our suitcases to deal with later.

"You have a beautiful home, Tori," Genevieve said as Tori took us down to the dining room.

She snorted. "Oh, I know. Sometimes I wish it weren't so pretty. I'd feel less guilty about making a mess." The aroma of baking bread wafted through the air, tempting my empty stomach.

We passed a small archway to the dining room, which had generously large windows along one wall and a long mahogany table in the middle. Lord Strongfoot was already seated, and to my surprise, so were two young girls, neither much older than ten.

"Gimme back my egg, Ria," one of them whined. She looked like the miniature version of Tori. The other, who had a hard-boiled egg smashed in her small fist, was fair haired with stout features. At our entrance, the two quieted and stared with large eyes.

"Ha! We should have visitors more often," Tori said,

patting her miniature on the cheek. "There's hardly a moment when these two don't shut up."

Genevieve and I sat.

"You didn't tell us you had little sisters, Tori," Genevieve said, smiling at the two petrified children.

Tori pulled up a chair noisily. "Oh, these two? Meet Victoria and Victoria."

Genevieve gave her a puzzled look.

"It was Pa's genius idea," Tori said dryly. She reached over to grab a roll from the center of the table as Lord Strongfoot lowered the newspaper he was reading.

"Darn right. Hit me like a ton of bricks. I say, if mother nature is going to be repetitive with me and give me three daughters, I'll do the same." Lord Strongfoot gave a bellowing laugh.

"Hence, I'm Tori, this is Vicky, and that's Ria," Tori said, pointing from herself to her miniature and finally to the one with the egg smashed in her hand. She looked exasperated, as if Lord Strongfoot had told the same story too many times to count. "Let's just eat."

"Can't I entertain our guests in peace?" Lord Strongfoot grumbled.

Tori turned to us and whispered, "Pa always gets grumpy when I don't let him bore people. No doubt he'll ask me to hoe the garden later, so you two are going to have to pretend to be occupied with something so I can join in. Hoeing is the worst," she said with a grimace.

Ria giggled. Half of the smashed egg was on the side of her face.

The rest of the day went on reasonably well. Genevieve and I decided to partake in the laborious task of unpacking and gladly recruited Tori to help her escape the dreaded garden work. She got so bored that she ended up hoeing the gardens anyway. Vicky and Ria mysteriously disappeared after breakfast, but glimpses of messy hair and tiny limbs around the corners told us that they were curious enough to spy. Genevieve put an end to it when she began to organize her undergarments. The two scampered off with shrieks of horror.

When we finished unpacking, Tori gave us a tour of the house. Hours passed with lighthearted conversations and walks along the city streets. I forced myself to be at ease despite the worries nagging the back of my mind.

When night fell, we were called yet again to the dining room for dinner with Lord Strongfoot.

"I must admit I never had too many guests over since we got this manor, so you two ladies are the first to get a taste of Strongfoot hospitality."

Genevieve and I sat eating our dinner of roast chicken, potatoes, and greens. Tori was seated to her father's right. There were no places set for Vicky or Ria, so I assumed the girls did not find formal dinners particularly amusing.

"When did you move in?" I asked, looking up at the fresco of bare-bottomed angels on the ceiling.

"Six months ago," Tori answered after swallowing a mouthful of chicken. "Around the time when Pa made Captain Greenwood his sword."

"Ah, yes, a fine sword that was," Lord Strongfoot said, stroking his beard. "For a finer man, if I must say so myself."

I raised my brow, thinking back to what Lydia had said about Captain Greenwood and his affair with the queen.

"It is awfully generous of the captain to grant you all this," Genevieve said.

"Not just generous, my girl. He is the most honorable man I have ever met, and I'm not saying that because he gave me this grand old house and a title of my own," Lord Strongfoot said with a wink. "There are countless stories about his bravery and comradery. There's never been a soldier quite as respectable as him. Fearless in battle and faithful to the king."

"And faithful to his wife, I hope?" I said, keeping my tone polite.

Lord Strongfoot looked at me from over the rim of his goblet, his bushy brows raised high. He took a swig of wine. "You've heard those nasty rumors about him and the queen, I suppose?"

I nodded, feeling somewhat ashamed.

"I must admit I had my doubts about the matter too. After all, how could they explain the unexpected birth of Prince Ash? Something like that can't be kept in the dark."

"And heaven knows how to prove someone's legitimacy," Tori mumbled over a forkful of greens. "There's really no saying whose son he is. It's all based on witnesses and word of mouth."

"Exactly. But after I met the captain, I knew he would never do such a thing," Lord Strongfoot said. He picked up a fork and speared a piece of chicken. "You would too, I think, but I doubt debutantes will meet any of the Royal Guard. Hardly anyone does. They're always on duty."

I pushed a carrot around my plate and wondered what Prince Ash thought about the whole affair. How could he possibly stand the notion that his supposed illegitimate birth impacted the way people viewed him, and even viewed the queen?

I paused. How would people view me, if they knew I was a witch? I shook my head and continued to eat. It was a ridiculous thought. If things went my way, no one would know.

I only hoped my magic would stay under control until Theodora and Rowena got rid of it.

9

"We have a tea social with the queen," Tori announced the next day.

Genevieve looked up from her sketch. We received a letter from the palace this morning containing the invitations and descriptions of the Season events.

"With the queen? I thought it was supposed to be with Duchess Wilhelmina," Genevieve said, closing her sketchbook.

"Apparently there's been a change of plans," Tori said. "Her Grace will be hosting the soirée instead."

"What's a swa-ray?" a small voice emerged underneath the coffee table. Vicky poked her head out, giving Tori a gap-toothed grin.

"None of your business, that's what," her sister said brusquely. "Why don't you go play with Ria?"

Vicky pouted. "Fine," she said. "You never have time to play with me anymore."

"That's because I have things to do. Now run along."

"Why don't *you* run along, you big, ugly—"

At the sight of me and Genevieve, Vicky darted under the table with a gasp. The three of us watched her make a stealthy escape out the parlor on all fours.

Tori shook her head. "Weird kid," she muttered.

The short carriage ride to the palace seemed to drag on as I thought about the duchess. It was a relief that I wouldn't have to see her again so soon, but something nagged at the back of my mind—the plume of scarlet smoke from the queen's goblet at the Debutante Ball. Was it magic? Or something else? I sighed. I wasn't sure if I wanted to know.

Tori, Genevieve, and I were escorted into the south wing of the palace where the royals lodged and personal gatherings took place. This, I heard a girl whisper, was the exclusive of the exclusive.

It was nearing afternoon when we seated ourselves underneath a large, ornate gazebo out in the Queen's Garden. Hedges, fountains, and hydrangea bushes were arranged tastefully around us. Five tables were set out, and the three of us managed to find seats with Olivia, who was silent at our arrival, and another debutante.

We didn't have to wait long for Queen Cordelia to appear.

She glided in, dressed in a gown of aqua blue and looking as regal and elegant as ever.

The twenty-five of us stood. "Good afternoon, Your Majesty," we said in unison.

The queen smiled. "Welcome, and good afternoon to all of you. Unfortunately, Duchess Wilhelmina is unable to join us at this moment, but I believe she will be roaming around later to meet you all."

I suppressed a groan.

"Before we begin tea, why don't each of you introduce yourselves?" Queen Cordelia said, gesturing to the table closest to her, which also happened to be the farthest from me.

Julianna went first. "It is a pleasure to meet you all. I am Julianna Alderidge."

"I am Tessa Donahue and I am positively enchanted to be a part of this year's Season."

"I am Samantha Faas. Delighted to meet everyone."

One after another, each debutante introduced themselves. Some appeared full of themselves, some out of their comfort zone, and some as stoic as a rock. When it finally came to our table, my hands were slick with sweat. For a moment I wished that I had already gone, or made an excuse to go to the powder room.

Tori stood first and cleared her throat. "I am Victoria Strongfoot, also known as Tori if we happen to be bosom friends. Absolutely spiffingly enchanted to be here this afternoon."

It took everything in me not to snort at her faux pompous air. Some of the debutantes looked scandalized, while a few had suppressed smiles.

Genevieve went next and executed her introduction with perfect dignity and grace. After the other debutante at our table, Rachel Estelle, did the same, I realized it was down to me and Olivia. The poor girl looked petrified. I took it as a sign to go next.

"Hello. I'm Amarante Flora," I said, opting for a quick curtsy. "Lovely to be here."

As I sat, Olivia stood shakily, tucking a braid behind her ear.

"I-I'm Bolivia…um, Olivia Sternfeld. Happy to m-m…"

The rest of her sentence faded into a whisper. I couldn't help but feel sorry for the girl as she sat and sunk into her high-necked dress.

The queen gave a warm smile Olivia certainly didn't see six inches into her collar.

"And that concludes introductions," the queen said, bringing the attention back to her. "It is truly a pleasure to have you all here today. I hope you will familiarize yourself with the palace and your fellow debutantes this afternoon, as you will be spending the next two months in each other's company. Now. Let us have some tea."

Waiters streamed in, bringing cakes and sandwiches piled on layered tiers. They poured the tea and set out bowls of sugar cubes. It wasn't long before I was chewing on a pastry. Genevieve quietly sipped her tea. Tori shoveled cucumber sandwiches into her mouth. Rachel was looking off somewhere, and Olivia had shrunken in on herself, hunched over so low that her nose touched the tablecloth. She gave the softest, high-pitched whine. I paused my chewing.

Rachel inched away uncomfortably. Tori was munching too loudly to notice and Genevieve seemed to be daydreaming about something.

I cleared my throat. "Olivia? Are you alright?" I asked in a low voice.

She looked up. Tears, among other fluids, were rolling down her face and gathering to the tip of her pointy chin. A large drop plopped into her tea.

"N-n-no," she sniveled. "I-I'm always…l-like this."

"You didn't do so bad," I said.

Olivia shook her head so violently that her braids whipped her cheeks.

"I-it's…I can't," she said. The rest of her words drowned into another high-pitched whine. This finally drew Genevieve and Tori's attention.

"Hey now, what are you crying for?" Tori said, setting down a half-eaten sandwich. "Embarrassed about your introduction?"

Her words, though blunt, were not unkind. Olivia stopped crying and looked at Tori with a quivering lower lip. She nodded.

Tori shrugged. "I was like you once. Terrified of people. But being a blacksmith's daughter toughened me up a few notches. My Pa always says fear holds everyone back. The way to get over it is not to become fearless, no, but to decide once and for all that you don't give a blooming crap about what anybody thinks of you. Makes life a lot easier, you know?"

Genevieve coughed delicately.

"B-but it's so hard to m-make friends and Mummy… Mummy wants me to marry."

My eyebrows raised at the thought of marrying Olivia off. I could hardly imagine the girl surviving a short stroll without a chaperone, much less being courted by a young man.

"You don't have to worry about the first part," Genevieve said warmly. "We're already your friends, Olivia."

Olivia stared at us, large eyes widening. "But I barely talk to you."

"It's not too late to start," I said.

The girl looked like she was going to cry again.

"So, what brings you to the Season?" I asked quickly.

Olivia, thankfully, blinked back her tears. "My mother says I should marry soon so Cedric wouldn't have to worry about me."

Tori raised a brow. "Either way you're still leeching off a man. Does it matter which one?"

"I wish Cedric was attending too," Olivia said with a sigh. "He'll have to eventually, when he inherits grandpa's fortune."

"He's not chaperoning you today?" Genevieve asked.

"No. I wanted to do this myself," Olivia said. She gave us a small grin. "And I'm glad I did."

Tea went on in peace. The queen was seated at the far table with Narcissa and Julianna who behaved more amiably than I had ever seen. Tori, Genevieve, Olivia, and I conversed. After an hour or so, we were allowed to leave the gazebo and wander about the Queen's Garden. The four of us took a stroll amongst the hydrangea bushes.

Unfortunately, we came up behind Julianna, flanked by Samantha and Tessa. None of them noticed us.

"Have you heard that Prince Ash is attending the Season on behalf of Crown Prince Bennett?" Samantha said.

Julianna scoffed. "Don't tell me you fancy him, Samantha. That's ridiculous."

"Absolutely ridiculous," Tessa said.

Samantha's face grew red. "Of course not," she said, raising her chin. "I still haven't forgiven him for soiling my gown."

I rolled my eyes. The way she looked at Prince Ash at the Debutante Ball said enough.

"It's unfortunate he's in the way of making an impression on Crown Prince Bennett," Julianna said. She smoothed the skirts of her peach dress and fluffed her hair.

"But isn't Narcissa engaged to the crown prince?" Tessa piped up.

Julianna scoffed. "Of course she isn't. That's just a rumor she spread herself, no doubt. Her chances are as good as ours," she said. "It helps that she's the duchess's daughter, but Her Grace has taken a liking to me in the past year. And Father has been increasing his influence in court."

I almost laughed. To think she switched her sights from Cedric Sternfeld to Crown Prince Bennett in a matter of weeks! I must've made a noise, for Julianna turned around. She gave an outraged gasp.

"You people!" Julianna narrowed her eyes at me. "What are you doing here?"

Tori crossed her arms. "If you haven't noticed, we're debutantes too."

"I wasn't talking to you," Julianna said in disgust, shouldering past Tori. "Amarante, have you come to gloat? Now that you've danced one dance with the bastard prince, you think you're better than us?"

It seemed that she hadn't gotten over her failure to humiliate me at the Debutante Ball. I rolled my eyes, having no wish to make a scene at yet another Season event. Instead, I focused on the cobblestone path where several loose rocks littered the perimeters, intending to walk past them without a word.

"Don't you dare ignore me!"

My vision swam for a second.

Just as Julianna stepped forward, a rock rolled beneath her slipper, glowing purple.

Her ankle twisted.

Then, the most unfortunate thing happened.

Julianna fell back and jabbed Olivia in the ribs with her elbow.

"Ack!" Julianna shrieked as Olivia lost her footing and fell bodily into the hydrangea bushes. Tessa and Samantha gasped.

"Olivia!" I rushed over to the bushes but an explosion of color assaulted my vision. I teetered on my feet as bursts of neon yellow riddled the back of my eyelids.

"Burning barnyards, are you alright?" Tori asked, taking Olivia's arm. Everyone was too busy fussing to notice my reaction. I blinked rapidly. The color melted away.

Petals of violet, pink, and purple clung to Olivia's gown as she stood, trembling. There was a body-sized dent in the bush she had fallen into.

"What in heaven's name is going on there?"

Duchess Wilhelmina strode down the path in a maroon gown, her shoes clacking against the cobblestone. My stomach turned. Julianna pushed herself up and curtsied.

"Amarante shoved me and I fell, Your Grace," Julianna whined. Tessa and Samantha nodded vehemently.

Tori almost growled. "Absolutely not," she said. "You fell on your own and rudely elbowed Olivia in the ribs."

Julianna's nostrils flared. "Watch your mouth when you're talking to me, country commoner."

"Look who's talking, you horse-faced, spoiled—"

"Enough!"

The duchess's voice boomed over the other two. Tori resorted to glaring venomously at Julianna, who was flushed to the ears. Duchess Wilhelmina looked to me.

"There always seems to be trouble when you're around," she said with a sneer.

I couldn't tear my eyes from where Olivia had fallen. I hadn't noticed it before, but lined between the hydrangeas were bushes of stinging nettle.

The neon yellow started pulsing before my vision again, and I looked to Olivia's exposed arms. Red splotches riddled with small bumps marred her skin.

"Look at me when I'm talking to you, Miss Flora," Duchess Wilhelmina said sharply.

I pointed at Olivia's growing rash. "We need to get her a physician, Your Grace," I said, hating how my voice wavered.

Samantha squealed. "Oh! That is disgusting."

Olivia whimpered when she saw the rashes on her arm. Her eyes brimmed with tears. "I-I'm so sorry, Your Grace, I didn't mean to," she whimpered. Tori gave me an incredulous look from over Olivia's shaking head.

"What is going on?"

Everyone curtsied again as Queen Cordelia appeared up the path.

"It seems that one of our debutantes has a talent for causing trouble," the duchess said, giving me a disdainful look.

"She—" Julianna whined.

"Your Majesty," Tori cut in before Julianna could say anything more. "Julianna tripped and caused Olivia to fall into the bushes."

Queen Cordelia nodded. "I see," she said. She gently put her hand on Olivia's shoulder. "What happened to your arm, my dear?"

Olivia's eyes welled with fresh tears and she began blubbering. Duchess Wilhelmina looked at her in distaste.

"There is stinging nettle between the hydrangeas, Your Majesty," I said, toeing the spiky leaves with my slipper. "They're planted all over. It's what caused Olivia's rash."

Queen Cordelia raised her brows. "Indeed? How odd," she said. "I'm quite sensitive to stinging nettle myself. Thank you, Miss Amarante. I will ask the gardener to remove them."

I blushed, surprised that she remembered my name.

Duchess Wilhelmina exhaled. "You are not fit to be in public right now, Miss Sternfeld. Have someone escort you inside."

Julianna's jaw dropped.

"S-Sternfeld?" she whispered, her face reddening.

The duchess surveyed the rest of us somewhat scornfully. "You may all go." She walked off.

I was sure Julianna would've shot me a withering look if it weren't for the queen's presence.

"There will be a physician sent for you, Miss Olivia," Queen Cordelia said.

Tori, Genevieve, and I escorted Olivia into the entrance of the south wing where a decrepit physician gave her a jar of ointment and a melted candy stick from his pocket. After gingerly applying the balm on Olivia's arms and wrapping it in gauze, we emerged from the building only to find that the debutantes had long gone home.

"Good riddance," I said. "I've had enough of the Season already."

Tori sighed. "Amen to that."

Nixgrass—When dried, bundled, and burned,
this herb releases a fragrance that will soothe
the senses and slow the effects of any poison.

2

THE
HERBWITCH'S
APPRENTICE

10

A letter came for me that night as Genevieve and I were getting ready for bed.

"Here you go," Tori said, tossing the rumpled envelope on my mattress. "Whoever sent it must've been in a rush."

"Who is it from?" Genevieve asked as Tori went off yawning to her own room.

I recognized my nanny's handwriting from the front of the envelope. "It's from Theodora," I said, trying to sound casual. Something told me that it wasn't merely inquiries about the Season.

"Are you going to read it now?" my stepsister asked, stifling a yawn.

I shook my head with a tight smile. "Maybe tomorrow," I said. I blew out the candle on our bedside table. "Good night, Gen."

"Good night."

I waited until my stepsister's breathing evened before pulling out the letter. Shifting closer to the sliver of moonlight by the window, I unfolded the parchment.

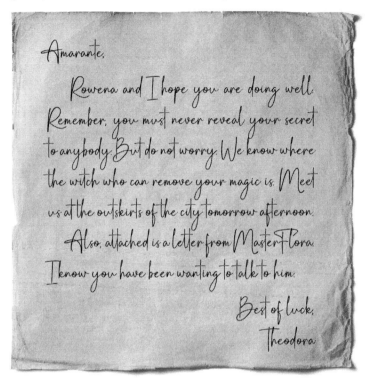

Amarante,

Rowena and I hope you are doing well. Remember, you must never reveal your secret to anybody. But do not worry. We know where the witch who can remove your magic is. Meet us at the outskirts of the city tomorrow afternoon. Also, attached is a letter from Master Flora. I know you have been wanting to talk to him.

Best of luck,
Theodora

There was another letter inside the envelope, this time covered with Papa's neat script.

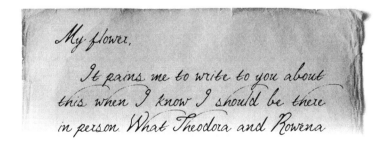

My flower,

It pains me to write to you about this when I know I should be there in person. What Theodora and Rowena say is true. I wanted to tell you about the circumstances of your birth the moment your Mama passed, but I was afraid. And selfish. I knew revealing the truth so late would change everything between us or even worse, put you in danger. I fear I will ramble on more than necessary if I continue writing. I will head back to Delibera as soon as I handle some business matters. Until then, take care and stay safe.

Much love,
Your Papa.

My throat tightened. Business matters always came first, so I wasn't surprised. How long until I'd see him again? A month? Two months? It was much too long to wait. I stuffed the letters beneath my pillow and shut my eyes.

The city of Delibera normally had mild weather year-round, but as I took a horse chaise to the outskirts of the city, the sun was sweltering. Mixed with the jitters that plagued me all morning, the heat was positively nauseating by the time I arrived. Theodora and Rowena stood near the familiar cluster of buildings as I made my way toward them. Their faces were pinched.

"How are you, dear?" Theodora asked, holding me at arms-length as if she were looking for fatal wounds.

I ignored the tightness of my stomach and the sweat soaking the back of my dress. "I'm fine," I said. "Are we going to see the witch?"

Both of them winced. "Not so loud," Rowena said, eyes flickering to a few passersby.

I lowered my voice to a whisper. "Does she live here?"

"Not really," Rowena said. She fiddled with the loose threads on her sleeves. "It's a lot to explain."

"I have all the time in the world."

Rowena sighed and took my elbow. We walked down the street, the two of them flanking me like they used to when I took walks as a child.

"The thing is, we have to go through another witch to find her," Rowena said. "The former is a gatekeeper of sorts."

I cocked my head. "Like a bodyguard? Do all witches have another witch guarding them?"

Theodora made a face that told me I had said something extremely foolish. "I'm sorry, dear. This must be confusing you."

Rowena snorted. "Never mind that. Let's hurry."

A short minute's walk led us to a very familiar building.

"The post office?" I asked, staring at the painted blue door.

Rowena shook her head and opened the one beside it. I exhaled. Of course. Miriam's Terrariums.

This time, the snail lady was draped in shawls of mustard and tangerine. A gaudy turquoise turban sat on her head and wobbled when she threw out her arms to welcome us. "Hello and welcome to…oh, it's you two again."

"Yes, Miriam," Theodora said, sounding almost annoyed. "We need to use the passageway."

"Really? I thought you swore never to step foot in the village again," Miriam lowered her arms and stared at me. "Unless it's because of her?"

Rowena stepped forward, blocking me from view. "That's none of your business. And we need you to take us to Lana."

Miriam tutted. "Ah, then it is my business," she said, throwing yet another shawl over her shoulder. Her brass bangles clinked together as she crossed her arms. "No one has passed through here for sixteen years."

"Which is exactly why we need to pass now," Theodora said.

The two stared at each other until Miriam broke her gaze.

"Very well," she said with a scoff. "Come along then." She strode through a beaded curtain and motioned for us to follow.

Behind the curtain was a small sitting area. We wove through the poufs and rugs that littered the floor, stopping in front of a poorly woven tapestry. Miriam lifted it out of the way, revealing a rectangular piece of brick wall. She pressed in five bricks in no particular order. The wall rolled back with a rumble. Before I knew it, a set of dusty stairs appeared, leading to a dark pit below.

"There's a passageway in your shop," I said stupidly.

Theodora patted my shoulder. "It leads to Witch Village," she said. "There are few such passageways throughout Olderea. This one happens to be the closest."

"They require very complex magic to make," Rowena continued. "Witches with great skill can materialize one on the spot and it'll take them wherever they wish. Most, however, can only use preexisting ones like this."

I suppose my nannies thought spouting trivia would distract me from the fear boiling in my gut and the nerves weakening my legs.

"Yes, yes. Hurry now," Miriam said, shooing us forward.

"You're not bringing a lamp?" I said in a small voice.

Miriam shrugged and grabbed a lamp from a low table. The light didn't penetrate far into the dense darkness, but it was still some comfort as Theodora and Rowena led me down the stairs. The air cooled as we descended. When the stairs ended, the ground beneath was rough and uneven. Theodora and Rowena's hands in mine were my only source of comfort.

"I can't see a thing," I said. Miriam's lantern was nothing but a weak blob of light, as if the darkness was suffocating the flame.

"That's the point," Rowena said in a cheery voice. I knew she was speaking so for my sake. "It discourages trespassers."

"How is anyone supposed to see where they're going?" I muttered.

"There are no real directions," Theodora said, squeezing my fingers. "We just have to walk forward until the passageway opens for us."

"Oh."

So this was magic. I couldn't help feeling intimidated as we proceeded blindly forward.

Eventually, a rectangular outline of light appeared before us, almost like a door.

"Ah, here we are," Miriam said. And then the darkness melted away.

A soft gust of wind swept in the scent of dew and freshly cut grass. I stumbled back into Rowena, appalled at what lay before me. Somehow, we were outside before a village on a hill. Huts and shacks spiraled up the mound, reaching the pinnacle in a chaotic crowd of straw, wood, and specks of green where trees and flora sprouted out from the crevices. It looked like a squatter village or an anthill, not quite man-made, but not quite natural either. I squinted up at the wisps of clouds floating through a cerulean sky.

"Welcome to Witch Village," Miriam said, discarding the lamp behind her. The cave from which we came had disappeared completely, leaving only a vast expanse of green fields that extended to the horizon.

"I thought the tunnel was underground," I said breathlessly. "We're outside."

She cackled, shaking her head. "Humans. I forget you grew up in ignorance."

"She grew up protected," Theodora said testily. "Now, show us to Lana, as you promised."

Miriam harrumphed. "Alright, alright. Come with me."

My nannies and I followed, traversing the field to the winding dirt path that led into the village. The path grew increasingly cramped as ramshackle structures and over-grown gardens crowded in. Laundry from clotheslines billowed gently in the breeze.

Rowena craned her neck to a short cottage behind us with a round yellow door, an unreadable look on her face.

"Want to stop for a visit?" Miriam asked without looking back.

"No," Rowena said. Miriam grunted.

I stole a look at Rowena, but I couldn't glean anything from her now impassive expression.

For the first time, I realized my nannies had lives outside of Papa's manor. Lives that started here, no doubt. Why did they leave to care for me?

Perhaps they would tell me another time.

"Where is everyone?" I asked instead. Other than the overflowing flora, the five of us were the only living souls to be seen.

Miriam glanced back at me. There was a glimmer of something in her eye. "We witches are reclusive people. Not as social as humans. Not as strict, either. Your rules and regulations are frivolous to us," she said. "But what you see here began when King Humphrey started the Non-Magic Age."

I looked up. The history of King Humphrey had never been taught to me from a witch's perspective.

"Two generations ago, to be precise," Theodora said from behind me. She sounded tired, but not from the exercise. "The witch Navierre was accused of poisoning the royal family after the sudden death of Queen Heather. Not a good look for the head of the royal inspection team."

"The trial was conducted in private. No doubt King Humphrey wanted to hide the lack of evidence." Rowena huffed. "Lucky for him, malicious rumors were beginning to spread about magic and witches anyway, so it wasn't difficult to condemn Navierre. And subsequently, all of witchkind."

"As you know, Olderea's Non-Magic Age meant that magic and all who associated with it were forbidden from freely roaming the lands. Plants with magical properties were uprooted. Witches were forced to leave. Most of us eventually went underground as there was no room for us in other kingdoms and no one wanted to transport witches," Theodora said. "Still, some stayed above, either to guard our passageways or for personal duties." She shared a look with Rowena.

"And you just let them push you out?" I said, perplexed. "Don't you have magic?"

"Magic is not for warfare. And I told you, witches are a passive people," Miriam said. "Passive to a fault."

Something akin to injustice swelled in my chest. "Did no one ask King Maximus to change things when he took the throne?"

Miriam laughed heartily. "Now you're getting some witch pride. Alas, just as magic runs in witch blood, hatred for magic runs in the royals'," she said. "It is because witches have powers they could never possess. Fear and jealousy are only natural for humans in authority. I am afraid witches will never see the light of day for a long time."

"But can't they come aboveground whenever they like?" I asked. "They could disguise themselves like you."

Miriam shook her head. "Guardians of passageways are very choosy about who they let in or out," she said. "Letting through one wrong person could lead to chaos."

"You would know, Miriam," Rowena grumbled.

The snail seller scowled. "That was a special case," she said. "And so it seems is this one."

I waited for her to explain, but she didn't say anything more. There was still one question that nagged me, though I was afraid to ask it.

"So, who was my mother?"

The silence suddenly felt uncomfortable.

"Her name was Seraphina," Theodora finally said.

She didn't continue and though a million more questions followed, I didn't feel it right to ask.

Seraphina.

At least that much I knew about her.

We walked for some minutes, the path growing increasingly steep as we approached the top of the hill. Miriam

finally stopped before a cottage with circular windows. A neat garden lined the perimeter and extended to the back. Miriam stepped aside.

"Here we are. Go ahead and knock," she said, giving a nod to my nannies.

"Any particular reason you won't?" Rowena asked.

Miriam frowned. "You know how Lana is with visitors. I have no wish to experience another wart jinx. It was horrible for my business and took months to wear off. People actually thought I was a witch."

"Oh for heaven's sake woman, just knock. Everyone knows a wart jinx can easily be fixed with fig root potion…"

Voices faded away as I stared at the door before me. It was emitting a soft aura the color of Papa's favorite sangria. Almost unconsciously, I stepped forward and touched the brass knob. Hot and cold prickles ran up my arm. The knob turned freely in my hand.

The three women stopped bickering as the door swung open. They looked at me in surprise.

"It was unlocked," I said.

"Oh." Miriam pursed her lips. "I could've sworn she put some type of nasty enchantment on it this time. Ah well. In we go."

I cautiously trailed behind her. It didn't seem wise to enter a witch's territory without permission. Especially a witch who was expected to put jinxes on her door. I shuddered, wondering who this Lana was and why, out of all the witches in Witch Village, my nannies chose her to help me.

It was considerably darker past the threshold, but bright enough to observe that the interior was circular and filled with strange knickknacks. The smell that lingered in the air was both acrid and sweet. A bubbling noise came from the closed door before us, underneath which a pale purple light shone.

The door burst open and the purple light flooded our surroundings. I staggered into Theodora, blinded.

A woman's firm voice reverberated through the room. "Intruders! State your business or prepare to be melted."

"Relax, Lana. So dramatic."

"Miriam." The name was spat out in distaste. "I thought you learned your lesson from the warts."

The snail shop owner sniffed and stepped aside. "I'm here with guests."

My vision recovered. Before me stood a tall, middle-aged woman, a bucket of something bright and bubbling slung over her shoulder. Her face reminded me somewhat of a strict school teacher, pinched and scowling.

"Who is this?" she asked when her gaze met mine. I froze.

"She's half witch," Theodora said. "She wants her magic removed."

There was a long, drawn out silence that I longed for someone to break. I stole a glance over Miriam's shoulder. Lana was no longer scowling, but her expression was nowhere near welcoming.

"So it's you two. Here to cause trouble again, aren't you? Haven't you done enough?" the witch said bitterly.

Rowena bristled.

"If you will just listen," she said, stepping forward. "I know we haven't been on the best of terms, but—"

Lana barked out a sharp laugh. "That is an understatement," she said. Swinging the bucket of liquid from her shoulder, she walked back to the room from which she came. My nannies followed, and I with them.

"I'll wait out here," Miriam said with a shrug.

If the previous room was odd, this one was even stranger. It was about the size of a large closet, but instead of clothes, it held a red brick oven and a myriad of shelves that spiraled up and up the rounded walls.

A large cauldron filled with something thick and viscous hung above a fire. Lana poured the contents of the bucket inside and to my amazement, the solution turned clear and fluid like water.

"I know you still have your grudges," Rowena said. "But Amarante needs your help. Just make a potion to remove her magic."

"And what do I get in return?" Lana said, hardly sparing any of us a glance. She took a pinch of something from a ceramic jar and sprinkled it over the cauldron. Pops of blue smoke erupted from the solution and disappeared in the air.

"Redemption," Theodora said stiffly.

Lana slammed the ceramic jar on the counter, rattling the shelves above her. "I do not take custom orders," she said. Her green eyes flicked over me. "Especially not from humans."

"She is half witch," Rowena said, scowling. "You know perfectly well that she is."

"And you are ruining my business," Lana said. "I sell what I wish to sell at the Witch Market and even there I don't get enough for my work."

"Listen—"

"Move," Lana said. "All of you. Except you, girl. Come here."

Theodora and Rowena backed away, dissolving my protective wall. I was exposed to Lana's scrutiny yet again.

I forced my legs to step forward.

"Can you tell me what potion this is?" Lana asked.

I glanced at the contents of the cauldron, noticing that the bubbling had stopped. The liquid was now the color of amber, shimmering and shifting in the firelight.

I shook my head.

"What about this? Do you know what this is?" She held the ceramic jar before me. It looked like tea leaves, but the smell was high and fruity. Blue flashed before my vision. *Repair.*

I shook my head again, my vision spinning from the scent. My mouth felt glued shut, as if I couldn't move a muscle under her glare.

Lana sneered. "I see." She filled a rounded glass jar with the contents of the cauldron. "Any witch would know that this is a basic antidote for mild poisoning. You, however, had no such knowledge."

I watched the liquid swirl inside the glass, too humiliated to say anything. Rowena wrapped her arm around my shoulders.

Lana corked the bottle. "I've seen enough to know that this girl is not a witch," she said. "Now get out. Do not trespass again unless you have a death wish."

"How could you?" Rowena said. "You owe it to Sera—"

"Do not speak her name!" Lana shouted. The bottles on her shelves rattled.

Rowena fumed. I cowered behind her.

"Very well, Lana," Theodora said, frowning. "But I daresay you'll regret it."

We found ourselves once again trudging along the dirt path, this time downhill. Miriam gave a loud sigh.

"I told you she was testy," the snail seller said.

"Typical," Rowena growled. "I never liked her."

Theodora shook her head. "Never mind that. What's important is that Amarante figures out how keep her powers under control."

"Can't you three help me?" I asked. "Can't you teach me how to use magic?"

They all exchanged glances. I was getting tired of not knowing what was going on.

"Are you sure you want to use it?" Rowena said, furrowing her brows. "It could be dangerous."

"If there's no other option, yes," I said. "I only need to know enough to keep it hidden. Like you and Theodora."

Theodora sighed. "No, I'm afraid we cannot teach you." She looked to Miriam. "Tell her why."

Miriam nodded. "Witches are split into two categories, generally speaking. Herbwitches have an affinity to the living world, to animals and plants. Charmwitches specialize in nonorganic magic, like enchantments and jinxes and protective spells," Miriam said. "You, my girl, are an herbwitch."

"What kind of witch are you?" I said.

"Me?" She winked. "I'm a businesswoman."

"What Miriam is trying to say," Theodora said irritably, "is that each witch specializes in magic from the organic world or the inorganic world. This simulation of outdoors, for example, is a blend of both kinds of magic."

I shook my head, barely understanding. "What do herbwitches do, exactly?"

"The most common is potions and plant magic," Rowena said. "Even then, each witch's magic is unique and works differently. For example, some witches can talk to plants. Some can merely grow them out of thin air."

"So you can't tell me what the colors in my vision mean?" I said.

Rowena shook her head. "That's for you to figure out, dear."

When we finally reached the field at the base of the village, Miriam summoned the passageway by mumbling a few words. I figured from that she was a charmwitch.

We traversed the tunnel yet again. This time I was too overwhelmed to be afraid of the darkness. I didn't know what to make of the stillness of Witch Village, Lana's anger, or Seraphina, the name that seemed to cause so much trouble.

11

The colors were getting difficult to control.

Flashes of chartreuse, yellow, and magenta flickered before my vision. The mount I rode didn't help my nausea. It was a spirited pony by the name of Thunderstorm, supposedly because her coat was as dark as a stormy sky. But I had been too distracted by the neon green fog on the stableboy's pants to pay attention to what he was saying.

"Calm down, why don't you?" I muttered into the beast's ear as we trotted through the trees. Thunderstorm shook her head, whipping my face with her long mane.

I rubbed my stinging cheek. It was still morning, that much I could tell from the crisp air. Murmurs, giggles, and the tinkling of bells from the other debutantes could be heard amongst the crunching of forest debris underfoot. This was the day of the hunting party, where gold ribboned young men went on murdering sprees of wild animals to win the heart of their favorite debutantes.

"Amarante? Are you alright?" Genevieve's voice sounded from my left. I didn't need to see her to know her brows were knit with worry.

"Quite," I said, keeping my eyes shut. Colors still danced before my lids, but it was better than the chaos I was faced with when my eyes were open.

"You look pale."

"Thanks, it's the lavender powder. Have you heard that fair complexions are in again?" I said, trying to keep my voice light.

My stomach lurched as Thunderstorm increased her pace. I peeked down at the soldier leading my mount, wondering why in the world he was speeding up, and instantly regretted it when a sharp flash of silver cut through my vision. I flinched.

"Are you sure you're alright?" Genevieve asked. "Is it the pheasant?"

Lord Strongfoot had served his signature, blisteringly spicy pheasant last night. My mouth was still stinging by the time we went to bed. That discomfort, however, was nothing compared to my current dilemma.

"Probably," I said. I couldn't very well tell Genevieve about the colors.

"I told you not to eat so much even if you were being polite," my stepsister said. "I hardly had a full bite."

"Aren't you hungry, then?" I asked as a burst of fuchsia bloomed in my vision.

"A bit. Good thing we'll be picnicking soon."

I was all too happy when Thunderstorm came to a halt. I opened my eyes gingerly.

"Miss?"

The soldier leading Thunderstorm extended his hand. A blinding, neon yellow dripped from his fingers. I shut my eyes and swung my leg over the saddle, but my foot came into contact with something solid.

"Oof!"

A thump and a clatter of metal sounded as I lurched off my mount, slamming bodily into the soldier who, it seemed, I had also kicked in the face.

Genevieve was the first to rush to my side. "Amarante! Heavens, are you hurt?" she asked. I couldn't help but look at her. Splashes of peach and rose surrounded her hair like a halo.

"No, I'm fine," I said. I turned to the soldier. He was now sitting up, a shock of red streaming down his nose into a sea of yellow. He gaped at me. "I'm so sorry," I said, but he scrambled off before I could say anything more.

"You should have stayed at Tori's if you weren't feeling well," my stepsister said, helping me up to my feet. My skirts were muddied by dirt and debris, and there was a sizable rip where the fabric caught on the soldier's armor. A few debutantes passed, snickering. My face burned.

"I'm fine," I repeated, brushing off my gown as best I could. Genevieve continued to say something, but I could only stare.

There were no more colors.

I looked around in wonderment. Why had it stopped?

"Amarante? Are you listening?"

"Huh?"

"You really ought to sit down. They're building the shelter right now so we'll have plenty of time to rest. Really, how could you go out in this state?"

The tents and shelter were built in about thirty minutes in the forest clearing. Sheets of canvas were stretched over wooden beams, providing shade from the emerging sun.

The debutantes were escorted to one such structure, where stools and tables were set out for our comfort. We spotted Tori and Olivia and joined them.

"What happened to you?" Tori said when we approached.

Olivia made a soft noise at the back of her throat. There was large hole in my riding skirt where my knee had scraped the road. Luckily, the trousers underneath were still intact.

"I'm perfectly fine," I said, plopping myself onto a stool.

"Was it Pa's pheasant?" Tori asked.

"It didn't really agree with her," Genevieve said delicately.

Tori shook her head and sighed. "Alas, not everyone can stomach a Strongfoot pheasant," she said. "Anyway, they say the hunting is going to start soon, though I don't see the point in telling us—we'll just be sitting here all day."

"We'll be picnicking and mingling," Olivia piped up.

"Like I said, sitting here all day."

I smiled at their banter, almost glad to have some semblance of normalcy, though attending the Season wouldn't have been my idea of normal three weeks ago. Never in a million years had I thought that I'd be seeing strange colors, that there were witches living underground, that they were forced to do so because of a king Olderea knew and loved.

I glanced at the makeshift dais some men had lifted in. Ornate chairs replaced thrones. Queen Cordelia was already seated, leaning on the arm of her chair. Prince Ash was nowhere to be seen.

"Miss Amarante! What happened to you?"

I turned my head and was met with the sight of the missing prince. Murmurs of "Your Highness" sounded from my companions.

"I fell off my horse, Your Highness," I said.

Prince Ash towered over me, dressed in a royal blue hunting coat and leather boots. His brows raised as he glanced at the hole in my skirts. I tucked my legs under the chair.

"I'm fine," I said, suddenly embarrassed.

He shook his head in bewilderment. "You kicked Michael in the face. You might have broken his nose, you know?" he said.

"I didn't mean to," I said, horrified.

I noticed that we were drawing some looks. Samantha was both glaring at me and shooting simpering smiles at the prince's back. Julianna merely sneered.

Prince Ash didn't seem bothered. "Come with me. They just put up the medical tent," he said, offering me his hand. His golden ribbon gleamed in the dappled sunlight.

"I don't know how to fix broken noses!"

He laughed. It was a pleasant sound, but it rang too loud for my comfort. "You're something. You can't fall off a horse without injuring yourself. Trust me. I've tried." he said.

"He's right, Amarante. You should probably check if you're hurt," Genevieve said softly.

Prince Ash smiled at Genevieve. "Come. Bandages await."

With a huff, I stood from my seat without taking his hand. Pain shot up from my right knee and for a terrifying moment, I stumbled. Prince Ash caught me around the waist before I hit the ground.

He tutted. "What did I say?"

"You can't fall off a horse without injuries."

He released me. "Nothing like a teachable pupil," he said, offering his arm. I took it begrudgingly and looked back to check if anybody saw my fall.

120

Nearly everyone's heads were turned. If Samantha was glaring before, she was glowering now. Julianna was fuming. Tessa sneered. Poor Olivia looked flustered and Tori, to my utter embarrassment, had formed a heart with her hands and pulsed it before her chest.

The medical tent couldn't be close enough. I limped as fast as I could, leaning heavily on Prince Ash's arm. When at last we entered the protective canvas walls, I threw myself on a nearby bench, nearly breathless with relief.

"Reselda? You have another patient," Prince Ash said to a woman in the far corner.

"Already? For heaven's sake, the hunt hasn't even started and we already have a broken nose and a…what happened to you?"

A middle-aged woman dressed in a healer's white frock stopped before me.

"Fell off a horse," I mumbled, chastened by her no-nonsense stare.

"And kicked a man in the face," the prince added almost cheerfully.

Reselda sighed. Taking my arm, she led me to a cot near the end of the tent where jars of herbs and ointments cluttered a table. "Where does it hurt?"

I pointed at my throbbing right knee.

"Very well. Let's have a look."

Reselda pushed my skirts away from the spot. I was horrified to see a scarlet stain blooming like a carnation on my trousers. "It didn't hurt when I fell on it," I said faintly.

"Of course it didn't," Reselda said. "Roll up your trousers."

"What?"

"Roll them up. Unless you want me to cut through them," she said. "And what in the devil are you still doing here?"

I was about to state my confusion before I realized she wasn't talking to me. Prince Ash stood to the side, blushing. Mortified, I pulled my skirts back over my leg. Trousers or not, I still felt indecent.

"I'll be waiting outside," he said, and promptly exited.

Reselda shook her head. "Boys," she muttered under her breath. "Wait here. I will get the bandages."

She disappeared behind a curtain that closed off the back of the tent. A second later, the front flap opened and Queen Cordelia herself entered, escorted by a servant.

"Your Majesty," I said, stumbling from my seat and executing a clumsy, one-legged curtsy.

"No use hurting yourself over formalities, Miss Amarante," the queen said. She took a seat at the bench near the entrance. "I suppose you're the one my son was looking for earlier?"

"I-I suppose so," I stuttered.

Reselda emerged with bandages before I embarrassed myself further. "Your Majesty," the healer said, dipping into a curtsy. "May I be of service?"

"Yes," the queen said. "I seem to have a headache from the heat."

"Are you usually sensitive to heat, Your Majesty?" Reselda asked.

"Not at all. I don't know what has gotten into me lately," Queen Cordelia, rubbing her temple. "Stress, perhaps. I reckon I'd be worse off if Wilhelmina wasn't organizing the Season for me."

"Understandable, Your Majesty," Reselda said. "I have a tonic that may help."

The healer disappeared behind the curtain again and emerged with an amber vial.

"Thank you, Reselda," Queen Cordelia said, taking the vial. "That will be all."

The healer nodded and turned her attention to me. She worked quickly, cleaning my wound with a stinging solution and wrapping the bandages firmly around my knee. "Any pain?" she asked. I stood from the cot and tested my weight on my injured leg. It throbbed a little, but otherwise was bearable.

"No. Thank you," I said.

"Good. The injury is minor—only a scrape and some bruising," the healer said. She handed me a small jar of ointment. "Apply this on the wound nightly to keep it from being infected."

I took it gratefully. "Thank you, Reselda," I said. "Oh, and if you see Michael—the soldier I kicked in the face— tell him sorry. Again."

Reselda broke into a smile, exposing a row of white teeth. "You're a nice girl," she said. "Now go on. I suppose the prince will want to know you're well."

I was all too aware of Queen Cordelia's stare as I limped slowly past her. "Be kind to him," she said, startling me. "He's more sensitive than he appears."

Without waiting for a reply, the queen stood and headed to the back of the tent. I hardly knew what to think of her words when I headed back to the debutante area of the camp.

When I rejoined Genevieve and the others, the stools were gone, replaced by patterned picnic blankets and baskets of food the servants had passed out. Tori was munching on a sausage roll as I picked at some fruit, lost in thought.

"So, how was alone time with princey?" she asked, her mouth full.

"His Highness kindly escorted me to the healer and I got my knee bandaged," I said.

"Please, anybody with two eyes and a brain can tell he's interested," Tori said with a snort. She paused and chewed. "Actually, that's not too many people."

"H-he caught you when you fell," Olivia said. Her dollish eyes widened as if she were the one who had been caught.

"Can we please stop talking about it?" I said, flushing as I recalled the queen's words.

A fanfare sounded before anyone could reply. Young men were gathered before the dais, armed with bows and arrows. I spotted Prince Ash in the midst of them. He caught my eye and waved.

Soon enough, the group dispatched on their horses. The debutantes tittered as they thundered past the clearing, dispersing into the forest. A flash of turquoise flitted over my vision and I winced. The colors were back.

A dull headache throbbed at the base of my skull. I began to close my eyes, but something was thrust under my nose.

"Amarante?" a sickly-sweet voice said. "Would you care for some punch?"

Lady Narcissa's figure was silhouetted against the morning light. Berry red fog billowed from her skin. She held a glass of punch toward me. A flash of acid green flitted across the surface of the drink. My headache sharpened and I shut my eyes.

"What are you doing here?" Tori asked, her voice brimming with disgust.

"I wasn't talking to you," the duchess's daughter said contemptuously. The rustling of skirts sounded. Someone sat next to me.

"Lady Narcissa," I said, forcing myself to meet her gaze.

"Please, call me Narcissa. We got off on the wrong foot, I'm afraid, and I am willing to extend a hand of friendship," she said. Tangerine orange and cerulean blue swirled from her mouth as she spoke. I didn't believe a word of it.

"Why the sudden change of mind?" Tori said from behind me.

Narcissa narrowed her eyes. Her hand of friendship didn't seem to extend very far. "I am merely here to present a peace offering," she said. "This is a glass of Mother's premium punch, imported directly from Aquatia. Take it or leave it."

I took the glass from her and set it down next to me, just so she would leave.

"Thank you," I gritted out. The acid green was nearly taking over my vision.

Narcissa stood, seemingly satisfied. "Of course. I hope you and I can be friends now, Amarante," she said with a false smile I could hear. I managed a nod.

"My, my. How could you refuse?" Tori said flatly when Narcissa was out of ear shot.

"She's scary," Olivia said softly.

Tori snorted, grabbing another sausage roll. "Yeah, about as scary as a paper tiger," she said as she chewed. "She's probably jealous Amarante has a prince's attention and she doesn't. Look at her, gone off to ask her mother to suck up to the queen."

A loud slurp sounded. The punch Narcissa gave me was gone.

I whirled around. "Tori, no!" I grabbed the drink from her hand. But it was too late—only half of the punch remained. Tori smacked her lips, acid green billowing from her mouth.

"What? She wouldn't give you a poisoned drink in broad daylight, would she?" she said, wiping her mouth with the back of her hand.

"I mean, no, I don't…"

I turned, frustrated. Somehow, in the back of my mind, I knew that the colors meant something. I recalled the flash of blue I saw in Lana's hut. Repair, it told me. The potion in her cauldron was an antidote meant to heal.

I was right.

A wild excitement rushed over me as I stared hard at the punch. What did the green mean? I waited, and a peculiar sensation emerged from the base of my head. *Laxative.*

"Tori," I said. "Let me take you to the medical tent."

"How did you know?" Tori moaned.

"You said it yourself," I said. "She can't be trusted."

"I'll have her head for a trophy!"

The symptoms of the laxative were rather explosive, to put it delicately. It was clear Narcissa had used a large quantity of fast-acting medicine, but Reselda had luckily given Tori something to combat it, along with several glasses of water. By the end of it, my friend was in a rotten, if not murderous, mood on the way back to the debutante shelter. The hunting party had returned with their game. Tori and I found a shaded spot away from the rabble of tittering debutantes and boasting young men.

"Careful," I said.

Tori growled. "I'll do whatever to get that b—"

She doubled over and clutched her stomach.

"What you need to do is sit down," I said. "I'll deal with Narcissa."

Tori stared at me incredulously. "You?" she said, leaning against a tree. "How? Stay silent until she dies of boredom?"

"I'm perfectly capable of confrontation."

Tori didn't look convinced.

A strange sort of confidence had overtaken me in the past hour. As I sat in the medical tent, I let the colors bloom from the cluttered table of ointments and herbs, enraptured. Slowly but surely, I deciphered the words that came from them. *Mend. Protect. Cleanse.* Some words were vague and some specific, and when I tried to decipher the lemon-yellow oozing from the canvas ceiling, nothing came. Still, there was progress, some semblance of control—and excitement—that wasn't there this morning.

I went back to the picnic to grab what was left of Narcissa's punch. Prince Ash was a few feet away, cleaning his bow as Samantha chattered and hovered over him like a hummingbird. I skirted around the pair and found Narcissa, who was sitting on a blanket at a far corner of the shelter, tossing bits of bread to a group of squirrels. She was relatively isolated, which I was grateful for. I tapped her shoulder.

"Amarante. I see you decided—"

I thrust the glass toward her, hard enough to fling the remaining liquid over her dress. Narcissa screamed as the punch dripped down her bodice.

"A peace offering," I said, twisting my lips into a smile.

Without waiting for a reply, I turned to the gaggle of shocked debutantes. My hands shook as I marched past them. There was power in confrontation, that I knew now. But where there was power, there was price. Narcissa ran to Duchess Wilhelmina, shrieking. For a second, the duchess's eyes met mine.

I had made a dangerous enemy.

12

The jingle of silver bells sounded. Through my fuzzy vision, the palace ballroom took form. Perfume and anticipation hung heavily in the air. I floated past nondescript faces and voices.

Then I saw her. A flash of wine purple eyes and a laugh sweeter than a nightingale. She was with a man, tall and familiar, but his face was a blur. I reached for her, but the closer I tried to get the further I drifted. Some invisible force pulled me back into the ocean of tulle and silk and featureless faces, suffocating me. I shoved and kicked, desperate to escape.

Fire and ice seared through my bones. An explosion of light flooded the ballroom, then everything disappeared.

I woke up.

A cotton quilt weighed over my face. The pocket of air I was breathing had long gone stale. Shifting in my sweat-drenched chemise, I sat up and blinked hard, wondering why my blanket felt ten times heavier and why it looked like a pile of ruffled fronds. And why they were glowing purple.

A fresh film of sweat dampened my neck when I turned to the window. The bird's-nest fern that sat in a pot on the windowsill had an explosive growth spurt. The pot lay shattered. From the cake of dirt that remained, thick tendrils of fronds snaked across the floor, up my bedposts, and wound themselves over my quilt. My jaw hung open. Was this what Theodora and Rowena meant when they said my magic was bound to show itself?

Genevieve's soft breathing brought me back to reality. Thank heavens she was a deep sleeper.

The sky had barely lightened. Slipping quietly from my bed, I began pulling the fronds into a heap on the ground. It was laborious work for someone who had just woken up and especially difficult with an injured knee. My leg and back ached by the time I shoved the hefty pile under my bed frame. I would have to take it outside later.

Light began to stream in through the window. I surveyed the room and deemed it satisfactorily un-magicked. But when I touched the quilt, a flash of vermillion sparked from the fabric. I clutched my hands to my chest, gnawing my lip. There was only one witch who could help me figure this out.

After pulling on a dressing gown and cloak, I penciled a quick note to Genevieve. Soon enough, I was out the window and through the gates of the Strongfoot's mansion with a leather pouch stuffed with fronds.

The pouch dug into my shoulder as I hopped off the horse chaise and marched through the buildings at the outskirts of Delibera. My thoughts strayed to the dream. Somehow,

I couldn't remember the whole thing—only snippets. The ballroom. A laugh as clear as a bell. Something that thrummed and vibrated my very bones. I had dreamed of a person but also a time and a place. And my magic. Swirls of purple emerged from my fingertips. My bag pulsed with the same energy.

I walked into the building I was looking for.

"Hello, and welcome—"

"Miriam, I need you to take me to Lana," I said.

She stared at me in shock. "Amarante? What are you doing here?"

"I have to see Lana now."

The witch looked askance and fiddled with her snail shell necklace. "You heard what she said last time, child. We've angered her enough."

I shook my head. "You don't understand. It's different now." I opened my bag and showed her the curling, engorged leaves of the bird's nest fern. Miriam raised her brows. "My magic is getting harder to control."

Miriam sighed. "Lana will have my neck if I bring back an unwelcome guest. You should leave. Go to your nannies and see if they can suppress your magic," she said.

"But I don't want to suppress it," I said. "Please. At least show me the way. You don't have to come with me."

"No," she said. "Your nannies will have my neck. I only have one neck! They'll split it three ways, the lot of them," she said.

I made an impatient noise at the back of my throat. "Fine, I'll go myself," I said, walking past Miriam to the back room. I pushed aside the ratty tapestry and narrowed my eyes. Five bricks glowed gold. I pressed them in.

"How did you—?"

The wall began to shift and part until it formed into the archway that led to the tunnel. I stepped in and turned back to Miriam whose jaw hung agape. "I'll be back soon," I said. "Don't worry. I won't mention your name to Lana."

The bricks resealed before she could say anything. Taking a deep breath, I walked forward in the dark, the gravel crunching underneath my thin slippers. This time I was not afraid.

A few minutes later, the rectangular sliver of daylight appeared before me. I reached out. My hand met something cold and spongey, and then the darkness melted away. Instead of overlooking the village from a distance, I found myself in the middle of a field of farmland. Witches hacked the dirt with hoes and pulled up beets by their purple and green stalks. No one seemed alarmed at my sudden appearance.

"Looking for anything, dearie?"

I started at the croaky voice. A positively ancient witch squatted a few paces behind me with a basket full of bell peppers. He had an impressively long beard, snowy white and adorned with a tangle of chains and beads that nearly concealed his toothless grin.

"Er, I'm actually looking for a person," I said.

"You've come to the right place," the witch said.

"I have?"

"Of course. When you want something urgently enough, the passageway will lead you to it," he said with a wink.

I spun around. This clearly was not where Lana lived. Perhaps she was somewhere here?

"I should get going," I said.

"Very well. But you should take your ration of produce before everything is gone."

I began to shake my head until I caught a glimpse of my own face in a puddle on the ground.

My eyes were purple.

I leaned in. A glimmer of something flitted over my cheeks. My freckles had turned gold.

The old witch gave me a strange look as I rubbed my face. "I-is this puddle enchanted?" I asked.

"Well, technically everything here is enchanted—"

A stiff figure emerged from behind a stalk of corn, hair streaked with gray. Lana.

"Sorry, I have to go!" I said to the witch before darting off. I thought I heard him grumble something about "witches these days" but wind rushed through my ears as I weaved through the rows of vegetables.

"Lana!"

She did not turn around. My view of her was obstructed by the heads of several people walking about. I dodged a few swinging baskets.

"Lana! La—Oof!"

Someone crashed into my shoulder, nearly toppling me over. Pain shot up my knee. I barely bit back a curse. After regaining my balance, I looked down at the person I had run into. It was a little witch girl, hardly more than twelve. She stared at me, her silver eyes a glaring contrast to her midnight skin.

"I'm sorry," I panted. "Are you alright?"

She nodded, but continued to stare. "I've never seen you here before," she said. "Are you new?"

"I'm sure you haven't seen loads of people here," I said. I didn't have time for small talk. Lana's head was getting further and further away. I rushed forward again, limping.

"No. I've seen everyone here. And I remember them too."

I glanced down. The little witch had followed. There was something familiar about her, but I couldn't quite place my finger on it.

"Alright. I am new. What of it?" I said.

"There's never anyone new."

"Shouldn't you be with your parents or something? Before you get lost?" I said, narrowly avoiding another collision with a young witch.

"I never get lost."

"You're awfully sure of yourself for someone so young."

"I'm Elowyn. What's your name?"

I exhaled loudly. Lana had disappeared. "I'm Amarante. And also lost," I muttered. How was I supposed to find my way back now?

Elowyn tilted her head. "You have purple eyes. My sister said she had a friend with purple eyes once."

I heaved a sigh. "Elowyn, was it?"

She nodded.

"Do you by any chance know someone called Lana?"

She nodded again.

A feeble ray of hope shone down on my situation. I felt foolish asking such a young child, but she was my only option at the moment.

"And do you know where she lives? Can you take me to her?"

Elowyn nodded yet again.

I nearly melted with relief. "Great. Which way do we go?"

Instead of pointing to a direction, Elowyn merely stretched out her hand. "Take my hand," she said.

"Er…alright." I took her hand.

Then, my stomach dropped to the ground and the field twisted away. In a blink of an eye, I was standing before the door to Lana's hut. I stumbled back.

"W-what happened?"

"We transported from one place to another."

Elowyn blinked up at me. I realized I was still clutching her hand and let go.

"How did you do that?"

"I'm a charmwitch," she said simply. "Didn't you know?"

I opened my mouth, but no sound came out.

Elowyn, seeing that I had nothing to say, shrugged. "Well, you're welcome. I'll see you around?"

I nodded and she skipped off without another word.

When I regained my senses, a figure was walking uphill towards me. It was Lana. Miriam's warning came back to me. I had to have a death wish to come back to Lana's cottage uninvited.

"Lana," I managed to say as she approached.

If she was surprised to see me, she didn't show it. A basket hung from the crook of her elbow, filled to the brim with glass containers and sprigs of herbs. She hardly spared me a glance.

"What did I tell you last time, Miriam?" she said. "This girl and her nannies are not welcome here."

Lana slipped into the cottage and slammed the door. A purple glow surrounded the handle, but I twisted it and entered.

"Miriam isn't here. It's just me," I said.

Lana set down her basket on a counter, her expression a mix of irritation and surprise. "That enchantment took me weeks," she muttered. She briskly removed the contents of the basket, glass clinking as it hit the wooden surface. "What is it you want, girl?" she asked. "I already told you I do not take custom orders from humans."

I bit my lip, cowed by her dismissive tone. "But I'm not," I said. "Not really." I let my bag fall to the floor with a thump. The silver bells of my bracelet jingled as I did this. Lana stiffened and turned, eyes flickering to the bag and then my bracelet.

"Look, I think I really do have magic," I said. "Last night, I…I had a dream and the plant next to my bed grew." I toed the bag, and the engorged leaves tumbled out.

Lana's face remained stony. "Perhaps you used too much fertilizer," she said and turned back around to busy herself.

I glared at her back, a surge of anger and frustration overtaking me. "Why are you so against helping me?"

"I do not teach humans."

"I'm half witch and I have magic," I said, marching over to Lana. "Last time when you asked me what those leaves were, I didn't know, but…I *knew*. I saw blue and the colors told me what it was. Repair. It said repair."

Lana began sorting through the herbs.

I clenched my jaw. "You're not listening to me!"

"Not everything is about you, girl," she said harshly. "Typical of humans, demanding favors when they need them and disappearing when they don't. You are selfish, like your—"

She stopped abruptly, and pinched her lips into a thin line. I stepped back, chastened. "No one told me I had a witch for a mother," I said. "Not even my Papa."

She was silent and did not react.

"I don't know what to do. Please help me."

Lana turned. There were deep creases along her forehead and frown lines around her mouth. "Put this over there," she said, flinging a sprig of herbs in my hand. I barely caught it before it hit the floor.

"Huh?"

"Are you deaf? Hang that over there," she said, pointing at the row of hooks above my head. There were already several different bunches wrapped in twine. I hung the one she gave me on an empty hook and looked over for approval, but Lana's head was bent over as she wrapped another bunch of herbs with a length of twine.

Several minutes passed in silence as she handed me each bunch of herbs to hang on the wall. I was too afraid to ask what was happening. When the last bunch of herbs was strung, Lana broke the silence.

"Follow me."

She traversed the room and revealed a short hallway behind a curtain. I trotted after quickly, noting that the interior of the cottage was a lot larger than the exterior suggested. The hallway opened up to a modest bedchamber. Everything inside was tidy and organized. Lana knelt before the bed and pulled a box from underneath the bed frame. It was small, with no embellishments or gilding, but she held it with great care.

"Tell me exactly what you've been experiencing with the colors," she said.

I took a breath and recounted the very first time I had seen the purple smudge with Rowena in the gardens, the situation at the hunting party, and finally the dream and the plants.

"You're experiencing the emergence of your magic," Lana said. "Most witches go through their Emergence much earlier, around five or six years old. It is a developmental process during which they discover their specialty of magic."

"Five or six?" I said, aghast.

"Theodora and Rowena have suppressed your magic for sixteen years, which is why you are late," Lana said. "Magic will ebb and change during a witch's Emergence. Your magic could be completely different at the end of it. All in all, Emergence is an unpredictable process. We usually have some sort of enchanted object to keep the magic under control."

"How does that work?"

"You channel your powers through that enchanted object. It keeps excess magic inside it, in case it expels outward unexpectedly," Lana said. She opened the box and thrust it toward me. Inside was a crystal pendant, deep wine in color, strung on a long leather cord. "Even after their Emergence, witches keep their enchanted object. They develop a bond with it. It becomes a part of them, just like their magic."

I glanced at it hesitantly. "Is that for me?"

"Who else would it be for?" Lana said sharply.

I gingerly lifted the pendant out of the box and dropped it over my head. It rested comfortably over my chest and hummed.

"Try it. Use your magic."

I looked at a windowsill and waited for a color to ooze out of it, but nothing happened.

"It's not working," I said.

Lana grunted. "Of course not. Come back out here," she said.

We traversed the hall to the front room. I focused my gaze on a bushel of herbs hanging from the wall. A pale green aura appeared around the leaves. I waited for a word to appear, but none did. Instead, a feeling overtook me and I knew exactly what to say.

"That plant. It's supposed to slow the effects of any poison," I said.

"Yes. Nixgrass. It can also be used in incense, to calm the senses when burnt."

I touched the crystal. "This is amazing."

"The crystal is merely a crutch. Soon enough you'll be able to control your magic on your own," Lana said.

"But what is my magic?"

"Magic is different in every witch, even amongst herbwitches and charmwitches," Lana said. "I happen to be particularly skilled at potion making. I know exactly what ingredients to use in exact quantities. You seem to understand what certain herbs and potions are through color."

I nodded. "So. Knowledge is our magic?"

"Indeed. Knowledge is power," Lana said, "but it can also be enhanced with more knowledge. All things can't be learned through our abilities. Take these." She grabbed several thick volumes from the shelves above her and handed them to me. My legs nearly buckled under the weight, and a sharp pain shot through my right knee. I winced. I had forgotten about my injury.

"Are you hurt?" Lana asked.

"I…fell off a horse yesterday," I said, setting the books on the counter.

Lana pointed to a stool and whisked off to her shelves. I took it as a sign to sit down, somewhat getting used to her behavior. After a few seconds of clinking and shuffling, she came back with a viscous amber substance. It was the potion from her cauldron last time. I hiked my dressing gown over my leg and unwrapped the gauze.

The sight wasn't pretty. I had forgotten to apply Reselda's ointment last night. Blotchy purple and green riddled my swollen knee. Lana dabbed the substance over the injury. I felt an instant cooling sensation and watched amazed, as the bruising disappeared before my eyes.

"A basic healing elixir," Lana said, corking the vial. "All witches learn to make it eventually."

I prodded my knee as Lana went back to her shelves. No pain. It was as if I hadn't fallen off a horse at all. A giggle threatened to burst from my throat. It was like magic. No. It *was* magic.

Lana dumped the pile of books onto my lap. I jumped.

"Do some reading," Lana said. "I expect you to finish them all before you come back. And don't let anyone see them."

"Come back? So you'll help me?"

"Why else would I give you my books?" Lana said. "And never take off that crystal. It will control your powers when you're in the midst of human society. I will contact you through it as well."

"Contact me?"

"It will vibrate when it is time for our next lesson. I expect you to arrive promptly when I call for you."

"Can I contact you through it?" I asked.

Lana frowned mightily. "Absolutely not. You are not to use magic above ground. And you are not ready for communication charms. Stick to your books."

I thumbed through the titles. *History of Witchcraft. Potion Making Volume I. An Index of Witchmade Herbs.* They were all worn, except for the first volume, *The History of Witchcraft.* The title was embossed with gold and I caught a glimpse of my reflection.

"Thank you…but I can't go back looking like this," I said, gesturing to my face.

Lana nodded. "Your witch traits have emerged. They are the physical marks of a possessor of magic," Lana said. She rolled up her sleeves, and I noticed that there were gold flecks on her elbow and fingertips, not unlike the gold of my freckles. With a wave of her hand, a shimmering mist settled over me and then dissolved. I checked my reflection again.

"Nothing happened," I said.

"Humans will not be able to see your witch traits unless you tell them what you are," Lana said. "All witches have this enchantment casted on them by one charmwitch or another."

"But I thought you're an herbwitch."

Lana sighed. "Charmwitches and herbwitches each have basic magic the other can learn. A charmwitch can learn to make basic potions. An herbwitch can cast simple enchantments. I refuse to waste any more time blabbering facts. You may leave."

"Well, thank you for everything," I said, standing up.

Lana turned her back to me again. "I will call for you in two weeks' time. I won't tolerate tardiness."

"Yes, Lana."

"And throw that bag of plants in my garden on your way out. I could use some fertilizer."

I returned when Genevieve was dressing for breakfast. She started at my sudden appearance.

"Amarante? Where have you been?"

I pointed to the note I had left on my mattress. "On a walk." I discreetly shoved my bag under my bed as Genevieve bent down for the note.

"A walk. At the crack of dawn? Dressed like that?"

I nodded, hoping she wouldn't question me further. Luckily she didn't, but the face she made told me that it wouldn't be easily forgotten.

"Hurry and get dressed," she said, tossing me a gown. I caught it, but not before the fabric hit me squarely in the face.

I recognized the gown Papa sent me for my sixteenth birthday. He was overseas, unable to attend my birthday celebration. I ran my fingers across the olive-green silk of the bodice. The square neckline was embroidered with shimmering bronze vines.

"What's the occasion? We don't have an event today, do we?" I asked.

Genevieve twisted her fingers. "No, but you are summoned to the palace."

I began to ask why, but realization dawned on me.

"Oh. Oh no."

13

It turned out that throwing punch at the duchess's daughter in front of an audience of debutantes was not something that could be easily overlooked. A letter arrived from the palace summoning me to the queen herself for disciplinary matters. My gut dropped to the floor.

"Don't worry, Amarante," Tori said. "I'm sure Her Majesty knows perfectly well what the duchess and her daughter are like."

"She and Queen Cordelia are bosom friends," I said. "You told us that yourself, remember?"

This did not seem to distress her. Throughout the course of breakfast, during which I barely stomached a blueberry, Tori encouraged me to "give that nasty Narcissa what's coming for her". Genevieve pulled me into a rib-crushing embrace as if I were being sent off to the gallows. Lord Strongfoot, after hearing about the matter, merely guffawed.

A carriage was called for me and I clutched the letter in my hand, crumpling and smoothing and crumpling the parchment until it felt like tissue. When I finally arrived at the south wing of the palace and showed the guards the crumpled letter, they led me to Lady Hortensia, whom I immediately recognized from her frilly gown. Her face was pinched in disapproval. I colored.

"Come along, Miss Flora," she said.

I followed Lady Hortensia down the hall of the south wing. Giant portraits of old, dead politicians with white beards and finery hung along the wall to my left. They seemed to glare down at me as I passed. After a couple minutes of walking down the lusciously furnished hall, we entered an archway that led to a wide chamber. Arched windows let in cheery daylight, a cruel contrast to my bleak situation.

"Wait here," Lady Hortensia said, gesturing to a small alcove before a pair of oak doors. "The queen will see you soon."

I took a seat on a particularly lumpy couch as the woman left with a sniff. I gripped the crystal around my neck with a shaky hand, willing myself to calm.

The possible punishments that loomed before me were unlike anything I dared to imagine. Would I be whipped? Shamed and disowned? Publicly beheaded? My fingers went to my throat. A beheading was a very viable punishment for throwing punch at the duchess's daughter.

My gaze wandered to the oak doors that led to the queen's study. Voices could be heard. Narcissa and the duchess were inside, perhaps overdramatizing the situation to reap a harsher punishment. I closed my eyes in frustration, wishing I were Elowyn so I could disappear and reappear elsewhere.

The doors burst open and the Whittingtons walked out. Narcissa was red in the face from fuming. Her Grace barely spared me a glance.

"The queen will see you now, Miss Flora," Duchess Wilhelmina said icily.

I swallowed and stood, careful to distance myself from Narcissa, who was glaring daggers at me.

"Prepare for the worst, city girl," she hissed, her slender shoulders shaking as I entered.

Queen Cordelia's study consisted of a sprawling desk and shelves of books that spanned the length of two walls. Before us was a stained-glass window depicting a mermaid at the shores of an aquamarine sea, tinting the carpeted floor with shards of multi-colored light. The queen herself sat behind the desk.

She looked up. For a moment, a scarlet aura rippled around her. It disappeared when I blinked.

I dipped into a low curtsy. "Your Majesty," I said, my voice hopelessly feeble.

"I suppose you know what you're here for, Miss Amarante?" the queen said with a firm, though not unkind, voice.

Shame colored my face. With Narcissa's glare burning into my cheek, I was sure I looked like one of Rowena's ripe heirloom tomatoes. "Yes, Your Majesty," I murmured.

"I am sure as a young lady of good upbringing," Queen Cordelia said, pressing her fingers together, "you are aware that splashing drinks on another debutante is a great offense."

It was difficult to meet her eye. If I did, she'd know I felt no remorse. "Yes, Your Majesty," I said.

"Well then. An apology is in order," the queen said.

I bowed my head. "I apologize."

"Not to me, child. To Narcissa."

THE HERBWITCH'S APPRENTICE

Duchess Wilhelmina scoffed. "Your Majesty, Miss Flora owes more than an apology. Perhaps an explanation for why she decided to soil my daughter's gown with the same punch Narcissa so kindly offered her before?"

"Well, I-I…" I stuttered.

"I was only trying to be friendly," Narcissa said, sniveling. I looked up, shocked at her drastic change of demeanor. The venom in her words before was gone. Now, she was all teary innocence.

"The punch was laced with a laxative, Your Majesty," I said, finding my voice. "Tori, Miss Victoria Strongfoot, could attest to that."

Her Majesty's brows raised ever so slightly. She turned to Narcissa. "Is that true?"

Narcissa's snivels crescendoed into a sob. "I offer you an olive branch and in turn you have struck me with it and tainted my name with nonsensical slander," Narcissa wailed. I stepped back, thoroughly appalled at her theatrics. If only she had used half that effort during the hunting party, I would've truly believed she wanted to be friends.

"Miss Flora, have you no decency?" Duchess Wilhelmina scolded, wrapping an arm around her daughter who was dabbing her nose with a lace handkerchief. "Your Majesty, I demand you to punish this young lady at once. I have never seen such an ill-mannered, nefarious girl in my life."

Queen Cordelia stared for a minute, not quite at me and not quite at the duchess or Narcissa. She looked more tired than thoughtful, the dark circles beneath her brown eyes deeper than they were before.

When she finally spoke, Narcissa's wails had quieted into whimpers. "You're distressed, Narcissa," Queen Cordelia said. "Wilhelmina, take her to rest, will you?"

A flash of irritation passed through the duchess's face, but disappeared as quickly as it came. "Your Majesty, I really—"

"Will you?" the queen repeated.

Duchess Wilhelmina curtsied deeply, hiding her expression. "Indeed."

She and Narcissa swept out of the room without another word, though their hostility was tangible when they slammed the door.

The queen folded her hands before her.

I curtsied again. "Your Majesty—"

"Rise, child. I have enough formalities to last me a lifetime."

I rose, surprised to hear that her voice was not brimming with anger. She motioned for me to sit in the chair across her. I sank into the velvet cushion.

"We have rules on how young ladies should act during the Season," the queen said. "Your behavior during the hunting party will be frowned upon."

I swallowed. "Your Majesty, I really didn't mean—"

"Next time you will do well to handle your affairs in a more private and ladylike way. Is that understood?"

My mouth gaped open. "P-pardon?"

Queen Cordelia sighed. She offered me a small smile, her almond eyes glimmering. "Growing up in a palace has taught me many things, both about myself and other people," she said. "But there is one thing I always keep in mind. Quarrels, no matter how badly you want to win them, are not worth their consequences. I will speak with Wilhelmina myself after this, so rest easy."

I nodded slowly, though not quite comprehending what she meant. "What about my punishment?" I asked.

"Ah, that," the queen said, leaning back in her chair. "You will dust the library this week, if you have no objections."

I shook my head, hardly knowing whether to be more surprised at the lax punishment or that the queen asked if I objected to said punishment.

"Good. And remember to pay extra attention to the east end, will you?" she said with a mysterious smile. "I'll have someone show you the way."

I nodded, speechless.

"Very well, you are dismissed," Queen Cordelia said.

I left the study with a servant who was to show me to the library. I followed her down the hall in a daze, hardly believing my luck. I had escaped a conference with the queen unscathed. To say I was relieved was an understatement—I was elated. Narcissa couldn't convince the queen to behead me after all.

When we reached the library, which wasn't too far from the queen's study, the servant thrust a duster in my hand and left, leaving me to wander the shelves alone with a ridiculous smile on my face. Luckily, there was no one there to see me, besides an old balding gentleman I assumed to be the librarian perched behind a tall desk. The nameplate in front of him identified him as Mr. Charles Northberry. He was fast asleep and snoring up a storm.

The library was a sprawling space with a domed ceiling, the walls lined with countless volumes of every size. Tall, narrow windows let in streams of daylight, illuminating the tops of the bookshelves. I squinted. There was hardly a speck of dust in the air, much less on the furniture.

I walked through the immaculate shelves to the east end, wondering why Queen Cordelia told me to pay extra attention there. Maybe the east end was neglected. Less than a half minute's walk led me to an opening. A comfortable corner with plush armchairs was situated next to a window seat surrounded by more books. It was not significantly dustier than the rest of the library, but there was company.

Prince Ash reclined on an armchair, his feet thrown over an ottoman. His hair, instead of neatly combed, was in a state of disarray. I stepped back, not expecting to see anyone—much less him—at the library.

The movement must've caught his attention. "Who's there?"

"Housekeeping," I said, hoping he wouldn't put down the book that obscured me from his vision.

Brown eyes emerged from behind the cover. "Ah. There you are."

"Your Highness," I said with a quick curtsy. "Er…were you expecting me?"

Prince Ash pulled himself up into a proper sitting position. "Yes, indeed."

"Oh," I said. I thought he really believed me to be a servant until he broke into a smile.

"Miss Amarante," he said, standing and giving me a smart bow. "You didn't think I've forgotten your face already, did you? What brings you here this fine morning?"

"I'm carrying out a punishment of sorts," I murmured.

He raised his eyebrows. "Is it for…?"

My cheeks burned. I supposed throwing punch at someone at a public party wouldn't go unnoticed. Shortly after the episode, I begged Tori to call a coach to take us back early. I didn't bother counting the people who saw the whole thing.

"Yes," I said, raising my chin and daring him to comment further. "I'm here at the queen's orders. She told me to clean the east end."

A peculiar look crossed Prince Ash's face. "Did she?"

I nodded, running my duster along the shelf next to me. It was spotless.

"Are you here to take care of the mice?" he asked.

I froze. "Mice?"

"That's right. But you won't have any luck. We've tried everything," the prince said with a shrug. "I don't mind them. They're quite cute."

I looked at him in disbelief.

"I'm joking," Prince Ash said, chuckling at my expression. He swung his legs down from the ottoman. "Come. You can help me instead."

I approached his corner, which was rather cluttered. A jacket was flung over the armchair and sheets of parchment covered in indiscernible scrawl littered the low table.

"What were you doing here?" I asked, tiptoeing through the paper.

"Filling up time, as usual," Prince Ash said, pulling on the jacket. "I was researching."

"Not debutantes, I hope?" I said, referencing our first conversation at the Debutante Ball.

"Not this time, though I've crossed many off the list since," he said, laughing. "I'm afraid my poor brother is going to be a bachelor for a long time."

A book lay face down on the seat. I picked it up. "History of Witches?" I said, shocked to see the title.

Prince Ash took it from me. "Just some light reading," he said, handing me a pile of books. "These go on the bottom shelf."

"What are you reading about witches for?" I said as I knelt. My voice wavered a bit, but he didn't seem to notice.

"If you must know," he said, "I'm trying to prove something."

"Prove what?"

"That I'm competent. To my father, anyway," Prince Ash said with a shrug. "Like I said, he doesn't let me help with kingdom affairs. I'm thinking if I show him I can solve this mystery—"

"What mystery?" I asked. I knew I was being rude, but I couldn't help it.

"Ah, apologies. I'm rambling like an idiot," he said. "You're familiar with Navierre's Trial, during my grandfather's time?"

His grandfather. King Humphrey. The king who began the Non-Magic Age and banned witches from Olderea after Navierre, a witch in the royal court, was found guilty of attempted regicide and beginning a witch rebellion.

My throat went dry. I had nearly forgotten Prince Ash was his direct descendant. My opinion of King Humphrey had certainly changed since discovering the circumstances of my birth.

"Yes," I said. "What of it?"

"Well, it's a bit of a family secret," Prince Ash said slowly, "but there hasn't been any hard evidence that Navierre committed the crimes he was charged with."

I stared, stunned.

"I know. It sounds bad, but there has to be evidence somewhere," the prince said quickly. "There are pages missing from my grandfather's journal. Someone probably wanted to hide Navierre's crimes. I hope to find them eventually."

"You're saying the Non-Magic Age happened on baseless accusation?" I said, aghast. My nannies were right. History about witches *was* skewed beyond belief.

"Not so loud," Prince Ash said, darting his eyes around. "It wasn't *completely* baseless. But that isn't the point. If I find that evidence, I'll finally win my father over."

"I suppose," I said.

I wanted to ask him why he was so sure that there was evidence, that perhaps it was King Humphrey who wanted to hide *his* crimes. But I held my tongue lest I offended him, or accidentally revealed myself. After all, he did just tell me a royal secret, though I hardly knew why he trusted me to keep it. I continued to shelve the books until he spoke again.

"Your knee," Prince Ash said almost hesitantly. He clearly didn't expect my curt tone or my silence. "Is it still hurting?"

I paused. Maybe he believed I thought him silly for wanting to win his father's confidence. "It's doing fine," I said, feeling slightly guilty. "Thank you, Your Highness. And I wish you the best of luck with your research."

I saw him glance at me from the corner of my eye. "You can call me Ash, you know. I have enough formalities to—"

"To last you a lifetime."

He raised his brows.

"You and your mother are very similar," I said.

He laughed. "I'm afraid we are."

"And what about your father?" I instantly regretted the words as they came out of my mouth. He stopped smiling and bent down to busy himself with gathering more parchment. I wanted to slap myself. He must've thought I was trying to weasel out information about his illegitimate birth.

"He spends more time with Bennett. My brother is the crown prince, after all," he said. There was hardly any emotion in his voice as he said this.

I thought back to the countless nights I had to spend alone when Lydia began etiquette lessons with Genevieve. I was only eleven at the time and I was forbidden to join lest I be a pest. As I got older, I started running from them instead.

We shelved the books in silence for several minutes. Somewhere along the way, the tension dissolved into a companionable silence as the sun climbed up the sky. When I tucked the last book into the shelf, I broke the silence.

"Is that all?" I asked, standing up.

"Seems like it." Prince Ash said.

"I should get going, then."

He nodded. I was halfway down the aisle of shelves before he spoke again. "Amarante? Make sure to come back next week. I have a feeling the east end will be particularly dirty by then."

I caught a glimpse of his smile between the shelves before he disappeared.

He called me Amarante.

14

Papa once told me that books were treasure chests of knowledge. It was the winter after I turned seven. We were in his study taking our tea near the warmth of the fireplace. The velvet drapes were pushed back from the window, heavy droplets of rain pounding against the roof and peppering the glass in clear, crystalline orbs.

I was leaning over his shoulder, watching him flip over the worn pages of a thick volume. The print was so small I had a headache looking at it.

"Papa, why must you read that book?" I whined, tugging his ears. "Can't we join Genevieve and stepmother in the parlor?"

He laughed, the sound like warm honey to my ears. "Lydia has her own plans with Genevieve, my flower," he said. He closed the book anyway, just to please me. I climbed onto his lap, glad to have his undivided attention.

"Would you like to learn how to read, Amarante?" Papa asked after a moment. I stopped playing with his cravat and looked up at him. He hadn't shaved that day, the whiskers on his chin shadowing his face.

"To read? Mrs. Handel said I was too young to learn," I said.

"You mustn't always listen to your governess," Papa said. He lifted me from his lap and set me down, reaching for a thin book on the shelf behind him. "Here," he said, placing the book on his desk. "I will teach you."

I stood on my tiptoes as Papa opened the covers to reveal vibrantly colored illustrations and large letters.

"That looks difficult," I said.

"Ah, but don't you know, Amarante? When you read, you will learn about the world, or be swept on fantastic adventures you could never imagine," he said with great zest, pointing at the window to the great beyond. The rain had stopped and a hint of golden sunlight peeked through the dense, gray clouds.

"Really?" I said.

Papa smiled his knowing smile. "The more knowledge you gain, the wiser you'll be. And books, my flower, are treasure chests of knowledge."

I had never been a great reader, regretfully, for I was easily intimidated by the books Papa so loved. He often read volumes on philosophy or economics, or novels as thick as my mattress. I never could imagine myself comprehending any of it.

As a result, the books Lana gave me sat under my bed for several days. I was almost afraid to let them touch daylight, as if they would crumble to dust if the sun made contact with the pages. But I knew that Lana's books were nothing like Papa's. Even after days out of my sight, they held my curiosity. I eventually asked Tori if I could take a peek at their library, where I stripped off the dust jacket of Lady Strongfoot's sappy romance novel to conceal what I was actually reading. This garnered some strange looks from Tori and Genevieve as I devoured the pages at every meal.

"Ah, the prime age for young girls to fill their heads with mush," Lord Strongfoot said when he noticed my undivided attention to what he thought was *A Sailor's Seduction: Tales of Romance at Sea.*

I was too distracted to be embarrassed. It turned out that Papa was right—books *were* treasure chests of knowledge. And books on witch magic were like pirate coves of rare gems and antique gold. My muddled ideas about magic and types of witches finally made sense. Like Lana had said, every witch's magic worked differently. Whereas one witch could hear the thoughts of plants and animals, another could sense their usefulness or purpose in a potion or charm. I thought about the colors I saw and how I instantly knew what they meant.

The crystal Lana gave me was another odd change. With each passing day, I became more familiar with it and sensed that it became more familiar with me. It hummed whenever I touched it, as if emitting its own energy. Slowly but surely, I called upon the colors with ease and made them disappear just as quickly. I knew the jar on Tori's desk emitting puffs of pale pink was meant to fade freckles and the tube of paste oozing indigo blue in Lord Strongfoot's pocket tamed his hair and beard.

I stopped being startled by my witch traits and instead began to admire them. My cheeks glittered as if brushed with gold dust. My eyes, instead of the dark earthy brown I was used to, caught the light in quite an entrancing way. Genevieve teased me for staring at the mirror more times than I'd like to admit. She once told me all young ladies go through a phase of admiring their own beauty. I was embarrassed, but admittedly during that time, I found my features more pleasing than I had ever before.

As the days passed, another letter came from the palace, this time notifying us of the next event of the Season: a talent show. Hosted by the music mistress Madam Lucille, it would require the debutantes, as well as select young men who wished to join, to showcase their personal talents to the attendees of the Season. For me, this was cause for some anxiety.

"A talent show?" Tori said. She looked positively delighted. "Prime time to whip out my old lute."

Genevieve decided to exhibit her watercolor paintings and do a live demonstration. Meanwhile, I was trying very hard not to think about all the things I was terrible at.

"I actually regret escaping stepmother's lessons," I moaned to an amused Genevieve. "Who would've thought this day would come?"

Lydia forced us to learn a multitude of ladylike arts, including playing the piano, painting, and embroidery, among other activities. I barely passed as mediocre on the piano and my embroidery was a definite disaster. Luckily, there were still two weeks to prepare.

Ash was similarly amused when I told him of my plight. I had returned to the library as promised and the two of us actually cleaned the east end, as he had requested the servants to leave the work for us.

"Why not try dancing?" he said, wiping the panes of the window with a damp rag as I swept the floor.

"You of all people should know I'm a mediocre dancer." I had gotten surprisingly comfortable in his company.

He tapped his chin. "Sing a song, perhaps? I could play the piano. We'll put on a good performance, you and I."

I leaned over on my broom. "Only if you play exceptionally loudly to mask my terrible pitch."

"Is there anything you're good at?"

"Gardening."

"Now there's an idea! How do you feel about flower arrangement?"

"That is not the same thing, Ash."

His face practically glowed. "You called me Ash."

I masked my embarrassment with a scowl. "Well, it's your name, isn't it?"

His silly smile didn't dissolve fast enough for my liking, so I spent the rest of the time in icy silence and calling him "Your Royal Highness" when I had to address him.

Though nothing came from the cleaning session, I decided to busy myself with Lana's books and forget about the blasted talent show until it was close enough to worry about. A week before the event, my crystal vibrated, calling me to my first lesson with Lana. I deemed it much more important and enjoyable than a Season event, until I discovered that it involved toads.

"Bring it over here."

I gingerly picked up the glass box in which a very large, very slimy toad sat and set it next to Lana. In addition to snails and cats, toads were creatures I absolutely detested, mostly because of their slick-looking skin and bulging eye balls. When I came into Lana's cottage first thing in the morning, I expected her to ask me about the reading she

158

had assigned, but instead I was fetching things for her and bringing them to her potion-making room. One of them happened to be a toad.

I didn't ask Lana what she was making, as she was too absorbed in her work to speak more than a few words at a time, the bulk of them commands. I stood to the side and watched her, fascinated, as she cut a wine-colored root into thin slices and scraped it into a stone pestle filled with a mixture of strange powders. I knew what each ingredient did. A good amount of them had detoxifying properties and some were meant to purify. Lana soon broke the silence.

"Open the lid."

I jostled out of my trance. She couldn't mean the toad.

"Well? Open it." Her jab at the glass box melted away all doubt.

It was ridiculous to moan about my phobia of amphibians to Lana, so I swallowed my fear and lifted the lid. The toad's eyes darted about, looking ready to leap out and attach itself to my face like a leech.

Lana selected a cotton swab from the multitude of tools before her and began stroking the toad below the chin. I watched with a mixture of disgust and fascination as a milky substance oozed from its back. Rings of fluorescent teal pulsed from the toad's skin.

"Is that…?"

"Toad venom." Lana ran the swab across the creature and then closed the lid. She wiped the gooey substance into her bowl and began grinding the mixture with a mortar. After a moment, she walked over to the stone fireplace where she had told me to prepare a small cauldron with salted water. It was boiling when she scraped the ground contents inside.

I looked at the concoction doubtfully, wondering why Lana was putting venom in a potion. I recalled that a neighborhood girl's dog died by toad venom a few years back and treacherously wondered if Lana was making poison. Was it for the Witch Market I had heard so much about?

"This is an antidote for mild poisoning," Lana said as if reading my thoughts. She stirred the cauldron with a wooden stick, looking every bit like the witch she was. Her face betrayed none of her thoughts. Though serious, she looked calmer than she did the first time I saw her.

"An antidote? With venom in it?"

"Have you not read anything I gave you?"

"I have!" I said, scrambling for the books in my bag. I didn't want to disappoint her. "But I only started the third one. On potion making."

Lana glanced at the book in my lap and raised an eyebrow. Only then did I notice the dust jacket of *A Sailor's Seduction* was still wrapped around it, depicting a very saucy image of a bare-chested man. I yanked off the jacket and shoved it back in the bag, blushing. "That was a disguise," I said.

The witch gave a nod. I thought I detected a twitch at the corner of her lips. "Potion making is the most important of the bunch, but I suppose you had to familiarize yourself with basic witch history first."

I recalled what the volume on witch history said about King Humphrey's Non-Magic Age. There wasn't a hint of malice in the passage despite being written by a witch. It could have been in a standard book on Olderean history. I wondered how the witches could be so compliant as to willingly leave because a human king said so. Though, I supposed that they managed to live perfectly well underneath their homeland.

"I'll try my best to finish it this week," I said earnestly. "I've been a bit preoccupied."

Lana's gaze strayed to my bracelet of silver bells. I had gotten so used to its weight on my wrist that I barely took off.

"I see," she said. "Well, no matter. I intend to teach you the basics of potion making today, anyhow."

She covered the cauldron with a lid and beckoned me to the main room, which I began to refer to as her storage room if anything else. The chamber was cluttered with herbs and bottles and papers. Lana pulled out a bench near the fireplace and gestured for me to be seated.

"Today we will cover poisons and antidotes, the former of which is the first thing that comes to humans' minds when they hear about witch potions," Lana said dryly. "If you were wondering why I put venom in the antidote, it is meant to work with the purifying ingredients to stagnate and at some point, reverse the effects of any mild poison. I find that poison itself, if used in small quantities, can be used for healing. Antidotes, too, can be poisonous if used in great amounts. There is a delicate balance between the two, and any small change can tip the scale."

I nodded, wishing that I had brought fresh parchment and a pen with me. My younger self would have scoffed, as my old governess's lessons were as dull as a barrel of turnips. But this was different.

"Mind you," she said, "making poisons with intent of killing humans or fellow witches alike is not allowed. No witch is allowed to use magic for malice. It is the only law we have."

"So you can't make poisons?" I asked, confused.

"We can," Lana said after a beat. "I suppose it's not a law. More of a code of honor, really."

Lana proceeded to list the most common types of witch-made poisons, which were only made to kill off pests or to get rid of mold, that wouldn't be fatal to humans or witches if ingested. Most of them could be cured with the basic antidote Lana had made out of toad venom.

"And you will find that all witch-made potions will linger on any object it touches," Lana said. "Magic always leaves a trace."

I asked her what she meant by that.

Lana went to her cupboard and pulled out a vial of murky liquid and a dented tin mug. I touched my crystal when she uncorked the vial. Rat poison.

"Watch carefully," Lana said. She dripped the poison into the mug, swirled it around, and poured it back into the vial. A puff of gold emitted from the tin when the poison made contact, then faded away. Lana went to her cauldron where she rinsed the mug with water.

"All witches can sense where a potion has been, in their own way. For you it will be visual," Lana said, tilting the mug to me. "Do you see anything?"

A pulsing gold aura emitted from the mug where the rat poison had been, even though it was clean. "I do," I said. "It's like a magical footprint."

"It is," Lana said. I thought I saw a hint of satisfaction in her expression. "And luckily, it is possible to extract and identify that footprint with a special extracting potion. Very handy for witches who forget the recipe of something they previously brewed."

"So you could make more rat poison appear from that mug?" I asked, amazed.

"That's right. You will learn how to make that extracting potion in the future," she said.

"Are there any other examples of magic leaving a trace?" I asked, wondering at the possibilities. "If a charmwitch casts a spell, does that leave a trace too?"

"Not quite. But magic works in mysterious ways. Sometimes things happen that even witches can't comprehend," Lana said. "Legend has it there was once a powerful witch who passed away. When she breathed her last breath, her enchanted object glowed and her body disappeared. The object was passed on to her granddaughter, who claims her grandmother has appeared before her many a time, as real and as solid as any living person."

I stared at my crystal, wondering if I'd be stuck in there if I died. Lana seemed to read my thoughts. "But of course, it is just a legend," she said. I realized she was looking at my crystal too. She tore her gaze away and cleared her throat. "Never mind that. It is getting late."

The strong sunlight streaming through the circular windows told me it was near noon. My stomach gave an embarrassingly loud growl as I bent over to retrieve my bag.

"Will you stay for lunch?" Lana asked just as I stood.

"If you will have me," I said, sitting back down. I'd be a fool to refuse Lana's hospitality after taking such pains to convince her to teach me.

Lana disappeared into another room, and before I could react, dishes of food shot out and skidded onto the table. She emerged and sat calmly, as if levitating dishes were not out of the ordinary.

"Go ahead."

A bowl of mixed grains sat before me. The other dishes held assorted vegetables and a hunk of steamed fish. I took a small bite, noting that the grains and vegetables tasted rather bland despite the spices speckling the surface. We ate in silence until we finished. Lana waved her hand and the empty dishes flew back into the room from which they came.

"Will I be able to do that?" I asked.

"Moving objects with magic? Yes, if you wish," Lana said. "It is like any skill. Some witches never bother learning it and some find it immensely useful." She gave no more explanation, and I didn't feel like prying. I still felt hungry, oddly enough, but I did not say so. Hopefully, there would be something for me back at the Strongfoot manor.

"Thank you for the meal." I lifted my bag over my shoulder again and slid off the bench.

"It's a poor meal compared to what you are used to, I'm sure," Lana said.

"Not at all, really. It was…er, delicious."

She laughed. I noted that it was the first time she had done so in my presence. "There is no need to lie. I am perfectly aware of how tasteless it was."

"The fish was fine," I said. It was. I had eaten my portion much too quickly after discovering that it had ten times more flavor than anything else.

"I got it from the Market," Lana said.

I was almost hesitant to ask. "The Witch Market?"

Lana nodded. "Illegal as it may be, we depend on it, especially for food. There are many shortcomings to living underground, no matter how much we make it look like the outside world." She glanced out of the small round window near the door, an almost wistful expression overtaking her face.

"Do witches get all their food from humans?"

"No. We have land for growing crops at the perimeter of the village. It is not nearly enough to feed an entire village year-round, so we use magic to grow more and grow faster.

And well…one could imagine the quality of rushed crops," Lana said.

So that's why I wasn't full after eating so much. It never occurred to me that magic couldn't accomplish everything.

Curiosity got the best of me. "When was the last time you went outside?" I asked. Lana's face stiffened.

"Last week," she said briskly. "To the Market."

She went to the counter again. She had bottled up the antidote in small glass jars and began putting them in a shallow wooden crate. "Speaking of which, we are going next week. I'll need someone to carry my wares."

"Do you often sell at the Market?" I asked.

Lana turned around, hands on her hips. "Many of us have to, unless we wish to have bland food and no supplies."

I felt ignorant and scolded as Lana loaded her wares. I had always heard the Witch Market referred to in whispers, a place where twisted people went to purchase twisted things. But now, despite not having been there, I saw it in a different light.

I decided to speak again. "But if it's illegal, how do you manage to go?"

Lana's lips pinched. "As powerful as your king is, he cannot control everything."

Your king. Not our. I supposed it was fitting, as witches have technically been banished from the kingdom. Yet it made me wonder if witches had their own sort of leadership, and if so, who? I asked Lana just that, and she laughed again, but this time it was mirthless.

"We have no king and no leader. We are a reclusive, independent people."

I recalled Miriam's words. Witches were reclusive to a fault. But I sensed, for some reason or other, that Lana did not take well to the snail seller's ideas.

15

A book fell from the top most shelf, almost smacking me in the face.

"Apologies! Are you alright?" Ash poked his head around the corner, his hair covered in a light coat of dust. We were cleaning the library again. Oddly enough, I had grown to enjoy the task.

"I'm fine," I said. I leaned my mop against the wall and picked up the volume. It was a hefty thing on finances. "Ah. Olderean Finances. My old governess tried to teach me out of that."

Ash took the book and disappeared behind the bookshelf. His hand emerged from the top as he put it back. "Really? Learn anything interesting?"

"I didn't learn anything at all," I said, dunking my mop into a bucket of soapy water. "She was an awful teacher. My Papa taught me the basics."

"Ah, perhaps the next kingdom-wide issue Bennett ought to tackle is decent governesses," he said. The creaking of ladder rungs sounded from the other side. "Mine was just as awful."

"You had a governess?" I said, unable to keep the laughter out of my voice. "Why not a regular tutor?"

"It was only for a year or so. And it was meant to be a punishment of sorts." Ash flashed me a smile from a gap between a few books. "I was eight, I believe. I was supposed to be studying with Bennett overseas but I slipped off the ship last minute. Needless to say, my parents were furious when they found me hiding in the throne room."

I laughed. "How did you manage that at eight years old?"

"A magician never reveals his secrets."

Of course he was a handful as a child.

"Tell me about your governess," I said, pushing the mop across the floor. The clean path of marble gleamed in the daylight. "What did you do to the poor woman?"

"Quite the opposite, actually," the prince said. "You should be asking what she did to me." He was still smiling, though his usual cheekiness was absent. "I don't think I've ever lived a bleaker year. It happened that my mother had to pay a visit to her cousins and my father was busy with his affairs as usual. I was completely under my governess's care, if care is even the right word. She expected me to dedicate every hour to my studies. Language, history, economics, politics, etiquette, and piano. I wasn't allowed to play outside for more than a few minutes each day. And if I disobeyed her…well I learned not to." He grimaced, but smoothed his features when he caught me staring.

"She didn't hurt you, did she?" I said incredulously. I've had my fair share of stinging palms, though the way Ash spoke suggested that he had far more than a quick smack on the wrist. Ash ran his thumb over a faint white scar across his knuckles. That said more than enough.

"I became very good at piano," he said, abruptly drawing away from the bookshelf. I suspected he didn't want me to see his face. "Excellent, if I do say so myself, but I detest it. Isn't that funny? I believe there is little point in mastering something if you end up hating it. Then the only reason you continue to do it is because you're a master, and not because you're truly passionate about it."

"Makes sense," I said. I certainly had never been a master at anything, but I knew Genevieve would not love drawing if she had been forced to do it.

Ash rearranged a few volumes, creating more racket than I thought necessary, and stuffed an etiquette book into the gap he had talked through. "I'm rambling, aren't I?"

I didn't want to push the topic. "Not at all," I said. I bent down to wring out the mop, making a face as dirty, sudsy water drenched my sleeves. I should have rolled them up beforehand. "Do you reckon Mr. Northberry will be satisfied with our work?"

"Tired already?" I was glad to hear the teasing tone return to his voice.

"No," I said. "Just hungry."

"I'll say," Ash said. He emerged from the other side of the bookshelf, this time fully, and handed me his handkerchief. I glanced at the pristine fabric embroidered with gold thread. His initials gleamed at the corner.

I held up my filthy hands. "You can't be serious."

He rolled his eyes. "Take it. I have more than enough to spare."

I reluctantly accepted and dried my hands. "I ought to go back. I can't miss another luncheon or I'll hurt Lord Strongfoot's feelings."

"I'll see you back, then."

I was going to protest, but he had already offered me his arm and didn't look like he was going to retract it. We left our cleaning supplies for the servants to take care of and passed Mr. Northberry, who as usual, was snoring up a storm at the front desk.

The halls of the south wing were relatively empty, save for several passing maids who pretended not to gawk at us. I only hoped they wouldn't start a rumor too atrocious. I probably looked ridiculous with my sleeves soaked through and skirts wrinkled at the arm of a prince, who at the moment didn't look too princely either.

As I was going to withdraw my arm and declare I go my own way, a guard rushed past us with a tray of tea, the fine porcelain clattering together haphazardly. But the noise wasn't the only thing that caught my attention. A faint wisp of cyan swirled from the spout of the teapot. I blinked, realizing that I had unconsciously reached for my crystal.

"Stop right there," Ash said. His voice projected across the hall. The guard was in such a hurry that he was already on the other end, but his shoulders hunched at Ash's command. He turned and trailed back at a considerably slower pace. I recognized him as the buggy-eyed guard Tori danced with at the Debutante Ball.

"Your Highness," the man said with a bow. He kept his head lowered when he rose.

"What is your name and why are you not on patrol?"

"Peter, Your Highness. I was sent to deliver Her Majesty's tea." He had a youthful voice, despite his large build. He couldn't have been older than myself.

"Look at me when I address you, Peter." Ash's tone and words reminded me very much of someone else. I couldn't put my finger on who, but it was clear he meant to intimidate. It was quite effective.

The guard raised his head, looking cowed. He was young indeed, and his round nose accentuated that, especially in comparison to Ash's sharper features. "Who decided to send a guard to deliver the queen's tea instead of a regular servant?"

"The head cook, Your Highness. There's been a shortage of staff with the arrival of the debutantes, so I was told to do the job." Peter provided this answer quite readily, but the tray shook. My hand itched to reach for my crystal again. Curiosity and wariness stirred in my gut. What was in that tea?

"There were several idle maids who passed a few moments ago," I said.

"And you are?" Peter said. His tone held much less reverence than it had when addressing Ash. He stared a little too boldly for my comfort.

Ash stepped in front of me. "There *were* several maids at leisure," he said. "We have four hundred staff members and a good many of them work in the kitchens. A shortage of staff is impossible, even with the debutantes. I will have to ask you what your tray contains and why you are in such a hurry."

"Merely the queen's tea and biscuits, Your Highness. I'm afraid I will be punished if I don't bring it to Her Majesty in a timely manner."

"You will not be," Ash said. "Have they been through the taster?"

"Of course, Your Highness."

I gripped my crystal and focused on the teapot. The cyan reappeared, this time brighter. *Arsenic.* I stifled my gasp. He was going to poison the queen! I stopped myself before I nudged Ash in warning. He was already suspicious of Peter. I hoped he wouldn't be convinced otherwise.

"Then you will not mind having some," Ash said. He clasped his hands behind him. They were clenched tight.

Peter flicked his buggy gaze around the hall before settling on the prince. "Your Highness, surely that would not be proper."

"That was an order."

I wasn't prepared for the crash when Peter dropped the tray and dashed down the hall. Ash was after him immediately.

"Guards!" he bellowed as he ran. I was rooted to the floor as members of the Royal Guard streamed in seemingly out of nowhere, pouring in from both ends of the hallway in their purple tunics. Swords were drawn and soon Peter was surrounded. He cowered on the floor before Ash, who was angrier than I had ever seen him.

"This man has committed treason. Take him away for questioning."

As several guards lowered their swords, Peter stood and laughed. "No need for that," he said, all trace of respect gone. He surveyed the circle of men around him with his buggy eyes. "I'll tell you whose orders I'm working under. Captain Maverick Greenwood."

Shock flitted through the guards' faces.

"What proof do you have?" one of them shouted.

Peter sneered. "Isn't it obvious? His affair with the queen has been put to an end. He's been poisoning her little by little each year out of spite." He stared at Ash. "And his own son won't acknowledge him as father."

Ash looked murderous. "Lies," he said. "How dare you lie in my presence?"

A shiver ran up my spine at his words.

"You've seen the proof yourself. The queen is getting weaker each day," Peter said. "Search the captain's chambers if you still don't believe me."

A muscle twitched in Ash's jaw. He made a motion and three guards split from the group, no doubt off to Captain Greenwood's chambers. To another, he said, "Take him away and question him thoroughly."

But Peter's body fell with a thump. The guards jumped back, widening their circle. I caught a glimpse of foam bubbling out of his mouth and someone holding a finger under Peter's nose. "He's killed himself!"

At that moment, the double doors to the queen's study opened a few feet before me. Out walked Queen Cordelia herself.

"What is going on?" Her Majesty said.

Ash stared at the unmoving body at his feet. "Someone is poisoning you, Mother."

Queen Cordelia swayed. I rushed over to steady her. The hand that gripped my arm was frighteningly white. "I've been afraid of this," she said. Her voice was so faint that only I could hear it. She turned to me, her expression almost pleading. "Who did they say it was?"

"Captain Greenwood, Your Majesty," I said hoarsely.

Her face drained of color and she swooned, buckling to the floor. Ash was instantly by her side.

"Somebody take the queen to her chambers!" he said. Several maids came at his call. They took Her Majesty by her arms and led her away. The red aura around her pulsed, now a bright scarlet.

The three guards who had left appeared, holding a fistful of letters and a box. "Poison, Your Highness. And proof."

Ash grabbed a letter, scanned it, and crumpled it. "Arrest him. Immediately."

"Yes, Your Highness!"

The guards streamed out of the hall, their faces pinched and ashen—faces of men about to arrest their own captain. I stared at the floor. It was a mess of broken porcelain and tea and soaked biscuits. The tea was still oozing cyan. The queen's aura had been red. The queen's drink had been red at the Debutante Ball—the drink the duchess had given her.

I didn't know how long I knelt there before Ash touched my shoulder. "Amarante," he said in a low voice. I realized then the hall was empty, save for us and Peter's body. No one had bothered to take him away.

"Search him," I said, standing up. "We have to search him."

He grabbed my arm before I could take a step toward the corpse. "I'm sorry you had to witness that. You should go home."

I shook him off and trotted over to Peter's limp form, running my hands over the dead man's chest and arms.

"Amarante, *what* are you doing?" Ash said, flabbergasted.

I'd never touched a man so liberally before, much less a dead one, but determination saved me from embarrassment. There was a lump at his side, and I pulled back his tunic to reveal a bulging leather pouch strapped to his waist. I pulled it off and dumped the contents onto the floor. Heavy golden coins spilled onto the marble.

Ash crouched beside me. "The captain paid him a hefty sum," he said, looking at the coins in disgust.

"It wasn't the captain," I said.

He exhaled. "I know the Strongfoots respect him. But Amarante, the proof is not in his favor."

I picked up a coin and flipped it over. It was stamped with an elaborate insignia—a snake entwined in roses.

"Is that…?" Ash said.

I knew the design too well at this point to mistake it. "The duchess's emblem," I finished. I recalled what Tori told me about illustrious families having gold stamped with their own emblem.

"Of course. This complicates things." Ash stood again and paced the width of the hallway. He stopped. "How could you have known?"

I set down the coin. "I thought I saw the duchess slip something into Her Majesty's goblet back at the Debutante Ball."

Ash knelt and gripped my shoulders. "You did? Why didn't you tell me?"

I faltered, startled by the urgency of his voice and stare. "I-I couldn't have been sure," I said.

He blinked and released his hold, but not before smoothing my sleeves. "I'm sorry. That was rude of me. Of course you couldn't have been sure."

"It's fine." I shoveled the coins back into the pouch. "I think there might be a way to find out. Have you got a royal inspector?"

16

Mr. Erasmus Lenard was the head of the royal inspection team, having risen to his post by being the only member. Ash said that King Humphrey didn't see the need for an extensive inspection team after pioneering the Non-Magic Age. I thought that was quite silly.

We soon found ourselves in the old man's laboratory, poorly lit and crowded with all sorts of gadgets and mysterious crates. The sheer quantity of strange things in the space reminded me of Lana's cottage, though the crumbling stone walls were much less welcoming.

"Damn traitors," the inspector grumbled. "I was about to submit a retirement request."

"I assure you, sir, my father will happily let you retire after this case," Ash said.

He snorted. "Erasmus will do, boy. I cannot have my first visitors in fifteen years call me 'sir'."

I gawked at the old man, wondering if he had been trapped down here for that long.

Erasmus caught my eye. "Who are you, missy?"

"Amarante Flora, s—er, Erasmus," I said, deciding to hold off on curtsying lest I offended him.

He snorted again. His eyes flicked to my dirty sleeves. "And here I thought they finally allowed women to do something useful," he said. "Fetch me a pair of gloves, will you?"

"Actually, I'm a witness," I said.

"And also a servant, aren't you?"

"She's a debutante," Ash intervened. "I'll fetch the gloves."

He disappeared around the corner, leaving me and the inspector in the cramped room. My determination dwindled as he bustled about his desk with clear authority despite his advanced age. How was I ever going to tell him about my theory if he thought I was a servant at first glance?

"That one fancies you, doesn't he?" Erasmus said.

I had enough teasing from Tori and Genevieve. The last thing I needed was the royal inspector teasing me too. "A platonic friendship between a young man and woman is very possible, sir," I said.

"Not during the Season, little flower."

"What did you call me?"

"You're named after the amaranth flower. Love-lies-bleeding, if you're poetic. Or depressed. I see very little difference between the two."

The old man was off his rocker. I glanced at the door, wishing Ash would come back so I didn't have to reply. Thankfully, the door swung open and he returned with a thick pair of gloves. I could've kissed him. Platonically, of course.

"Took you long enough," Erasmus said, pulling on the gloves. He shuffled to the table where a sample of the tea and the poison found in Captain Greenwood's chambers lay. "You want me to find out what these poisons are?"

"Yes. And if they're the same."

I shifted on my feet. "It's arsenic!" I wanted to say, but I didn't. So I sat on a barrel at the corner of the room, leg bouncing, as Erasmus tinkered with his contraptions. Ash leaned over the table, watching the inspector's process with clear interest.

Erasmus made a low noise and held up a needle. The tip was black. "Arsenic," he grumbled. "How original."

Ash's face paled. "Will my mother be alright?" he said.

"It depends on how much she's had and for how long," Erasmus said. "I'd say the damage is done."

"Is there a remedy?"

"I don't get paid to answer stupid questions, boy. That's the physicians' job."

Ash did not look pleased.

"We don't know if the queen is poisoned with arsenic," I said, standing before he could say anything rude.

Erasmus raised a bushy gray brow. "And why is that?"

I told him of what I had seen at the Debutante Ball and our suspicions of another culprit. I did not mention the duchess's name. "Can you detect what was in Her Majesty's goblet at the ball?" I said.

The inspector stared. "How do you expect me to detect something that is long gone?"

Blood crept involuntarily to my cheeks. Ash was staring at me too. "W-well, er, I have a theory," I said, almost sounding like Olivia.

Lana wouldn't take well to me claiming her teachings as my theories, but the witch wasn't here to scold me. I relayed to Erasmus the idea of all things leaving a trace. Surely that rule applied to both magic and non-magic things. There simply had to be some way to draw out the poison without an extracting potion.

"So," I said. "If you could find a way to separate the lingering poison, I'm sure you could figure something out."

The inspector laughed. It sounded more like wheezing than anything. "What ideas you have! It's like you've learned from a witch."

"Amarante does not associate with witches," Ash said, frowning.

"What do you know?" Erasmus said, removing his gloves. "Fetch me another pair of gloves. And bring the queen's goblet while you're at it."

I would've found the exchange funny if I weren't sweating so much. I eased a little when Ash exited.

"So. Have you learned from a witch?" the inspector asked.

"Not at all," I said, trying my best to appear nonchalant.

Erasmus narrowed his eyes. "Humph. You think like one. Fifty years ago, this room was full of witches. They made up the bulk of the investigation team."

"Witches worked in the palace?" I said, aghast.

He nodded. "Elsewhere too, but in the palace, they held the most important positions. Inspectors and physicians. I was a mere youngster when I worked alongside them."

"But," I said in a small voice, "didn't everyone think magic was dangerous?"

Erasmus scoffed. "Magic? Dangerous? I forget what ignorance the youth grow up in these days. Magic is *knowledge*, girl. Those witches knew more about medicine and alchemy than every human physician combined."

My face was still hot, but for a different reason entirely. "Did they?"

"I knew an old witch, Navierre. Yes, *the* Navierre, whose trial started the blasted Non-Magic Age. He was the one who discovered the contagious nature of the common cold. And his wife was the most talented herbwitch in her day. She could whip up antidotes in minutes." Erasmus obtained a faraway gaze and then shook his head. "Bah. It's all over, thanks to that cursed old King Humphrey. The inspection team dissolved and now all the royals want from me is an occasional sleeping draught! I'm bloody tired of it."

I suspected the inspector wouldn't have spoken so liberally if he weren't on the verge of retirement.

Erasmus leaned over, a sparkle glinting in his heavy-lidded eyes. "Did you know how Humphrey died?"

I shook my head.

"The old boy choked on candied pineapple." He guffawed. "Can you believe it? What a way to go! Served him right for banishing those poor witches."

I let out a giggle as Ash came in with another pair of gloves and something wrapped in brown paper.

"What's so funny?"

Telling him that we were making fun of his late grandfather choking on candy did not seem appropriate, so I remained silent and Erasmus gestured for the gloves. Ash unwrapped the parcel and gingerly placed the queen's jeweled goblet on the work table.

"The kitchen maids said they cleaned it thoroughly since the Debutante Ball," Ash said.

Erasmus resumed his gruff demeanor. "I did not ask, boy. Now move back. I have to work in peace."

Ash looked as if he was going to say something but thought better of it. He joined me by the barrels. One of them creaked as he sat. "The old dingbat didn't make you uncomfortable when I left, did he?"

I smiled. "Erasmus? He's not so bad."

A few minutes of silence interrupted by occasional grunts and curses from the inspector passed. It wasn't long before he removed his gloves again.

"There's definitely poison," he said as Ash and I approached the cluttered table. "Though I have no idea what it is."

"What do you mean?" Ash demanded. I didn't think he meant to sound so rude, but Erasmus harrumphed.

"There is irregular texture inside the goblet," the inspector said, tilting it toward us. "But I will need some time if I want to extract the particles of poison, if there are any left."

Indeed, on close inspection, the bottom of the goblet was rougher compared to the smooth edges, as if something had corroded it. It was so subtle that it could've been mistaken for embellishment on passing. I touched my crystal. A golden glow emitted from the rough patches, but quickly faded into a red aura. My fingers were stiff as I let go of my crystal. Every other substance I had sensed with my magic had some useful property or other. But this was entirely different. The sickening scarlet fumes had but one purpose—to kill. And a witch had made it.

Ash shook his head and looked to me. "You were right then."

"That means someone framed Captain Greenwood," I said.

Erasmus furrowed his brow. "I'd investigate thoroughly if I were you. Whoever did this is exceptionally crafty. The poison was coated on the edges and insides of the goblet." He pointed to a spot on the rim that had the same rough patch.

"What does that mean?" I said.

"The poison was not in the drink. It was smeared on the goblet beforehand."

Ash and I left Erasmus's laboratory in grim spirits. It was well past noon, but I had long forgotten about rushing to the Strongfoots' luncheon. How could a witch create such a deadly poison? How did it get into the hands of Duchess Wilhelmina?

"I can't believe the duchess is capable of doing all this," I said, more to myself than to Ash. How could the woman who stressed the importance of eating salad with the correct fork commit treason?

"She's more than capable," Ash said, surprising me. His face was stony.

I stopped walking. We lingered in the hallway before the endless row of portraits I had passed a week ago. Ash stared at the painting before him, which depicted two men and two women, all young and exceptionally good-looking. The placard underneath read: *Prince Maximus Median, Princess Cordelia Arcia, Miss Wilhelmina Bellerose, and Lord Maverick Greenwood.*

It was odd to see Queen Cordelia and King Maximus so young, but even stranger to see the duchess's face smooth and radiant and smiling.

Ash looked at the floor. "Do you remember my governess?"

I nodded.

"She was Duchess Wilhelmina."

News of Captain Greenwood's arrest spread like wildfire. The morning after, articles about the queen's poisoning were plastered all over the newspaper. Lord Strongfoot was enraged.

"The captain would never do such a thing!" he said, crumpling the morning's news into a wad and tossing it behind him. Vicky and Ria began kicking it around the parlor. "Slanderous, I say. Slanderous!"

Tori furrowed her brow, her nose buried in her copy of the post. "You can say that again, Pa. I don't believe a word. It says Greenwood has been slipping the queen arsenic for months when she allegedly put an end to their affair. Their affair is bogus! Merely a rumor some sharp-tongued snake started to stir up trouble."

"Even if it were true," Genevieve said, "I doubt he would do anything to harm Her Majesty. That is far too cruel."

"And treasonous," Tori added.

Lord Strongfoot stood from the sofa. "I must write to King Maximus. He of all people should know the captain's character."

He departed immediately, leaving us anxious for news. I had yet to tell Tori or Genevieve about witnessing the entire fiasco with Ash. I decided to keep quiet, at least until Ash gathered enough evidence to prove Duchess Wilhelmina was the real culprit. It all seemed too surreal. We spent the rest of the morning attending to our own affairs, though Tori's lute playing seemed less spirited than usual and Genevieve couldn't concentrate on her book. At noon, Lord Strongfoot still did not return, but a mail boy came with letters. One of them was from Lydia, which appeared to be written that very morning.

My dear Genevieve and Amarante,

Have you read the articles about that wicked Greenwood poisoning Her Majesty? I was so shocked I spilled tea all over the dining table and stained my gown—the one with the pretty beading along the sleeves.

Anyway, I hope no one respectable was there when that happened. I do not like the idea of the two of you witnessing such messy affairs. To think a traitor was within the very palace debutantes reside! I shudder thinking about it.

Genevieve, dear, I hope you are spending the bulk of your time with Mr. Sternfeld and his sister. The Season ends in a mere month so manage your time wisely. And Amarante, keep talking to Prince Ash. I heard from Lady Thornbrush's daughter that she spotted him with some girl at the palace library. She thinks her very plain, and though you are no great beauty yourself I reckon you will have better luck with His Highness, seeing that he danced with you at the Debu-tante Ball. That is all. Be good.

All my love,
Your Mama (and stepmother)

I barely scanned the contents of Lydia's letter before passing it on to Genevieve to read. Another letter caught my attention. It was addressed to me with the royal seal.

Amarante,

I hope this letter finds you well. What you've found yesterday has been invaluable. I've written to Bennett and my father about the duchess's gold and what Erasmus discovered. My father believes Her Grace might have been framed and advises me not to expose her lest she is wrongly accused. I am to handle this whole affair in a quiet manner.

I regret that Captain Greenwood's arrest was so rushed. My mother is recovering in bed. I suspect her weakness is equal parts shock and poison. The physicians managed to improve her condition, but I do not know how effective the medication will be when they are treating the wrong poison.

Captain Greenwood will have his trial once my father and Bennett return. In the meantime, my father has put me in charge of this case. I hope by then I can turn the tables

> *and expose the true culprit. Meanwhile, I have something I need your help with. Meet me at the library this afternoon around three. If you cannot, write me and tell me when you are free.*
>
> *Yours,*
> *Ash*

I stuffed the note into my dress pocket before Genevieve looked up from Lydia's letter. My stomach twisted at the reminder of yesterday's events. The duchess could very likely get away with her crimes. The silly part of me was embarrassed that he had signed off his letter with "yours" when there were so many other options. I fetched my boots from the doorway and laced them on. It was two-thirty in the afternoon and a walk to the south wing would take half an hour. I'd be able to gather my thoughts then.

"I'm going for a walk!" I called out, already past the threshold.

"Dressed like that?" Genevieve followed me, squinting at the sweltering sun and frowning at my wool spencer. It was considerably cooler indoors. "You've been going on an awful lot of walks lately."

I unfastened the buttons and thrust it into her arms. "I enjoy the exercise. I'll be back in a couple of hours."

I hated lying to my stepsister, but I couldn't possibly tell her everything from the lessons with Lana to the duchess's crimes.

My face was flushed by the time I entered the library.

Mr. Northberry was still asleep at his desk when I made it to the east end.

"You called?" I said, panting.

Ash looked up from his seat and smiled. "I have a plan to make the duchess expose herself."

17

A couple days later, I found myself back at Lana's, this time burdened with a heavy load.

"Come along."

My arms were burning. The wooden crate filled with Lana's general antidote seemed to grow heavier with each step I took. The passageway's uneven ground did little to help the matter.

Lana had a personal passageway in her garden that led to the Witch Market. I was half-tempted to ask why she couldn't have made hers with a smooth ground, but I was beginning to realize that magic couldn't solve everything—and that Lana did not take well to complaints.

"How many passageways are there to the outside?" I asked instead.

"An infinite amount as long as there are witches to conjure them," Lana said. "There are many that lead to the same destination. The public ones have guardian witches."

"Like Miriam?" I said.

"Unfortunately," Lana said.

I wondered what Miriam did to garner so much distaste from Lana and my nannies.

After a minute of walking, the door-shaped light finally appeared before us. Instead of walking straight out, Lana knocked on the door in an elaborate rhythm. On the other side, a key turned and the door swung open. My eyes watered from the sudden flood of brightness.

"Ah, Lana." A short, stumpy witch with a long white beard stood behind the threshold. I recognized him as the witch from the crop fields.

"Ferdinand," Lana said in greeting.

"Have you brought more of your extra sticky glue? I had a shelf fall off yesterday and I cannot be bothered to nail it back."

"I'm afraid not." Lana pushed her way out, clearly in no mood for small talk. I followed, coughing when I inhaled a lungful of stale air. We were in a dusty basement of some sort, overtaken with crates and barrels. The walls were high and lined with square windows.

"Who is this?" Ferdinand said, peering up at me. He didn't seem to recognize me.

"My apprentice," Lana said before I could introduce myself. I made up for her curt response with a smile and a half-curtsy and rushed after her as she climbed the short steps to the exit.

"Apprentice? I never took you as the type to take an appren—" Ferdinand's words cut off as the door swung shut behind us. I felt bad for being so rude, but thoughts of manners left my head when I took in the sight before me.

We were in a narrow street sandwiched between red-bricked buildings. Wagons and table displays made of ramshackle crates lined the street, leaving barely enough space for a horse-drawn cart to pass through.

The street itself was crowded with people—witches and humans alike—chattering and shouting and bartering. Despite the crispness of the morning, the air was thick with sweat and incense. We were still somewhat underground, as the walls stretched up high and the road was unpaved.

This was the infamous Witch Market.

"Where's our stand?" I shouted.

"Just around the corner."

I squinted past the hustle and bustle, trying to see where the corner was. The street seemed to stretch on forever. My arms felt like they would fall off any second.

Lana glanced at me. "Here!" She waved at a passing witch with a cart full of crudely-made wagons. He pushed one down to her and proceeded through the crowd. Lana gave the wagon to me.

"Thank you," I said, but she was already halfway down the street. I hurried behind her. A few men with scarred faces and wild beards were mixed in the rabble. I wasn't eager to mingle with the likes of them.

Lana and I walked on for a minute or so before I saw the corner she was talking about. It opened up to a slightly wider street with a stone archway at the end of it through which people were entering.

Humans, I noted. Not witches.

I wanted to peek in and see what lay beyond, but Lana stopped before an empty stand and set our crates onto the table. A piece of canvas was pulled over the top of four narrow posts, sheltering us from the strengthening sunlight.

"You may help me handle the wares and the payments," Lana said.

I nodded and joined her behind the stand, seating myself on the hard bench.

"How long does the Market stay open?" I asked.

"All day, every day," Lana said. Her eyes flicked to my wrist, where my bracelet of silver bells gleamed. "Do you have somewhere to be?"

I did. But I shook my head anyway. I would have to make up an excuse for Ash later.

A hunched, wrinkled woman approached us with a pole over her shoulder. Two large baskets hung from either end, reeking of fish.

"What have you got this time, Lana?" the woman croaked, squinting at the glass jars of antidote.

"Antidote for mild poisoning," Lana said. "Works wonderfully if you've eaten bad seafood."

The woman harrumphed. "Is that a jab at my fish, you old witch?"

I was both appalled and amused that someone had the guts to call Lana an old witch.

"Not at all, Nina," Lana said. She smiled—actually smiled. "And what have you brought?"

"Fresh salmon from the river," Nina said, reaching into her basket to pull out a limp fish the length of my forearm and thrice as wide. "Isn't she a beauty?"

"Quite. Two for two?" Lana said.

Nina squinted at the jars, holding one of them up to her wrinkled face. The antidote gleamed prettily in the light.

"I would've suggested two for three but these seem useful. Very well, two for two it is," the fisherwoman said. She pulled out two sheets of wax paper from her basket and wrapped the fish in each. Lana did the same for the antidotes and they exchanged their wares.

An hour passed and we had sold a good amount of our stock. In exchange, Lana got three heads of cabbage, a spool of twine, a hefty jar of honey, and five sticks of cinnamon.

I loaded all this into the empty crates and set them on the wagon. By the time the sun was high in the sky, we were down to three jars of antidote.

"This was a particularly good day," Lana said. "I hardly expected it."

"Why?" I asked. Lana seemed to have more than a few regulars.

"The Royal Guard has been preventing people from entering. There's been several arrests, so I've heard."

"Ah." I thought back to the poor fellow who got thrown in prison after being accused of dabbling in witchcraft. Perhaps he just wanted some extra sticky glue.

The sound of horse hooves broke through the chatter. A cart rolled in through the arch, carrying a mass of something covered in a canvas sheet. The driver rolled to a stop near our stand. Judging from his skinny limbs and crooked stature, he was quite elderly. Despite that, he leapt nimbly onto an empty crate and struck a dented pot with a piece of wood. Witches approached the cart—many of them were smiling.

Lana was not.

"Who is that?" I asked, glancing at the elderly man.

Lana exhaled and cleared off the remnants of her wares from the table. "A human under the impression that he is our hero," she said. "There are many such people. I don't like the idea of humans here if they're not going to buy something."

I watched the man pull off the canvas from his cart, revealing sacks of grain, crates of ruddy fruit, and barrels of other goods. Two other men began handing out the goods to the witches who had formed a line before them.

"He's giving away food. For free," I said.

"He fancies himself a philanthropist."

I did not expect the venom in Lana's voice. "Isn't that a good thing? Being a philanthropist?"

Lana let her crate drop to the floor with more force than necessary. The remaining glass bottles clinked. "Humans will never view us as equals. Witches will either be feared or pitied—there is no in between. I don't care for either treatment. But if I had to choose, I'd rather be seen as a monster than a charity case."

"You don't think there's anyone out there who truly wants to help?"

"Oh, of course they want to help, but for their sake and not ours. Helping us witches allows humans to revel in their own greatness and generosity."

I stole another glance at the cart-driving philanthropist. A group of young witches laughed in delight when he gave them a box of strawberries. Beside them, a dark-haired young man walked with his head down and shoulders hunched.

I scrambled down the bench, bumping into Lana.

"What is the matter with you?"

"Nothing," I said, nauseated.

My suspicions were confirmed when the young man raised his head to look about with darting brown eyes. It was Ash—and I was a mere five feet away from him.

With unnecessary violence, I wrapped my scarf around my face until everything but my eyes was covered. Just as I finished, Ash fixed his gaze on me.

We had met a mere three days ago at the palace library for one of our meetings discussing his plan of exposing the duchess. It was a strange and desperate plan, but the mad part of me thought it might work and agreed to help. We met up frequently ever since. I was sure by now he had become more than familiar with my features.

Ash stared. I stared back, unable to move and terrified his lips would form my name.

But he merely made his way over to our stand.

"Hello," he said, smiling stiffly at Lana and then me. I lowered my gaze. "Do you happen to have any…er…"

"If you're looking for nefarious poisons and voodoo magic, I'll have to disappoint you," Lana said flatly, as if young men asked for poison every day.

Ash shrugged. "Is there anyone else who…?'"

I nearly felt Lana's glare simmering in the air. "No, sir," she said, "and if there is a witch who sells such things, I am not acquainted with them nor do I have the desire to."

The prince finally seemed to realize the awkwardness of the situation. No doubt he was here to investigate the origins of the poison Erasmus found and decided the Witch Market was a reasonable place to start.

His disguise, however, was a poor one. His shirt and trousers were of too fine a material to blend in with the rough, dirt-streaked rabble of the Market. And the way he glanced about and jumped whenever someone brushed his shoulder made it clear it was his first time in magical company.

"May I inquire what you're selling?" he asked.

"A general antidote," Lana said brusquely. "Heals minor cuts if applied topically and minor illnesses if consumed."

Ash nodded slowly.

"You are clearly not familiar with purchasing from our kind, so I would appreciate it if you would leave. You are holding up my line," Lana said.

There was no line, except for the massive one before the elderly man's cart.

Ash looked over his shoulder. "Ah, I apologize. I…er… have something for your trouble," he said, fishing out an apple from the pouch at his hip. It was in the shape of a flattened gourd and had a yellow stripe down the middle. "It's a little strange looking. But delicious, I'm sure."

An agonizingly long moment passed with Ash's arm outstretched and Lana pretending he wasn't there. Stifling a laugh, I took the apple from him to spare his feelings, but instantly regretted it when he turned his attention to me.

He stuck out his hand. "Much obliged, Miss…?"

I stared at his hand, knowing that I couldn't possibly speak.

Lana came to my rescue. "She is my apprentice."

"Ah, much obliged, Miss Apprentice."

I shook his hand briefly before the bells or my laughter gave me away.

He seemed confused at my silence, so I pointed to my throat and shook my head.

"You're mute?"

I nodded. Lana did not object, nor did she give any indication of speaking again. Feeling it only right, I grabbed one of the remaining antidotes and gave it to him.

"Thank you," he said, inspecting the jar. "I'll give it a try." With another stiff smile, Ash turned and disappeared behind the massive line.

Lana and I didn't exchange a word until we were back in the basement where Ferdinand was waiting for us. His inquiries and comments were ignored until they were cut off yet again by the slamming of the door.

When we were finally in the safety of the dark passageway, I pulled my scarf down to my neck.

"That was…someone I knew," I said.

"Someone who wouldn't take well to knowing you're a witch, I suppose?"

"I don't know," I said honestly. "He's usually very kind." Miriam told me hatred for magic ran in royal blood. But I couldn't imagine Ash hating me. I felt the apple in my pouch bump my leg with every step.

Lana harrumphed. "Don't be fooled, child. Helping a witch and being a witch are two very different things. He and the other foolish philanthropists will be commended for their charity. You, on the other hand, will be shunned."

When I returned to Miriam's shop, I had an extra jar of antidote Lana told me to keep. It was another gruff act of kindness I appreciated but didn't comment on, lest she scolded me for speaking nonsense.

"You took longer this time," Miriam said when I emerged through the portal.

I rubbed my back and shifted the pouch on my shoulders. "Lana took me to the Witch Market."

"Did she? What was she selling?"

Before I could tell her, Miriam took the jar from me. She unscrewed the top, dipped a finger in, tasted it thoughtfully, and dipped her finger in again.

"A general antidote," I said. "You can have it if you like."

"I couldn't," she said, smacking her lips.

"Really. I insist."

It was a little past noon. I was once again close to missing lunch at the Strongfoots'. As I made my way to the exit, the door burst open and I nearly stumbled into Theodora and Rowena. They looked equally shocked to see me.

"Amarante? What are you doing here?" they said in unison.

I opened my mouth but no sound came out. I had completely forgotten to tell them about my lessons with Lana. It had practically been a week!

Ashamed that I had neglected them, I filled them in on my visits to Witch Village.

Rowena's face turned thoughtful when I finished. Theodora furrowed her brow.

"We were just here to see Lana again, for your sake," Theodora said. "I thought she wanted nothing to do with us. Why the sudden change of heart?"

"Maybe the old bat needed a servant and decided to take Amarante," Rowena said.

Theodora turned me around as if, once again, looking for fatal wounds. "Are you alright, then? We tried to write last week, but your stepmother sent the staff into a frenzy."

Rowena chuckled. "Somehow she found out that Master Flora is returning and insisted on cleaning every inch of the house. He won't arrive for another month, for goodness sake," she said. She pinched my cheek and widened her eyes. "My! Your witch traits have emerged!"

My stomach twisted at the mention of Papa's return, but I masked it with a shrug and a smile. "Yes. And I have been doing fine. Lana gave me something to keep my magic under control," I said, lifting the crystal from my bodice.

My nannies exchanged a look so quickly I barely noticed. I thought I detected a hint of sadness in Theodora's lined eyes. "Well, dear, I'm glad you are doing well. Just remember, you can come to us anytime. If you no longer wish to learn magic…" she trailed off, but I shook my head.

I wasn't going to quit my apprenticeship any time soon—not after everything I had seen, and especially not after what I learned from Erasmus's investigation. If this morning wasn't evidence enough, Ash didn't have a chance finding out what that poison was. It was up to me.

After a warm goodbye, I returned to the Strongfoots' just in time for lunch. Lord Strongfoot was still bothered by Captain Greenwood's framing, but he seemed to regain a bit of his cheeriness when he told us what he had heard at the palace.

"They say Her Majesty is recovering mighty fine," Lord Strongfoot grumbled over his roasted turkey leg. "Maybe once she's well she'll pardon the captain."

I doubted that'd be the case, but no one dared to contradict him lest he wither into stormy depression again.

After dinner, I stewed over Ash's plan. We had gone over it several times, but I was still uneasy.

Whether or not it would truly expose the duchess, we would have to wait and see.

18

So, what are you doing again?" Tori whispered in my ear. I barely made out her words over Julianna's operatic singing.

The crate on my lap shifted as I leaned over in my seat. "You'll find out."

Tori winced when Julianna hit an inhumanly high note that reverberated within the theatre. Even Genevieve, who had high tolerance for opera, grimaced. Olivia pulled her braids over her ears. When at last Julianna ended her song with a powerful vibrato, the theatre erupted in applause, concluding the first performance of the evening.

Madam Lucille emerged from the velvet curtains as Julianna curtsied low.

"Wonderful, simply wonderful! What a voice!" she exclaimed, giving Julianna an appraising look. Julianna tossed her hair as she returned to her box, which was unfortunately in front of mine.

"You were amazing, Julianna," Samantha gushed, bunching up her skirts to let her pass.

Julianna sat primly, smoothing her satin gloves as she was bombarded with compliments from the girls in her box. She was awfully pleased with herself for someone who had damaged multiple pairs of ears.

"I know. Mama had me trained by professionals when I was a little girl," Julianna said. "How fortunate I was to learn the arts instead of wasting my girlhood away in dirt and dusty studies." She gave a tinkling laugh, throwing her head back far enough to look at me.

I narrowed my eyes, wishing I could tip the contents of my crate on her frustratingly stunning gown. But I couldn't risk losing my supplies. And there was no saying how long it would take to get the rest.

In the box on the second level, Ash stood out from the red velvet seats in a suit of emerald green. He was talking to the queen but occasionally glanced down at the sea of boxes below. Duchess Wilhelmina and Narcissa sat behind him. I leaned forward, trying to catch his attention with my stare alone, but found that it only strained my eyes and garnered a contemptuous glare from Samantha.

"Next is Lady Victoria Strongfoot, playing the lute," Madam Lucille announced.

Tori jumped up from her seat and squeezed past me and Olivia, a hefty lute in her hands. "Wish me luck, girls."

She didn't stay to hear our good lucks, though, and bounded down the steps.

"How do you think they'll take it?" I murmured to Genevieve.

"I'm sure she'll do fine," she whispered.

We had woken up to the sound of Tori's lively lute

playing for over a week. Neither Genevieve nor I had the heart to tell Tori that her lute needed desperate tuning. Despite our urgings for her to borrow a palace lute, she insisted on using hers, which once belonged to Lord Strongfoot when he almost became a minstrel.

The sound of a stool dragging across the stage could be heard through soft murmurs. Tori arranged herself on the seat, lifted the lute onto her lap, and began to play.

The first notes were miraculously in tune. It sounded like a simplified version of an old folk song, but as Tori continued, the tempo increased and became a spirited jig one might hear at a tavern. Her fingers danced deftly across the strings. Despite the occasional sour note, it was altogether a pleasant and of course, very lively, performance.

"She's doing well," I said, surprised.

"She might've done better with another lute," someone whispered to my left. I glanced over. It was Ash. I had hardly noticed him come in.

Genevieve and Olivia looked startled at the unexpected guest. Ash smiled at them in acknowledgment and ignored Samantha's simpering gaze below him.

"Amarante. Care for some air?" he asked, tilting his head to the exit.

I nodded and said to Genevieve, "I'll be back in a bit."

Tucking my crate under my seat, I followed Ash out of the box. Luckily, we were sitting on the outer edges of the theatre so no one noticed us slip behind a curtained alcove near the exit.

"Do you have them?" I said, my palms dampening.

"Just caught them," he said, pulling out a wooden box nestled beneath a corner table. There were several holes punched into the top.

I took it gingerly as faint squeaks sounded inside. "Thank you. I suppose."

"Don't worry. They're quite cuddly," Ash said, grinning.

"They're rodents!"

"Be glad they aren't rats. Those are the worst. Once I found one the size of a cat inside my—"

"Please stop," I groaned.

Ash dipped his head in acquiescence. "I'll leave you to it then. If you need help, scream."

"That's comforting."

With a bow and another smile, he was gone. I looked down at the box and suppressed another groan. Holding it away from me, I managed to return to my seat. My new possession drew inquiring stares from both Genevieve and Olivia.

"It's for my act," I whispered.

My stepsister smiled. "You're still not going to tell us what it is?"

"You'll find out."

Tori finished her song with one final flourish. She rose and bowed as everyone applauded.

"What a horrendously antiquated piece," Julianna said with a sneer as Tori returned to our box.

Neither of us paid Julianna any mind. I was much too nervous to argue. I knew it was my turn before I heard my name.

"Next, Miss Amarante Flora will be performing...a scientific demonstration," Madam Lucille said, pulling a face.

I began the treacherous descent to the stage with my arms full of my supplies. I was immensely glad of the velvet carpet, which gave my slippers more grip than they would have otherwise. I climbed the stairs. The table and

two glass terrariums I had requested were already set up when I approached.

It was deathly silent when I unloaded my crate.

Two small porcelain dishes, one in each terrarium. A flask of water. The box Ash gave me, right at the center.

When everything was in place, I took a deep breath and spoke.

"Tonight, I will be showing you all a mystery. A mystery you will be eager to solve."

I shot a quick glance up at Ash, who flashed me an encouraging smile. I wanted to strangle him with his own necktie. The lines he wrote sounded ridiculous. But there was no time to change them, so I continued.

"Inside this box are two mice. One will have a very different fate than the other."

I lowered the box into one terrarium and slid the lid open. A tiny white mouse scurried out. I tried not to shriek as I let the other into the next terrarium. I put the box down.

"Both will drink out of the same flask." I opened the flask and filled each dish with water. Murmurs rose as I waited for the blasted mice to drink the water. It took longer than I anticipated. One of them drank a bit. The other was busy sniffing around the terrarium, exploring every corner except the one that actually held something of interest.

When at last the stubborn mouse drank, I stepped back and waited for the sleeping draught to kick in. I waited some more. The murmurs grew louder. Somebody coughed. The curtains rustled behind me.

"Now, what is this, Miss Flora?" Madam Lucille demanded, poking her head out. "I must object to the rodents. They are horrifying."

I threw a worried glance at the terrariums. Both mice were still scurrying around. Had I remembered to use Erasmus's sleeping draught at all?

"Madam, if you'll wait a little longer—"

Madam Lucille frowned, emerging fully from the curtains. "That is quite enough, Miss Flora. What are you trying to do, speaking so cryptically? It's quite unbecoming."

Both mice were still awake. I was sure my cheeks were red enough to be a beacon. "Madam—"

The music mistress shook her head. "The theatre is a place for art, Miss Flora, not spectacle. Now, if you would like to sing a song, perhaps—"

"Look! One of them stopped moving!" a voice that sounded suspiciously like Ash's rung out from the seats. I looked. The mouse on the left was no longer moving. I deflated with relief. Madam Lucille gasped.

"Yes. This mouse has felt the effects of a sleeping draught while the other remains awake," I said, assuming as grandiose an air as possible. "How could it be, when both drank the same water from the same flask?"

Murmurs ran through the audience. They seemed properly intrigued. Madam Lucille retreated into the curtains with a huff.

"You slipped it in when we weren't looking!" someone shouted.

"The mouse was drugged beforehand!" another gentleman hollered.

"You're a witch!" a debutante exclaimed.

My heart nearly leapt out of my throat at the last comment, but another voice stopped me from blubbering and exposing myself.

"Do not keep us in suspense, Miss Flora." It was Duchess Wilhelmina. She had stood from her seat, her face impassive. "Tell us."

I bit my lip. "I coated one dish in sleeping draught before pouring the water."

Oohs and ahhs filled the theatre, but the ruckus quieted when Her Grace clapped slowly. "What a clever little trick, Miss Flora. I wonder where you got such an idea."

I swallowed, feeling the intensity of her stare despite her distance. I trained my gaze past her on Ash. His eyes were on the duchess. "It's nothing, Your Grace. I just thought it would be an entertaining riddle."

"Indeed. But such riddles, I'm afraid, are not appropriate for young ladies like yourself," the duchess said, staring with half-lidded eyes. "It seems like a part of some…scheme."

"Forgive me, Your Grace," I said. "I mean nothing by it."

The back of my gown was slick with sweat. I wanted to slap myself for my own foolishness. What did I expect? That the duchess would stand and expose her crimes once she saw her own tricks performed before her?

"Now, Wilhelmina. It was just a harmless demonstration," Queen Cordelia said. She gave me a smile. Her cheeks were hollower than I remembered them. "I found it amusing. Thank you, Miss Amarante."

I curtsied low. "Thank you, Your Majesty."

Madam Lucille reentered with her list and I scampered off, leaving the mice and the crate for the stagehands to deal with. My heart pounded at doing something so bold. Tori slapped my back when I returned to our box.

"What a show!" she said. "No wonder you didn't want to tell us. I didn't expect that at all."

"Will the mice be alright?" Olivia asked, furrowing her brow as the stagehands carried the terrariums away. "I would hate for them to be harmed. They look so cuddly."

"I'm sure they'll be fine," I lied.

"Any reason why the prince of all people fetched you mice?" Genevieve said. Her tone was more teasing than serious, which calmed me.

"He offered."

"Did he now?" Tori asked, wiggling her eyebrows. "What else did he offer?"

Julianna and Samantha turned to glare at us. "Will you be quiet?" Julianna snapped. "Some people would like to enjoy the show without your blabbering."

The talent show ended at half past nine. We all filed out the west wing to wait for our carriages. On my way out, Ash pulled me aside at the threshold so we were concealed by a row of potted plants.

He grinned, his face illuminated by the gas lamps along the hedges. "You were fantastic."

I laughed. "Thank you. But it didn't do much."

"No," Ash agreed. "But it was a warning. The duchess looked livid."

"That's not enough to stop her, is it?"

Ash shook his head. "No, it isn't," he said in a low voice. His grin faltered. "And now, if she is the culprit—which I have strong reason to think she is—she knows that you know."

I shrugged. It wasn't as if Duchess Wilhelmina and I were on good terms to begin with. "And the queen? How is she?" I asked.

"The physicians are trying," he said. "My mother is showing signs of recovery, but I don't know how their antidote will work when they're treating the wrong poison."

I opened my mouth, about to recommend he use Lana's general antidote, but remembered that I shouldn't know about it. "You'll find a way," I said instead, tugging the strap of my pouch.

I tugged a little too hard. The contents spilled out onto the grass. My flask, and to my horror, the misshapen apple Ash had given me at the Witch Market. I had forgotten to remove it the other day.

My blood froze as he knelt to pick it up. I remembered Miriam's words.

Hatred for witches run in royal blood.

For a moment, I forgot I didn't believe that.

I snatched the apple from him and shoved it in my bag.

Ash furrowed his brow and grinned. "You're quite violent with apples, you know?"

I pressed my lips together, not knowing whether to laugh or cry in relief. He hadn't recognized it. I bent to retrieve my flask instead, glad that it was dark.

"I really like apples, that's all." It wasn't entirely a lie. But it still didn't make much sense. Ash merely looked perplexed. Luckily, he didn't comment on my odd behavior.

"I'll see you in a week, then?" he said.

I returned his smile. "I'll see you then."

19

Lana stirred the contents of her cauldron. The murky substance shifted to pale green and developed a viscous quality.

"This is the extracting potion I mentioned from our first lesson," Lana said, adding a pinch of crushed herbs into the mixture. There was a recipe book next to her, though she rarely glanced at it during the demonstration.

The open fire beneath her cauldron was making me sweat buckets, but not a trace of perspiration lingered on Lana's forehead as she tapped her ladle on the rim. Fat droplets of extracting potion splashed back into the cauldron. "Potion making is a skill every witch needs to learn."

"Even charmwitches?" I asked.

"Yes. All witches can do it. Think of it as cooking. Everyone can follow directions, but there is a difference between a person who cooks and a chef," Lana said. "Inventing new potions requires skill as well as a magic unique to herbwitches."

"Is there anything charmwitches can do that herb-witches can too?" I asked.

Lana set aside her ladle with a clatter and wiped her hands on her apron. "Yes, levitation. Most witches learn that out of the womb. However, you've yet to learn the skills essential to an herbwitch," she said. With a wave of her hand, a new cauldron replaced the old one. "No more dillydallying. Try making the extracting potion yourself."

I perspired more, but not because of the heat. "Am I ready?"

I'd only ever read about potion making in books and the only magic I had done was see colors. And that was completely involuntary.

Lana continued organizing the space. A dish of chopped lavender whizzed past my head, narrowly missing my face.

I certainly hadn't learned to make things levitate either.

She finally turned when the only thing left on the counter was a leather notebook.

"You will never be ready unless you start," she said, pushing the recipe book toward me. "Now go wash your hands."

I felt even more incompetent crouching amongst the bushes behind Lana's cottage, scrubbing my hands with the ice-cold water that gushed out a low faucet. If I had been born a real witch, I could have easily filled a dish with water with a flick of my wrist. With a sigh, I dried my hands on my skirts, trying not to be too disappointed. It wasn't as if I could practice magic outside of lessons.

When I went back inside, dishes and jars of ingredients waited for me on the counter. Lana pointed at the recipe book without a word, looking very much like my old governess.

I obediently read it.

Ingredients:

2 cups water
Rinds from five limes
5 tbsp crushed lentils
3 drops brittlebrush oil
1 tsp azoola extract

Directions:

Pour in water and bring to a simmer. Drop in rinds, thinly sliced. Mix crushed lentils with brittlebrush oil and add the mixture to the cauldron. Let potion sit for five minutes before splashing azoola extract. Stir counterclockwise for three minutes. Let the potion rest for ten minutes.

"Is that all?" I said, bewildered. It looked like something straight out of Theodora's cookbook, except for the strange ingredients I had never heard of. "Can't humans make potions too, if they have all the ingredients?"

"Of course not," Lana said. "It may seem as straightforward as any recipe, but only witches can truly bind these ingredients together in a way that makes them work. You will find that you pour some of yourself—your own magic, that is—into the cauldron every time you make a potion."

I nodded, though not fully comprehending. Pouring a bit of myself into a cauldron did not sound appealing.

213

"Well? What are you standing around for?" Lana said. "Fetch the water."

Grabbing an empty pitcher, I went to the faucet again, grumbling quietly so Lana wouldn't hear. I simply *had* to figure out how to levitate objects.

By the time I filled the cauldron, I realized why Lana compared potion making to cooking. On paper, the instructions seemed easy enough. The challenge was carrying them out.

"You're slicing them too thickly."

I fumbled with the scalpel and went back to a thicker piece rind. I sliced off a miniscule portion of it, nearly impaling the tip of my finger in the process. My cheeks burned.

The witch made a noise at the back of her throat. "Never mind that. The water is simmering."

I scraped the lime rinds into the cauldron. They landed with a splash, sending a few drops into the fire. "Sorry," I said sheepishly.

"The lentils and brittlebrush oil." Lana motioned to the counter. "Not a moment to waste. And please be careful with the oil. That is my last vial."

I glanced at the glass vial that was no larger than my thumb. I decided to handle the lentils first. "You can't get more?" I measured out the five tablespoons and poured them into a mortar.

"Supplies are hard to come by. Even the witch-made ones," Lana said. "Plants with magical properties are overlooked in favor of growing regular crops, which don't turn out well anyway." There was a hint of bitterness in her voice.

"Oh," I managed to say. My hands shook as I dropped three drops of the bright green oil. The scent was a mix of peppermint and chives. It fizzed when it soaked into the lentils. I immediately screwed the cap on and began crushing the concoction with a pestle.

Witch Village was in trouble. The way Lana made it sound, they were worse off than they were in the past. My thoughts strayed to the royals. Did they know how witches are living? Would they care if they knew? Would Ash care if he knew?

I hesitated. Surely his opinion of witches would not be favorable if he finds out the queen fell ill with a witch-made poison. I ground the mixture harder. There was no way I could tell him what I knew without exposing myself.

The next best thing was to prove Duchess Wilhelmina guilty.

Lana made it clear the week before she did not condone meddling in human affairs, especially royal affairs. But I was determined. I had scoured my potion-making book for something that may help, but to no avail. My last resort was to ask Lana.

"I've been wondering," I said, keeping my voice casual, "how many kinds of potions are there?"

"There are many. Herbwitches invent new ones every day."

"Is there a potion that just…kills?"

Lana was silent for a moment. "You're speaking of poisons. Not the ones for critters, I presume?"

I shook my head.

"I'd be lying if I say not a single witch has created a poison meant to kill humans," Lana said. Her voice was grave. "But none of them have made it into the hands of non-magic folk. Except one."

My interest peaked. Could there only be one witch-made poison above ground? "What is it called?" I asked.

"Manbane." Lana's face looked grimmer than I had ever seen it. Her eyes flicked to me, sharp and suspicious. "Why are you asking?"

Questions of what manbane did and what it was made of died on my lips. I'd be a fool to prod her.

I shrugged. "No reason. Is there a potion that makes someone tell the truth?"

I felt Lana looking at me. "Yes, there is," she said slowly. "But it requires a rare ingredient."

"Really? What?"

"Gold."

Perhaps I could use some of my own jewelry once I beg the recipe off Lana. But my plans were crushed when she spoke again.

"Five pounds of pure gold."

I choked on my saliva. "Five pounds?" I said, sputtering.

"That's right," Lana said in a clipped voice. "Five pounds. No more, no less."

I gripped the pestle a little harder. "Can we make it?" I ventured to ask.

She snorted. "Only if you bring five pounds of gold, girl. Now finish up the lentils before the water boils over."

The next fifteen minutes I spent sweat-drenched and nervous as I worked under Lana's scrutiny. It was as if my limbs had forgotten how to function as I trembled and slipped and poured, but there was a new sensation I experienced amongst it all. My fingertips tingled as I went through the motions. A hazy swirl of purple-red filled my vision and drizzled into the cauldron like rain on a summer day.

So that was what Lana meant by pouring a part of myself into the potion.

By the end of it all, I had a glass of cloudy green liquid before me. Lana set hers beside it. Compared to hers, mine was two shades too dark and much too lumpy. My embarrassment mounted even as Lana assured me that potion making took years of practice to perfect.

"Let us test these, then," Lana said. She rummaged through her cupboard and brought out two empty jars. I recognized them as the containers she used for her general antidote. A subtle golden glow emitted within them.

Lana uncorked her potion and poured half of it into a jar. Almost immediately, the green liquid turned amber.

"Is that the general antidote?" I said, widening my eyes.

"That's right. The extracting potion turns into the potion it's extracting, if done correctly. If I had more of it, I wouldn't have to make another batch of antidote."

"Can't you make more? It seems like it'll save a lot of time."

Lana shook her head. "I don't have enough brittle-brush oil to make big batches. It's ridiculously rare as well, so no witch in their right mind would use so much for an extracting potion." She paused and gestured to my vial. "Try yours."

Expecting the worst, I poured my attempt of the potion in the other jar. Nearly all of it vanished when it made contact. A miniscule drop of amber liquid rested at the bottom.

"If you made it right it would retain the same volume," Lana pointed out.

I sighed in dismay. "Sorry I wasted your brittlebrush oil."

When I returned to the Strongfoots', the house was empty. The butler informed me that Tori and Genevieve had gone for a stroll in the palace gardens and that Lord Strongfoot was in town with Vicky and Ria. I retired to my room, where I gazed glumly at my failed potion in its lumpy glory.

The shade of green reminded me of when Lydia taught Genevieve and I to embroider strawberry vines. Mine ended up looking like asparagus stalks. My stepmother scolded me for not possessing an artistic eye like Genevieve.

Afterward, I had gone to Papa and asked him to excuse me from Lydia's lessons. He consented. I stayed terrible at embroidery ever since. Was my apprenticeship with Lana going to end up the same way?

I shook my head. No. This was different. This mattered. And most importantly, this was enjoyable. I never found pleasure in anything my stepmother forced me to learn, but learning magic with Lana was something I looked forward to, despite her occasional crabbiness.

Lana said potion making took years of practice. If it was practice I needed, it was practice I would get.

I burst out of my room, failed potion in hand, and was halfway to the kitchen until I realized what I was holding.

An extracting potion. Erasmus. He needed to extract the poison from the queen's goblet. He couldn't possibly do it without magic.

Without another thought, I grabbed my things again and headed off to the palace. When I arrived, I flew down the halls and winding stairs and burst into Erasmus's laboratory.

"Did no one teach you how to knock?" the inspector demanded.

He was lounged on an armchair with a book that looked suspiciously like *A Sailor's Seduction*. The room seemed to have accumulated twice as much clutter the last time I had visited.

"You're right," I said, out of breath.

"No one taught you how to knock?"

I sucked in a breath. Erasmus needed to know. He was the only person I trusted with my secret. "You're right that I was taught by a witch. Actually, she's still teaching me. I'm an herbwitch's apprentice."

Erasmus stared, his whiskered jaw slack. No doubt Lana's concealment spell was dissolving before his eyes, revealing my witch traits. "Well. I suppose we have a lot to discuss."

As Erasmus attempted to clear some space around his work table, I told him everything—how I discovered my magic, what I saw at the Debutante Ball, how Lana taught me about extracting potions and the concept of magical things leaving a trace.

"Aha!" Erasmus exclaimed after listening to my story. "So, you think the duchess used a witch-made poison on the queen."

"I do. And I can prove it to you," I said, holding up my extracting potion. "May I?"

"You may," Erasmus said eagerly. "It's been much too long since I've seen magic in action." He hovered over my shoulder as I poured the rest of my potion into the queen's goblet.

Like earlier, most of it vanished, except for the tiniest drop of a blood-red liquid veined with indigo. "I think it's called manbane," I said, my voice wavering.

Erasmus took the goblet and inspected the drop. "You think? Did your witch instructor tell you what it does, exactly? Or if there's an antidote?"

I shook my head. "She didn't want to talk about it," I said.

Erasmus hummed. "Poison is always a touchy subject for witches. Probably because they're always accused of making them. Well, no matter. We'll just have to test it ourselves."

"Ourselves?" I said, stepping back.

Erasmus ducked under the desk. Shuffling ensued. A second later, he popped up with a board and a metal cloche in hand. "I've been saving this critter for a while." Squeaking sounded from within.

I sighed. "Is that another palace mouse?"

Erasmus lowered the board into a crate on the ground. A white mouse scampered out and began exploring the box.

"I'll feed it the poison and we will see what happens. Proportionately, it should be the same dosage as the queen's," Erasmus said. "Hand me the goblet."

I obeyed and crouched down as the inspector held the jeweled cup to the crate. The mouse climbed in the goblet, and then out. Another look at the goblet told us it had ingested the manbane.

"And now," Erasmus said, "we wait."

And so we did. Seconds turned into minutes. Minutes turned into hours. It wasn't long before both Erasmus and I grew bored of watching the mouse scurry around the box.

I furrowed my brows. "Nothing is happening," I said, slumping onto a barrel. "Maybe it's my extracting potion. I didn't brew it correctly."

Erasmus frowned and removed his spectacles. "Hold your horses," he said. "Queen Cordelia hasn't fallen over and died after being poisoned. Perhaps this manbane is insidious. The victim merely appears asymptomatic, but feels the effects over time. There are many such poisons."

"There are?" I said.

He nodded. "I've seen many a great witch struggle with some spell or potion or other—but they eventually figure it out. It takes practice, little flower, like all things. But I'm sure your potion has done the job, albeit not the best—ack!"

Erasmus jumped out of the way just as a large gray rat scampered across his feet and dived into a hole in the opposite wall.

"Blasted rodents!" he cursed, brushing off his trousers.

I cringed. "I should probably get going then," I said, hopping onto the stairs in case the rat decided to come back. I fancied I saw a pair of eyes in the hole. "Keep me updated?"

"I will. And also," Erasmus said as I was about to turn, "don't tell your prince that the poison is witch-made. I don't think letting everyone know that a witch is the cause of Queen Cordelia's ailment would do any favors for witchkind."

"It isn't a witch, it's the duchess! And…and he isn't my prince!" Though I knew he was right, I couldn't help but be indignant.

"The royals would sooner imprison a witch than they would a duchess, little flower," Erasmus said, his face grim. "Promise me you'll keep this, and your identity, a secret."

I sighed. "I know. I promise."

When I told the Strongfoot's cook, Jasmine, that I wanted to help with the meals, she laughed at me.

"I am sure, Miss Flora, that you'll find something else to amuse yourself with," she said, gesturing dismissively with a wooden spoon.

But I was adamant. After pestering her for hours, she finally caved and let me help with dessert.

"I didn't plan on making any tonight, so you can do what you like," Jasmine said, handing me an extra apron. I thanked her profusely and set to work after the rest of the kitchen staff took their break.

Theodora had made her raspberry tarts in front of me so many times that I had learned the recipe by heart. Thankfully, I had some experience baking them, but they never tasted quite as good as Theodora's. It never occurred to me that the exquisite taste of all Theodora's food was due to her magic. I was eager to try it myself.

I spent the entire afternoon and the earlier part of the evening sifting and mixing and whisking. It was all very standard, but the most peculiar sensation overtook me as I made the tarts—very much like the sensation of making that potion at Lana's cottage.

My arms and fingers tingled and my chest felt warm. Even without touching my crystal I saw a pulsing purple aura seeping into the dough from my hands. I was using magic. And it felt good.

By the time dinner was served, the tarts were ready.

Jasmine and a couple of other kitchen maids peered over my shoulder as I plated the pastries. They were not immaculately shaped like Theodora's. Some had too much filling, others had too-thin crusts, and I had forgotten to sprinkle sugar on several. But I knew I had done a decent job.

I plucked one off the plate and invited the others to do the same. One bite and I knew I had done it. The peculiar, zingy aftertaste in Theodora's tarts was present, though while hers tasted more mellow, mine tasted of something zesty.

"This is…not bad at all," Jasmine said, her dark eyebrows shooting up to her hairline.

I smiled. It was as good of a compliment as I could get from her.

Tori and Lord Strongfoot, on the other hand, were more enthusiastic in their commentary.

"By golly, I'm never letting you leave," Tori said, reaching for a third tart.

Lord Strongfoot reached for his fifth, a shower of crumbs and sugar falling from his beard like snow as he took a bite. "I'm almost afraid to say it, but Amarante, these are better than my wife's custard pie!"

For the next couple of days, I spent my time in the kitchens. Jasmine had begrudgingly allowed me to help out with daily meals. What I lacked in skill I made up for in magic, and though no one knew why the food tasted marginally better, it was agreed that my presence in the kitchen had something to do with it.

As I continued to read Lana's book on potion-making, I realized that precision was a skill that did not come magically. But I was building on that very skill under Jasmine's watchful eye. By the end of the week, I figured out how to mince and slice evenly and knew exactly how long it took for onions to cook through. It was only a matter of time before my growing confidence in the kitchen translated to potion-making, something I was sure Lana would be satisfied with the next time I saw her.

But as I learned the skill of measuring and slicing and timing, something else was nagging the back of my mind. I did not know how to levitate objects. It seemed like a pointless skill to acquire. I certainly wouldn't be able to make things fly around outside of Witch Village—yet I wanted to master it. For the first time in my life, I had something special and I had every intention of making the best of it.

One night when Genevieve was asleep, I attempted to move a perfume bottle. It was on the vanity a few feet away from my bed. I positioned myself at the foot board, my arms crossed under my chin, and stared hard at the tiny glass bottle.

Nothing happened. I shifted and slipped my crystal out of my nightgown. Magic pulsated underneath the smooth surface.

I knew now that there was eucalyptus oil in the perfume meant to calm nerves. But it still did not move. I analyzed the bottle, squinting for details in the darkness which the moonlight barely chased away. It was skinny at the top and fatter at the bottom, like a pear. The glass had a textured surface and the knob at the top of it was a perfect, smooth sphere.

I thought about tipping the bottle over by its skinny top. Magic thrummed in the crystal. The perfume bottle wobbled.

I smiled so widely my cheeks ached. The bottle did not tip over and it certainly hadn't moved the direction I wanted it to, but it did not discourage me any less. It was a start, and more importantly, it was a sign—a sign that I was capable.

The next morning, I woke up with dry eyes and sore cheeks and a plethora of misplaced items on the vanity.

"Why are you smiling?" Genevieve asked as she helped me into my dress. Her brow raised when she caught my gaze in the mirror.

I only grinned. "I think I'm actually getting good at something."

20

Between the four wings of the palace was a sprawling square of space with trimmed lawns and flourishing flower hedges. It was there we gathered the next morning beneath a large gazebo.

"Now, I want all of you to pair up," Lady Hortensia said, projecting her high-pitched voice. "There are eight boats, so only sixteen can go at a time."

In the center of all the greenery was an enormous manmade pond, bordered by tastefully arranged rocks and willow trees. A row of canoes bobbed near the edge, awaiting pairs of debutantes and young men for a morning of rowing and mingling.

"Actually ma'am, there are twelve boats," Edward Thornbrush piped up, his cheeks as red and freckled as ever.

Lady Hortensia smiled at him, an expression that did not flatter her heavily powdered face.

This morning she was dressed in a gown of gauzy

fabric, not unlike Miriam's shawls, embroidered with iridescent butterflies. It was almost blinding in the dappled sunlight. I glanced behind her shoulder and caught a glimpse of Ash standing in the shadows.

"The pond is only so large, Edward," Lady Hortensia said with a girlish giggle. "If we use all twelve there will be no semblance of privacy."

Olivia whimpered next to me. I couldn't blame her. The woman was making a chaperoned event sound like an excuse to canoodle.

"Don't worry. I'm sure your brother will go with you if you're nervous," I said. Cedric was also in the crowd of young men, made obvious by his height and lack of gold ribbon. Though from the glances he was throwing at Genevieve, he may have regretted not having one.

Tori stuck her head out from behind my stepsister. "But you'll deprive the poor man of Genevieve's company," she said, voicing my thoughts.

"Tori!" Genevieve said, her face pink.

"She's right," I said. "I'll go with Olivia instead."

Tori pouted. "But what about Princey? You'll leave him all alone."

"His name is Ash, Tori."

"Oho! You're on first name basis?"

I resisted the urge to bury my face in my hands, lest Lady Hortensia ask me what the matter was. Olivia giggled. At least she wasn't nervous anymore.

"Eight young ladies and eight young men, come with me to the boats," Lady Hortensia said, gliding down from the gazebo. Her face stretched into another smile as she passed Ash, fluttering her fan before her face. I was surprised he wasn't blinded by the erratic flashing of her gown. "Your Highness has the first pick, of course."

Ash walked over to me and offered his arm. "Amarante?" he said.

Lady Hortensia's smile dropped.

I was about as embarrassed as Olivia was when I took his arm. Tori made one of her pulsing hearts again, which I tried very hard to ignore. Genevieve was bombarded by Edward Thornbrush before Cedric could move. I tossed him a sympathetic glance.

When everyone paired up, Lady Hortensia brushed brusquely past and marched down to the pond. The group followed. Narcissa walked behind me at the arm of a blushing youth. Her stoic expression and his flustered one was quite a match.

"Any progress with the case?" I asked Ash in a low voice. I thought I felt Narcissa's glare at the back of my neck, but brushed it off when I found her looking elsewhere.

"Not yet," Ash said, his brows furrowed. There were dark circles under his eyes. "I've been thinking…"

We walked further, but he didn't continue.

"Yes?" I prompted.

Ash sighed. "The duchess knows you're suspicious of her. What if something happens to you?"

"I'll be fine," I said. "She can't possibly do anything to me without raising suspicion."

For all Her Grace knew, I was merely a nosy debutante who posed no real threat. And if things went favorably, it would stay that way.

When we lowered ourselves into a canoe, Ash paddled us to a secluded area shaded by the foliage of a willow tree. A couple of swans floated in our midst. One of them hissed at us. I shifted away.

"As long as you're safe," he said, giving me the slightest of smiles.

I felt a little breathless. The rocking of the canoe, no doubt. "Any updates?" I managed to ask.

"Ah." His smile melted away. "The physicians are worried their cure isn't working."

I swallowed, desperately wanting to tell him to use Lana's antidote. But my tongue was glued to the roof of my mouth. "How bad is it?" I said instead.

"Heaven knows what that poison is. A week ago, my mother started having nightly fits. They only pass when the sun rises," Ash said, his voice wavering.

"What?" I sat straighter. "What kind of fits?"

"It's awful. She keeps screaming and clawing at nothing. We had to restrain her from hurting herself and—"

I shook my head. This pained him to talk about.

"How many people know about this?" I said.

"Just me and the physicians. And now you. My mother didn't want my father or Bennett to know the severity of her condition just yet," Ash said, furrowing his brow. "If Erasmus can't figure out what the poison is, I don't know if we'll ever find a cure. And Captain Greenwood will still be blamed. It's a whole mess."

Dread settled into my stomach like a lump of undigested potatoes. I wondered if the queen's symptoms were the same as Erasmus's mouse. I almost wanted to tell Ash everything, but I stopped myself. "Have you talked to the captain yet?"

Ash shook his head. He tugged at his ribbon, nearly unfurling it from his wrist. "No. But I will soon," he said, exhaling. "Will you join me?"

"Am I allowed?"

"I understand if you don't want to," he said quickly. "I'm sorry you got tangled in all of this in the first place. You're just a debutante—"

"Of course I'll come," I said. I knew how important it was to him. After all, he was in charge of the case and there was so much on the line: his father's respect, his mother's life, and of course, the innocence of witches. But the last was for me to worry about.

"Thank you," Ash said, gaze softening. He leaned forward and gripped the sides of the canoe. I blinked, startled at his sudden proximity.

What a lovely deep brown his eyes were.

A flush appeared on his cheeks, as if he had heard my thoughts. "Amarante, I've been wanting to—"

Then, the boat flipped over.

Icy water knocked the air out of my lungs. My knees hit the bottom of the pond and I scrambled to stand, my nose barely out of the water. Before I could get a lungful of air, something white and feathery smacked my face. A bevy of swans had surrounded us, hissing and beating their wings. A few nipped at my hair.

"What the—" A mouthful of pond water choked me as I lost my footing. Ash grabbed my waist and I clung to his sleeves, gasping for breath. The swans kept beating the water.

"Good heavens, what are they feeding these birds?" Ash exclaimed, shooing away the animals. Miraculously, they scattered, except one who wouldn't let go of my hair. I shut my eyes, willing it to go away. It eventually did, but not before ripping out several strands from my scalp.

Ash's laugh rumbled in my ear. "Don't tell me you're afraid of swans."

I retched at the taste of pond scum in my mouth. "I am now," I said, rubbing my head. "They flipped the boat over!"

Our fall created quite a splash, in multiple senses. Lady Hortensia looked almost scandalized as we pulled up with a pool of water in our boat and both of us drenched from head to foot. I was ordered to clean myself up while someone was sent to fetch towels and a change of clothes for His Royal Highness. Lady Hortensia began fussing over Ash before he could speak.

I decided to make my escape, lest the lady blamed the

disaster on me. Tori rushed over as I wrung my skirts out under the gazebo.

"Can't you attend one of these events without something disastrous happening?" she said, picking off a sopping piece of moss from my hair.

I sighed. "It appears not."

From the east entrance beyond the pond, a squire ran toward us, evidently in a hurry. I thought he had come with Ash's towels, but he was empty handed besides an envelope tucked in his sash. I was all surprise when he at last approached me.

"Miss Amarante Flora?" the squire asked.

At my affirmation, he handed me the envelope and departed before I could ask him any questions.

Tori peered over my shoulder. "What's that?"

I began to shrug until I recognized the name scrawled on the corner of the envelope.

Erasmus Lenard.

No doubt it was the results of our manbane experiment.

"It's nothing," I said to Tori, tucking the letter into my pocket. I hoped it wouldn't be destroyed by my damp skirts. "I should go inside and clean up."

"You need any help? I happen to be very good at wringing out water—"

"No thanks, Tori," I said, already up and running. Tori was a small figure when I considered myself a safe distance away. There was a wall of hedges behind the pond, a section of which there was nothing but a charred stump. I figured it was the hedge Ash said he set fire to. Wedging into the gap, I opened the letter.

The water from my skirts made the ink bleed, but it was still legible.

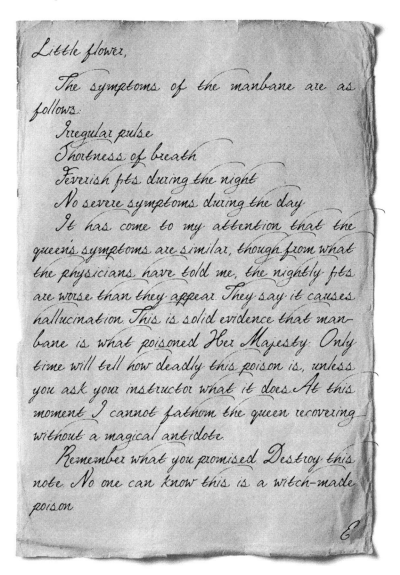

Little flower,

The symptoms of the manbane are as follows:
Irregular pulse
Shortness of breath
Feverish fits during the night
No severe symptoms during the day
It has come to my attention that the queen's symptoms are similar, though from what the physicians have told me, the nightly fits are worse than they appear. They say it causes hallucination. This is solid evidence that manbane is what poisoned Her Majesty. Only time will tell how deadly this poison is, unless you ask your instructor what it does. At this moment I cannot fathom the queen recovering without a magical antidote.

Remember what you promised. Destroy this note. No one can know this is a witch-made poison.

E

I crumpled the note and stuffed it back into my soaking pocket. Erasmus hadn't explicitly said it, but I knew he wanted me to ask Lana to make an antidote for manbane. Queen Cordelia had no chance of recovery if the physicians didn't know it was a witch-made poison. And if they did know, there was no saying what could happen to witchkind.

I bit my lip, both fear and thrill churning in my stomach. Could the recovery of Queen Cordelia be on my shoulders?

"Amarante?" Ash emerged behind my hedge, staring at me curiously. It took my all not to yelp. "What are you doing here?"

"Getting...dry," I said. I inched into a patch of sunlight.

There was a towel around his neck and another on his arm, which he offered to me. "Sorry about all this. I should have paid more attention to the boat."

I took the towel gratefully. "It's not your fault. It was the swans."

Ash laughed. I was reminded of how his chest rumbled with mirth when we were submerged in the pond. I blushed.

"They were acting strange," he admitted, "but I really don't think they could flip over a whole boat."

I decided not to contradict him. It was an irrelevant detail compared to what sat in my mind now. There was no doubt about it—I had to ask Lana about manbane and convince her to make an antidote.

A swan's bugle blared into my ear as one swooped down from the hedges and flew past me. I screamed and stumbled backward into Ash, knocking us both down to the grass.

"What is wrong with those creatures?" I bemoaned, too distressed to be annoyed at Ash's cackling or embarrassed that my back was flush against his chest. He had taken the brunt of my fall.

"Perhaps they like you," he teased, sitting us both up. "That one followed you all the way over here."

"It did? And no one thought to tell me?"

"It's a swan, Amarante. What's the worst that could happen?"

"Well, I—apologies!" I jumped up to my feet, realizing that we were in a most compromising position. I cringed to think of what Lady Hortensia would say if she saw me practically sitting on the second prince's lap.

Ash looked relatively unbothered as he stood.

"Never mind that. Come," he said cheerily, offering his arm. "I think we're both overdue for a change of clothes."

21

A few days after the Disastrous Swan Incident, my crystal called me yet again to Witch Village for another lesson with Lana. I was eager to show her the progress I had made in the past few weeks, but more urgently, I was burning to ask her about manbane.

When I arrived at Lana's cottage, though, she was standing outside with a basket on her arm. "We're visiting a patient today," Lana said before I could greet her.

"A patient?" I asked, trying not to sound too disappointed. "Are you the village physician?"

"Hardly," Lana said with a humorless smile. "But I help when I can. She is an old friend."

There was silence after that and I didn't try to fill it up with questions or conversation despite the urgency I felt. She seemed more solemn than usual, which couldn't mean anything good.

After weaving through stone buildings and passing a cramped courtyard, we arrived before a tiny wooden shack with a yellow door. Lana knocked once. A faint voice came from within and we entered.

The interior was much bigger than the exterior suggested, a patterned rug carpeting the floor. A witch about Lana's age lay along a worn couch. She had dark skin peppered with gold and silver hair tucked in a cotton bonnet. Her legs were covered in a thick quilt.

"Ah, Lana," the witch said.

"Beatrice." Lana set her basket on a side table and took a seat next to the woman. "Any changes?"

"Your health potion worked wonders," Beatrice said. Her smile seemed familiar, but I couldn't place where I had seen it. "I'm more energized than usual."

Lana nodded. "You've been taking it regularly?"

"I have. Elowyn is adamant I keep it up. I'm afraid I would've forgotten if it weren't for her." Beatrice's gaze shifted to me. "Hello. Who are you?"

I dipped my head. "Amarante Flora, madam. I'm Lana's apprentice."

"I never thought we'd meet," she said. "You're familiar with my daughters, I reckon?"

Her silver irises matched another's perfectly. "Elowyn and…?" I trailed off.

"Rowena."

"Oh!" I widened my eyes. So that's why Elowyn seemed familiar. I curtsied. "Lovely to meet you. Rowena is like family to me."

Beatrice nodded, looking wistful. "I haven't seen her in sixteen years."

"I brought you a new treatment," Lana said abruptly, moving to a stool. "Amarante, the nixgrass."

Why hadn't Rowena seen her mother since I was born? Did she leave her family to take care of mine? My heart twinged at the thought, but I obeyed Lana and pulled out the herb bundle, a match, and a candle.

"How have you been feeling lately?" Lana asked.

"A little short of breath," Beatrice said, tucking her hands into her quilt.

I lit the nixgrass and set it on the table. Yellow smoke spiraled upward, perfuming the air with its calming scent.

Lana motioned for her basket. I gave it to her. "Ideally I'd prescribe fresh air, but the nixgrass will have to do," she said.

Beatrice exhaled. "I do miss summer mornings," she said ruefully.

Lana fished out a couple of apples. "Here. Apples are good for the lungs," she said, putting them in Beatrice's lap.

"Oh, Lana. I couldn't."

"Take it. I got it from one of those annoying fellows at the Witch Market," Lana said gruffly. "You ought to get some proper food in your system. It has been helping the others."

So there were other witches suffering like Beatrice because of the lack of fresh food and air. It never occurred to me that witches could get sick.

The smell of something burning jerked me out of my thoughts. My sleeve was on fire. I barely had time to shriek before Beatrice flicked her hand and put out the flames, leaving a gaping, charred hole in the muslin.

"Thank you," I said sheepishly.

"I remember your mother wearing that," Beatrice said.

I blinked. "Wearing what?"

"That crystal pendant. Ah, yes, her enchanted object. She never took that off."

My mouth parted. I looked to Lana. Her lips were pinched. They always were when she wasn't pleased with something.

"We ought to get going," Lana said, standing.

Beatrice looked at her. "You haven't told her?"

Lana took her basket and traversed the room without another word. I scurried after, giving Beatrice an apologetic look before ducking out the threshold. I barely slipped out when Lana shut the door. She was already halfway down the street when I straightened. I ran to catch up.

"What did Beatrice mean?"

"Nothing. She was simply overtired."

I frowned, looking down at my crystal. "She said this was my Mama's."

Lana kept walking. "She was overtired."

Her voice was so firm that I didn't speak another word on our walk back. Her pinched lips and creased brow were enough to force me to swallow my curiosity, no matter how difficult it was.

After all, it was a waiting game with Lana. She drove me away the first time I met her. Now, I was her apprentice. I would get my answers eventually.

When we were back in her cottage, I dared to speak again.

"I've been practicing," I said, wishing my voice didn't sound so small.

The walk must have quelled her mood. Lana grunted. "Potion-making?"

"And levitation," I said. "See?"

I focused on a small vial on the counter and hovered it in the air.

"Very good. That was expensive," she said, taking it and putting it into a cupboard.

"Oh." My face reddened. "So, is this all for today's lesson?"

Lana was silent for a moment.

"Yes," she said at last. "You may go."

"May I ask you a few questions first?"

She continued rummaging through her cupboard. "What is it?"

"Can you tell me more about manbane?"

Lana stopped rummaging.

"I was reading the potion book you gave me," I said quickly, "and I was wondering why it didn't mention any poisons."

"I told you. Witches do not make poisons for malicious intent. It is the one law we have," Lana said.

"I know," I said. "But shouldn't there be something about the one poison that made it into human hands?"

Lana exhaled. "If you must know," she said in a low voice, "manbane drains years of life. Each day the victim is poisoned, a year is taken from their life. It is painful and insidious. Each night passes in agony and each day with exhaustion. Eventually it kills the victim. But not before inflicting terrible damage on their psyche."

Perhaps it was the breeze from the window that caused the chills running up my spine and down my arms. Or perhaps it was the emotionless way Lana described the horrors of manbane.

To think the queen was suffering through such a poison! Was Duchess Wilhelmina really capable of inflicting such horrors upon someone she called a friend? And the thing that bothered me most…

"What kind of witch would make such a poison?" I asked.

"Perhaps," Lana said, her voice still stiff and emotionless, "one who was caught up in negative feelings. Perhaps they have repented."

"Is there an antidote then?" I asked. "Surely there must be if they have truly repented."

Lana closed the cupboard. "There is not an antidote, nor will there be any use for one. It has been years since manbane got into human hands. The victim, if there is one, would be long gone by now."

I bit my lip. "She isn't."

Lana whirled around. I had never seen her so pale. "What are you saying?"

"Queen Cordelia," I said. "She was poisoned by manbane recently."

Her mouth thinned. "How can you be sure?"

I told her everything I had found out, from the scarlet smoke at the Debutante Ball to the results of Erasmus's lab experiment to the investigation with Ash. I told her of the manbane I had extracted with my extracting potion. I told her that if no one in Witch Village made an antidote for the queen, she would not survive.

Lana stared hard at the spot above my head. "Foolish girl. You should have never told that inspector of your magic. And why are you so concerned about a human queen?"

I blinked rapidly, taken aback by her response. I knew she disliked royalty, but I didn't know her hatred extended this far.

"If only there's a recipe for the antidote, I could make it myself," I said. "You don't have to—"

"You didn't make any foolish promises, did you?" Lana interrupted.

"What?"

"You didn't tell that prince you would save the queen?"

I shook my head. "No, but I'm the only one—"

"Good. Then you are under no obligation to do so. I suggest you remove yourself from this mess. Leave it to the human physicians."

"They won't be able to save her," I said, growing helpless.

"Neither will you," Lana said firmly. "Manbane antidote does not exist."

"But—"

"Close the door on your way out."

I did. My gut was in tangles as I half walked and half ran down the path from Lana's cottage. If there was really no antidote, Queen Cordelia was doomed to suffer until the manbane killed her. My gut clenched. How could I tell Erasmus? And worst of all, how could I tell Ash?

22

reakfast came with letters. Lydia wrote us again, rambling about the Season coming to a close and offering to send us better jewelry to wear to the upcoming soirée. I hardly got through half of it before abandoning it for another note from Ash. Tori and Genevieve shot me some looks at the sight of the royal seal, but I let them believe what they wanted.

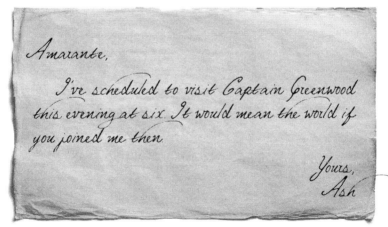

Amarante,

I've scheduled to visit Captain Greenwood this evening at six. It would mean the world if you joined me then.

Yours,
Ash

The two of them were shamelessly giggling when I told them I was going to take another walk.

"I…I'm going to visit Olivia!" I said in an attempt to stop Tori's guffaws and Genevieve's sly smiles.

Tori only snorted. "Alright. Say hello to Prince Ash for us."

Lord Strongfoot burst in before I could defend myself. He looked as if he had just rolled out of bed, waving a newspaper around frantically. "Girls, I just read the most confounding news."

"What is it, Pa?" Tori asked, wide-eyed.

"They say the queen was poisoned by a witch!"

I gaped as Genevieve gave a soft gasp.

"How awful," my stepsister said, pressing her fingers to her lips. "But how did they find out? Was anyone arrested?"

Lord Strongfoot shook his head, mussing his already mussed black hair. "They didn't find a culprit, if that's what you mean. But the physicians say the poison was unlike anything they've seen and concluded that it was witch-made. Who would've thought!"

I was frozen in my seat. Everything seemed to be spiraling out of control. There was no manbane antidote, and now this. How did the physicians know the poison was witch-made? Erasmus couldn't have told them, and the note he sent me had long been destroyed in my damp dress pocket.

And who could have possibly leaked this information when it was supposed to be a private case?

"Just because the poison is witch-made doesn't mean a witch did it," Tori reasoned, chewing on a piece of bacon. I could've kissed her.

Lord Strongfoot nodded. "You're right, my girl. We mustn't forget the Witch Market. That's why old Greenwood is still imprisoned. But I've heard more people are asking for his pardon now that this bit of news is out," he said. "Can't blame them. I'd choose a witch to be imprisoned than the captain any day."

I lowered my head and buttered a piece of toast I didn't intend to eat. My fondness for the former blacksmith didn't keep me from feeling offended, but I knew he only wished the best for his benefactor.

At this point, there was only one thing I hoped for—that Captain Greenwood would be able to clear his own name without ruining an innocent witch.

The palace dungeons were rumored to be an intimidating labyrinth of cramped cellars and dank air that sucked all the life out of a prisoner. Those who were proven guilty lost all defiance and those who refused to admit their crimes did so after mere hours of being locked up. I could see where such rumors originated when Ash took me through the iron wrought gates and down the dark pit.

Though it was only a few hours after midday, there was not a hint of light aside from the torches. Square grates lined the ceiling, but they were too high up and too small to illuminate anything.

"Take one of these to better see the gorgeous scenery," Ash said, handing me a torch from the wall. The firelight flickered over his grin as he gestured grandly to our squalid surroundings.

I took it, feeling too grim to smile at his jokes. "How long are we allowed in here?"

"Thirty minutes, at most. Though we could get away with an hour. I am a prince, after all."

We passed a set of hefty wooden doors guarded by two men. They bowed and pushed them open.

"Here comes the not-so-pretty part," Ash said into my ear.

I swallowed as we stepped over the threshold. Moans and cries of prisoners echoed from the long hall. A draft brought the odor of unwashed bodies and other unpleasant things. I pressed my sleeve to my nose, inching closer to Ash.

"Your Highness! Save me!" A hand shot out from one of the cells, caked with grime and grasping for Ash's leg. He sidestepped gracefully.

"No can do, sir," Ash said. "I believe you murdered somebody six months ago."

"Where exactly did you keep Captain Greenwood?" I whispered as we proceeded down the passageway. I was shaking involuntarily, trying to avoid eye contact with the wild-eyed prisoners. I thought I saw a woman chewing on her foot.

"Not too far," Ash replied. "Cell number one hundred fifty-six."

I glanced at the numbers nailed atop the cells. The furthest I could see was sixty-two. Something touched my arm. I yelped, but I had only brushed Ash's elbow.

He turned to me, lips twisting. The scoundrel was on the brink of laughter. "Are you scared, Amarante?" he teased. Someone's shrill scream pierced the air.

I scowled heavily. "Of course not. I promenade amongst half-crazed criminals and murderers daily."

His face lost a bit of its mirth. "Unfortunately not just criminals and murderers," he said.

"What do you mean?"

"Some of them are citizens who couldn't afford to pay taxes or were caught with illegal goods."

I bit my lip. "Like from the Witch Market?" I ventured to ask.

"Precisely," Ash said. He shook his head. "Many of them couldn't help it. They have no choice when they are too destitute to pay for little else but food. I only hope they haven't been harmed by witch-made items."

I thought about Nina and her fish. Was her family so poor that she had to trade for medicine at the Witch Market? It was a good deal for her—I knew Lana's antidote worked wonders, even more so than a regular ointment that costed gold. Yet magic was unlawful and Ash spoke of it with such distaste.

"I didn't know you sent people with witch-made items to the dungeons," I said.

Ash heaved a sigh. "It came with the Non-Magic Age. Once I find evidence of Navierre's crimes, my father will reinforce the anti-magic laws—"

He paused abruptly at my scowl. He probably mistook it for disinterest. "I'm sorry, I shouldn't be talking about this with you."

If anything, I was the most fitting person to talk to. But I knew I couldn't say so.

"It's fine," I said instead.

His grin reappeared on his face. "Well, if you're still scared grab on to me." He took my arm and wrapped it around his.

For a moment, I forgot my offense.

We traversed deeper into the dungeons, taking a sharp left turn. The cells were different now. Instead of barred gates, thick wooden doors obstructed the cells and their prisoners. There were two narrow slots cut into each, one a window and one an opening for food. A guard stood watch before each door. They bowed as we passed. Ash acknowledged each of them with a nod until we stopped in front of cell number one hundred fifty-six.

"Your Highness," the guard said.

"Henry. I would like to see Captain Greenwood."

"Of course, Your Highness. But…" Henry looked at me. I hastily let go of Ash's arm, which I was clutching like a toddler would a stuffed toy.

"She's with me."

"Very well, Your Highness. Take your time. Call if you need help."

"That won't be necessary, but thank you."

The guard unlocked the door and let us inside. I shifted uneasily, upsetting the hay strewn on the floor. The cellar had a high, grated ceiling that let in watery light. A man stood in the far corner. He fell to his knees at our entrance.

"Your Highness," Captain Greenwood said, bowing his head.

"Please rise, Maverick," Ash said.

"I cannot. I am too ashamed."

"I know you're not the one who poisoned my mother," Ash said, lowering himself to the floor. "How are you?"

"I've survived worse than this. Henry is a good and loyal guard."

"I want to help."

"That means the world, Your Highness," Captain Greenwood said quietly. "But I'm afraid the true culprit will not reveal themselves or let me go free so easily."

"Do you know who did it?" I asked.

"And you are?"

I curtsied. "Amarante Flora, sir."

"She's joining me in my investigation," Ash said. I knelt next to him.

The captain nodded. "I see."

It occurred to me that I had never seen the captain in person. He was a little past middle-aged with a straight nose and specks of silver in his dirty blond beard. Lydia said he was an infamous flirt in her day. But all I saw was an exhausted man who looked at Ash with the reverence of a dutiful guard.

"So, do you know the culprit?" Ash asked.

Captain Greenwood sighed. "I'm afraid you wouldn't believe me if I told you," he said.

"You have nothing to lose," I said.

"You're right." The captain gave a mirthless smile. "Duchess Wilhelmina Whittington."

Ash let go of a breath. "We had our suspicions."

Captain Greenwood looked up. "Really?"

"Yes. But why the duchess?" I said, furrowing my brow. "The queen trusts her. They're friends, aren't they?"

Ash thinned his lips.

Captain Greenwood sighed and said, "Ah. I suppose you don't know. Not many do."

"Know what?" I asked.

"Back when we were all younger, Wilhelmina fancied Maximus," the captain said. "She was envious of nearly everything Cordelia had. How could she not be? She was merely a servant and Cordelia…well, she was to be the future queen."

I found myself blushing at the thought of Duchess Wilhelmina in love with the paunchy King Maximus. Ash looked similarly bothered, but urged the captain to continue.

"But jealousy is a dangerous thing, especially in someone like Wilhelmina who was headstrong and ambitious

and stubborn. I saw it eat away at her. I was shocked to hear the things she said about Cordelia. But after a while, she became quieter. I thought she finally let go of her spite when she married Duke Earnest Whittington." Captain Greenwood shook his head, as if dismissing his own folly. "But then the duke died and, well, she became Wilhelmina again. She disregarded morality for gain, both financial and social. By the time I became captain of the Royal Guard, she was unrecognizable. A part of me knew she wouldn't stop at merely being a duchess. I'm not surprised she has harmed Cordelia at last."

I pressed a hand over my mouth.

"I see," Ash said hoarsely.

Captain Greenwood gave a sigh. "I dislike recounting the past. But if it will help, I am glad. Now tell me. How exactly did you discover she was behind this?"

"I saw her giving something to the queen at the Debutante Ball. And the guard who was caught slipping poison into the queen's tea—the one who framed you—we found the duchess's coins on him," I said.

"Ah, Peter. His morals have always been questionable." He shrugged. "But to think he would die for Wilhelmina's schemes is odd indeed. He had no sense of loyalty in the regiments."

"And he killed himself right after exposing you," Ash said slowly.

I recalled Peter's limp body. "Unless he didn't actually kill himself," I said. Both men looked at me in surprise. I colored at the scrutiny, but replayed my suspicions. "Think of it. Why would a man with no loyalty die for the duchess's sake? Especially right after being paid such a hefty sum."

Ash nodded. "You're right. The coins were still on him when he did the deed."

Captain Greenwood stared at the straw-littered ground, seemingly deep in thought. He was awfully quiet for a man who finally had hope shine on him. Perhaps he didn't dare believe it.

Ash stood and paced the cell. "But the mortician proclaimed him dead. He was sent to his family for burial on a mortuary wagon. He didn't deserve it, after his act of treason," he said bitterly. "But Mother insisted."

"Maybe there's a potion that makes someone appear dead," I said quietly. I wished I had thought to use my magic sight when Peter was unconscious.

Ash stopped pacing and Captain Greenwood looked up. "Are you speaking of witchcraft, Miss Flora?" the captain said. I couldn't decipher his tone.

"I'm being foolish," I said, looking at the floor. "Witches wouldn't meddle in human affairs."

"You speak as if you know that for sure, Miss Flora."

I raised my eyes to meet the captain's gaze and instantly darted them away. He was a little too sharp for my comfort.

"Amarante brings up a valid point," Ash said. "The physicians said my mother was poisoned with a witch-made poison. If Duchess Wilhelmina had dealings at the Witch Market, she must have made more than one purchase. I'll send a few men to ask around."

My stomach turned. At least Ash didn't immediately think to blame a witch as culprit.

"You ought to check with Peter's family first," Captain Greenwood said. "Make sure if he is dead or alive."

The tension in my gut eased. Perhaps Peter *was* dead. Perhaps he was foolish enough to die for the duchess for a reason we weren't aware of.

Ash ran a hand through his hair. He looked tired. "You're

right. As of now, all we have are suspicions. But I will find a way to get you out of here."

Captain Greenwood smiled. "Thank you, Your Highness. Promise me you won't do anything foolish."

"I won't."

The captain looked to me. "And you too, Miss Flora."

I was surprised to be included, but promised as well. We concluded our meeting soon after, but I lingered behind as Ash stepped outside to converse with Henry.

"Sir, do you think they'll let you out if the duchess confesses her crimes?" I asked.

Captain Greenwood raised a wiry brow, no doubt surprised that I had stayed. "I would imagine," he said. "But the chances of that happening are slim."

I nodded. A truth potion would solve almost everything. Captain Greenwood would be saved and the duchess would be exposed. And Ash would not suspect witches.

Everyone would be safe, that is, except the queen. I felt sick thinking about what would happen to her. But there was still a chance for justice.

"This may seem a little forward, sir, but I was wondering if I could borrow five pounds of gold."

He threw his head back and laughed. "Asking a dead man for gold? You must be jesting, Miss Flora."

"You aren't dead, sir," I said, embarrassed. "But it's not for my personal use. I'm trying to help."

"And I suppose you won't tell me what you're going to do with it?"

I hesitated and shook my head.

"Very well. I have nothing to lose," he said with a grumble. "I will send a note to my wife. She'll see to it you receive your gold."

Out of all the possible responses, I did not expect him to agree. "Thank you, sir!"

After telling him Tori's address, I exited Captain Greenwood's cell and joined Ash outside. Luckily, he didn't ask any questions, and he and I traversed the shadowy halls of the dungeons yet again. I prepared myself for the gruesome sights this time, but it did not make the trip any more pleasant. Still, I refrained from clinging onto Ash's arm for the sake of my pride. I was all too glad when we made it outside. The air was a great deal fresher.

An owl hooted. The sun had set hours ago. Time was imperceptible in the dungeons.

"I ought to go back. The Strongfoots and my sister are expecting me."

Ash nodded. His profile was silhouetted by the lamps along the exterior of the east wing, but I saw the creases under his eyes and the stiff set of his jaw as clearly as I would in daylight. His features softened when he turned to me. "Will you be fine on your own?"

"It's a fifteen-minute walk, at most. And shorter by chaise, which I'll be taking," I added quickly when he raised a brow.

"Good." He paused a few moments before speaking again. "What did you say to the captain?"

I shifted my weight, glad it was dark enough to hide my flushed cheeks. I felt like a schoolgirl caught committing some petty crime. "It was nothing. I told him…not to worry, and that he's in good hands."

Ash smiled. It was a ridiculous for a girl to tell a grown man who had seen all sorts of violence not to worry. Luckily, he didn't comment on it and merely took my hand. "I see. That's kind of you."

"Thank you. Well, good night," I said. His fingers were very warm.

Ash released my hand and tucked his behind his back. "Good night."

I began walking away before I did something foolish like kiss him.

Then, a voice stopped me in my tracks.

"Amarante. My mother would like a word with you."

I turned. Narcissa strode out the entrance of the east wing in a velvet gown, a servant trailing behind her. Her heels clicked against the marble in sharp, staccato steps. Her face was icy.

"Lady Narcissa," I said. How had she known that I was here? I exchanged a glance with Ash. His expression was guarded as he dipped his head in greeting, even though Narcissa hadn't addressed him.

"It is late. Would Her Grace be so kind as to schedule a meeting for tomorrow?" I said, keeping my voice as civil as possible. What could the duchess possibly want with me?

"My mother is a very busy woman," Narcissa said. She flicked her gaze from me to Ash. "And clearly you have no objections to staying late in the company of nobility." She said the last word as if she didn't mean it.

"You will have to excuse Amarante," Ash said. If he was insulted, he didn't show it. "It is late."

Narcissa's nostrils flared. "Are you defying my mother's orders?"

I wondered if she knew she was talking to a prince.

Ash looked calmly at her. "Not at all. Amarante merely wishes to meet Her Grace at another time."

"Do you know how scandals start?" Narcissa flicked open her fan. "With a rumor. Or in this case, the truth. What would people say if they hear about a lowly merchant's daughter sneaking off to the dungeons with the bastard prince at night?"

"Are you threatening me?" Ash growled.

I pulled his sleeve, restraining him from stepping forward. "I doubt rumors of the prince punching the duchess's daughter would be any better," I whispered.

He frowned.

"I'll go," I said to Narcissa. She smiled and closed her fan.

"Amarante," Ash warned.

I shook my head. To Narcissa, there was no reason for us to think the duchess would do anything to harm me. I had to act oblivious. Ash seemed to realize this and reluctantly stepped back.

I tried to calm my hammering heart as I followed Narcissa down the hall. What if the duchess did try to harm me? Did she know that Ash and I were on her heels? Everything pointed at her as the culprit for poisoning Queen Cordelia. I didn't want to think what a woman capable of killing her queen would do to someone as insignificant as me.

We at last came before a set of double doors. The servant bowed her head as Narcissa and I entered.

23

Duchess Wilhelmina herself was stretched out on a chaise longue, a crystal goblet filled with scarlet liquid glittering in her hands. Misty was curled up at her foot, a ball of midnight fur.

"You brought her." The duchess's deep voice filled the room.

"Yes, mother."

I couldn't help but notice that Narcissa seemed more subdued in her mother's presence. My knees were shaking as I lowered myself into a curtsy. "Your Grace."

Duchess Wilhelmina set her goblet on the low table before her and regarded me. The silk of her deep red dressing gown gleamed in the candlelight. Something sinister lurked beneath her usual finery.

"It appears that Cordelia did not punish you satisfactorily after behaving so horribly at the hunting party," she said.

"Your Grace?" I said. The issue had long been resolved. What could she mean by bringing it up again?

The duchess traced the rim of her goblet with a finger. It went around and around and around. "I am sure, Miss Flora, that you believe in justice?"

"I hope everyone does, Your Grace."

The duchess's finger paused. "Yes," she said softly. "One who has done wrong must be punished."

My spine stiffened as I took in the flickering candle-light, the heavy velvet drapes, and the closed double doors. Misty mewed and stared at me with acid green eyes.

"What shall it be, Mother? Shall she be whipped?" Narcissa's gloating words almost made me jump. I had forgotten she was standing there.

"Are you a savage, Narcissa, or are you a noblewoman?" Duchess Wilhelmina said. She hardly spared her daughter a glance. How differently she treated Narcissa in public! I would've felt bad for the girl, if she hadn't just suggested that I be whipped. I didn't let myself relax, though. The duchess may be opposed to whipping, but what of other, lesser forms of torture? The old thumbscrew? A night locked away in a closet? Or perhaps her area of expertise: poison.

"My purpose for bringing you here is to right a wrong. You never received the punishment you deserve. What do you suppose it should be?"

Was she seriously asking me? I decided to go for the safest answer. "Whatever Your Grace deems appropriate," I said.

Duchess Wilhelmina pointed at the servant girl behind Narcissa. "You. You're dismissed. Pack up your things. Someone else will be taking your room."

The girl squeaked. She was clearly distressed but curtsied

low nonetheless. Without a word, she was gone. I watched in disbelief.

"Mother!"

"Never fear," the duchess drawled. She gestured to me. "Here's the replacement."

"Y-your Grace?" I stuttered. Narcissa seemed equally appalled.

"Mother, you can't make—"

"There is nothing I can't do," Duchess Wilhelmina said, eyes flashing. Her gaze was sharp and calculating as she sat up. "You, Miss Flora, will move here to the palace in the servant's room. You will do Narcissa's bidding and attend to her every need. You will not tell anyone about this. From now to as long as I say, she is your mistress and you will do everything she tells you. Is that understood?"

This couldn't be legal.

Me? Playing servant for Narcissa for heaven knows how long? Impossible. "But, Your Grace—"

"Are you defying me, Miss Flora?" the duchess said softly. Ice shot up my spine at her very gaze.

I forced myself to bow my head. "No, Your Grace."

"Defying me is a very grave mistake. Don't think I'm not aware of your frequent visits to the outskirts of the city," Duchess Wilhelmina said. She resumed tracing the rim of her goblet. "You disappear every week, do you? A certain shop called…ah, what is it? Miriam's Terrariums."

I froze. How did she know?

The duchess leaned forward, eyes glittering. "Would it surprise you, Miss Flora, that I find that particular shop as interesting as you do?" she said. "Maybe your friends would find it so too. But it would be a shame if everyone knew about its…charms."

My mouth seemed to dry out.

"Your Grace, please." My voice was hoarse.

"I wonder how poor, darling Ash would react when he finds out you were the one behind his mother's death. How would he feel if he finds out you were a scheming witch all this time, getting close to him and misleading his little investigation to finish off the queen?"

I sucked in a breath. She knew. She knew I was a witch. And somehow, Narcissa did too. "How did you find out?"

The duchess scoffed. "I am not so foolish as to tell *you*, girl. You will do as I say or you will feel the consequences. And I repeat—you will not tell anyone about this unless you wish for death."

"Yes, Your Grace."

"Get out of my sight. You will attend to your duties first thing tomorrow."

I curtsied.

Narcissa was glowering at me when I rose, seemingly not as content as I thought she would be. Why wouldn't she enjoy seeing me suffer and treating me like her servant? I swept out of the room before I burst into tears.

Footsteps echoed in the hall. Ash was pacing by a nearby column dimly lit by flickering torches. I hurriedly wiped my eyes, glad to see there was nothing there. Yet.

"What are you doing here?" I asked.

He paused and crossed his arms. "You didn't think I would let you go into the lion's den by yourself, did you?" he said. "What did she want?"

I opened my mouth and closed it again. "Nothing. She warned me not to disrespect Narcissa again," I said. It was partially true.

He looked like he was going to prod me more.

I sucked in my cheeks. "You should go check on the queen. Make sure she's getting better."

A crease appeared between his brows at the mention of his mother. "Right," he said. He glanced at me again. The firelight from the torches danced in his eyes. "I should go. I'll have a horse chaise called for you."

I suddenly wanted to tell him everything. The duchess as good as confessed her crimes. But no doubt he would question what Her Grace held over me. Did I have the courage to tell Ash I was a witch?

But before I could make up my mind, he was gone.

It was tricky business explaining to the Strongfoots why I had to temporarily move out of their manor and why Genevieve wasn't coming with me.

"My nannies missed me so much they fell ill. I ought to go visit them."

Tori had said, "Amarante, I say this because I care about you. What kind of grown woman has nannies?"

I had to explain to her my relationship with Theodora and Rowena, their actual roles in the house, and how I still called them my nannies for old times' sake. Genevieve offered to come home with me.

"Oh, it'll only be for a week or so." I forced myself to sound bright.

In reality I had no idea how long the arrangement would last. One week? A month? Until the end of the Season? Whatever it may be, I had to pack light to go through with my ruse.

I ended up bringing four dresses, under which I smuggled all of Lana's books, and other essentials. The day before, a hefty package came for me from Captain Greenwood's manor, full of the gold he promised. I packed that with me too and deflected Tori's questions. I felt horrible for lying. I almost wanted to jump off the horse chaise as Genevieve and Tori waved goodbye.

It was hardly dawn when I arrived at the east wing of the palace. I was led to the servant's quarters by a stern-looking matron in charge of the staff who introduced herself as Madam Josephine. She had an incredibly beaky nose and wore a high-necked dress. Right away I didn't expect her to take well to my pleads of mercy.

"Lady Narcissa will be expecting you in her chambers in half an hour," the matron said as we walked down a narrow hall.

"So soon?" I said, half-carrying, half-dragging my luggage behind me.

Madam Josephine harrumphed. "That is considered late for a servant. It is the highest honor to serve a noblewoman. Though it is beyond me why the duchess chose you." She stared as I tried to tug my suitcase out of a divot in the ground. It released gracelessly.

It appeared Madam Josephine wasn't acquainted with my situation. I didn't bother to explain.

We eventually reached the end of the narrow hall. She pointed at a decrepit door that had fallen off its top hinges. I had to lift the door by the knob to get it open. And what greeted me inside was not worth the work.

"Your room," the matron said. She shoved a wad of rough fabric in my arms. "Change quickly. I have other things to attend to after I show you to Lady Narcissa's chambers."

What Madam Josephine referred to as my room appeared to be a small abandoned kitchen turned into a bedroom by a group of drunk youngsters yet to find apprenticeships. A dingy cot nestled in the corner with a rickety nightstand at its foot. There was nothing else in the room except for a partially-boarded up brick oven. My jaw went slack. Was this where Narcissa's previous servant lived? It had to be the ugliest room in the palace.

"What are you standing there gaping for?" Madam Josephine said sharply.

"But Madam, there has to be a mistake. Aren't I to serve Narcissa?"

She barked a laugh. "Don't tell me you expected to be her lady's maid," she said, her lips peeled back in a sneer. In addition to her beaky nose, she had very horsey teeth. "I was told that you are nothing but her personal scullery maid. You will sweep her floors and wash her dishes and empty her chamber pot."

"I will *what*?"

My question was ignored. "If you take more breaks than those given to you, Lady Narcissa will personally see to your punishment," the matron said. "Take it from me, girl. She is not merciful."

24

After donning the servant's uniform, I followed Madam Josephine to Narcissa's chambers. It was a long route with too many twists and turns and staircases to count. By the time we arrived, my feet were aching. I surveyed the ornate rug and cushioned chairs, wishing I could sink into any one of them. Madam Josephine, however, executed a deep, steady curtsy.

"I have brought your maid as you instructed, milady."

Narcissa didn't bother turning around. She was seated before her vanity in an elaborate lace gown. Another maid was combing her hair. "You may leave, Josephine."

"Yes, milady."

I was almost sad when the woman exited, even when she shot me a glare.

"Amarante. I underestimated how much I enjoy seeing you like this." Narcissa finally turned around. Her hair fell in silky auburn waves down her shoulders. "Kneel."

I resented her a little more as I knelt.

"What are you going to do, Narcissa?" I asked warily.

The maid beside her gasped. "How dare you speak to Her Ladyship that way?"

"Karen is right." Narcissa stood from her seat and glided toward me, her eyes narrowed. "You must remember you are nothing but a lowly servant now. When a servant addresses her mistress in such a way that servant is punished. Stick out your hand."

I kept my hands firmly tucked behind my back.

Narcissa scoffed. "Still playing strong, are you? You heard Mother loud and clear last night. Serve me or be ruined."

How could they threaten to slough their crimes onto me when they were the treasonous ones? I wanted to shout at her, but I didn't. I would have to have a death wish. So I stuck out my left hand.

"You have the hand of a lady. How unfitting," she said with a sigh. "We'll have to change that. Bring me a needle, Karen."

The maid rushed over with a pin cushion full of needles. They varied in length and width, but they were all undeniably sharp. My arm shook as Narcissa selected the thickest of the bunch. She admired the point for a second before pricking the back of my hand and scraping it across my skin.

I cried out. She didn't go deep enough to draw blood, but it hurt beyond belief. It wasn't until I blinked back my tears did I realize she had written something.

NW. Her initials, in angry red scratches on my hand.

Narcissa stuck the needle back into the cushion and wiped her fingers on the handkerchief Karen offered her. "Now it'll be easier to remember I own you."

I clutched my throbbing hand to my dress. She had carved her initials on me like she would on a wooden doll! "You're *demented*," I spat out.

She tilted her head. "Did I not make it easy enough? Stick out your other hand."

I stumbled back. Before I could express my defiance, a knock sounded on the door.

"Lady Narcissa? You are summoned to the Queen's Garden to accompany Lady Hortensia and Her Grace for breakfast."

Narcissa shooed Karen away and grabbed my wrist.

"Very well," she said to the door. She dragged me around the corner to a fireplace, her strength surprising, and shoved my head into the ashes. My forehead banged against the grate. The charred wood chips stung my face. I jerked back, eyes burning and mouth full of cinder. I was overtaken with the desire to shout again—and box Narcissa in the nose at the same time.

"Enjoy," she said with a smirk. With that, she glided off to the door.

I sat, nursing the bruise on my head, when Karen placed herself before me.

"Lady Narcissa says you are to listen to me when she is absent," she said. I suspected that her haughty expression was a rare occurrence, but only because she didn't have many people she could use it around.

I nodded stiffly.

She pinched my chin and smeared more of the ash onto my face.

"What are you doing?" I said, twisting out of her grasp.

Karen snickered. "Lady Narcissa says you are not to be recognizable."

I stared. "You know I'm a debutante," I said, touching my cheek. My fingers came off dirty.

The maid raised an eyebrow. "Yes. But I know you're

nothing more than a merchant's daughter. You're hardly worth anything."

"Is that so?" I said. "Then what are you worth?"

"Insolent girl!" Karen struck me across the face.

I glared, cheek stinging, as the maid wiped her hand off on my dress.

"The chamber pot needs scrubbing. Take it outside and come back for your next assignment. Supplies are in the servant's hall."

I found Narcissa's unnecessarily luxurious chamber pot already empty, but it did not make the smell any less offensive. There was nothing pleasant about my experience as I navigated the palace. I was told by a guard that scullery maids were not allowed to roam the main halls. Apparently, there was a separate web of hallways for servants who did the unpleasant work. The way the guard wrinkled his nose at me clearly meant he thought I was one of them.

He was not entirely wrong.

I wandered the narrower, darker halls for a considerable amount of time before I finally found an exit. Madam Josephine had not shown me the way back, so it took several hours to find the servants hall, raid the closet for a pail and brush, and scrub Narcissa's chamber pot outside where several other maids were doing the same task. Many of them were stouter and older than I was and went in with gusto with their sleeves rolled up to their elbows.

I wanted desperately to use my magic as I scrubbed the inside of the porcelain with the rough brush. The handle needed a good sanding.

By the time I had worked off the stains, my hands were covered in splinters and the older maids had long gone inside after snickering at me. My back ached and my feet were numb. The hand on which Narcissa had carved her initials was throbbing. The other was sore from the splinters. I could not recall another time I was in such a condition.

Narcissa was nowhere to be seen when I came back with the cleaned chamber pot. I was glad of it, but Karen's pinched face was not much better.

"What took you so long?" she demanded as I entered.

"Cleaning the chamber pot like you ordered."

The maid snatched the porcelain pot from me with a glare. "You must have been taking breaks. It's been three hours."

"I merely got lost."

She sneered. "Lady Narcissa will not be happy to hear that you've been lazing away. You will not have a lunch break today."

My stomach clenched. I had no appetite after my odious task, but I knew I would be suffering later.

"Very well, Karen," I said.

She looked surprised that I hadn't put up more of a fight, but she recovered quickly. "You will call me Mistress Karen," she said, putting her hands on her hips.

"Very well, Karen."

Her face reddened again and I resisted a grin. At least in that regard I could defy her.

Unfortunately, my cheekiness did not do me any favors for the rest of the day. My next task was to bathe Misty, which proved to be more difficult than scrubbing the chamber pot. The feline's hatred for me had not faded in the least when I unceremoniously dumped her into her bath water. I emerged with deep scratches on my arms and a drenched dress.

After that, I was sent to town to purchase the specific lavender-scented soap Narcissa wanted. I was turned out of the shop more than once, but after wiping off some of the cinders with my spit and straightening my dress in the alleyway, I was allowed to purchase the soap. I bought myself a bar with the money Karen gave me, just to spite her.

The sky had darkened when I returned to Narcissa's chambers, dirty and exhausted. I was told to stand as she supped.

"How did you like your first day, Amarante?" Narcissa said, stirring her soup.

I made no answer. I couldn't see her face but it was clear she was gloating. The aroma of her dinner wafted beneath my nose, tantalizing me. My stomach let out a pitiful growl.

She laughed. "Karen tells me you haven't eaten today, isn't that right, Karen?"

The maid bobbed her head and smiled. "Yes, milady."

A thin gold chain glimmered around her neck. I narrowed my eyes. No doubt she had been rewarded for treating me as badly as possible.

"You may have my leftovers," Narcissa said. She picked up a buttered roll and bit into it, chewing slowly. She set it down. "Then you may retire for the night."

My legs trembled with relief. I had been running errands for the better half of the day. But my relief soon turned into annoyance when the minutes ticked by and it became abundantly clear Narcissa was eating as slowly as possible.

She took a spoonful of soup, ate half of it, and put the rest back in the bowl. She took miniscule nibbles of the rolls. Her salad, she ate one leaf at a time. It was nearing midnight when she finally set her napkin down and gestured for me to take the tray. I bent over and took it.

"You may go," Narcissa said, reclining in her seat. "Karen. See her out."

The maid ushered me out of the room. "Don't be late tomorrow or you will be punished."

I wanted to say doing this was already punishment, but I was too exhausted and merely went off.

The dinner tray was as good as empty. Narcissa left a drop of soup, a crumb of bread, and a piece of garnish from the salad. I ate them all as I returned to my room, which looked smaller and drearier in the dark. After putting the dishes into the scullery, I collapsed onto the hard bed and fell into uneasy sleep.

The next day was not easier even when I expected what was to happen. My entire body ached when I was dragged out of bed by Madam Josephine who informed me that I was late once again. I hated the woman a little less when she thrust a warm roll into my hands and barked at me to be on my way. I devoured it in seconds.

Karen took great pleasure in my late arrival and had the honor of rapping my knuckles five times on each hand. I was then told to draw a bath for Narcissa. It took many trips to the pump to fill her unnecessarily large bathtub and hours to heat it up. When Narcissa was finished and dressed, I was to drain the water and give the tub a thorough scrub with the small brush Karen provided me.

After that was the stables. I groomed Narcissa's horse and cleaned its stall and nearly had my hand bitten off when I tried to give the creature an apple.

Several days passed this way under Karen and Narcissa's tyranny. I found myself ducking out of sight when I recognized the debutantes roaming the palace grounds, especially when I saw Olivia and Cedric. My limbs constantly ached. My tasks became more and more ridiculous.

When my crystal pulsed on the fourth day of servitude, I was in the middle of polishing Narcissa's windows with my sleeve under Karen's scrutiny. I stilled.

"Well? Get on with it!" Karen said from her place on the chaise longue. Narcissa had gone out for the afternoon, but I suspected that she would not take well to her maid reclined like a lady on her seat.

I tucked the crystal deeper into my bodice. "I have to relieve myself," I said.

Karen huffed. "You can wait."

"It's an emergency."

She made a face. "Fine. Make it quick."

I rushed from the room and ran to the servant's hall to grab the parcel of gold from my room. With the gold in tow, I called a horse chaise to the outskirts of town. The ride took fifteen minutes and I relished sitting down for once. When I arrived, I burst into Miriam's shop.

"Welcome to Miriam's—my goodness." The witch stared at me in shock.

"Can you tell Lana that I cannot make it today?" I said.

"I'll pass on the message, but—"

I dumped the parcel on her table, rattling the snail-ridden tree branch. "And please give this to her."

Miriam stared. "Very well, but what—?"

"Great. See you later!"

I was out the door and back on the chaise before she could say anything. There was little traffic on the way back, though several flocks of pigeons crowded the streets. The driver narrowly avoided them. I rushed back to Narcissa's chambers before thirty minutes was up.

Karen gave me a dirty look. "What took you so long?"

I feigned embarrassment. "I'm not sure you'd want the details."

This disgusted Karen enough that she left me well alone as I polished the remainder of the windows.

When Narcissa returned that evening she had a smile on her face. I stood warily as she cut her chicken into small cubes.

"Mother is hosting the soirée tomorrow night," she said. She took a sip of her wine. "You will have to attend, of course."

I almost laughed. Attending another Season event was the last thing on my mind.

"You expect me to go like this?" I said, spreading my arms. The servant's uniform Madam Josephine had given me was wrinkled and stained. The rough fabric was torn where Misty had clawed me. I couldn't imagine the state of my hair.

Narcissa rose from her seat and circled me like a hawk. Her scrutiny made me uncomfortable, as if she could pounce at any moment. "I admit I didn't think you would last this long," she said. "Karen. Come here."

The maid hurried over at her call and bobbed a curtsy. A new set of pearls shone from her earlobes. "Yes, milady?"

"Draw a bath for Amarante. Tonight, she will be taking your chambers."

Karen's jaw dropped. "B-but milady! You can't possibly—"

"Are you refusing my orders?" Narcissa narrowed her eyes.

"No, milady," Karen said. She exited the room, but not before shooting me a poisonous glare.

I would have gloated if not for my confusion.

Narcissa leaned back in her seat. "You will be made presentable. After all, we cannot have your friends thinking something is wrong," she said.

I felt a pang at the mention of my friends. A part of me wished I was brave enough to tell them the truth before any of this happened. There was no way I could pretend everything was fine when it wasn't. Genevieve especially would see right through me. And Ash. He would wonder why I hadn't been frequenting the library.

"I trust that you will not speak to them," Narcissa said.

"What?"

"You will pass the event with me," she said, taking another sip of wine. "You will not be allowed to wander."

My anger rose. "That wasn't a part of our agreement."

A flash of irritation crossed Narcissa's face. "Do you think I want to spend this much time around you?" she said in disgust. "You are a threat to my mother, Amarante. She wants you contained so you will be contained."

"Are you going to make me your slave forever?" I said, raising my voice. "Aren't you tired of having a traitor for a mother?"

Narcissa slammed her hand on the table, rattling the silverware. "I'd rather my mother be a traitor than a witch," she spat. The venom in her words stung me. She downed the last of her wine. "Do as I say or everyone will know what a monster you are."

"The only monster here is you," I said.

I barely had time to react before Narcissa slapped me hard across the face.

"Say that again," she hissed.

Karen came back in at that moment. "The bath is ready, milady," she said, her voice strained.

Narcissa stepped back. Her expression was once again a blank canvas. "Clean yourself," she said, turning her back to me. "Tomorrow you will look like royalty."

25

The gentlemen were gawking at me. It was the second most uncomfortable thing at the moment, the first being the ridiculously tight gown and itchy lace gloves Narcissa lent me. My scalp ached from Karen's rough combing.

As promised, I entered the palace parlor with Narcissa. My arms were tucked behind me. The black lace did wonders in concealing the scratches and calluses that I had acquired, but I felt as though the scrutiny of the room could cut through fabric.

I kept my head down as I followed Narcissa to the card tables where the duchess was standing with a few older women. They left when we approached.

"Narcissa. You brought her."

I curtsied, though paying respects to Duchess Wilhelmina was the last thing I wanted to do.

"Yes, Mother." Narcissa's face was unreadable.

The duchess smiled but it didn't reach her eyes. "Miss Flora, I do hope you enjoy tonight's festivities. I'm afraid it will be a while before you get a chance to do so again."

To others it may have appeared the duchess was speaking of the next Season event which wasn't for another ten days, but I figured her real meaning. I wouldn't be released from my punishment any time soon.

"I will try to relish it, Your Grace," I said stiffly.

"Good." Duchess Wilhelmina glided away and gave her daughter a look I couldn't decipher.

A woman from the card table began conversing with Narcissa, which gave me the freedom to look about the room. I recognized Tori in the gaggle of debutantes by the sofas. Genevieve was with her and they appeared to be distracted, no doubt wondering where I was.

I hadn't even sent them a note this week. My palms dampened and I shrunk back into the shadows, hoping they wouldn't recognize me. I hardly recognized myself.

"Ladies and gentlemen, may I have your attention?"

The sound of silverware on a wineglass rung through the parlor and the murmur of conversation stopped. The duchess stood at the front of the room. "As you all know, the Season is coming to a close with the Masquerade Ball, just in time for the arrival of Crown Prince Bennett. The Choosing Ceremony will take place directly after, where debutantes and gentlemen may pair up and announce their courtship."

Gasps and giggles sounded from the debutantes in the front.

"Not only will His Highness be attending, but he will choose a young lady amongst you to court. That young lady will have a chance of becoming the crown princess consort." The duchess looked at Narcissa when she said this. No one noticed, as they were too busy chattering among themselves. I thought I saw Samantha swoon onto a sofa.

"Of course, there is no guarantee that he will select one of you at all," the duchess continued, "but I understand that picking a future queen is strongly suggested by Her Majesty herself, given the unfortunate circumstances."

The chatter lowered to murmurs. I smiled mirthlessly. Being queen seemed less appealing when it involved possible assassination.

"Recent events have complicated this Season, but it is my hope, along with the other mentors and the queen, that we will end with a plethora of young couples and a future queen. Thank you, and enjoy tonight's gathering!" The duchess smiled and set down her wine glass. She was immediately swarmed by a handful of debutantes, one of them Julianna, who seemed more than eager to discuss the Masquerade Ball.

Narcissa gripped my wrist. "Stay here. I have an image to uphold." She smoothed her skirts and paused to give me a look. "In fact, stay here all night until I tell you to move. You know the consequences if you don't."

With that, she went off to her mother, leaving me by the card tables where several gentlemen were still gawking at me. I seated myself on the bench behind me and avoided their gaze. Cedric was a table away, chatting with Olivia. They hadn't noticed me yet and I prayed they wouldn't. At the moment I was more than happy to pretend to be a statue the entire evening. I couldn't imagine facing my neighbors or friends or stepsister.

Staring at the floor proved to be too difficult a task for my wandering eyes. I eventually found myself searching the room for Ash. After several seconds I spotted him by a potted plant. He was concealed by the broad leaves of a small fig tree. Given his sulking stance and lack of company, I figured he was less than thrilled to be here. His mother was being poisoned and he was at a soirée hosted by the culprit, whose daughter had a solid chance at becoming his brother's fiancée. It was ridiculous.

Our gaze met through the gaps of the plant. I ducked my head. Had he recognized me? I risked another peek and deflated with relief. He was looking somewhere else now. Unfortunately, my relief did not last very long.

"Amarante?" Olivia's soft voice nearly had me flying off my seat.

She and Cedric seated themselves beside me as I cracked a smile. "Cedric. Olivia. How lovely to see you two," I said, keeping my voice as unaffected as possible.

"You look beautiful," Olivia said, widening her eyes at my dress.

I smoothed the deep red fabric of my skirts which felt more suffocating by the second. "Oh, thank you. It's, er, a rental."

"Genevieve was looking everywhere for you," Cedric said. "I'll bring her over." He rose from his seat.

"Wait!" I said, forcing my smile wider. "Why don't we chat a while?"

He raised his brows but sat back down.

"How has everything been, living at the palace?" I said, looking to each of them.

"Oh, it's been lovely," Olivia said. "The gardens are beautiful. They let us roam around wherever we like."

Cedric described the palace views and the delicious meals they had each day. The conversation dwindled at Olivia's third description of the rose bushes near the pond and Cedric's talk of the weather the other morning.

"I think your sister has a lot she wants to speak to you about," Cedric said after a moment of awkward silence. He rose from his seat again but this time I made no effort to stop him.

My palms were slick with sweat. Narcissa and the duchess were on the far side of the room conversing with a group of debutantes and Lady Hortensia. Their backs were turned to me, which did little to ease my anxiety.

"What does 'NW' stand for?"

I jumped. "What?"

Olivia's nose was inches away my left hand. I jerked away.

"You have it written on your hand," she said.

At least she thought it was written and not scratched on. I shrugged, trying to ignore the perspiration on my back. "Northwest," I said. "I have to remember which direction my home is from the palace."

I had no idea if home was northwest from the palace, but neither did Olivia. She looked perplexed, but didn't question me further. It was then Cedric came back with Genevieve and Tori.

"Gosh, it's been ages since we've seen you!" Tori said, wrestling me into a hug.

"I missed you, Amarante," Genevieve said. She looked lovelier than ever in a satin gown of sea foam green. It appeared that Cedric hadn't failed to notice, judging from the way he was staring at her.

I felt tears spring to my eyes. "I missed you too. And you, Tori, along with the rest of your family."

Tori squinted. "Are you crying? It's only been a week, for goodness sake."

"It felt much longer than a week," I muttered, quickly blinking away the moisture.

"How are Theodora and Rowena doing?" Genevieve asked, taking a seat next to me.

"They're still sick," I said. "I think it'll be a while before they recover. Maybe until the end of the Season."

My stepsister furrowed her brow. "That's awful. I ought to go back with you."

I shook my head profusely. "You really shouldn't. The replacement cook stepmother hired is struggling. I don't think she'll be able to handle an additional person."

"Alright. Should I write them, then?"

"No need! I'll pass on your regards," I said.

Tori squeezed in between me and Olivia. "When you were gone, Prince Ash sent you a load of letters," she said with a suggestive look.

I cringed. "Did he?" It then occurred to me that I hadn't given Ash an excuse for my absence.

"That's right. After the fifth letter I had to write a note saying you weren't there. I bet that's why he's looking so mopey."

Ash was looking mopey. He was still behind the fig tree, but Samantha had approached him. No doubt she was trying some last-minute flattery before the Masquerade Ball.

"You should go to him," Genevieve said.

I blushed in spite of myself. "I don't feel like getting up."

"Oh, excuses, excuses," Tori said. She pulled me out of my seat. I threw a panicked glance at Narcissa. She was still conversing. The duchess was nowhere to be found. I trembled to think what she would do if she found out I defied her daughter.

"No, really. I would much rather stay here," I said, easing myself out of Tori's grasp, which proved to be no easy task. Her fingers were like steel.

"Come on, Amarante! I never took you for a coward," she said.

Our movement must've caused some disturbance, for Ash turned and caught my eye again. This time his brows raised in recognition and he excused himself from Samantha. I held back a groan as I sat back down.

"We'll step aside for a moment," Tori whispered loudly. She took Olivia by the arm, leaving Cedric to take Genevieve. It seemed like her matchmaking skills weren't wasted during my absence.

I frowned at their retreating forms as I became increasingly aware of the princely figure approaching me. I didn't look at him until he cleared his throat.

"Amarante," Ash said.

"Hello." I rose, and feeling Narcissa's glare, curtsied to avoid her gaze.

Ash looked thrown off at the sudden formality. I wanted to give him an apologetic look but found I couldn't meet his gaze either.

"You look nice," he said, clearing his throat again.

"Thank you. It's a rental."

"I wasn't talking about the dress."

I felt another blush crawl to my cheeks. "Would you like to sit?"

He took a seat on the bench. "Tori says you went home this week."

"I did. My nannies were sick," I said. I hated how easily the lie came the second time around. "Sorry I didn't get your letters."

"It's alright. We can talk now," Ash said. "I'm looking for Peter right now. I'll have to check the Witch Market—"

"I don't think this is the best place to discuss this," I said, fiddling with my gloves. I felt Narcissa's glare again. She was closer now.

"You're right. Let's get out of here."

I gripped the bench when Ash offered his hand. "Oh. I…I can't go."

He tilted his head. "Why not?"

Narcissa walked over. I decided to let her do the talking, which probably wasn't the best idea.

"She wants to stay with me," Narcissa said. "Your Highness."

Ash gave me a questioning look, but I turned my head away.

"After all, my mother worked very hard to put this soirée together. It would be rude to leave in the middle of it, wouldn't it?"

"It would," I said quietly. "I'm sorry. I would much rather stay."

I kept my head turned, but hearing Ash's voice was enough to make me miserable.

"I see. I won't keep you from enjoying the gathering." With a stiff bow, he was gone.

Narcissa narrowed her eyes. "What were you two talking about?"

"Nothing. Nothing at all."

26

Perspiration dampened my back as I sprinted to Miriam's shop the next afternoon, wiping the ashes off my face. I had thrown on a clean gown before setting out, though the sleeves were already soiled with grime. My crystal pulsed incessantly. I was late. Lana would not be pleased.

"Amarante? Is that you?"

I skidded to a stop at the sound of Olivia's voice. She was several paces away, rolling leisurely in a horse chaise with her brother. I froze. There was no avoiding the confrontation now.

"Olivia! And Cedric. Hello," I said nervously when our paths intersected. The driver looked at me with a mixture of alarm and disgust. Narcissa was especially heavy-handed with the cinders today.

"Goodness, what happened to you?" Cedric exclaimed, half-rising from his seat. Olivia looked like she was going to stop the driver.

"Nothing. I, er, accidentally fell into a fireplace!" I said, backing away. "Please don't delay your trip for me. I'll see you later!"

Before either of them could reply, I darted around the corner and waited for them to pass. When the sound of hooves and wheels faded away, I slipped into Miriam's shop, my heart pounding. Hiding so many things at once was getting difficult.

Miriam raised a brow at my disheveled appearance. "This is the second time you showed up like this," she said, following me to the back room. The air felt stuffier than usual. "I hope you're not in trouble and not telling anyone. Because that would be idiotic, dear."

I pressed in the usual bricks. My sigh of exasperation was drowned out when the wall rolled back into the tunnel. "I'm fine, Miriam. Don't tell Theodora or Rowena, alright?"

Miriam huffed and let the tapestry drop.

I was wheezing for air by the time I arrived at Lana's cottage. She was standing outside with an irritable expression. "Good heavens. Have you been hired as a scullery maid?"

Even if she was the only person I could tell without consequence, I didn't.

Lana merely shook her head at my silence and opened the door. "Come inside. We've wasted enough time."

"Can we make the truth potion today?" I asked as Lana rummaged through her cupboard. "Miriam sent you the gold."

The parcel was sitting on her counter, untouched. Lana's shoulders stiffened when she glanced at it. "How did you come by this?" she asked, her tone accusing.

"I acquired it fairly."

Lana continued rummaging through the shelves. She behaved the same way last time, avoiding my gaze and my questions. I was tired of her evasive behavior.

"I told you not to meddle in human affairs," she said.

A flash of irritation came over me. What business did she have telling me what and what not to do? "Give me the instructions. I can make it myself—"

"I lied." She slammed the cupboard and whirled around, eyes flashing.

"What?"

"I lied about the gold. You don't need gold to make truth potion," Lana said. She barked a mirthless laugh. "I told you that to discourage you. I know whatever you're planning involves the royals and that prince. You're better off minding your own business."

"You *lied* to me?" The thought of Lana lying didn't sit well with me. I trusted her. She was my teacher, my mentor.

Lana frowned. "I did it to protect you. You don't know what you're getting yourself into."

"What I'm getting into is none of your business!" I said, clenching my fists. "You don't understand. People will suffer if I don't have that potion."

She slammed her hand on the counter. "Witches suffer every day," she said, voice booming in the small space. "And yet humans do nothing. *Nothing.* They care nothing for us, Amarante, can't you see? They are vermin upon this earth, destroying everything for their selfish desires. That prince will find you repulsive. Why are you helping him when he will kill you if you reveal yourself?"

I stumbled back, struck by the hatred in her eyes. Ash would never go so far as to *kill* me.

"How dare you!" I shouted. "What right do you have to speak to me that way?"

"Do you know what that enchantment on my door was when you first came to me?" Lana asked. "Do you know why you were able to pass when everyone else couldn't?"

I bit my lip hard enough to draw blood. What could she possibly mean by changing the subject?

She exhaled sharply when I didn't answer. "It was meant to repel all but my own blood."

"What do you mean?" I demanded.

"Your mother was my sister, Amarante," Lana said shakily. "You are my niece."

And then everything made sense. Why Theodora and Rowena insisted on taking me to Lana specifically. The look Beatrice had given her. Why Lana had Mama's things. I felt like somebody was squeezing me so tightly I couldn't breathe.

"Fraternizing with humans led to Seraphina's death. She was so foolish. That silver bracelet ruined everything," Lana said, pointing a trembling finger at the chain of bells around my wrist. "She conceived with your coward of a father who never told you the circumstances of your own birth. Then she killed herself when they found her out. She killed herself to protect you and that man. Humans are cruel, worthless creatures. That queen deserves to be poisoned."

"How could you say that?" I said, my voice breaking.

"Not only that," Lana said. A dark look came over her visage. "I created manbane."

The floor spun.

Lana took a shuddering breath. "And when you came to me, I knew I shouldn't have accepted you. But I couldn't help myself. I am your aunt, Amarante, and I…I cannot have what happened to your mother happen to you."

"You're no aunt of mine." I nearly spat the words out. "You insult my Papa. You say humans are vermin upon this earth. You refuse to cure an innocent you poisoned! You are *wicked*."

I snatched my bag and fled from Lana's cottage. She didn't call for me and I didn't care to look back. My vision was too blurred with tears. I flew down Witch Village, ignoring the passersby. How dare she lie? How could she have kept everything from me all this time? To think I respected her! To think I wanted to make her proud!

The traverse through the tunnel for once felt too short. I wasn't done fuming when Miriam received me in her back room. She gave me an appraising look. "So. She told you?"

I gave a stiff nod and wiped my eyes. My sleeves came away wet.

"Must've done it in a darned awful way, then," Miriam said with a snort. She pulled out a porcelain tea set from a low shelf. "Care for some tea?"

I sank down into a pouf before a low table as Miriam clattered about, levitating the tea cups and shooting a spout of flame underneath the kettle.

She arranged herself before me. Her gaudy brass jewelry gleamed in the dim lamps hanging from the ceiling, a welcome distraction. I didn't wish to see her face. No doubt she pitied me, or was guilty for lying to me from the start.

Miriam, Lana, Theodora, Rowena, and Papa. All of them lied to me.

The water in the kettle simmered. I stared at my tea cup. It had snails painted on it and the rim was dipped in gold.

Miriam heaved a mighty sigh. "Seraphina...She was one of those young witches too curious for their own good."

I said nothing, but she continued. "She was no older than you when she got the bright idea to pretend to be human and explore their world. She came to me, of course, because I liked assisting the young and curious." Miriam

chuckled. "I didn't see the harm in letting her roam around a bit. But that silly girl wanted more. She wanted to attend the Season.

"I didn't think she'd pull it off, but in a fortnight, she had a false identity and went off to the palace with some money she magicked. There, she fell in love with your father. Lana hated the match. But Seraphina didn't care."

Mama had always been a figment of my imagination, an empty space I knew should have been filled but simply wasn't. To hear her story was like filling that space. Even in my current state, I hungered for more. "When did Papa know?"

"When she became pregnant with you. Once she had you, the facade she built to attend the Season began to crumble. Magicked money isn't permanent. Eventually a dressmaker did some digging and found holes in her story. It wasn't long before he was blabbering about it to the public.

"Your father wanted to escape the kingdom, but Seraphina refused. Delibera had become her home. She couldn't bear for you to live as an outcast, or risk exposing the location of Witch Village. She took her own life before the authorities figured out her identity. I had to tell Lana the news myself. She didn't like me very much after that."

I closed my eyes. Papa's absence made sense now. Perhaps he couldn't bear to see me after what Mama did to protect us.

"But Theodora and Rowena," I said. "Who were they in all this?"

"They were your mother's closest friends. They offered to raise you. At your father's request they suppressed your magic for sixteen years. I don't think either of them expected you to come to Witch Village. It was Seraphina's wish to not see you suffer the same fate she did."

"You knew. When you first saw me, you knew who I was," I said, warming my shaking fingers with the steam rising from my tea. "Why didn't you say anything?"

Miriam shrugged. "It wasn't my place."

I shook my head. It didn't matter anymore. I couldn't change my family's past. But there was still one thing I could do.

"Miriam, do you have the recipe for truth potion?"

27

She raised a thick brow. "What do you need that for?"

"Do you have it?"

"Yes." She looked like she was going to object, but got up from her seat nonetheless to a shelf of spherical terrariums. There was a secret compartment underneath, from which she handed me a folded piece of paper.

"What do you need it for?" she asked again, but I had already crossed the beaded curtain.

Sudden knocking at the front door stopped me in my tracks.

"Open up. Royal business."

Miriam walked over. She peered out of the narrow slot, then withdrew with a frown. "I really hope this has nothing to do with you."

I didn't answer as she opened the door. Soldiers dressed in the purple of the Royal Guard marched in, towering over the witch's short frame. If Miriam was intimidated, she didn't show it.

"Hello, gentlemen. May I interest you in some snails? Buy two and get a terrarium free."

The leader, a man with a very long nose and large feet, motioned for the other guards. Three of them began to search the shop.

"We're here to look for evidence of witches or witch-related items," he said, looking down at her. "Meanwhile, I need you to answer some questions. Have you come into contact with any witches recently or in the past few months?"

Miriam gasped. "Witches? My goodness, sir! You don't expect an old woman like me to meet any witches and survive the encounter," she said, pulling her shawls tighter around her shoulders. "I merely sell my little pets for a living."

The guard looked around the room, cringing visibly. No doubt he was thinking the same thoughts I had when I first stepped foot in Miriam's shop. "I see. Then do you have any useful information about the whereabouts of the Witch Market?"

She pressed her fingers to her lips. "You mean that awful place where curses and poisons are bottled and sold like raspberry jam?"

"That's right."

"I assure you, sir, if I knew anything of it, I'd go to the authorities straight away," Miriam said, looking earnestly at the guard. "I do not sleep easy knowing there are witches out there selling such heinous things."

The guard grunted and shook his head. "Unfortunately, it is the world we live in, madam," he said.

I figured why Miriam was made guardian—she was an impeccable actress. As the guard asked her another question, I inched toward the doorway, desperate to leave. I had been gone for longer than I wanted. No doubt Karen already tattled to Narcissa about my absence.

But as I was about to cross the threshold, I came face to face with Ash.

His eyes widened. "What are you doing here?" he said, walking into the shop.

I took a step back, too surprised to talk.

"Your Highness," the guard said, bowing. "I was questioning this shop owner." He darted a glance at me. "Er, I will question her next."

Ash took my arm, his fingers burning through my sleeve. "No need. She's with me."

Miriam's jaw fell as she looked from me to Ash. I avoided her questioning gaze and followed him outside. There were several horses waiting on the cobblestone with another guard. Ash led me to a lamp post, far enough to prevent eavesdropping.

"What are you doing here?" he repeated. The lamp light cast harsh shadows across his features.

"I…I was shopping for a snail," I said. It was a horrible lie. No one in their right mind would buy anything from Miriam's shop.

"You've been crying."

I lowered my head. "I haven't."

"Amarante." Ash took my shoulders, forcing me to look at him. "Why won't you tell me what's wrong?"

I moved away with a laugh, my cheeks aching from the fraudulence. "Nothing is wrong. I didn't find a snail I like, that's all."

He didn't smile. "Last night and now this. You're worrying me."

"I don't know what you're talking about," I said, turning around. "Listen, I have to go."

Ash grabbed my hand, squeezing my knuckles as he did so. I sucked in a breath. My reaction did not go unnoticed.

"What is this?" he said, staring at the welts on the back of my hand. They had not yet healed from yesterday's raps.

Before I could come up with an excuse, Ash pushed up my sleeve and revealed the angry red scratches I had acquired in the past week.

I yanked my arm away. "It's nothing. I fell this morning." The lie came smoothly, but my throat seized at his expression.

"Let me see your other arm," he said, stepping forward.

I stepped back as he advanced, holding both my arms behind my back. Narcissa's initials were still scratched on my other hand. I didn't think Ash would take long to figure out that "NW" didn't actually stand for northwest.

"I promise it's nothing," I said, but Ash looked determined. My back hit a wall of a building.

"If it's nothing, why are you hiding it?" he demanded.

I didn't expect the moisture that sprung to my eyes. I wanted to tell Ash that nothing had gone right after my meeting with the duchess. But I knew if I did, he would have no wish to help me. I blinked, feeling hot tears run down my face.

Ash looked taken aback. He stepped away. "I'm sorry. I didn't mean to scare you—"

I shook my head. "Can you trust me?"

His eyes softened. "I do trust you."

"Then understand I have my reasons. I…I want to go home." My voice broke. I missed Theodora and Rowena and poking fun at our neighbors with Genevieve. I missed when all I worried about was filling up time. I even missed Lydia's ramblings.

Ash pulled me into a hug. I buried my face into his shoulder and sobbed like a baby. His scent of evergreen and peppermint was a comforting familiarity in a sea of confusion.

"I'll take you home," he said.

"No. I'll take a horse chaise."

"Fine. But mark my words, I will find out what's wrong," he said. After a second, he gently kissed my knuckles and left.

Ash's words repeated themselves in my head as I rolled down the street in the horse chaise. His kiss burned the back of my hand like a promise—a promise I hoped he wouldn't keep.

My eyes were swollen when I leaned over and told the driver to switch our route to the palace. He turned the horse around, reentering the outskirts of the city from the opposite side.

It was so late by the time I returned that I didn't bother to check back in with Karen. The only thing that mattered now was setting things right.

I had to fix Lana's mistake no matter what it took. She was wrong about humans, especially Ash. He needed my help.

I looked over the recipe Miriam gave me. The directions seemed simple enough, but it would take three days to make. Most of the ingredients could be acquired in an herb garden, but several of them I would have to beg off Miriam.

The next morning, I rose early and stuffed my pockets with sage and rosemary from the cook's herb garden. Madam Josephine seemed surprised to see me on time as I passed the servants' hall on the way to Narcissa's chambers. I did my chores in silence as Karen boasted about her new ring. I wasn't even upset when Narcissa left me nothing but a few crumbs of bread for dinner.

After dropping off her dishes in the scullery, I picked out a small pot that still had remnants of vegetable stew and smuggled it into my room. The leftovers served as my dinner. I slept easier that night knowing that in a few short days, I'd make the duchess confess her crimes and finally be freed from servitude.

I readied the brick oven in my room with a grate and a few coals I had stolen the next day. For the small pot, I fashioned a wire handle so it could hang like a witch's cauldron. The day after that, I paid a visit to Miriam.

"You want what?" the witch asked, frowning at me through her gauzy veil.

"Pheender leaves," I said. "Do you have any?"

Miriam snorted. "You think I have something as expensive as that lying around? And what do you need it for anyway? To make someone vomit?"

More specifically, to make someone vomit words. I suspected she was feigning ignorance. She herself had given me a potion recipe a few days before. After pestering her for half an hour and even offering to purchase a snail, Miriam finally gave in.

"Fine! I'll get you everything you need," she said, scowling. "But you owe me an explanation. For everything."

I sighed. "Only if you promise not to tell anyone," I said, sinking into a pouf. "The truth potion is for the duchess."

I explained helping Ash with the case, the framing of Captain Greenwood, and how the duchess found out I was a witch and forced me to be a scullery maid for her daughter.

Miriam threw back her veil when I finished. "All this

time you were in trouble and you didn't say anything?" She looked livid.

"I am now," I said in a small voice.

She shook her head. "What you need to do is ask your aunt for the manbane antidote."

"So," I said with a frown, "you know Lana created manbane."

Miriam sighed. "I do. And I understand how you must be feeling, but Amarante, your aunt isn't the same witch she was when she made that potion."

"She is not my aunt."

"Fine," Miriam said after a moment of glaring. "Since you insist on being stubborn, I have something that might postpone the effects of manbane for a few days."

She rummaged through a hidden compartment underneath a chest of drawers and pulled out a familiar container. It was the general antidote I had given her so many weeks ago, untouched.

"Lana makes the best of the best," she said when I made a face.

I took it with a sigh. It seemed that I couldn't escape Lana even if I tried.

That same night, I began making the truth potion, pouring every bit of my focus into it. I lost hours of sleep sitting beside my makeshift potion room, fanning the coals to the right temperature and snuffing out embers before something blew up. My only companions were the occasional mice and roaches that scurried through poorly patched holes along the walls. I was too tired to be disgusted by them.

My knuckles suffered extra raps the next morning for my lethargy. I told myself that every bruise was worth it as

Karen fawned over a new necklace. If things went my way, her jewelry box would never be filled to the brim.

On the third night, I ran into a problem. The recipe required a hair from the person forced to tell the truth.

I had to find a way to acquire a strand of Duchess Wilhelmina's hair.

My chance came when Karen decided to take advantage of Narcissa's frequent absences.

"I have an appointment in the city," she said. She was dressed in a fine gown, adorned with all the jewelry she had earned since I began working. "If you peep a word about it to milady, I will tell her you've been careless with your work."

I was all too glad to see her leave and even wished her a good afternoon. If only mine could be as enjoyable.

I dropped the mop I was using somewhat reluctantly. The duchess's suite was right beside Narcissa's, easily accessible through a shared door near the fireplace. Narcissa used it frequently to visit her mother. I knew for a fact it was always unlocked. That made the first part of my job easy.

Now came the difficult part—actually going inside.

The duchess's schedule was a mystery to me, though I never took her as a woman who lounged among her wealth all day. I pressed my ear against the door and waited. When no sound came, I slipped in. The chamber was empty. I began to search.

Finding a strand of hair in a very large, well-kept suite proved to be a difficult task. There wasn't a speck of dust on the furniture or a streak of dirt on the floor. I looked under pillows and cushions and rugs.

Not a single hair in sight.

After overturning the living space, I mustered up the courage to enter the duchess's bedroom. It was ridiculously lavish like everything else in the suite, furnished with a canopied bed, a polished mahogany vanity, and a large armoire with a full-length mirror. The scent of soap in the air told me the bed sheets had been freshly laundered.

I scowled at the pristine pillows and set to work on the vanity drawers. But drawer after drawer was filled with brooches and rouge and powder.

At last, I found a golden hairbrush at the bottom. I nearly crumpled with relief. The bristles were full of brassy red hair. Pulling off a clump, I stuffed it into my pocket.

Just as I celebrated my success, a hiss came from the doorway.

I dropped the hairbrush, sending a perfume bottle crashing to the floor.

Misty stalked into the room, her back arched and tail stiff in the air.

I backed into the vanity.

The cat continued toward me. Her acid green eyes were more unsettling than usual. There was a glint of intelligence in them, right beside the more obvious glint of malevolence.

The corner of the vanity dug into my lower back.

"Good kitty," I said, trying to shoo her away. My voice was horribly shaky and only seemed to agitate her further. Was my hard work doomed to be destroyed by a cat?

Misty pounced.

Sharp claws pierced through my dress, biting into my shins. I shrieked and tried to shake the feline off, but only kicked drawers open. Glass bottles and jewelry flew out like cannonballs. Misty scrambled up my legs. Before her fangs could sink into my arm, I flung her onto the bed.

She landed amongst the pillows, hissing. Instead of attacking again, she turned her tail up and fled the room.

I stared open-mouthed at the chaos that marred the once immaculate room. Shattered glass bottles glittered from the tiles like hazardous snow, dotted with sapphire necklaces and diamond brooches. A pot of rouge had overturned on the rug, staining the brocade a bright poppy red. A deep dent scarred a drawer I kicked away, the wood splintered.

Sweat pooled into my palms. The duchess would no doubt know someone had intruded.

After making sure the commotion didn't bring anyone inside, I cleaned up the best I could, shoving the drawers back in and throwing the glass shards out the window. The rest I swept under the rug. I hoped the gardener wouldn't notice the broken perfume bottles in his pansies.

When I exited, Misty was pacing before the door that led back to Narcissa's chambers. She arched her back when I took a step toward her. I shuddered, turning to the exit instead. I'd rather risk the short trek down the hallway than another round of feline attack.

I slipped out, noticing too late that I had company. And this time it wasn't a cat.

"This is the girl I was talking about, Sir Hughes," Narcissa said, crossing her arms. Behind her were four armed guards and a smug-looking Karen. "She is the thief."

28

My arms were twisted behind my back before I could react.

Sir Hughes, the bulkiest guard, stepped up and looked me up and down. He had a thick mustache that drowned his mouth.

"She certainly looks like a thief," he said with a sniff. "Don't worry, milady. I'll have her thrown in the dungeons with the rest of her kind."

"I haven't stolen anything!" I protested, attempting to wriggle out of the other guards' grasp. They held tight. "I'm innocent!"

Sir Hughes grunted. "Search her."

One of the guards behind me nodded, but I shot him a withering look.

"I'll do it," Karen said. She looked extremely pleased with herself as she patted down my arms and legs. When she reached my pockets, her smile spread even wider. "There's something here!"

The only things in my pockets were a wad of hair and a day-old dinner roll. I knew that for a fact, so I was surprised to say the least when Karen pulled out a glittering ruby bracelet.

"T-that wasn't there before!" I said as Sir Hughes's mustache drooped down in displeasure.

"Nice try," he said gruffly. "Bold of you to steal from the duchess. Too bad you're not smart enough to get away with it. Take her away, men."

"Wait!" Narcissa and I said in unison. I gaped at her, but the look on her face wasn't one that wanted to help. "This isn't her first time sneaking into my mother's chambers. Perhaps she has more in her room."

Sir Hughes nodded. "Then let us search there too."

The guard holding me shoved me forward. "Lead the way."

My legs felt like limp noodles as I made the trek down the hall. It was clear Karen set me up. She and Narcissa knew I'd be snooping around Duchess Wilhelmina's suite. But how? And where did that ruby bracelet come from?

It didn't make any sense. And now I was leading a procession of armed guards and snobbish girls into my room with my arms tied behind my back. There was no doubt Narcissa had more jewelry planted there, otherwise she would've let the guards take me straight to the dungeons.

My situation grew more and more hopeless until I spotted a familiar figure at the end of the hall. It was Ash. And he was walking toward us.

Sir Hughes and the guards bowed as he approached. "Good afternoon, Your Highness."

Ash looked right past me. "What's going on?"

"A thief was found in my mother's suite," Narcissa said

before Sir Hughes' mustache could quiver. "I believe she's an acquaintance of yours?"

Ash met my gaze and his eyes widened. "Amarante! Why are you dressed like that? Release her immediately!"

"I apologize, Your Highness," Sir Hughes said. "This girl was caught stealing from the duchess. We are to search her rooms for more stolen items. Good day, now."

"I did not steal anything," I said again, emboldened by Ash's presence.

"Of course you didn't," he said. He turned to the guards. "Release her. She's not a thief. She's a debutante."

"In that case she's a thieving debutante," Karen said, snickering. She coughed when Ash stared at her. "Your Highness."

I swallowed, my throat dry. "Just search my room," I said.

It was clear Narcissa wanted Sir Hughes to uncover the jewelry she placed there. My only hope was that Ash could convince them I was being framed.

"See? She might as well have admitted to her crimes," Sir Hughes said with a shrug. "Let's go, men. Good day, Your Highness."

Ash shooed away the guards behind me and untied my hands. "I'm coming with you."

The mustached guard shrugged again. "It's all the same to me. Make sure you've got a good grip on her. Thieves are slippery."

It was a tense walk to the servant's hall with a tenser silence that marching feet or clearing throats couldn't break. I knew Ash wanted to ask me a million questions. I hardly knew the answers to the ones I was asking myself.

Madam Josephine scurried out of the way as we marched down the hall to my room.

"Well," Narcissa said. "Get on with it."

I took a breath and pushed open the door. But instead of jewelry, my room was littered with herbs and vials of witch-made ingredients I could have sworn I put away. The pot still hung over the oven, filled with the truth potion. My blood froze.

"What is this?" Sir Hughes bellowed. "What have you been doing here?"

The guards streamed into the room, inspecting the potion ingredients. "Witchcraft!" one of them bellowed, holding up a jar of pheender leaves.

Naricssa swooned and Karen caught her. "A witch!" she cried, pointing a shaking finger at me. "You must be the one who poisoned the queen!"

"Narcissa, this was not part of our deal," I said. "The duchess *promised*."

"What deal?" Narcissa said.

"She said if I served you—"

"Nonsense! You are changing the subject on purpose. You poisoned the queen!"

"I would never hurt Her Majesty," I said, running into the room. "I have an antidote for her!" I grabbed the bottle of general antidote from my bed stand and held it out.

Sir Hughes and the guards recoiled. I looked desperately at Ash. His face was unreadable.

"Ash, please—"

"You've been getting close to the prince on purpose," Narcissa said. She had abandoned her shocked guise, but no one noticed. "You pretended to be helping him when in fact you were the culprit all along."

I shook my head, backing into my bed as the guards advanced. "No, I can prove it! I wasn't making poison. It's a truth potion! Duchess Wilhelmina is the one poisoning the queen. You have to believe me!"

Narcissa gasped. "How dare you taint my mother's name?" She gestured around the room. "This is evidence enough! You're using magic."

"A thief and a witch and a traitor." Sir Hughes frowned. "There's a special place in the dungeon for your kind. Seize her."

The guards grabbed me again, but this time more gingerly. It was clear they were frightened. My pleading fell on deaf ears.

"Stop," Ash said quietly.

Relief flooded through me. There was still hope. But when I tried to meet his eyes, he kept them firmly on the ground.

"Amarante. Is it true you're a witch?"

I opened my mouth to answer. Then I realized my situation.

I was in a room full of people who detested magic and those who possessed it. Ash hadn't asked the guards to release me. He asked if I was a witch. There was fear in his manner—something I never expected would be toward me.

My voice broke. "Yes."

"There. She admits it," Narcissa said almost gleefully. "Throw her in the dungeons where she belongs."

Sir Hughes motioned for the guards to take me away. "Your Highness, it would be perfectly understandable if you would like to personally—"

"No." Ash shouldered his way past the guards and past me. "I'm finished here."

And he was gone.

They dragged me to the dungeons and threw me into a windowless cell of stone. Save for the grate in the high ceiling, there was no light. Darkness fell when they slammed the door.

I collapsed onto the straw-littered floor at the sound of heavy chains and a lock clicking shut, numb to everything but my thoughts.

Ash believed Narcissa's lies. Had Lana been right about the royals all this time? He let me shoulder the crimes of the duchess after all I had done to help him. After all the evidence we had found. I never had a chance to explain myself.

If only the guards knew the potion in the cauldron wasn't poison. If only there was someone who could clear my name. I sat up.

Erasmus.

Erasmus could do it. He could tell them I wasn't a traitor. He was the only person in the palace who wasn't afraid of witches.

I scrambled to the door and pounded it, ignoring the splinters digging into my flesh. "Is anyone out there? Please let me see Erasmus Lenard, the royal inspector!"

My plea was met with silence. Echoes of the other prisoners' cries seeped in through the stone, but no answer to my request. I banged the door again. "Please! Someone call for Erasmus Lenard! I'm innocent and I can prove it!"

The slot above my head slid open.

"Quiet down," a gruff voice of a guard said. I didn't recognize the bushy brows and creased eyes, which was a good sign. Maybe he didn't know I was a witch.

"Please, sir! There's been a misunderstanding. I've been wrongly accused. I can prove my innocence if I see Erasmus Lenard, the royal inspector."

The bushy brows lowered. "You're the witch?" he said. "The one who has been poisoning Her Majesty the queen?"

"I-I didn't poison Queen Cordelia!" I said. "I can prove it—"

"You're a witch?"

"Well, yes, but—"

The guard snorted. "Then it doesn't matter if you poisoned the queen or not. Either way your trial and execution are in one week, when the king and crown prince return from overseas."

The air seemed to be sucked out of my lungs. "What? Trial *and* execution?"

"That's right. Save your breath for the king. I don't want to hear your jabbering." He began to close the slot, but I stuck my fingers in before he could.

"B-but sir, I'm begging you—"

The guard's eyes narrowed. "Make any more noise and you'll be executed tomorrow."

He slammed the slot closed. I yanked my throbbing fingers out and kicked the door in frustration, stubbing my toe. Tears welled up in my eyes and fell down my face in fat droplets.

I had one week. If I didn't prove my innocence, I'd die. And if I did, I'd die. All because I was a witch.

Lana had been right all along. Witches could never live among humans. They could never trust us, especially those with power.

How could I have been so blind? Of course Ash felt the same way about witches—he was a prince. He *wanted* to be involved in royal business. And he was taken aback by the idea of me associating with witches. Even after what I had done to help him, he still believed Narcissa over me.

"Miss Flora? Is that you?" A faint voice came by the wall I was sobbing against. I paused.

"Who is it?" I said hoarsely.

"It's Greenwood."

The captain's voice was just as I remembered. From a gap between two stones, a sliver of an overgrown beard and crinkled eyes appeared.

"I'm guessing you heard everything," I said, embarrassed to be caught in hysterics.

"I did." To my surprise, there wasn't a hint of fear or disgust in his tone. He sounded almost defeated. "I suppose I'll be joining you in a week."

I sank onto the floor and hugged my knees. "No, you won't. You'll be released. There's no reason to keep you here when they have me. I'm the witch and therefore the only culprit."

"Make that two culprits. I, too, am a witch."

I paused. Had I heard him wrong? "Pardon?"

"I am a witch," the captain said simply, as if he hadn't shocked me to the core. "Or, was. I had my magic removed, but I've hidden the fact for far too long. It's only fair for me to bring it up at our trial. You mustn't shoulder the burden alone."

"W-what?" I sputtered. "Why aren't you down in Witch Village? Why did you decide to stay here?"

"Simple. I was curious and then I fell in love," he said.

Curiosity and love. It seemed that all they did to witches was kill them.

I laughed bitterly. "Do you regret it?" I said. "Was your wife worth the trouble?"

"It...wasn't my wife," he said. "It was Wilhelmina."

Yet again, I found myself at a loss for words.

The captain continued. "She was a different woman once, if you can believe it. Jealousy ruined her. I will always treasure our love, even if it was fleeting." He sighed heavily. "The only thing I regret is leaving my daughter with her."

"You had a daughter?" I said.

Dread pooled into my gut when I realized who she was.

"Yes. You know her as Lady Narcissa."

My fists clenched. I dug them into the floor. "Narcissa is half witch."

"Yes. An herbwitch, to be exact. She was born between two worlds, but was as carefree as any other child. I'd let her use her magic when she visited me. She had a wonderful way with animals," the captain said wistfully.

Animals. Narcissa had a way with animals. "How did her magic work, exactly?" I said.

If he noticed how tense my voice was, he didn't show it. "She could read their thoughts and feelings and persuade them to do things for her. One time her favorite kite got stuck in a tree. She asked the pigeons to retrieve it," Captain Greenwood said with a chuckle.

"Would it be possible for her to convince swans to flip over a boat? A cat to do her bidding? Or maybe mice to spy for her?" I said stiffly.

"Yes. I would imagine she could," he said, "but Narcissa never used her magic for harm. She had the kindest heart. She used to help the neighborhood squirrels prepare for winter."

It was difficult to imagine the snobbish, cruel Narcissa as the girl Captain Greenwood was talking about. I didn't have the heart to tell him that the duchess had stripped all the good from their daughter, so I merely grunted.

One thing was clear, though. The duchess and Narcissa were behind everything. And they made sure a witch would be blamed for all of it.

I did not know how many hours passed when I woke up to a noise at the door. A tray clattered in through the lower slot. The contents rolled onto the ground—a stale hunk of bread and a bowl of watered-down porridge.

My stomach turned. I was in no mood to eat, but I reached over nonetheless.

"Psst. Little flower."

There was only one person who called me that. "Erasmus?" I scrambled to the floor and peered through the slot.

Sure enough, it was the inspector.

"I heard through the grapevine you wanted to see me," he said, squinting through the poor lighting. He was sprawled on the floor too. There was no sign of guards around him. "They found out, huh?"

"Yes." I shifted closer on my elbows, ignoring the straw digging into my skin. "I wanted to see you but it doesn't matter now. They're going to kill me in a week."

Erasmus grumbled. "I see. To think I wasted a dose of sleeping draught to hear that."

A thunderous snore sounded from outside.

"Thank you for visiting, anyhow," I said. "You're the only person in the palace who isn't afraid of me."

"What about that prince of yours?"

My throat tightened at the mention of Ash. I wiped the spilled porridge away with a handful of straw.

"Ah. I see." Erasmus harrumphed. "I'll give him a good talking to after this."

"Don't bother," I said quietly. I shut my eyes and sighed. "But since you're here I have a favor to ask."

Erasmus left shortly after with instructions to notify the Strongfoots what had happened. Genevieve would have to pass on the news to Theodora and Rowena.

My heart ached to think how they would react. My nannies would no doubt blame themselves for not taking my magic away in the first place. Too little too late. I had made the choice to be a witch. Magic was in my blood.

And I loved it.

If only I had listened to Lana. If only I hadn't been so stubborn, so adamant to prove to her that I could use my magic to help humans.

I curled into a ball and buried my face between my knees. Moisture soaked my dress. Whether it was my tears or the porridge I left untouched, I did not care to know.

Pheender leaves—Characterized by their rounded shape and white spots, these rare leaves can induce severe vomiting when crushed and consumed...and serve as a useful ingredient in an herbwitch's crafty potion.

3

THE
UNFADING
FLOWER

29

I was in the ballroom again. Dancers swirled through my periphery but I was focused on someone else.

Papa.

He stood beside the refreshments table surrounded by a gaggle of women I didn't recognize. Silver bells hung from their wrists.

I pushed forward, trying to get his attention. "Papa!"

He kept chattering with his companions. Then I noticed he wasn't wearing his spectacles and his hair was not streaked with gray.

A woman whispered something into his ear. He threw back his head and laughed. His smile was unlined.

There was only one explanation—I was dreaming. But it didn't feel like a dream. The floor beneath me was solid. I smelled the perfume in the air and the enticing aromas from the refreshments table. The dancers' dresses brushed my arms. I looked down. I was wearing the copper embroidered gown Papa had given me for my sixteenth birthday.

Whether it was a dream or something else didn't matter. Papa was paces away. I needed to speak with him. As I took a step forward, the women around him turned their heads.

Then I saw a woman in a purple dress—the woman I had dreamed of so long ago. This time, I knew who she was.

Mama emerged from the crowd of dancers and rushed toward the refreshments table. She was beaming, her face flushed and shiny from dancing as she piled puff pastries onto a tiny plate. I stared as I had never stared before. She was mere inches away from me, solid and alive.

As a child I often wondered what she looked like. Papa described her as lovely with laughter as sweet and clear as bells, which wasn't nearly enough for a seven-year-old to paint a mental picture.

I was shocked to see how much she looked like me. The freckles on her cheeks. The thick eyebrows. The brown hair. She haphazardly stacked another pastry onto her plate. It was like looking into a mirror.

She continued down the refreshments table, now closer to Papa. His gaze was fixated on her. The distance between them shrunk as she kept piling tarts and sandwiches onto her plate until she finally bumped into him, sending her tower of snacks tumbling back onto the table.

The unknown women around him dispersed and so did the rest of the dancers. It was only Mama and Papa. His lips formed her name. The ballroom disappeared and I fell through the floor.

Then, I was back home, standing amongst the marigold bushes. Mama and Papa rushed through the gate, laughing and holding hands. My late grandparents were smiling by the door as the two of them embraced. The scene changed again.

We were in the crop field surrounding Witch Village.

Papa looked around in wonder as Mama tugged him along.

Then it was another scene. Mama lay in a bed, her belly swollen.

The next scene depicted the birth of a wailing child. The rest flashed by in lightning speed.

Lana shouting.

Mama crying.

Papa alone in his study with me in his arms.

Mama in the dungeons. Then darkness.

I shut my eyes.

When I opened them again, I was inside Lana's cottage. Soft daylight streamed in through the circular windows and the smell of chrysanthemum tea perfumed the air. I gripped the bench I sat on.

"Lana?" I called out hesitantly.

"Your aunt is not here, darling. I hope you're not too disappointed."

I stared, paralyzed, as my mother walked in through the door. Her eyes crinkled as she smiled. They were the same shade as mine.

"Mama?" I whispered.

The hands that took my fingers were as warm and soft and solid as I hoped. "Yes, darling. It's me," she said with a voice as soothing and sweet as honey.

I threw my arms around her, burying myself into her embrace. She smelled like roses.

"There, there," she said, gently stroking my hair. "Look at how you've grown."

I pulled away and blinked away my tears. Papa was right. She was lovely. "Is this real?" I said, my lip trembling.

"It's as real as that crystal around your neck," she said, seating herself beside me. The crystal hung loose over my dress, glowing brighter than ever before.

"Now dry those tears. Tell me what's wrong," Mama said.

I rested my head on her shoulder. "Everything is wrong. They're going to kill me because I'm a witch. You're visiting because I'll be with you soon, aren't you?"

She patted my cheek and chuckled. "Silly girl. I'm visiting you because you're in trouble and you won't do anything about it."

"There's nothing I can do, Mama. Lana was right. Witches don't belong with humans. Helping them only landed me a death sentence."

Her eyes saddened. "Darling—"

I shook my head and stood. "You showed me your life with Papa. Sure, you were happy," I said, smiling at the memory of their meeting, "but it ended much too soon. If that isn't proof, I don't know what is."

"I chose my own path and I do not regret it," Mama said. "You still have time to choose yours."

"What is there left to choose? I chose to be a witch among humans and look where that led me. They think I poisoned the queen."

She tilted her head. "You speak as if you aren't one."

"Aren't what?"

"Human," she said. "You forget you're also human."

I stared at my hands. "But my magic—"

Mama pressed my hand between hers. "You thought witches were horrid creatures before you realized you were one. And now that you've embraced your witch side, you speak as if you're no longer human."

My mouth opened, but no words came out. "Which one am I, then?" I finally said.

She laughed. "Darling, you don't have to choose. You're both."

"It doesn't matter," I said, hanging my head. "They only see my magic."

"Then show them everything else," Mama said. She lifted my chin. "Show them how bold and clever and kind you are by getting yourself out and saving the queen."

Tears pricked the back of my eyes again. "Lana said none of that matters if I'm a witch."

Mama rolled her eyes. "My sister has very pointed opinions. She's too blinded by her biases to see hope. That is largely my fault. But if anyone can change her mind, it's you."

"How?" I said. "I can't do it alone."

"I will always be with you, darling. I always have," she said, pointing to my crystal. "Everything leaves a trace. Lana was right about that."

Mama had been with me all along. I pressed the crystal to my chest, my vision blurred with tears. "Thank you, Mama. You're all I have left."

She shook her head and smiled. "Not just me," she said. "Your friends and your sister are at the door."

"What?"

Then, Mama and Lana's cottage melted away to darkness. I reached out, but my arms only touched stone and straw.

I opened my eyes to the dingy surroundings of my cell and the sound of voices.

"You have ten minutes," a guard said. "Scream if you're in trouble."

Something that sounded exactly like Tori's snort echoed through the dungeon. "Yeah, like that would happen."

I scrambled up as the door swung open, revealing Tori, Genevieve, and Olivia.

30

Genevieve threw herself into my arms first.

"How could you have hidden this from me?" my stepsister demanded, her sobs smothered by my hair.

Tori crossed her arms. "And me," she said. "All this time there was a witch in my house and no one noticed?" She looked serious, but her tone was teasing.

I could only stare at them.

"Amarante?" Olivia said softly from behind them. "Are you alright?"

Genevieve pulled back and took my hands. Tori quirked an eyebrow at me.

I shook my head, hardly knowing how to react. "Aren't you scared of me?"

"Scared?" Tori said, making a face. "I never believed that fear mongering nonsense about witches in the first place. Pa raised me better than that."

Genevieve's eyes brimmed with tears, but she wiped them away and smacked my shoulder. "I don't care what you are, Amarante. You're still my sister."

"And you're my friend," Olivia said. She fidgeted, as if embarrassed to be speaking at all. "I knew there was something wrong ever since the soirée, even if you didn't tell me."

I lowered my head. "I haven't been completely honest," I said. Tori snorted. "I owe you the truth. All of you."

Taking a breath, I told them everything, from the scarlet smoke to working as Narcissa's scullery maid. I told them about my fight with Lana and how making the truth potion led to my arrest. In a lower voice, I revealed how Narcissa used her magic to sabotage me. I didn't want Captain Greenwood to hear what his daughter had done. He had lost enough.

"And now I need your help to escape," I said after I finished my tale.

All three of them looked astonished. I could hardly blame them. Even I had difficulty processing all that had happened in the past two months.

Tori was the first to recover. "Anything to get those rotten Whittingtons what they deserve," she said, slamming her fist into her palm. "Really! The audacity of Narcissa to order you around and frame you as a thief and traitor!"

I winced as her voice boomed through the cell. Hopefully, Captain Greenwood was asleep.

"We'll help however we can," Genevieve said, her face earnest.

"Do you need us to tell Prince Ash?" Olivia said.

I scuffed the floor with my heel. "No need," I said. "He can't do anything for me."

Tori scoffed. "Don't tell me he didn't try to stop your arrest after all you did for him!"

The last thing I wanted was to talk about Ash. I pressed my lips together. "Never mind that," I said. "Tori, find Erasmus, the royal inspector."

"You mean the ugly-haired old fellow who told us about you?" she said.

I nodded. "I need him to bring me some of my truth potion, if it's still there. And a vial of his sleeping draught." I turned to Genevieve. "Gen, can you pay a visit to Miriam? Her shop is right next to the post office."

"Absolutely," my stepsister said. "Anything for you."

I gave her hand a squeeze. "Tell her what happened. And tell her I'll see her soon, if things go according to plan."

Olivia rocked on her feet, looking at me expectantly.

"Er…Olivia, you can choose to join Genevieve or Tori, or both of them if you prefer," I said.

She frowned, but nodded. "Very well," she said. "Will you be alright on your own?"

My lips twitched upward. The tuft of straw I was eying swirled in the air in a figure eight. "Of course. I'm a witch."

It was never truly quiet in the dungeon. The guards snored, the prisoners moaned, and the rodents squeaked. A rat scurried across my cell and wriggled into a hole in the wall.

Normally, I would've been terrified. But worse things awaited beyond the dungeon walls. I hoped I'd be ready to face them within the next hour.

My pockets hung heavy with two vials—Erasmus's sleeping draught and my unfinished truth potion. Both were still covered in a greasy film of lard. Erasmus had hidden them in last night's stew.

I pulled out the sleeping draught and pressed my ear to the door. Shortly after Tori, Olivia, and Genevieve's visit, two new guards were stationed outside my cell. Luckily, they were a loud pair. Even their snores were deafening. It made it easy to determine their schedule. Each night they dined before my door and passed out drunk until midnight. Tonight, if all went according to plan, they wouldn't awaken till morning.

"Care for a game of cards over dinner, Ken?"

"And leave the witch's cell unguarded? Have you gone mad?"

"It's been four days. She would've escaped by now if she meant to."

"Well, Ronnie, maybe she already has. We've never locked a witch up before. Perhaps there's a reason for that. They'll just end up using some voodoo or other to magic themselves away."

"That's hardly *our* fault, then, is it?"

There was a pause. "I suppose not."

"Cards it is. I'll deal."

"Hold on. We ought to check if she's still there."

"Alright. You do it."

"*Me?* You do it."

"No, you."

Ken gave an exasperated sigh. "How about we both do it?"

"Fine."

"On the count of three?"

"One. Two. Three!"

I scrambled a few paces back from the door as the food

slot lifted open. Two pale faces peered in, one bearded and the other freckled.

I gave them my sweetest smile. "Hello there."

The slot slammed shut, followed by screeches that rivaled even the maddest of prisoners. A moment of silence passed.

"She seems rather charming, don't you think?"

"Shut up, Ronnie. Just deal the cards."

I waited several minutes before raising the slot a hair's width to peer out. Ken and Ronnie were several feet away, seated across from each other at a square table. A sparse dinner of bread and cheese sat before them, a single jug of ale at the far side. The two started playing cards.

I uncorked the sleeping draught. Slowly but surely, I levitated two fat drops of the clear liquid from the vial. They rippled as I pushed them through the slot and toward the guards, low on the ground.

"Damn you!" Ronnie slammed his fist down onto the table.

I jumped, almost letting the droplets splash.

Ken took a swig of ale and guffawed. "Serves you right for challenging me to cards."

"Again! Again!"

I continued to push the sleeping draught forward as Ronnie gathered the cards and dealt them again. My eyes strained. The droplets were now making a perilous trek under the table in the space between the guards' legs. My magic wavered. One of the droplets dribbled and transferred some of itself onto the floor.

I clutched my crystal and pushed. They swept high into the air. Too high.

Ronnie stopped dealing and squinted. "Did you see that?"

"See what?" The droplets hovered above Ken's head. I pushed them higher against the far wall.

"Pesky flies," Ronnie grunted, passing his companion another card.

Ken scoffed. "Wanted to slip yourself the good cards, didn't you?"

The dealer's face nearly grew as red as his beard. "I did not!"

"Did too."

"Did not!"

The sleeping draught spiraled down into the jug as the guards bickered. They disappeared into the ale on contact. I closed the slot and let go of my breath, my eyes tingling and thrumming with magic. It felt wonderful.

Now it was time to wait.

It wasn't long before the bickering ceased and snores thundered through the dungeon. I peered out again, more than relieved to find both Ronnie and Ken unconscious on the table. A ring of keys gleamed at Ken's belt.

I unfastened the key wrought of black iron. The next thirty minutes were dedicated to the tricky business of predicting exactly where the monstrous iron lock was on the outside. I knew it was roughly in the middle of the door, but I had never tried to move an object I couldn't see.

Frustration mounted, but half an hour of guesswork led to a satisfying click and the heavy clinking of unraveling chains. I ignored the pain in my neck and pushed open the door.

I had done it. I was free. Even the air outside of my cell smelled fresher. I crept out and closed the door behind me. With a sweep of my hand, the chains wound themselves back up and the lock refastened.

"Miss Flora?"

I nearly stumbled over myself, until I realized who it was. "Captain Greenwood?"

A pair of gray eyes appeared at the slot of the door next to mine. "I heard everything the other day. My daughter. Is it true?"

The heaviness of his voice told me he already knew it was. I nodded anyway, not knowing if it would appease or upset him.

He heaved a great sigh. "I guess it was expected, leaving her alone with Wilhelmina," he said. He focused on me again. "But I still believe there is some good in her. There must be."

"Captain..."

"Please, if you see Narcissa, promise you'll take her away from her mother," he said.

He spoke of her as if she were a little girl. Maybe in his mind she was. The thought of carrying Narcissa away from the duchess now was ridiculous at best and impossible at worst. But I didn't have the heart to refuse Captain Greenwood.

"I will try," I said.

"Thank you, Miss Flora. I wish you luck. Make things right again—for all of us."

His sorrowful gray eyes disappeared and I was alone once more. Heaving a sigh myself, I replaced the key at Ken's belt and hurried out.

My muscles were stiff as I half walked and half ran down the unguarded hallway that led to the barred cells. There would be a great many guardsmen at the exit. But I had magic at my fingertips. I felt powerful, like I could get away with anything.

But any semblance of confidence deserted me when I stumbled into an armored figure.

Before I could scream, the guard clamped a gloved hand over my mouth. A metallic smell filled my nostrils. I kicked and twisted, but the arm wrapped around me refused to budge.

"It's me."

I stopped struggling and turned to my assailant. He had taken his helmet off. Even in the darkness of the dungeon, I knew those eyes. And that nose. And mouth. And every other part of the face that had haunted me for the past four days.

I slapped him.

Ash stumbled back as my palm met his cheek with a sickening crack.

I glared, my hand stinging. It took all my willpower not to cry. Even then, tears seeped out. "Why are you here?" I demanded, wiping my eyes furiously. "I thought you were finished with me."

Ash flinched. "I—" He shook his head. "I'm here to rescue you. But it seems you've done a decent job yourself."

I searched his face for any sign of deceit, but he looked earnest—even sorrowful—despite the red mark blooming on his face. I thought back to his passivity at my arrest. The distrust and betrayal in his eyes. Where were they now?

"Amarante—"

"This isn't the place to talk," I said coldly, hoping my tears weren't as noticeable as they felt. There would be time for explanations later. I stuck out my arms. "Get on with it."

A ghost of a smile graced his lips as he pulled out a length of rope and tied it around my wrists, tight enough to look convincing but loose enough not to hurt. I was immensely glad when he put his helmet back on. I didn't want to see his face.

The grates overhead let in just enough of the fading daylight for us to navigate the rest of the dungeons. As we passed the endless hallways of open cells, I recalled the first time I had come here with Ash to question Captain Greenwood. It wasn't long ago, yet so much had changed.

Ash stopped when we drew nearer to the exit. Two armed guards stood watch on either side. He stopped and unfastened his cloak. I was enveloped in his scent when he threw it around me.

"Just in case they won't let you through," he said quietly, pulling the hood over my head and fastening the drawstrings. His fingers paused. "Your eyes. They're purple."

"Yes, they are," I snapped, turning my face away.

It seemed like he was going to say something else, but didn't. He took the rope around my wrists and led me around the corner.

"Where you off to?" a guard asked when we approached the gates. Beyond, the short tunnel opened to the back of the east wing. Even the last bits of daylight were blinding to me.

"This one's got a hearing," Ash said in a deep voice, tilting his head to me. I kept my head down, making sure the hood hid my features.

The guard narrowed his eyes. "A hearing? The king has yet to return."

Ash flipped a gold coin into the guard's hand. "Indeed."

He grunted and pushed open the gate, tucking the coin into his pocket as we passed. My heart pounded as we climbed the stairs out to the palace grounds. My lungs nearly wept from the fresh air. The paved path felt wonderfully smooth under the soles of my boots.

We trotted across the grounds, ducking whenever a servant or gardener appeared. Ash led me to a row of tall hedges across the pond we had unceremoniously fallen into. The sun had fully set, plunging the land into a purplish haze. A few swans were silhouetted on the water, flapping and bugling. I knew now they had been under Narcissa's influence, but I still had no love for the creatures.

Ash pulled off his helmet and kicked it underneath a hedge. Heavy clunking followed as he did the same to the rest of his ill-fitting armor.

"You really like disguises, don't you?" I said.

He paused. "Being a prince is very limiting," he said.

"Being a witch is even more so."

He straightened his shirt and met my eyes, his stare unwavering. "Yes," he said. "I would imagine."

I looked askance, suddenly finding the grass very interesting. I wanted to scream at him. What could he possibly mean? Why had he decided to believe me after falling for Narcissa's lies?

"Olivia told me," Ash said, answering my unasked question.

I looked up. "What?"

"She told me everything yesterday. Everything." Ash's voice was strained. He raked a hand through his hair. "Why didn't you trust me with the truth?"

"Because I couldn't let you know I was a witch!" I exploded, clenching my fists. "And I was right. You didn't want anything to do with me when you found out."

Silence pervaded the air before he spoke. "Is that what you thought?" he asked quietly.

How dare he be so calm after what he'd done? The urge to scream at him resurfaced, but he spoke again before I could.

"First you somehow knew to search Peter. Then you ask Captain Greenwood for gold. At the soirée you stayed with Narcissa. Then I find you at an obscure snail shop at midnight with cuts all over your arms. And you went to the palace when you said you were going home. What was I supposed to think when Narcissa piled all those accusations against you? Don't you see, Amarante? I couldn't defend you because I didn't know what you were hiding from me."

I stared. Ash had been more observant than I thought, but he was right. I never realized how my actions must have looked from his perspective. But a part of me was still injured. It was the injured part that spoke.

"After all this time you've known me, you still thought I was capable of poisoning your mother. You said you trusted me, but you didn't."

Ash parted his lips. He looked away.

My gut sank, but I forced the feeling away. "There's something else you should know. Captain Greenwood is a witch. He's Narcissa's father."

"Narcissa...she's a witch?" he said.

"The animals were under Narcissa's control. The mice and the swans. And her cat. It was all her."

He pressed his lips together. "Was she the one who...?"

"No," I said grimly, answering his unfinished question. "It was the duchess. But my aunt...she's involved too."

"Amarante—"

"She didn't mean any harm," I said. Somehow I wanted to defend Lana, even if it meant further lowering myself in Ash's esteem.

Ash touched my shoulder but withdrew it when I tensed. "You don't have to tell me everything right now. Just know that I trust you. I will always trust you."

"Thank you," I whispered. I didn't know whether to believe him or not.

He looked past the pond. "I reckon you had a plan to stop the duchess before I interfered," he said.

I sighed and straightened my shoulders.

"I did," I said. "I wouldn't mind some help."

31

Ash didn't ask any questions during our ride to Miriam's shop. If he was bursting with curiosity, he didn't show it, but he eventually spoke when I knocked on the door.

"This isn't really a snail shop, is it?" he said.

The door swung open. "Yes, it is, sonny. It's just that no one has had the good sense to purchase anything yet." Miriam stood at the door frame, looking ridiculously short compared to the prince. She crossed her arms and glared at me. "I thought you were imprisoned."

I pulled Ash inside without waiting for an invitation. "We need to go to Witch Village. Now."

Miriam gave him a grave look. "The last time I let a human pass through it resulted in death and heartbreak," she said. "Are you trustworthy?"

Ash looked to me, his brows drawn. He wanted me to answer for him, but his distrust still stung. That was something I wouldn't easily forget. Yet he agreed to follow me here even when I told him of Lana's role in the poisoning. Though I sensed his discomfort, he was trying. And that was enough for me.

"He is."

Miriam sighed and made her usual route to the back room. Ash and I followed. She activated the bricks, revealing the gaping black passageway that only a month before I had been afraid of entering. Now, everything depended on where it led.

"Good luck with whatever you're up to," Miriam said. "But if you end up dead, it's not my fault."

I knelt and embraced her, burying my nose in her shawls. Her scent of incense and lavender oil was overwhelming up close. "Thank you. You've done more for me than I could ever repay you for."

Miriam looked flustered when I pulled away. "Well, get on with it," she said in a wavering voice, shooing us into the passageway.

When the wall sealed itself, Ash took my arm. His hold was as tight as mine was during our visit to the dungeons.

"I can't see a thing," he said.

I smiled in spite of myself. I didn't want him to believe I had forgiven him, so I was grateful for the lack of light. "It discourages trespassers from going any further," I said. "There are no real directions. We have to walk forward for long enough until the passageway opens."

"Fascinating! We could use something like this for the treasury."

Eventually the door to Witch Village appeared. I pushed it open. Hundreds of lights gleamed from the hill, the sky bejeweled with stars. Ash's jaw hung open as he took in the fields of crops and the village in the distance.

"We're not actually outside," I said. "It's magic."

He nodded in awe as we made our trek toward the hill.

Eventually, I spotted Lana's cottage at the end of the winding road. The circular windows were bright, meaning she was home and awake. A lump appeared in my throat when we approached. She had removed the enchantment on the door. I stared.

Ash waited a beat. "Are you going to knock?"

"You do it."

He tapped his knuckles on the wood. It swung open.

But instead of Lana, someone else stood at the threshold.

My lips parted. "Rowena? What are you doing here?"

She glared at me, but the tears that welled up in her dark eyes betrayed her feelings. "I thought you were rotting away in the dungeons, you ungrateful girl."

I embraced her. Her arms held me tight.

"You came back." Elowyn poked her head out behind her sister's skirts. Her eyes widened when she noticed Ash. "Who's that? He's handsome."

Ash cracked a smile. "Prince Ash of Olderea," he said with a smart bow. "You're quite handsome yourself."

Elowyn darted back inside with a squeak.

Rowena released me and stared at Ash. "It looks like we all have some explaining to do."

Lana was absent when we gathered inside on the benches near the fireplace. I told Rowena everything that had happened, though this time Ash jumped in to insert his part of the story.

After the duchess assigned my punishment, Ash set out to find Peter, who turned out to be alive. He was hiding in the outskirts of the forest with plans to flee the kingdom. When he was cornered, he admitted to using a witch-made sleeping elixir, but still refused to reveal whose orders he had been acting under.

"No doubt the duchess is threatening him with the death of his family," Ash said darkly.

With no other choice, Ash ordered his men to interrogate shops rumored to be associated with the Witch Market, hoping to trace down the witch who sold Duchess Wilhelmina the poison. His search was cut off when I was accused and imprisoned.

"So, why are you here?" I asked Rowena after we finished.

"Olivia Sternfeld told me and Theodora everything," she said.

Olivia again. I couldn't have been more grateful for her newfound bravery.

Rowena sighed and glared at me. "Theodora went to Lord Strongfoot and I came here to notify Lana. All of us were trying to come up with a plan to rescue you. How did you escape?"

"I managed," I said. "But now we need to save Queen Cordelia and expose the duchess."

She thinned her lips. "Amarante, they all know you're a witch. They won't want your help."

"Rowena—"

"Look what they've done to you," Rowena said, taking my hands. They were covered in dirt and grime. The scratches and bruises inflicted by Karen and Narcissa were still red and angry. I had almost forgotten about them.

Ash looked at my arm, then looked away. "She's right," he said in a low voice. "You shouldn't go back to the palace. It's too dangerous."

"What about the queen?" I demanded. "How will you save her? How will you expose Duchess Wilhelmina?"

"I'll manage," he said with a tight smile.

"Listen to him," Rowena said. Her eyes were rimmed red. "Lana agreed to let you stay here. Theodora and I will stay too. You'll be safe again."

"You want me to hide here for the rest of my life," I said, disbelieving. I turned to Ash. "And you think you can save your mother without a witch-made antidote. You're both insane."

Rowena looked at a loss for words.

"Amarante, listen—" Ash started.

"No. You listen." I gave him a hard look. "I spent ages helping you with this case. Why aren't you letting me help now?"

"They were going to execute you!"

"Because of Narcissa. Because of the duchess," I said. "I was making a truth potion that day. I wanted her to confess. It would solve half our problem. Captain Greenwood would've been freed."

"And then what?" Rowena interjected. "Everyone knows it's a witch-made poison. A witch will still be blamed, even if it isn't you."

"I refuse to cower when I can fix this," I said.

A voice came from the back. "You're right. But not without me."

Lana strode in, her olive eyes flooded with unreadable emotion when they fixed on mine. "I was the one who caused this. Fifteen years ago, I created a foul poison and sold it out of spite for humans.

"A woman bought a vial from me—the only one I ever sold. Even then I realized the error of my ways. No human deserves what that vial contains."

I stood. "Lana."

"I'm sorry, Amarante," Lana said, shaking her head. "I was a fool. A hateful, bitter fool. I need to set this right."

Tears welled up in spite of myself. "What changed your mind?"

She touched my arm. "You. And Seraphina. She never strayed from her morals. Neither did you." Lana turned to Rowena and Ash. "Give Amarante a chance. She is not one to be protected."

"But…but they'll kill her!" Ash sputtered.

"They won't if she saves the queen," Lana said.

Rowena sighed. "You're right. Seraphina would've wanted this."

My throat tightened. "Thank you."

Lana turned to me. "Now. I reckon you need my help."

The next thirty minutes I spent finishing my truth potion, which involved boiling the duchess's hair over high heat until it dissolved. I only had a small vial of potion, so I was careful with the flames lest it all evaporated. By the end of it, I had half a vial of coppery liquid.

I pressed it into Ash's hand. "Make sure Duchess Wilhelmina ingests this during the ball."

"I will," he said.

We were out in Lana's garden before her personal passageway. She had altered it to lead just outside the palace grounds after I told her Ash must go back for my plan.

"Rowena and Elowyn will show you there," I said. I turned to the door to get them, but paused at Ash's expression. I sighed. "What is it?"

"I never apologized," he said.

I merely stared.

"For everything," Ash continued. He paced the length of the garden, shoulders tense as his boots dug into the dirt.

"I put you in danger. I let you in on the investigation when I knew you were just a debutante. And when you needed my help most, I abandoned you. All this happened because of me. Amarante, you suffered because of me."

He glared at the ground, his hands twisted in his sleeves. I had never seen him so agitated. His face said it all. Guilt. Anger. And if I wasn't mistaken, self-loathing.

"Ash, I…" I shook my head.

There were too many things I wanted to say. But I merely folded his hands between mine. "You're ruining Lana's basil. She'll throw a fit." With a small smile, I squeezed his fingers and let go.

Rowena and Elowyn bustled out the back door at that moment.

"To the palace we go, then," Rowena said to a bewildered Ash, clapping her hands together. "We'll lead the way."

Lana was in the potion room when I returned, brewing the antidote in her cauldron.

"Any luck?" I said.

She stirred the contents. "I believe I'll be able to whip something together by morning," she said. The counter was a mess of vials and herbs.

"And it'll cure the queen?"

Lana pressed her lips together and sighed. "Not entirely. It will heal her for the time being, but her lifespan will be much, much shorter."

"Isn't there anything more you can do?" I asked.

"Well, I am missing an ingredient," Lana said, crushing

a sprig of nixgrass with her mortar and pestle. "Do you remember our first lesson?"

I nodded slowly. Antidotes needed a bit of poison in them to truly work. "Manbane. You need more manbane," I said. "Can't you make more?"

"I vowed I would never again," Lana said, shaking her head. "But even if I were to, I no longer have the ingredients required for it. They were exceptionally foul."

I paced the room, wishing I hadn't sent Ash off so soon. "The duchess must still have some," I said. "We could search her rooms for it and—"

Lana set her mortar down and crossed her arms. "You must have a death wish," she said.

Frowning, I mirrored her pose. "Queen Cordelia has to be saved. How can I tell Ash we had a chance to heal his mother but didn't take it?"

"*He* can take that chance. You were at death's door several hours ago, have you forgotten?"

I opened my mouth to protest but realized she was right. I couldn't enter the duchess's suite again unless I wanted to be executed on the spot. But I certainly couldn't let Ash do it alone.

A smile crept to my lips when I thought of a solution. "I can't go with him, but someone else can," I said. Lana gave me a look. "Can you disguise my face like you did with my witch traits?"

"Make you look like a completely different person?" Lana shook her head. "But I know someone who can."

Ferdinand arrived within minutes, looking as decrepit and cheery as ever with a large box in his hands. After complimenting Lana on her various household items and sturdy shelves, he set to work on me. He smeared an odd-smelling ointment on my forehead and cheeks and murmured things I didn't understand. I hardly felt any difference when he proclaimed he was done and thrust a mirror into my hands.

"It'll only last for a couple of hours. Whatever you must do, do it quick."

I was too entranced by my reflection to hear much of anything else he said. A stranger stared back from the mirror. She had straw-colored hair and no freckles. Her face was longer, her lips thinner, and her nose rounder, but she had my eyes.

"Ferdinand, this is amazing! Thank you," I said, shaking the old charmwitch's hand profusely. He shrugged and blushed.

"This stuff entertains my grandchildren. Never thought it'd be useful to anyone, but I'm mighty glad you appreciate it." He rubbed his hands together and leaned back in his seat. "Now. I could use a cup of tea."

A few strong words from Lana sent him out the door without tea. Barely a minute passed when Rowena and Elowyn came back. They started when they saw me, but I quickly explained to them my plan.

"I'm going to need transportation back from the palace," I said, giving Elowyn a hopeful look. She gladly accepted, but Rowena, who did not look pleased when I told her my plans, put her hands on her hips.

"What makes you think I'm going to let you waltz into the very place you should avoid?" she said.

"I'll be fine, Rowena. I have my disguise. Besides, with Elowyn it'll be quick in and quick out."

She looked like she was about to protest again, but to my surprise, Lana intervened. "She has grown, Rowena. Let her go."

Rowena wrung her hands and sighed. "Fine. But if you land yourself in trouble again, I will personally see to your punishment."

I beamed.

Elowyn and I took Lana's passageway, as charmwitches were not allowed to transport above ground from Witch Village.

"I'm sorry I'm making you walk so much," I said as we strode through the pitch-black tunnel.

She giggled. "Don't worry about it. This is the most excitement I've ever had." We walked a little longer before she spoke again. "Do you mind if…I accompany you and Prince Ash?" Her voice was hopeful, but there was a hint of sheepishness as if she expected me to say no. She was right.

"Elowyn, it'll be dangerous. What if someone finds you?" I said. I pictured her gold-streaked hair and silver eyes. She had no reason to have a concealment spell cast on her if she never went above ground. "You don't exactly blend in."

She let go of a breath. "But I want to help."

"You are helping," I said, reaching over haphazardly to pat her head. Luckily, my hand met soft curls. "Besides, I don't think your sister would appreciate both of us running into danger."

"I have an invisibility tonic from Ferdinand," she said. "I've been saving it for a special occasion."

"Elowyn…"

"Please! I'll stay out of sight for as long as we're in the palace. It'll only be for a little while, until you find the duchess's manbane."

I held back a groan. The girl was relentless. I had to admire her for it no matter how much it irked me. Escorting Ash was perhaps her first taste of the world above ground.

No doubt she insisted on following him all the way into the palace and got what she wanted. What was the harm in one more trip?

"Alright. Fine," I said. "But you have to promise to stay invisible and do exactly as I tell you."

Elowyn squealed and wrapped her arms around my middle. "I promise! Thank you!"

I was glad at least one of us was in a good mood. We emerged from the passageway outside palace grounds. Before I could whisper to Elowyn about sneaking past the guards, she grabbed my hand and transported us to the middle of an unfamiliar room.

I lurched forward, gasping for breath. "Elowyn! You really should warn me before—"

I stopped and stared at the indigo carpet and velvet drapes. A lavish, though untidy, double bed was in the center, elevated on a rounded platform.

"Where are we? I thought you could only transport to places you've been," I said.

"Prince Ash's room."

I sputtered. "You followed him to his *room*?"

Elowyn looked at me innocently. "He said I could. He also showed me the ballroom."

Before I could give her a lecture about the impropriety of the offer if given by anyone else in other circumstances, a door swung open and Ash himself walked out in nothing more than a pair of breeches. He stumbled back at the sight of me. "Who in the blazing fires are you?"

I was too mortified to do anything more than stare at the ground, so Elowyn answered for me. "That's Amarante. She's in disguise."

"Amarante?" Ash said. He gaped at me, no doubt marveling at the effect of Ferdinand's magic.

"What are you doing here? And why are you disguised?" He took a step closer, but I turned away.

"We'll talk when you're dressed," I said as evenly as my embarrassment allowed.

"Oh! Er...I'll be a moment."

The door shut. I deemed it safe to look up again.

"He's rather fit for a prince," Elowyn whispered loudly. "My grandmother told me all royals are fat and lazy."

I was still somewhat flustered when Ash emerged, this time fully dressed and with a faint blush on his cheeks. Elowyn and I explained to him how Lana needed manbane to complete her antidote.

The look on his face mirrored Rowena's. "I'm not letting either of you go in there," Ash said. "It's much too dangerous."

I frowned and Elowyn crossed her arms. It seemed that both of us were tired of being told no.

"I look like a completely different person and Elowyn will be invisible," I said. "Is that enough for you?"

32

It was enough. We found ourselves outside the duchess's suite. The hallway was quiet, barely illuminated by a few candles from the sconces along the wall.

I craned my neck over Ash's shoulder. Elowyn crouched behind me.

"Where is everyone?" I whispered. The lack of servants felt odd. Surely *somebody* was recruited to guard the duchess's suite after I was caught.

"Asleep, perhaps." He sounded doubtful. "I don't know how we're supposed to get in."

"I can go," Elowyn said. She dangled a small vial of clear liquid on a cord around her neck. Her invisibility tonic.

"Can you pick locks too?" Ash reached over and wriggled the doorknob. "There's no way—"

The door opened.

"What are they playing at?" I said, suspicious.

I turned to Elowyn, but she was nowhere to be seen.

A soft touch at my elbow made me jump. She had ingested the tonic.

"I'll see if anyone is in there," she whispered.

"Be careful," I said.

Ash and I watched as the door opened slightly. A few seconds later, there was another touch at my elbow. "It's empty."

"It's probably a trap," I said, frowning as I recalled the last time I snuck into the duchess's suite.

"Trap or not, this is as good an opportunity we'll get," Ash said with a sigh. "Elowyn, can you keep watch out here and alert us if someone comes in?"

"Okay. I'll knock on the walls like this." A short rhythm sounded from the wall beside him.

He nodded and we slipped into the suite. It was dark and silent, like the hallway. I peered under the furniture to check if Misty was hiding, waiting to pounce.

When I confirmed the absence of the accursed animal, I exhaled. "Okay. We're looking for places she would store poison." I recalled the manbane I had extracted from Queen Cordelia's goblet. "It should be a dark red, like blood, with streaks of indigo."

We set to work. Ash flipped over the cushions of the seats and I searched the other half of the room, clutching my crystal. There was nothing in the cabinets or drawers but baubles and perfume. Poofs of pink and baby blue and lilac littered the air, but no scarlet. There was one jar that emitted maroon fumes, but it was a treatment for foot fungus. I put it back immediately.

THE HERBWITCH'S APPRENTICE

"It's likely in her bedroom," Ash said, replacing the top of a storage ottoman. "She'd keep something like that close to her."

We approached the door that led into the duchess's personal chambers. I pushed it open. The hinges were silent. I peeked inside, grateful for velvet draperies drawn over the windows on the opposite wall. Someone had cleaned up the havoc I wreaked at the vanity.

I set to work on the armoire, feeling the base and the sides for any hint of a secret compartment. The wood was smooth all the way around. I even tried rifling through the ridiculous quantity of gowns stuffed inside it, but there was nothing but lace and silk and beading.

Ash didn't seem to be faring any better underneath the bed frame. He emerged, hair and clothing rumpled. "Nothing. Nothing at all. It's like she doesn't keep anything in here," he said. He sneezed. "Except dust."

I tried my best to shut the armoire. "We could check the lavatory," I said, leaning against the doors. It was unlikely the duchess hid the poison in her chamber pot, but at this point I was desperate.

Ash's face softened. "Calm down, Amarante. We still have time."

I shook my head. "We need the antidote before Queen Cordelia gets worse."

"She is a strong woman," he said offering a half-hearted smile. I held back my tears. The situation never felt more hopeless.

"Not strong enough to survive manbane," I said.

"I gave her the potion you gave me at the Witch Market."

I thought back to our encounter. "You knew that was me?"

"I figured it out eventually," he said, smiling.

348

"Ah."

"Plus, it was the same potion you said would help before you got arrested. I figured I give it a shot. She's doing better. We've bought ourselves time."

"My aunt made it," I said, feeling a little warmer. Ash had trusted me enough to give his mother Lana's general antidote. I took a breath, reenergized. "Let's hurry." I traversed the room and was about to turn the knob when I heard a rhythmic knock.

The door of the suite opened.

"Have you got your gown, Narcissa?"

"Yes, Mother."

"Good. You must look your best tomorrow night."

My heart leapt out of my throat as I exchanged a panicked glance with Ash. They were back.

Ash gestured frantically to the bottom of the bed, but I shook my head. The bed frame was too elevated to be a good hiding place. I opened the armoire. The lower half had just enough room for one person to lay in comfortably.

Or in our case, as I found out very soon, for two people to lay in uncomfortably. I hardly wedged myself inside before Ash threw himself on top of me, shutting the doors in the process. We were plunged into darkness, save for the tiniest sliver of light in the gap between the doors.

Duchess Wilhelmina and Narcissa's conversation became muffled. I strained to listen, but I was more or less immobilized by Ash's overbearing weight. He had pinned my braid down with his elbow. I winced and reached to pull it out, but found that there was no space between us. My face burned. I felt his breath acutely on my cheek.

Luckily, circumstances did not require me to speak, for I was more tongue-tied than I ever had been in my life—and not only because the air was squeezed out of my lungs.

"…you know what to do when the time comes?" Duchess Wilhelmina grew louder. She was coming closer.

"I do." There was a pause. "Must I be the one to do it?"

"One day, Narcissa, you will learn that some things are better done yourself."

"But I have no experience with such things. It'll be better for a mercenary to do it, someone who is trained and bound to succeed—"

"Are you afraid?" The duchess's voice was dangerously sharp.

"N-No, Mother, I want everything to work. That is all," Narcissa said.

"I will not tolerate fear, Narcissa," Duchess Wilhelmina said. "It is too late to go back. Ever since you helped me plant that poison at the Debutante Ball, you have lost your tolerance for fear. Do you understand?"

My breath hitched. No doubt it was Narcissa who caused the infestation of pigeons as a distraction for Duchess Wilhelmina.

"Yes, Mother."

A door opened. The door to the duchess's chambers. My blood turned to ice as footsteps grew louder. Figures moved at the gap between the armoire doors. I caught a glimpse of Narcissa's back and the duchess's skirts.

"Tomorrow I'll see the end to Cordelia," Duchess Wilhelmina said. "Those silly physicians are doing a poor job at keeping her alive. I ought to do them a favor and take her off their hands. One last dose and she'll be through."

"Is there enough?"

I peered through the gap. The duchess's face was now visible.

"More than enough," she said, pressing a hand to her necklace. I squinted. Scarlet smoke billowed from the seams of the locket. So that's where she kept it! My heart pounded against my chest. How would I get my hands on the duchess's locket?

Narcissa took a breath. "Mother, what if we get caught?"

The duchess stilled. The silence felt dangerous. "We will not," she said. "Every meddlesome person has been taken care of. That Amarante girl is nothing but a wicked, raving mad witch in everyone's eyes. And Greenwood is an immoral adulterer who would do and say anything to save his lover. In the end, our hands are clean. And the blame is put on those filthy witches who get what they deserve."

I clenched my jaw. The duchess had a surprise coming for her.

"Maybe we shouldn't kill the queen," Narcissa said. "Maybe we should let her die. She's had enough of the poison."

"No," Duchess Wilhelmina said sharply. "I will not have her live as long as I have the power to kill her. Cordelia has been a thorn at my side for thirty long years. Once you are queen, Narcissa, I will take her place. She must die now."

"But Mother, what if Bennett does not choose me?" Narcissa said. Her voice sounded oddly desperate. "What if he chooses someone else? He doesn't love me. He hardly knows me."

"Foolish girl! Of course he doesn't. Love has nothing to do with choosing a bride," the duchess said. "And he will have to choose. You are the most obvious choice."

"V-Very well."

"Compose yourself, Narcissa. You have followed me this far," the duchess said, looking imperiously down at her daughter. "It will not be in your favor to change your mind, do you understand?" It was a threat. Loud and clear.

Narcissa bowed her head. "I understand."

"I thought I raised you well," she said. "But it appears you have inherited your father's weakness."

Narcissa visibly stiffened, but the duchess continued to speak. "Once I thought witches were stronger because of their magic, but it becomes increasingly clear it has the opposite effect." She chuckled. "It's better this way. The strong can control the weak and put their powers to much better use, isn't that right, Narcissa?"

"Quite right, Mother," Narcissa mumbled.

"You are using your magic to seize power, as you ought to. You should be proud."

"Yes, Mother."

"Look at me when I'm talking to you, Narcissa, and stand straight. You know I hate your slouching."

Ash shifted, and the armoire creaked. The duchess's skirts drew nearer.

And the doors flew open.

"You!"

Duchess Wilhelmina dragged Ash out by his collar.

"How did you get in here?" The question was nearly spat in his face as she held him up with surprising strength.

Ash wrenched away, stumbling back. The duchess's face twisted in confusion when she saw me. "Who are you? Where is the witch girl?"

Ferdinand's magic had protected me. I didn't want

to think what the duchess would've done if I weren't disguised.

"She's in the dungeon," Ash said with convincing bitterness. "But not for long."

Duchess Wilhelmina sneered. "That one is a poor replacement," she said, jutting her chin toward me. "Not as pretty, don't you think?"

Ash ignored her. "You are charged with treason."

The duchess took a threatening step forward. "Am I?"

Something flashed in Ash's eyes. His hand went to the scar on his knuckles, but he hardened his gaze. "I'm not eight years old anymore, Your Grace."

"So you're not," the duchess said. "Still, Cordelia was clueless enough to leave you under my care. It is your word against mine. She will never believe you."

Ash set his jaw. "Surrender now and I will be merciful."

"Narcissa. Lock the doors," Duchess Wilhelmina said.

Narcissa, who stood frozen, fled from the room. The sound of locks clicking came afterward. She did not return, but the duchess did not seem to miss her presence.

"I made sure nothing will be pointed back to me." The duchess sneered. "The royals unknowingly assisted me in my plan for two generations. Witches' words will never be trusted and that silly boy Peter will not reveal me as long as I have my men watching his parents."

Ash fumed. "You will be exposed if it is the last thing I do."

She guffawed. "Do you think you will prevail when I have spent ages perfecting my revenge? I am a great storyteller. Stories got me into the palace. Stories made me a duchess. I'm quite fond of one in particular. It's about a prince born from the wrong father. His mother was a promiscuous woman. All the kingdom knew it was so, but she insisted the boy was legitimate. Yet everyone whispered behind closed doors. I am sure you're familiar with it." She looked straight at Ash. His fists trembled.

I barely constrained my outrage. The duchess was the one who started the rumor of Queen Cordelia's affair? Had she planned to frame Captain Greenwood before I came along?

"You won't get away with this," I said. I hardly believed my own words. We were trapped with no witnesses other than ourselves. There was no evidence against the duchess and from the current situation, no way to make her confess again.

"On the contrary, I already have," she said, a smile curving her blood red lips. "I think we're due for another story. How about a tale of a wicked witch seducing a prince for her own gain? Driven mad by his desire for her, he was willing to poison his own mother. In the end, both of them met a tragic demise."

"You are deranged," Ash said in disbelief.

The duchess laughed again. "By all means, call me whatever you like. In the end, I'll still be the one in power." She flicked her gaze away from us. "Take care of them."

I barely registered the shadowy figures behind me before something bashed into my head and I lost consciousness.

I awoke to a throbbing headache and someone tugging on the ropes around my arms. I turned, but no one was there. I was tied to a bed post. Ash was similarly bound to the other side of the bed. My hair hung over my face, brown again. Ferdinand's magic had worn off.

The door to the duchess's bedroom was ajar. Two large, rough-looking men stood on either side with heavy swords in their hands, no doubt the cause of my headache.

There was another tug. The knot at my wrists unfurled.

"Elowyn?" I said under my breath. A tap on my arm confirmed her presence.

On the other side of the bed, Ash groaned, just coming to. The ropes around his wrists loosened as well. He gave the air beside him a grateful look and turned to me. He jerked his head to the burly guards at the door. I shrugged hopelessly. Was it even possible to get past them?

Before I could ask Elowyn her opinion, the door of the suite opened. I recognized the light steps as Narcissa's and tucked my hands behind me, throwing the ropes over my wrists so it appeared I was still at her mercy.

"I would like a word with the prisoners," Narcissa said to the guards. They grunted and let her enter, but watched with beady eyes. She glared and said in a clipped tone, "In private."

With some reluctance, they closed the door.

"What do you want?" I said warily.

Narcissa stood for a few moments without saying a word. She didn't seem surprised at my presence.

"If you mean to scare us you are doing a very poor job," Ash said dryly. He too had wrapped the rope around his hands. His back was stiff against the bedpost.

Narcissa ignored him. "How dare you do this to me?" she said in a wavering voice. She paced the length of the room, an object in her hand. She was gripping it so tightly her knuckles were as white as bone. "How dare you push me to my limits?"

My blood turned to ice when I realized it was a dagger. I looked to Ash. He had noticed too, his face pale.

"Narcissa, calm down," I said, inching away from her. She was still pacing, her steps agitated like a caged beast's.

"All my life I've followed my mother's orders without question, and this is where my craving for approval leads me." Narcissa barked a mirthless laugh and unsheathed the dagger. It was wickedly sharp, nearly as long as her forearm. She turned to us.

Ash placed himself in front of me. "Rethink this, Narcissa," he said. "Please." Though his voice was level, I detected a hint of panic.

His plead was ignored. Narcissa stared down at him icily. "Turn around."

Ash set his jaw. "Leave Amarante alone."

I groaned in frustration. This was no time for silly heroics. Discarding the rope, I stood and faced Narcissa. "You're not a murderer, Narcissa."

She sheathed the dagger. "What did you think I was going to do?" she asked with a scowl. "I'm here to release you."

"What?" Ash said, flabbergasted. "Why?"

Narcissa scoffed. "So this is your opinion of me?"

"You haven't done anything to change it," Ash retorted.

I recalled Captain Greenwood's description of his daughter and the hesitancy in Narcissa's manner during her conversation with the duchess. Hope blossomed in my chest.

"Are you saying you want to help us?" I said.

I must've chosen my words poorly, for the look Narcissa gave me was withering. "I never said that. I will merely set you free with the possibility of you thwarting my mother's plans tomorrow night."

"Perhaps you could increase that possibility by letting us know her plans," Ash said.

Her lips twisted. "Didn't you eavesdrop on us earlier?"

"Only bits and pieces."

Narcissa clenched her teeth. I was afraid she would decide to use her dagger in a different manner after all. "After the Masquerade Ball, the crown prince will choose me as a possible bride. I am to kill him after we are married. Mother will finish off the queen shortly after I'm chosen."

Ash clenched his fists. I cut in before he said something rash and ruined our chances of getting Narcissa's help.

"Then we'll make sure you won't get chosen," I said. "We'll interrupt the ball before the Choosing Ceremony."

"How will you do that?"

I exchanged a look with Ash. "That's for us to know and you to find out," I said, deciding it was better to keep the details to myself. "We only need one thing from you. The duchess's locket."

Narcissa bit her lip and then nodded. "I'll bring it to you at the masquerade."

"Can we leave now?" Elowyn's disembodied voice said. I jumped. I had nearly forgotten her presence.

Narcissa looked around the room warily. "Who was that?"

"Our transportation," Ash said.

Of course. Elowyn could easily get us out. I was hit with a wave of relief. Magic was no longer off-limits to me above ground. Her hand grasped mine.

"Make it look like we escaped," I said, pointing to the curtained windows. Narcissa nodded.

As the room twisted away, the last thing I heard was the crash of a chair smashing through glass.

Elowyn, Ash, and I appeared at the outskirts of town. The streets were dimly lit by the street lamps and all was quiet.

I had never been more grateful for Elowyn's charmwitch magic.

"Are you alright?" Ash asked me once we were safe inside Miriam's shop.

After being lectured by the snail seller about being gone for so long, Miriam provided us with tea and blankets and retired to the back room, muttering something about reckless youths.

"I suppose," I said, touching the throbbing part of my skull. "And you?"

Elowyn patted her own head. "I'm okay," she said before Ash could answer. I chuckled.

"I don't think it would be wise for me to go back to the palace," Ash said, warming his fingers with his teacup. "Not when it's dark, anyway."

Miriam's voice came from the back room. "You're more than welcome to stay here, sonny. As long as you don't snore. I detest snoring."

Ash assured her that he didn't snore and thanked her for her hospitality. I expressed my gratitude as well, glad that he'd be safe. Heavens knew what would have happened if the duchess saw Ash after our escape.

"Elowyn and I should get back to the village," I said, shrugging my blanket off my shoulders. "Rowena and my aunt are probably worried." And I was in desperate need of a bath after my days in the dungeons.

"And I'm starving," Elowyn said with a sigh. "I'll wait over there." She skipped through the beaded curtain, leaving me and Ash alone.

I stood. "Good night, then."

Ash bit his lip, looking as if he wanted to say something. Instead, he briefly touched my cheek. "Good night, Amarante."

33

When Elowyn and I returned to Lana's cottage, Rowena demanded to know what had happened. Elowyn was bursting to tell the entire story, but I whispered to her it was better if Rowena didn't know, lest we got another round of lectures. That convinced her to keep quiet.

After a simple dinner of bread and cheese and a long overdue bath, sleeping arrangements were made. But I could only lie awake in my cot, wondering at Ash's unspoken words and hoping my haphazard plan would work.

It was nearing noon when Lana shook me awake.

"I have something for you," she said. I didn't have a chance to ask any questions before she swept out of the room.

After splashing water on my face, I found Lana in her own chamber where she had given me Mama's crystal. A magnificent gown of the same color hung in the armoire, with a silken bodice and gauzy sleeves. Amaranth flowers of wine and gold bloomed down the skirts and brushed the embroidered hem. I recognized it immediately.

"It's beautiful," I whispered.

"She wore this at her Debutante Ball," Lana said, trailing her fingers along the fabric.

"You're giving it to me?" I asked, touched.

"Who else would I give it to?" she said gruffly.

It was clear Mama's things meant the world to her. First the crystal and now this. Tears stung my eyes and I threw my arms around her.

"Thank you, Aunt Lana."

Her stiff demeanor melted and she patted my back. "Of course."

Evening came quickly enough, and after Lana instructed me on how to incorporate the manbane into her unfinished antidote, Rowena and Elowyn helped me get ready for the masquerade. Mama's dress, to my surprise, fit perfectly. Elowyn weaved flowers into my hair and Rowena gave me a matching mask.

"There," Rowena said, pushing me in front of a full-length mirror.

I pressed my hands to my lips, shocked to see how much I looked like Mama.

Elowyn sighed. "You're as pretty as a princess," she said. "Too bad Ferdinand has to change that."

"Just to be safe," Rowena said at my look of confusion, "I asked him to cast an enchantment to make you unrecognizable to everyone, except for the people you tell."

I nodded, my anxiety easing. "Thank you," I said, tears threatening to spill again. "Where would I be without you two?"

Elowyn smiled. "Worse off, I suppose."

I arrived when they announced the crown prince.

"His Highness, Crown Prince Bennett!" The herald's high voice was muted by the heavy tapestry I appeared behind.

"Good luck," Elowyn whispered. With a wink, she vanished.

I crept out from behind the tapestry, making sure I hadn't attracted the attention of the musicians. Luckily, they were busy playing a stately march as the crown prince descended the stairs. The music and chatter and glitter of the ballroom overwhelmed my senses, a stark contrast to the dingy dungeons and the muted surroundings of Witch Village.

I hurried from the balcony through the archway and descended the narrow staircase that led to the ballroom floor. It was difficult to see out of a mask, but I managed to slip into the crowd without tripping.

The guests tonight were a mix of debutantes, their families, and courtiers who wanted to take part in the festivities. I touched the beaded border of my mask. Ferdinand's enchantment would only last till the hour before midnight.

The crowd was still fixated on Crown Prince Bennett when I spotted Narcissa's coppery hair. She was behind the front row of guests gaping at the crown prince, who was now making a stately trek to the dais.

I huffed. He was moving slower than one of Miriam's snails.

It seemed an eternity until he sat. The king stood and began to give a speech about youth entering society. I tucked myself into the shadows beneath the stairs. My eyes were on

Queen Cordelia, who looked frailer than ever before. Her eyes were hollowed and her skin was pasty. A sickly air hung about her that even the rouge on her cheeks couldn't hide. I didn't need my crystal to tell she was dying.

When the orchestra commenced the first dance of the night, someone tapped my shoulder.

"I'm not dancing," I said without turning around.

"I didn't think you would." Narcissa crossed her arms over the glittering bodice of her white ball gown. An elegant feathered mask covered a quarter of her face, which did little to conceal her stony stare.

"How did you recognize me?" I said, touching my mask again.

"You're the only one hiding like a criminal," she said. "And I saw you at the orchestra balcony. Could you be any more careless?"

My brows raised at her words. I hadn't forgiven her for my time as her scullery maid, but I held back from saying something rude. "Do you have it?" I asked instead.

Narcissa thinned her lips. "No," she said. "But I will."

I felt for the flask of unfinished antidote Lana had given me that morning. It sat in the pocket of my dress, weighing as heavily as the duty on my shoulders. "Then hurry up," I said. "I need it before the ceremony."

Narcissa glanced at the grandfather clock on the other side of the ballroom. It read half past nine. Only thirty minutes before the Choosing Ceremony and one and a half hours before my disguise wore off. The duchess would not be fooled by a mask that barely covered half my face.

"I told you I will," she said. "Don't move too much lest I waste time looking for you." With that, she swept off and I was left with the familiar desire to box her face.

I stepped out from under the stairs into the light. The

refreshments table was inches away. I took refuge behind the towers of puff pastries and candied pineapple. It was surprisingly crowded due to the attendance of older people whose empty stomachs mattered more to them than appearances.

A gentleman in a phoenix mask picked out a glazed pastry. His thick black hair gave his identity away easily enough, though he was also throwing frequent glances at me. When he eventually meandered next to me, I sighed.

"Yes, it's me."

Ash looked relieved. "I thought I was seeing things," he confessed, scanning my face. "That is amazing!"

I would have gladly explained Ferdinand's magic if there weren't more pressing matters at hand. "Is everything ready?" I asked.

He nodded as he chewed on his pastry. "The mentors will make a toast soon—it's Season tradition. I made sure the duchess's goblet is coated in truth potion."

"Good," I said, taking a puff pastry for myself. My stomach had been much too knotted for lunch despite Lana and Rowena's urging to get me to eat something. Only now was I feeling the consequences. "Narcissa is getting the locket."

Scanning the ballroom again, I spotted Genevieve dancing with Cedric. I smiled, glad that despite the circumstances, my stepsister was enjoying herself. But my survey brought no hint of Narcissa. A seed of doubt planted itself in my brain.

"Don't worry," Ash said, noticing my unease. "If she did decide to desert us we still have the truth potion. The duchess has no chance of leaving tonight unscathed."

But Queen Cordelia's life depended on that locket.

Minutes ticked by. The duchess was nowhere to be found and neither was Narcissa. I grew tense when the grandfather clock read five minutes to ten. The mentors had yet to gather before the dais. Eventually, the herald came and whispered something into Ash's ear.

"I have to go," Ash said. "The ceremony is starting."

He left for the dais before I could reply. When he took his seat, I spotted Tori coming toward the refreshments table.

"Tori!" I said when she was close enough. "It's me."

She looked up through a sapphire peacock mask. "Amarante?"

We ducked behind a fountain of chocolate. "Remember what you're supposed to do," I said in a low voice. "I'm counting on you."

Tori nodded, sticking a strawberry into the chocolate and popping it into her mouth. "Don't worry. I got it."

She swept away just as Queen Cordelia stood.

"Thank you all for coming tonight," the queen said. "This ball marks the end of the Season, which has been quite eventful, to say the least." Murmurs went through the crowd as Her Majesty gave a grim smile. "But I hope to end the summer with positivity and hope, mainly, with the Choosing Ceremony."

A glimpse of a feathery white dress drew my attention to the far archway. Narcissa had entered and oddly enough, with Misty in her arms.

"Many lucky debutantes will be paired with the dashing young gentlemen they have met during the course of these two months. They will be announced and intertwine their bells and ribbons per Olderean tradition…"

Narcissa scanned the crowd, her eyes settling on Duchess Wilhelmina who was standing with Madam Lucille and Lady Hortensia.

"By the end of the ceremony, my eldest son will reveal his choice of a possible bride among the debutantes…"

Cheers went through the ballroom. Narcissa set Misty on the floor.

"…before we commence the ceremony, our mentors would like to say a word about their experiences this Season."

Narcissa paused and swept her skirts over her cat. I let go of the breath I was holding and looked over to Ash. He looked similarly relieved. I wished he would have remembered that the mentors spoke right before the Choosing Ceremony and not thirty minutes before.

Duchess Wilhelmina and the two other mentors stood before the dais and took the goblets offered to them. The white-blue glow around the duchess's goblet confirmed that she had the truth potion. My stomach tensed in anticipation.

Lady Hortensia was the first to speak. She praised the debutantes for their beauty and wit and charms and commended the gentlemen as handsome and well-bred. She praised the queen, the duchess, and the courtiers' generous donation that made the event possible. She probably would have praised the maid who dusted the vases in the ballroom if Madam Lucille hadn't coughed and told her it was quite enough. Lady Hortensia raised her goblet and sipped.

Madam Lucille's speech was much shorter in comparison, but I still did not have the patience to listen to her rave about the talents and graces of this Season's young ladies. Eventually, she too raised her goblet and drank. It was fifteen minutes till eleven when it was the duchess's turn to speak.

"It has been an enchanting experience mentoring this year's debutantes…."

The rest of the duchess's words faded as I focused on her goblet. Time seemed to slow. I didn't know how long I stared before she tilted her head back and let her lips touch the rim of the goblet. She swallowed.

Then, a voice shouted from the crowd, "Who poisoned the queen?" To my utter amazement, it was Olivia's.

Tori jumped onto a stool on the far side of the ballroom. "Who poisoned the queen?"

"Who poisoned the queen?" Genevieve said from beside her.

All at once, everyone began to speak.

"What is this?" King Maximus said, rising from his throne.

"Why, I have never heard such disrespect!" Lady Hortensia exclaimed.

"Young ladies, you ought to be ashamed!" Madam Lucille said.

The duchess said nothing. Her eyes were wide open and her lips were pressed tightly closed. I gritted my teeth. The truth potion made one tell the truth, but only if one spoke. She would never confess her crimes if she weren't forced to speak.

The clock read one minute till eleven. "Duchess Wilhelmina, will you not answer?" I shouted. "Who poisoned the queen?"

"How dare you wreak havoc during this celebration?" King Maximus said. His voice boomed through the ballroom and I ducked behind a tiered stand stacked with sandwiches. The guests around me were giving me scandalized looks, so hiding was futile. "All of you will face punishment for your brash mouths. Guards!"

"Father, wait!" Ash's shout cut through the noise as

members of the Royal Guard streamed in. "Duchess Wilhelmina has not answered."

The king glared at him. "Do not tell me you are a part of this scheme, boy."

"The duchess has no reason not to clear her name, Father," Ash said coolly.

King Maximus's face pinched in annoyance, but he turned to the duchess. "Wilhelmina, put an end to this foolishness."

Her face turned an unflattering shade of puce. She was biting so hard on her lip I thought she would draw blood. The grandfather clock chimed. The deep, melodic peals reverberated through the quieting murmurs. When it reached the eleventh, she spoke.

"I poisoned the queen."

Dead silence ensued. The remaining chime resounded, louder than the ones before. The king stared. Queen Cordelia clutched the arms of her throne, her face drained of color.

"Is this true?" the queen said.

Duchess Wilhelmina pressed her hand to her mouth, then shakily removed it. Something in her mien changed, like a snake shedding its skin. Suddenly she stood straighter, her eyes shone with defiance, her lips twisted into a depraved grin. "It is, Cordelia," she said. "I want you dead."

Gasps and shrieks went through the crowd. Lady Hortensia fainted right there on the steps, but nobody came to help her. Madame Lucille stumbled back. The king was still frozen in shock.

Crown Prince Bennett's face was a picture of rage. "What is the meaning of this?" he said. "How dare you do this to my mother?"

She smirked. "I wanted you dead too, boy. Both you and your mother would've been gone in a week if my plans weren't spoiled."

Ash stood slowly, his gaze never leaving the duchess's, as if she were a wild animal. There was no saying whether she would flee or attack. "You confess to framing Captain Greenwood and Amarante for your crimes?"

"Yes." Duchess Wilhelmina gritted her jaw and narrowed her eyes. "She's here, isn't she? That witch girl is here. How did she escape? How?"

A shard of fear stabbed my gut. I ducked lower, but the movement caught her attention. Her eyes met mine.

"You!" she screeched, pointing straight at me. "You have spoiled my plans you wretched girl. Guards, seize that witch!"

I backed away, but the guards did not move. They were eying both the duchess and me, seemingly torn between which one of us was more dangerous. She snarled in frustration. Then she charged for me.

The rest happened in a blur. A yowl and a streak of black slammed her to the ground. The duchess screamed.

"Get off, you cursed cat!"

Misty clawed her face and yanked off the locket. Before the duchess could raise a hand against her, she bounded to me, a golden chain dangling from her teeth. I had never been happier to see the feline when she dropped the locket into my hands. I gave Misty's head a pat. "Good girl."

Without a second glance, I fled for the staircase to the orchestra balcony. I abandoned my mask behind me—there was no sense in wearing it when my identity was known—and reached for the flask in my pocket.

Screams exploded in the ballroom. I didn't turn back to see. There was only one task on my mind—to finish the manbane antidote. I remembered Lana's instructions clearly. One drop of manbane was enough for the antidote. It must be stirred counterclockwise for two minutes to truly incorporate.

I burst into the balcony. The musicians had taken cover beneath their music stands. A violin player started at my entrance.

"Mind if I borrow this?" I said, plucking the bow out of his hands. He answered with a squeak.

There was a vase of marigolds on a pedestal. I tossed the flowers and emptied the water. The opening was narrower than I would've liked, but it would have to do. I squeezed the antidote into the vase and pried the locket open with shaking fingers. A tiny vial of scarlet liquid rested inside, nearly empty.

As I hovered the vial over the opening, the duchess's burly accomplices swarmed in and attacked the wall of guards that encircled the dais. Queen Cordelia was missing, and so was the duchess.

Someone below shouted at me. Before I could decipher their words, a hand clamped down on my shoulder.

"Give it to me! Give it to me!" Duchess Wilhelmina's crazed face was inches away from mine. A drop of manbane fell into the vase.

I jerked away. "Give it up!" I told her, clutching the locket behind me. "Your crimes have already been—"

My eyes widened at the sight of an unconscious Queen Cordelia crumpled behind the duchess. Had she been dragged up the stairs?

The duchess lunged for me. I evaded her again. My back hit the railing and I teetered.

"She's going to fall!" somebody squealed.

That distracted me enough. Duchess Wilhelmina

wrenched my arm from behind me. Pain shot up my shoulder and the locket clattered to the floor. She cackled and snatched it.

"Goodbye, witch."

She shoved me. The world turned upside down and for a terrifying moment, I was falling. And then my hand caught the bars of the railing.

"Amarante!" It sounded like Ash. I didn't look down to check.

The duchess had forced Queen Cordelia's mouth open and was holding the vial over it.

My fingers began to slip. I swung my other hand up to grab the railing when Ash barged in and knocked the locket out of her hand. It slid across the marble.

"No!" Duchess Wilhelmina screamed. She scrambled to retrieve it. I struggled to pull myself up, ignoring the burning of my arms. Ash grabbed my wrists and hauled me back onto the balcony. I barely caught my breath when the duchess charged for the queen.

"Get away from my mother, monster!" Ash lunged for a music stand and jabbed her shoulder with it. Sheet music went flying as the duchess howled.

I clutched the vase and began stirring counterclockwise with the bow.

"Slow, steady stirs," Lana had said. "Otherwise it will not be done properly."

I didn't know if I had the capacity to do anything slowly or steadily at the moment, but I forced my arm to still as I drew wide circles at the bottom of the vase.

"What is she doing? What are you doing, witch?"

"Slow and steady," I muttered to myself. I did not look up. I had to trust Ash to keep the queen safe and the duchess away as I worked.

Magic pooled from my chest to my fingertips and seeped into the violin bow like honey dripping from a comb, filling the antidote. A purple-red haze flooded my vision, rippling with magic. The scuffle was merely at my periphery as I stirred. But my stomach wrenched when I heard Ash cry out.

"Mother, stop!" It was Narcissa. "Stop this at once, please!"

"You ungrateful girl! How dare you betray me?"

"What you are doing is wrong, Mother."

"I knew it! You are weak! Weak like your good for nothing father!"

And then something very strange happened. An explosion of emerald green magic burst through my vision. Out of nowhere, a bevy of swans swept into the ballroom, their bugles and flapping deafening as they swooped past me and swarmed the duchess.

"What? Stop! Narcissa, stop this! How dare you—!"

Mice flooded in from the staircase, squeaking and scurrying. "Let me go! Give that back, you stinking vermin!"

The locket appeared at my side on a bed of moving white mice. One of them pushed it toward me with tiny paws. I took it and tucked the locket into my pocket. With a final stir, I knew the potion was done.

The sight that greeted me when I looked up was rather bizarre. Duchess Wilhelmina lay unconscious beside the queen, her skin pecked and bruised and bitten. The pond swans had made themselves comfortable on the seats of the musicians, many of whom had fainted. The mice cascaded down the steps. Narcissa stood before it all, looking breathless and bewildered with feathers in her hair. Ash was nursing a large bruise on his forehead.

I pushed the vase toward him. "It's done," I said. He gave me a weak smile.

The stillness was interrupted when the Royal Guard marched up the balcony. Two seized the duchess and one of them grabbed me.

"Your Highness, are you alright?" Sir Hughes said, helping Ash up.

He winced and touched his forehead. "Quite." He gestured to me. "Release Amarante at once. She saved my mother."

Sir Hughes looked down at Queen Cordelia, who was still unconscious, and tutted. "No, she didn't. And anyhow, that girl is a witch and is a danger to us all. We must imprison her again, this time with more security."

Ash began to shake his bruised head but seemed to think better of it. "You don't understand—"

"Now, now, Your Highness. What you need is some rest," he said.

I stepped forward, but my guard restrained me. "Give Queen Cordelia the antidote quickly," I said to Ash.

He grabbed the vase. "Sir Hughes, take my mother to her chambers."

"Understandable, Your Highness. First let me take care of this madwoman and this witch. And these birds."

Ash widened his eyes. "Wait, don't—!"

That was the last thing I heard before something slammed into my head and I lost consciousness.

34

A mouse was nibbling my hair when I opened my eyes. I jerked up. My head spun and my eyes strained to take in my surroundings. I was back in the dungeons.

Memories flooded back all at once. The Masquerade Ball. The duchess's confession. The scuffle that ensued afterward. Then nothing. I brushed off the straw on my skirts and pounded the cell door.

"Release me at once!" I shouted. "Take me to Prince Ash! I must speak to the prince!" I didn't cease my pounding until the slot above my head slid open. Ken peered in, his brows furrowed in displeasure.

"How long have I been in here?" I demanded.

"Two days," Ken said. "And hopefully many more."

He closed the slot but I pried it back open. My head swam. "There must be some sort of misunderstanding," I said. "The duchess confessed her crimes. I saved Queen Cordelia!"

Ken guffawed. "You? Save Her Majesty?" he said between wheezes. "Then I am a princess in disguise!"

I stared at him in disdain as his freckled face turned puce. When he recovered, he said, "Look, witch. The duchess might have confessed her crimes but that doesn't excuse you from yours. Ol' Captain Greenwood's name was cleared and that's all that matters to me. I suggest you make yourself comfortable because no one is looking for y—"

"Royal summons for the witch Amarante Flora to the throne room!" someone hollered.

I harrumphed as Ken's mouth fell open. He grumbled as he unlocked my door. Captain Greenwood stood waiting for me with a couple of other guards, one of them I recognized as Peter. He was back in uniform, which meant that he, too, had been pardoned. It seemed that I missed quite a bit.

Captain Greenwood's eyes crinkled when he saw me. "Thank you," he whispered, offering his arm. "Thank you for bringing my daughter back to me."

As he escorted me out of the dungeons, I felt lighter than I had ever before.

But my mouth grew dry when we entered the throne room. I marveled at the sheer amount of people present. King Maximus and Queen Cordelia sat on their thrones, flanked by their sons. Ash gave me a wink. To the side, there was a congregation of old men dressed in politicians' emerald robes, no doubt the king's council. Most of them wrinkled their nose at my entrance, but several were smiling. Erasmus was among them. He gave me an enthusiastic wave.

Debutantes and strangers filled the rows of wooden benches near the doorway. I spotted Olivia and Tori in the crowd and caught a glimpse of Genevieve's blond hair. To my surprise, Lana was sitting near the front along with Elowyn, Rowena, and Theodora.

I *had* missed a lot.

They all gave me encouraging looks when Captain Greenwood brought me to the center of the room.

Silence fell. I was suddenly aware of the debris clinging to my hair as I curtsied before the dais.

"Miss Amarante Flora." The king's voice boomed through the throne room. "Do you know what you have done?"

Was that a trick question? I looked to Ash, but he had hidden his face with his hands, as if exasperated. "Please enlighten me, sir. I mean, Your Majesty."

King Maximus stared at me, his heavy brow and heavy mustache making him look extremely displeased. What was there to be displeased about? Queen Cordelia looked healthier than ever. I began to sweat.

"You have used witchcraft in my kingdom. You have given strange elixirs and potions to unknowing subjects. You have hidden your identity and deceived my son. All this you have done in my palace," the king said, his voice crescendoing with every word. "Do you know the consequences of such actions?"

"Your Majesty, please—"

"Do you?"

I swallowed. "No, Your Majesty."

King Maximus sat back. "No matter. You do not need to know them. You have exposed Wilhelmina's wickedness and saved my queen."

My knees felt ready to collapse. "T-thank you, Your Majesty."

"You have shown that magic is not what we assume it to be," he said. "Prince Ash has uncovered the late King

Humphrey's old journals. The trial of Navierre is not as it seems. He was framed and executed because my father was jealous of the power the witches held. He banished witch-kind for selfish reasons."

A collective gasp went through the king's council. One of them stood. "How do we know that's true?" he said, arching a graying brow. "What if that witch girl is manipulating the prince?"

Ash gave the man an icy look. "You will speak of Miss Amarante with respect, Sir Jean. As for verifying the truth, I will be happy to show you my findings whenever you wish."

This seemed to satisfy Sir Jean enough, but he still shot me a glare when he sat.

King Maximus grunted. "Very good. Now, Miss Flora, you will be rewarded for your merits. I grant you the honorary title of Princess. And as princess, I offer you a betrothal to the crown prince."

Exclamations exploded across the throne room.

"A witch as the crown princess? Impossible!"

"The crown prince is far too handsome for her!"

"Say yes, my girl!"

The last cry sounded oddly like Lydia, but I didn't bother checking the audience for my stepmother.

"Why?" I sputtered. Me? Marry the crown prince? The very thought was absurd.

"Prince Ash has lauded you over the other debutantes. I would've had doubts," the king said, giving me a glance I didn't care to look into, "but you have proved yourself brave and loyal. Despite your lowly status, you will make a good queen."

Ash looked as shocked as I felt. Surely he didn't think his praise of me would result in this.

Shaking my head, I said, "I'm afraid I must decline, Your Majesty."

"Why is that? Do you prefer my other son?"

"No!" I blushed, pretending not to notice how Ash sat straighter at the suggestion. "I do not intend to marry at all."

Then there was silence again. King Maximus harrumphed. "Perhaps I was too hasty. What is it you want, then? Gold?"

"No, not gold," I said, looking to Lana and Elowyn and my nannies. "I…I want witches to be able to roam Olderea again."

The king paused, looking grave. "It seems it is my turn to decline, Miss Flora."

My face fell. "But you said magic isn't as dangerous as you thought. Navierre's trial—"

"Olderea is not prepared for the change after so many years," King Maximus said. "There is no room for an entire population of witches to reappear. No jobs and no houses. The people will protest."

"But Your Majesty, if you will please listen—"

"Do not grow too bold, Miss Flora. I am still king."

Queen Cordelia, who had sat without a word the entire time, touched the king's elbow. "Let the girl speak, Maximus. She is worth listening to." She gestured to me. "Miss Amarante."

I took a deep breath and told them about Witch Village and the unwholesome crops, the lack of fresh air, and the limited supplies. I explained the witches' reliance on the Witch Market and how the restrictions were cutting them off from all sorts of goods. Lastly, I told them that witches could hold their own, but must be allowed to roam above ground for basic necessities without fear of being imprisoned.

King Maximus was quiet when I finished, preoccupied with stroking his beard. He glanced at the queen. "What do you say, Cordelia?"

"I say it is time to end the Non-Magic Age," Queen Cordelia said.

"Perhaps with work, this is plausible." The king gave a slow nod. "Then, Miss Flora, I grant you your wish."

Cheers, mixed in with some grumbling, erupted in the throne room. I beamed and curtsied low, the applause and shouts like music to my ears.

When I turned, Elowyn and my nannies were smiling, and there were tears in Lana's eyes.

35

My arms burned under the weight of a crate filled with clinking containers of glue and sloshing potion bottles.

"I'm sure you could buy a cart and a horse of your own now, Aunt Lana," I said over a bottle.

"Nonsense," my aunt said. She was several paces away, burdened only by a light satchel. "Where will I ever put them?"

"In Papa's stables," I said, narrowly missing a divot in the paved road. "You know you're always welcome at home."

It had been four months since my hearing with King Maximus and three months since he passed the decree ending the Non-Magic Age. All the witches in Witch Village had been above ground at least once. The bolder ones stayed and applied for work. Others emerged only for the Witch Market, which had moved next to a major marketplace in Delibera. Witches were now paid in coins and allowed to purchase from human vendors.

We were headed toward Lana's stand in the marketplace that morning. It was ridiculously early, but there was still quite a bit of traffic. I recognized Beatrice with Rowena and Elowyn and waved at them. They were setting up a shop of their own, selling charmwitch trinkets.

"I don't know," Lana said. We finally arrived at her stand and I set the crates down. "I am not sure that is the wisest idea."

"Papa came home from Aquatia last week," I said in a singsong voice.

My aunt scowled. "Help me unload, why don't you? I have twenty orders of extra sticky glue to fulfill. No sense in keeping people waiting," she said, unwinding her scarf. Then her expression softened ever so slightly. "Aquatia, you say?"

I nodded, setting down the final pot of glue. "He had business there. I suppose he'll go back soon, now that Olderea is open to magic again. Perhaps magic Aquatian wares will pop up in our marketplaces."

"Never mind the wares," Lana said. I looked up, surprised at the enthusiasm in her voice. "Think of the books and knowledge we witches could get from such a kingdom! I don't believe a single Olderian witch has ever step foot in Aquatia."

"Would you go if you could?" I asked.

Lana's eyes glimmered. "Of course. But," she said, tucking a strand of hair behind her ear, "I don't see that day coming anytime soon. Sea travel is expensive and I haven't made a fortune quite yet."

By the time the sun was high in the air, our stock was gone. I helped Lana pack up. When she started toward the path to Miriam's shop, I stopped her.

"You really ought to come back with me," I said, holding her elbow. "Papa has been asking to see you."

I could see the conflicting emotions on her face. When she didn't reply, I said, "Maybe he'll tell you all about Aquatia."

The muscles on her arm eased, though her expression didn't change. "What makes you think I'd ask him, of all people?"

"Aunt *Lana*."

She heaved a sigh. "Very well, if you'll stop pestering me. But don't expect anything out of it," she said, turning around.

I beamed.

Papa was in his study when I returned home with my aunt in tow.

I led her through the pristine parlor and up the stairs, past my stepmother's room and down the hall. Lydia had made herself scarcer than ever since Papa returned, though I suspected it was because she was channeling all her energy into planning Genevieve's wedding.

It was lucky for both of us, as my stepmother was still a bundle of nerves around magic. Plus, she still hadn't forgiven me for not marrying Crown Prince Bennett. The last thing I needed was my stepmother's hysterics when she saw an actual witch from Witch Village in the house.

"So. Here we are," I said, gesturing to the mahogany door of Papa's study.

Lana stood before it, looking as if she had tasted something sour.

I gave her a look and knocked lightly against the wood. "Papa?"

"Come in."

He was at his desk per usual, his spectacles low on his nose. He looked up at my entrance.

"Done helping your aunt, my flower?" he said.

"Even better," I said, opening the door wider to reveal my companion. "I brought her."

Lana stood as stiffly as ever. I tugged her inside. Surprise flashed across Papa's face, but melted into a welcoming smile.

"Lana," he said.

"Julien."

My crystal glowed, warming my skin. Both Mama and I knew that their conversation must be had alone. I backed out of the study and closed the door, humming as I made my way down to the gardens. Just as I passed the marigold bushes, I spotted a mail boy standing behind the gates.

"Letter for Miss Amarante Flora," the boy said, holding out an envelope.

I trotted over and took the letter, recognizing the royal seal. "Thank you," I said, turning on my heel.

I had barely touched the wax before the mail boy said, "Did you really kill the evil duchess with your witch magic, miss?"

I held back a smile. It seemed that the wild rumors about what happened at the masquerade hadn't ceased entirely.

"No one killed anybody," I said, turning back and putting my hands on my hips. Duchess Wilhelmina had been sentenced to a lifetime in prison immediately after the masquerade. The king and queen had pardoned her life on behalf of their previous friendship. She deserved much, much worse, in my opinion, but I wasn't going to discuss my thoughts on justice with a little boy. "Now run along. Idleness rots the mind."

The boy pouted but complied. When his figure was a mere dot at the far end of the street, I went back inside and opened my envelope. It was a note from Queen Cordelia, summoning me to the palace.

Lana descended from the stairs just as I read the letter twice over.

"Well," she said, tucking her hands behind her back. "I suppose investing in a horse and cart isn't a bad idea after all."

36

After bidding Lana goodbye and telling Papa about my royal summons, I hopped onto a chaise to the palace, wondering what the queen could want with me. We hadn't been in contact for months, not since my hearing. Had something gone wrong with her recovery?

Queen Cordelia sat across her great mahogany desk when I entered her study. The light streaming in through the stained glass gave her a blue-green halo, a welcome contrast to the sickly scarlet I had gotten used to. Her expression was serene, but there was a sparkle in her eye.

"Your Majesty," I said, curtsying. "You wanted to see me?"

"I did. You've come just in time for tea," the queen said, pushing forward a plate of biscuits as I sat.

I thanked her and took a biscuit. She looked well enough. It couldn't possibly be the antidote, could it?

Queen Cordelia smiled. "You're doing well, I hope?"

"I hope you're doing well too, Your Majesty," I said quickly.

She laughed. "Rest easy, I've never been better. I wanted to propose an opportunity."

"Opportunity, Your Majesty?" I asked. I recalled the offer of marriage to the crown prince. Last time I asked, Ash said his brother decided to postpone his matrimonial affairs for another few years after the trauma of the masquerade.

Queen Cordelia nodded. "But before I talk about that, I must ask you a question," she said. "How do you feel about my son?"

My mouth gaped open before I could stop myself. A few biscuit crumbs tumbled out. I brushed them away, flustered. "I hardly know the crown prince, Your Majesty, and frankly it seems a bit silly to marry him to *me*, of all people—"

"Not Bennett, Amarante," Queen Cordelia said, laughing. "I meant Ash."

"Oh," I said. I closed my mouth lest I spewed crumbs at her face.

The last few months, despite being busy, had given me more time to think. The royals had been working nonstop on policies to restore witchkind to Olderea. It ate up quite a bit of time, especially for Ash who was by far the most eager. He and I hadn't been able to see each other quite as frequently, but whenever we did, he was more attentive than usual. I didn't miss the looks he gave me, or the friendly hugs that lasted a touch longer than proper.

"I'm fond of him but...I don't know, Your Majesty," I said honestly. I had been avoiding the topic. It made me far too nervous for my liking. What could the queen mean by bringing it up?

"He fancies you," Queen Cordelia said, shocking me with her frankness. "I'm merely curious if you feel the same, but it seems I've made you uncomfortable."

I merely blushed.

"I'm asking because of the opportunity I mentioned," she continued. "If you accept it you won't see him for a long time."

My curiosity piqued. "What is the opportunity, Your Majesty?"

"As you know, Captain Greenwood is grateful for what you've done for him and insists on rewarding you."

"I thank him, but my Papa and I have refused," I murmured. After Narcissa returned to his care, he had begged to send me a reward. Neither Papa nor I thought it was proper. I still had the five pounds of gold that went unused, which he refused to take back.

A corner of Queen Cordelia's lip twitched ever so slightly. "So he said. But I've decided to take a trip to Aquatia next month to reunite with my sister Nerissa, and my nephews, Noah and Gabriel. They're about your age now," she said, a wistful look in her eye. "Plus, it'd be a wonderful opportunity to see how magic is incorporated into their kingdom. Olderea could learn a lot. I wish to have a traveling companion. Captain Greenwood is more than happy to fund your trip if you join me."

"Me?" I said, appalled.

The queen nodded.

"But why not His Majesty, or the crown prince, or Ash?"

"Alas, they're busy with the kingdom. I trust they can hold Olderea together for a year while I visit my family."

I let the information wash over me. The last time I had traveled outside of the kingdom was with Papa as a child.

He would tell me stories of how I assisted him in selling his wares and charmed merchants with my laughter. This time, I'd be with Aquatian royalty, experiencing a kingdom full of magic. No doubt it'd be exciting. But far away. Very far.

"My Papa just came home," I said slowly. "My sister is engaged to be married. And my aunt is setting up her shop."

Queen Cordelia nodded. "Understandable," she said. "It can be daunting, leaving everything and everyone you know. Sometimes a call to adventure isn't quite enough to convince someone to leave home."

I polished off my biscuit and thought about what Lana had said about Aquatia. Clearly, it was a world of knowledge when it came to magic. There was no saying what there was to learn. The longing in her eye was enough for me to understand that she wanted to go. I shifted in my seat. Wherever Lana went, I went. At least it had been that way for the past few months. I was her apprentice after all.

"Do you think I could bring my aunt?" I asked.

"Of course," Queen Cordelia said, smiling. "Is this a yes?"

A tingle of excitement shot through my spine when I thought about exploring what Aquatia had to offer with Lana. Of course, I had to tell everyone first. And one person in particular.

"I'll have to think about it," I said, smoothing the non-existent wrinkles on my skirts.

"Take your time," the queen said graciously. "The trip isn't until the end of next month. By then I'll expect an answer. You are excused."

"Thank you, Your Majesty." I stood and curtsied.

When I was halfway to the door, she said, "He's in the library."

I blushed and thanked her.

My hands were shaking when I entered the library. Mr. Northberry's snores weren't nearly loud enough to mask the heartbeat pounding in my ears.

I rounded the corner to the east end. Ash's lean form was sprawled over the armchair, drowned in a pile of books and loose papers.

He sat up when I approached, scattering the papers. "Ah, Amarante! I wanted to ask you something,"

"Ask away," I said, forcing myself to sound calm.

"You said witches could grow crops three times faster than normal," he said. "We could use that for the troops stationed at our borders. Food supply is always an issue amongst regiments there."

I was glad for the distraction. "Magic grown food won't be as filling," I said.

"Of course. But it will sustain them until their stocks are replenished, won't it?" Ash said.

I sat on the armrest of his chair, as I always did when we met at the library. His proximity felt different this time.

"You're right," I said. "Ferdinand is looking for a job, actually. And he worked his magic in the fields before. You could consult him."

"Perfect!" Ash scribbled something in his notebook and tucked it away, giving me his full attention. The smile on his face was bordering radiant. "I never realized how much Olderea was missing when it didn't have magic. Did you know there hasn't been a single attempted robbery in the treasury ever since Miriam came and conjured that dark tunnel?"

A smile crept over my face. His enthusiasm was contagious. "That's great," I said, bumping his shoulder. "What else have you been occupied with?"

"Developing the new policies with Father and Bennett. Nice to be included," he said with a lopsided grin. "And you?"

I recalled Queen Cordelia's offer and what I was here to talk about. The trip to Aquatia was a wonderful opportunity, but I would miss Ash terribly whether I considered him a friend or something more. My smile dimmed.

"What's wrong?" Ash said.

"Well," I said slowly, "Queen Cordelia wants me to go with her to Aquatia. For a visit. Maybe a year or so."

He blinked. "Really?"

"She said she wants to observe how magic plays a part there. And reconnect with her family. She's been dying to see them, I'm sure. Did you know you have two cousins? I never really knew mine but I suppose that's just negligence on my part—"

"Amarante, you're rambling."

I snapped my mouth shut, feeling blood rush to my cheeks. Why was I so nervous? I was telling him about a trip, not proposing. The thought of proposing to Ash made me blush even more.

"So, the trip. You said it'll be a year?"

"That's what Her Majesty said," I said. "Unless she decides to stay longer. I heard there's all sorts of different creatures in Aquatia. I'm sure it's very charming in person. Not to mention my aunt would love to visit."

Ash chuckled. "You really want to go, don't you?"

"Oh! Of course I do," I said, throwing my hands up. "But I love it here. Olderea is my home. I'll be leaving Genevieve and Tori and Olivia and my nannies and Papa and... and you."

He looked up, as if surprised he was included at all. I didn't wait for a reply before continuing, "And magic is just being reincorporated into the kingdom. It'll be silly of me to leave right now. There's still a long way to go and I want to be there for it all. And Miriam is renovating her shop, which desperately needs help—"

"But you still want to see what Aquatia has to offer," Ash interjected before I further made a fool out of myself.

I groaned and twisted my fingers in frustration, garnering another laugh from him.

Ash gently pried my hands apart. After a moment's hesitation, he pressed something into my palm. It was his Season ribbon, slightly creased and discolored from wear.

The palace had hosted another Choosing Ceremony a few days after the masquerade. Several matches were made, including Cedric and Genevieve—despite the fact that Cedric didn't have a ribbon. Most others discarded their tokens, as they didn't want to remember the disaster they experienced at the ball. It seemed that Ash had kept his. He could only mean one thing by giving it to me.

"Amarante. I don't know if I've made it clear, but I like you. I like you a lot," he said, intertwining our fingers. His voice didn't waver. I was simultaneously stunned by his directness and horribly jealous of his courage. "I could love you, if you give me the chance. Blazing fires, I'm already halfway there."

I braved a look at him. Ash was staring at our conjoined hands. "I only want to know if you feel the same way."

His cheeks had the slightest flush when he met my gaze. I was sure mine was three times redder.

"I'm sorry," I said, easing my hand out of his and wiping it on my skirt. The ribbon fell onto his lap. "I'm sweating all over you."

Ash looked askance. "Apologies. I didn't mean to pressure you." Mortification was written all over his features as he fiddled with the ribbon.

Then, it was as if my limbs grew a mind of their own. I grabbed Ash's face and kissed him full on the lips, nearly falling on top of him in the process. He responded instantly. It was a clumsy kiss, but it was a proper one nonetheless— one that melted me to my very bones.

We stared at each other, lips swollen, breathless and dazed. A loud whoop sounded from behind a shelf.

"About time!"

"Mr. Northberry?" Ash sputtered.

The old librarian emerged with a stack of books in his arms. It was jarring to see him standing and even more so to hear something other than snores from him. "Don't mind me," he said with a cackle. "The assistant gardener thought it'd take you two nine months to confess. I said six. I won!"

He shuffled off before I could ask what he won. I turned back to Ash and had the satisfaction of seeing his cheeks as red as mine. Somewhere along the way his arms had encircled my waist. He didn't remove them. I didn't want him to.

"So," he said.

I cleared my throat. "So."

"Was that a yes, you do like me, or did you have a sudden seizure?" Ash asked.

"A bit of both," I said sheepishly.

He laughed. I never realized how much I loved the sound.

"I do like you," I said. "It's just…there's a whole world waiting for me out there. Queen Cordelia's offer is more than I could hope for."

"Don't fret," Ash said with a smile. "I only wanted an answer, and you gave it. Thank you."

Then he kissed me again.

37

I fiddled with Ash's ribbon on my wrist as I waited outside Papa's room. Lydia was making a big ruckus down the hall, telling Genevieve that wearing the slightest hint of white before her wedding was bad-mannered and presumptuous. My stepmother never pointed out the slightest flaw in Genevieve, but I supposed that having her daughter's engagement party at the palace would have such an effect on her nerves.

Papa opened the door, clean-shaven and impeccably dressed. His eyes brightened when he saw me. "Ah, you look beautiful, my flower. Is that your Mama's gown?"

I nodded and spun around. "Aunt Lana gave it to me," I said, lifting the purple skirts. The hem was adorned with golden embroidery.

"Our invitation still stands, you know," Papa said. "She's as much an aunt to Genevieve as to you."

"You know Lana," I said with a shrug. Even after her reconciliation with Papa, she was hesitant to accept our invitations for tea, dinner, or anything, really. Cedric and Genevieve's engagement party was no different.

"Nonsense! She must come. Besides, you still have to tell her about your trip," he said with a small smile.

The other night, I told Papa about Queen Cordelia's offer. We were in his study as usual, the setting sun turning the sky a dusky purple.

"After all these years, my flower, I am glad you've occupied your time with something useful," Papa had said. "Your Mama would be proud." He heaved a sigh. "I only wish you didn't have to find out about her on your own."

I recalled Papa's absence and sparse letters. I felt so lost then, despite Theodora and Rowena's efforts. But I had since found solace in my apprenticeship with Lana and discovering what it meant to be a witch myself. If Papa had been there, he would've tried to protect me from it all. Perhaps I would've wanted his protection back then, but that was no longer true.

I took Papa's hand. "Don't be sorry. I had Theodora, Rowena, and Lana to guide me. And Mama," I said, touching my crystal. It emitted a warm glow.

The wetness in his eyes reflected the purple light of my pendant. "But of course."

Today, Papa was smiling. "Well, what are you waiting for?" he said.

Before I could reply, my stepmother shouted from below. "Hurry now! Before we're late to our own party!"

Genevieve rushed past me in a powder blue gown. She was flushed pink, her eyes shining. "We better do as Mama says, if we want her in the best of moods tonight," she said between breaths.

I exchanged a look with Papa. "Maybe Aunt Lana will show up after all," I said to him.

"Maybe," Papa said, straightening his cravat. He offered me his arm. "Well, my flower, let us go before your stepmother flies off the handle."

The carriage ride to the palace was full of tension and excitement. Genevieve stared out the window for most of it, most likely thinking about Cedric as Lydia talked her ear off. By the time we arrived, the banquet hall was already scattered with guests.

Olivia and Tori met us at the entrance. "Look at you, the radiant bride!" Tori exclaimed, turning Genevieve around to admire the lace and beading of her gown.

"Thank you," Genevieve said, laughing.

"Have you tried the candied pineapple?" Tori asked, showing us her napkin filled with the crystallized fruit. "It's phenomenal. The palace cooks really know what they're doing. Next time Pa hosts an event he will have to hold it here. But he'll probably be too distracted by the food to be a proper host—"

Olivia elbowed her out of the way. "Cedric's out in the hallway," she said, dragging Genevieve out of Tori's grasp. "I'll show you."

Tori sighed dramatically as the two went off. "Ah, young love. Distracts you from what's most important," she said, looking down at her sweets. She popped one into her mouth. "So. Who are you looking for?"

I stopped my wandering gaze. "My aunt," I said. "Have you seen her?"

"Nope. But I think someone else wants to see you," Tori said, tilting her head to the left. I recognized Narcissa's fiery hair behind a pillar. She was throwing glances my way.

"I suppose," I said with a sigh. Genevieve insisted on inviting everyone to her party, even our not-so-amiable acquaintances. Julianna was invited too, but I had yet to see her face anywhere. She avoided me like the plague ever since the masquerade and my hearing with the king, which certainly was a blessing.

I wandered over to the pillars where Narcissa stood alone, Misty in her arms. Her brow was creased. Her expression didn't change when she noticed me.

"Amarante," she said curtly. Misty purred as Narcissa rubbed the spot behind her ears.

I nodded in acknowledgment. "How are you?"

"Fine."

"Won't you join us?" I said.

She shook her head. I wondered why she kept throwing glances at me if she didn't want to talk. And why she looked more miserable than usual. Surely her life improved after moving in with Captain Greenwood?

"You don't have to pretend we're friends," Narcissa said just as I decided to leave.

I stopped. "Sorry?"

"We're not friends," Narcissa said again.

"I know." She certainly hadn't gotten friendlier in the past few months. "But we're not so different," I said.

She barked a short, mirthless laugh. "Yes, we are. You're a hero. I'm just a witch who helped her traitor mother."

"Narcissa—"

She shook her head again. "Look at me," she said, "and look at everyone else. They're afraid."

As much as I tried to deny it, I couldn't. The guests, most of them Lydia's friends, were eying Narcissa like she was gunpowder about to explode.

My words lodged in my throat. I had my fair share of fearful looks, but after my hearing, I was mostly met with enthusiasm and sometimes even awe. My cheeks colored.

"You don't have to stay, if you don't want to," I managed to say. "I'll tell everyone you aren't feeling well."

She gave a small nod. The closest I'll ever get to a thanks, no doubt.

Captain Greenwood sauntered over to the pillar with two glasses of punch. "Miss Amarante," he said, eyes brightening. A bit of liquid spilled over the sides as he came to a stop. "Splendid venue, is it not? I heard the candied pineapple is to die for."

I mustered a smile. "So have I."

The captain handed Narcissa a glass and patted Misty's head. "I heard from Queen Cordelia you decided to accept her offer," he said. "Are you excited for your trip next month?"

"I am," I said. "I can't thank you enough for your generosity, Captain Greenwood."

"And I can't thank you enough for your deeds," he said. "Ah! I almost forgot. I believe your aunt is waiting for you outside. She looks a bit lost."

"Aunt Lana is here?" I asked, perking up.

"You better go meet her before she changes her mind and disappears," he said, chuckling. He placed a hand on Narcissa's shoulder. "Come, my girl. I suppose you're tired of all this standing. There are some heavenly cushions in the other room."

The faint smile on Narcissa's face as the chattering captain led her away was enough to untangle the knot in my stomach. I let go of a breath and ran back to the entrance.

"Aunt Lana!" I called out.

She stood at the foot of the stairs, dressed in a stiff beige gown and looking very out of place amongst the luxury of the palace. I met her halfway down the steps.

"You came," I said with a grin.

My aunt shrugged, rattling the basket on her arm. "I had nothing else on my schedule," she said, adjusting her bonnet. She handed me the basket. "Here. I had some extra sticky glue left over. I suppose your stepsister and brother-in-law would find it useful in the future. Toddlers are very destructive."

"They'll be delighted," I said, accepting the gift. I gave her a sidelong glance as we climbed the stairs. "By the way, I have good news."

Lana raised an eyebrow. "Miriam is closing her shop?"

I laughed as we entered the banquet hall. "I'll tell you later. But for now, we have a party to attend."

Minutes before the Welcome Banquet, Prince Ash gets into some tomfoolery.

ASH

The jacket looked terrible on me.

I stepped back, squinting at my reflection in the window. The embroidered hem was reminiscent of the coat made for me for my seventeenth birthday. Much too gaudy. But it wasn't as if Aidan had a say in what he and the rest of the waiters wore.

Beyond the glass panes of the west wing, Aidan was loading his things into the carriage I had called for him in the courtyard. There was a large, silly grin on his face as if he were the happiest man alive.

Perhaps he was. It wasn't every day a waiter was given a handful of gold in exchange for their uniform.

Rolling my shoulders in the too-tight jacket, I raked my fingers through my hair, making sure to create knots for good measure. No one would suspect a prince to have knotted hair.

"My dear, *what* are you doing?"

I yanked my hand out, wincing. My arm was still sore from sword practice that morning, but I smiled as Mother came down the hall. The sunlight illuminated her satin gown and cast long shadows on the marble tiles.

"Radiant as ever, Mother," I said, bowing.

She stopped in front of me, eyebrows raised. "Well?"

There was no use lying to her. "I thought I'd do Bennett a favor and take a peek at this year's debutantes."

Mother gave me a stern look. "Do not terrorize those girls, Ash. It is a monumental time in their lives. I doubt anyone would appreciate your meddling, unless you plan on marrying one of them."

I chortled. "Unlikely. Besides, aren't you the least bit curious about the future crown princess?"

"All in good time, my dear," Mother said. She gave me a sidelong glance. "But I suppose you ought to get acquainted with them sooner or later. Your brother and father are set to leave in a week."

"Is this permission to meddle?"

"No," she said, brushing a strand of hair away from my face. "A harmless peek during the banquet is one thing, but I cannot fathom what you are planning to do dressed as a waiter who apparently does not own a comb."

"I can't learn much from a peek." I mussed my hair again. "Bennett would appreciate more detailed notes, I'm sure. He *did* ask me to attend the Season on his behalf."

"Why the rush? You'll be introduced to them all during the Debutante Ball."

"One does not behave the same way to a prince as they would a waiter. Besides," I said, pouting, "I'm bored."

Mother pressed her lips together, but a corner twitched up. "Your father won't be pleased. And neither will Wilhelmina," she said. "You know how particular she is about these events. You'll ruin it for her."

"It was ruined when she decided to host it," I muttered under my breath.

"What was that, dear?"

I pasted on a smile. "Nothing. Where are you off to? Let me escort you."

"No need. I merely have some letters I want to send to your aunt."

"Aunt Nerissa?" I inquired.

Mother nodded. A slight crease appeared between her dark brows. "Hopefully one of them will get through. The anti-magic policies your father enforced make it difficult to correspond with my own sister."

"It's for the safety of Olderea," I said quickly. Then, realizing that Father was not here to give his grunt of approval, I lowered my voice to a murmur. "To limit magic from foreign kingdoms and such."

Mother patted my cheek, her palm soft but firm. "Don't forget your half Aquatian. Magic is in your blood, even if it does not show itself."

I shrugged, uncomfortable. Father had tightened anti-magic laws after a member of the palace staff was caught coming from the Witch Market. Mother objected, or at least tried to. Father heard nothing of it.

Sometimes I wondered if they would stay married if international peace did not depend on their union.

Mother shook her head and smiled. "I ought to get going. And it seems you ought to make your way to the kitchen."

"Right," I said, attempting to pull my sleeves down to my wrists. "I'll see you tonight at dinner."

She raised a brow. "Please don't ruin the banquet."

"Hardly, Mother. It'll just be a little mischief."

"*Ash.*"

I took her shoulders and steered her toward the exit. She felt thinner than I remembered. "*Alright.* I promise. Duchess Wilhelmina's banquet will proceed unscathed."

After sighing and smoothing my hair, Mother went off. I turned on my heels and made my way down to the kitchen, glad to see the sun flooding the hallway in a golden glow. There was plenty of time to get things sorted.

I descended the steps to the kitchen. The place was abuzz with palace staff running to and fro. No one stopped to acknowledge my presence.

"Nadia, the chicken is burning!" came a bellow. The west wing's chef, Ricardo, rounded the corner, his apron streaked with rich sauces and flour. His sweat-covered brow furrowed when he laid eyes on me.

"Good evening, sir," I said brightly.

"What in the blazing fires are you doing down here?" he demanded.

Ricardo never addressed me formally. I was grateful for that. To him, I was still the mischievous child who swiped apples from the kitchen when no one was looking, royal or not. I glanced at the bowl of gleaming red fruit on the counter, noting their presence.

"I was wondering if you needed an extra hand," I said.

The chef's sharp eyes darted around the hubbub of the kitchen. "Where's Aidan?"

I shrugged. "He quit."

Ricardo scowled. "*Quit?* He has a sick mother to take care of. He can't quit."

"He made twice his lifetime's wages this afternoon. I'm sure he'll be fine."

"Twice his lifetime's…? Good heavens, boy. You can't just hand out fortunes like candy."

I rested my elbows on the counter next to a servant girl kneading dough. "What's the use of giving lectures about finances to a prince?"

"*What's the use?* You'll eat your words when someone robs the treasury clean," he said with a growl. "Now kindly leave. It's bad enough I have one less pair of hands. I don't need you clogging up my kitchen and distracting my girls. Get your wits together, Kara. You're drooling over the dough."

The servant girl, who until that moment was staring at me with her mouth agape, ducked her head and began kneading twice as fast.

I rubbed the back of my neck. "Listen, Ricardo, I just need one job. Please. Anything will do."

"The duchess will have my head if a frog jumps out of the plum pudding," he said darkly. "Take your mischief elsewhere."

"There won't be frogs this time," I said. "One harmless job is all I ask. I won't draw attention to myself. Promise!"

"You're not leaving until you get it." Ricardo's words were flat.

A smile tugged at the corner of my lips.

Heaving a sigh, Ricardo handed me a crystal water pitcher. It looked delicate wrapped in his meaty fingers, so the weight surprised me. My sore arm throbbed.

"You're to refill the water glasses. You will not set amphibians loose in the banquet hall and you will leave those debutantes alone. Hear me?"

I nodded.

"Good. Now stand outside with the others and wait until you're called."

"Yes, sir." I bowed and went off, holding the water pitcher in both hands. My cheeks nearly ached from smiling when I found the other waiters standing in a file outside. I placed myself at the end and slipped the apple I had swiped from my pocket, admiring the ruby red skin.

If only Ricardo remembered that my promises to him were usually empty.

They didn't call for us until twenty minutes into the banquet. It gave me plenty of time to think, the act of which never led to anything exciting.

Was disguising myself taking it too far? The courtiers would no doubt whisper about my questionable conduct. Mother had enough on her plate. And Father certainly did not need to be proven right about his thoughts on my inadequacy.

The murmur of conversation swelled as I followed the waiters into the banquet hall, my palms clammy. I was sure they had figured out who I was in the time we stood together, but none spoke to me. Perhaps they were too busy wondering which of their old items I would want to exchange for a handful of gold.

Water pitcher in hand, I scanned the dining table. Duchess Wilhelmina's fiery hair stood out at the head, flanked by two older women and Narcissa. The duchess's daughter looked as if she sniffed something putrid. Typical Narcissa. I couldn't blame Bennett for wanting to avoid *her*.

The rest of the seats were occupied by debutantes. They were all rather pretty, but Bennett was never a great admirer of the fairer sex. He wasn't a great admirer of anything, really, except dusty old books on Olderean history. I held back a sigh. It was always duty with him. No wonder he jumped at the chance of joining Father's diplomatic travels instead of attending the Season himself.

I approached the middle of the table with my water pitcher. The other waiters stood a respectful distance from the debutantes, extending their arms to refill glasses. I tested the weight of my pitcher and mirrored them. My wrist strained as I filled someone's glass.

Moving over to the next seat, I reached past a debutante with an unusually tall hairdo. I marveled at the intricacy of the braids and pins. A long ostrich feather poked out from her chignon, all but inches away from my nose. I felt a sneeze tickle the back of my throat. Just as I restrained it, I noticed too late that my pitcher had dipped too far.

The debutante shrieked as water flooded her glass and dribbled onto her skirts, darkening the violet silk. She swiped the liquid frantically as I stepped back.

"What have you done?" she demanded, glaring at me with surprising animosity. "This dress is worth more than your yearly wages, you clumsy cow!"

It took everything in me not to snort. I glanced at her place card. *Miss Samantha Faas.* Definitely not the future princess. Bennett would be horrified.

"Apologies, Miss Samantha," I said with a bow. I offered her the napkin draped over my arm, which she snatched, used, then threw back at me.

I hadn't planned on doing something quite so drastic as spill beverages on debutantes, but since it already happened, there was no helping it now.

I proceeded down the table to a debutante in a yellow dress. She had witnessed the scene, I was sure of it, but didn't have the good sense to avert her eyes. I suppose she didn't know that in the palace, one was to ignore such situations. No one cared a whit about how nobles treated the servants.

I reached past her shoulder and emptied the pitcher into her glass.

Ice clattered down the table and rained into her lap. She shot up, knocking her chair to the ground in the process.

"Apologies!" I exclaimed. I felt a twinge of guilt at her mortified expression. Perhaps Mother was right. I was ruining everyone's time.

"Good heavens, what is going on?" Duchess Wilhelmina stood from her seat at the head of the table.

I bowed to avoid her glare. "It was my fault, Your Grace. An accidental slip of the hand." I straightened, though hesitantly. As expected, the duchess grew red when she saw my face.

A familiar surge of fear shot up my throat, but I forced it down.

Duchess Wilhelmina took a shuddering breath. Her voice was dangerously low. "Show the young lady to a place she can clean up. Then leave at once."

I bowed again. I beckoned to the debutante, dimly aware of her following me as I exited the banquet hall. Once we were safe outside, my face colored with shame. She was probably on the verge of tears because of me. I didn't know how to comfort girls. Blazing fires, when had I last *talked* to one?

"Er...are you sure waiting on the upper class was the right career choice?" the debutante asked.

A smile split my face at the unexpected question. So! She was fine after all. And had a healthy sense of humor.

"You're not angry with me?" I asked, glancing over my shoulder.

The debutante shrugged. "Not particularly." She held her drenched skirts away from her legs, making a face. "I would appreciate a napkin, though."

I shrugged off my jacket. "Here. Take this."

I turned around and handed it to her. She had dollish eyes and a smattering of freckles across her cheeks. They grew red when I grinned at her. She was rather pretty. I reckon she thought the same of me.

After she dried off, we reentered the banquet hall, and I escorted her back to her seat. The duchess was back talking to her peers, no longer paying me any attention. I allowed myself a sigh of relief.

Bending to lift the debutante's chair upright, I peered at her nameplate. *Miss Amarante Flora.* Not nobility, so not crown princess material.

She sat and thrust my damp jacket into my hands. I set the water pitcher before her.

"Enjoy the banquet, Miss Amarante," I said in a low voice. Then, unable to help myself, I threw her a wink.

Bennett would have to do without her.

ACKNOWLEDGMENTS

Coming out with an illustrated edition of *The Herbwitch's Apprentice* only a year after its original publication was completely unplanned. In 2021, I jumped headfirst into indie publishing and made some mistakes along the way I've been itching to fix.

As a result, rebranding and illustrating this edition became my senior project during my last semester at Otis College of Art and Design. This was truly a passion project. Special thanks to my professors Bill Eckert and Ursula Burton for being my mentors, giving great advice, and supporting me along the way.

Thanks again to all my beta readers: Cassandra, Henrietta, Samantha, Charity, Christine, Sabrina, and Emilie. You guys made Amarante's story that much better.

Thank you to the wonderful community of independent authors and readers I found on Instagram this past year. I never thought my book would end up in so many hands, or receive so much positive feedback.

Enormous thanks to Enchanted Ink Publishing for making my dreams come true and formatting this book beautifully.

And of course, thank you to Esme. You have never stopped inspiring me.

ĮREEN CHAU

is a long-time artist, writer, and above all, a lover of stories. She is located in the Bay Area where she hopes to become a children's book illustrator. When not reading, writing, or drawing, Ireen can be found browsing the internet for memes and watching YouTube commentary videos. Visit her Instagram page for more art and news about future projects.

@theherbwitchsapprentice